THE SONG OF THE WILD GEESE

THE SONG OF THE WILD GEESE

THE GEISHA WHO RAN AWAY VOLUME ONE

INDIA MILLAR

Red Empress Publishing
www.RedEmpressPublishing.com

Cover Design by Cherith Vaughan
www.ShreddedPotato.com

ALSO BY INDIA MILLAR

Secrets from the Hidden House

The Geisha with the Green Eyes

The Geisha Who Could Feel No Pain

The Dragon Geisha

The Geisha Who Ran Away

The Song of the Wild Geese

The Red Thread of Fate

This World is Ours

Haiku Collections

Dreams from the Hidden House

This book is humbly dedicated to Benzaiten; the Japanese goddess of good luck for both writers and geisha. May both she and you enjoy the words herein!

PREFACE

"Living only for the moment, giving all our time to the
pleasures of the moon, the snow, cherry blossoms, and
maple leaves. Singing songs, drinking
sake, caressing each other, just drifting, drifting. Never
giving a care
if we had no money, never sad in our hearts. Only like a
plant moving
on the river's current; this is what is called
The Floating World."

Tales of the Floating World
Asai Ryoi, 1661

PROLOGUE

*I*t would not be truthful to say I do not remember my mother. My family. Of course I do. It is just that their memory is dull somehow. Perhaps the best way I can describe it is to say that they seem to me as if I am looking at them through a silken screen. They are there. I can see their features, but they are slightly blurred somehow. Not quite real.

Of course, many people would say that I am confused. That the life I led with my family was real, and each day since I left them has been the dream. But they do not know. They cannot be expected to understand.

I think my mother was a pretty woman. She always seemed so to me, at any rate. And my father never took a concubine, so he must also have found her pleasing. Of course, we were poor, so it may be that he simply could not afford a concubine rather than a matter of choice. But I don't recollect Mother ever complaining that he spent money they didn't have on courtesans—or even common whores—so perhaps he was a contented man, after all.

Not that I understood about concubines or courtesans

in those days. I was a mere child, the only daughter in a family of five brothers. It may have been simple neglect. After all, what was the point of trying to teach a mere girl anything about life, or anything else for that matter? But I was soon to learn differently.

In fact, I began to learn the day that my new life began.

ONE

Adults can never
Truly remember childhood,
Be it good or bad

I was eleven years old on the day that Auntie visited our humble village. In fact, it was a week before my twelfth birthday when she took me away from my home and brought me here to the Floating World, to the Green Tea House, so that my new life could begin.

"Do I have to go, Mama?" I can hear my voice now, plaintive with confusion and worry. "Have I done something wrong? If I'm good, will you come and bring me back home again?"

Mother's face was stone, not like her normal, smiling expression at all.

"Are you hungry, Junko?" she asked. I had no need to think about it. Of course I was. Breakfast—and supper the night before—had been a small bowl of plain rice. My brothers and father, being men, had a small portion of vegetables as well.

"Yes," I said simply, even as I wondered what my empty belly had to do with this strange woman whose fierce expression already frightened me out of my wits.

"We are all hungry, dear. But if you go with Auntie here, then we will all eat. You will never be hungry again, and you will be given nice clothes to wear and you will live in a lovely house. You would like that, wouldn't you?"

I said yes, of course. Put like that, there was no choice. So I went quietly with the woman Mama called Auntie, and did not try to jerk away from her grip as she marched me away from our village. I was bewildered as well as frightened. I had never seen this woman before. How could she be my Auntie? But after a while, curiosity overcame fear and confusion, and I asked her—very nicely—how long it would be before I could go back home. She laughed at me.

"Oh, I think it might be quite a while, child," she said. I puckered my face in an effort not to cry and she slapped me —quite hard—on the back of my head. "Don't pull faces. It will give you wrinkles."

I didn't believe her, but that was the last time I pulled a face for many, many years.

Odd how lessons learned in childhood stay with a person, isn't it?

I thought that we walked for a very long time. I tried to distract my mind from worrying about what was happening to me by skipping on my shadow, and I remember clearly that it grew shorter and shorter as we walked, which of course made it far more difficult to try and touch it. It had shrunk to almost nothing by the time Auntie stopped. In fact, she stopped so suddenly I went ahead of her and she jerked me back with a fierce tug on my hand.

"Are you hungry, child?" she asked. The same question

mother had asked hours and hours ago. It made me want to cry and I couldn't speak. I nodded and she shook me.

"I asked you a question. When I ask you a question, I expect an answer. Are you hungry?"

"Yes," I said simply. Although truth to tell, I was so anxious by then that my stomach was seething with fear rather than hunger. But it seemed rude to say no.

I was shocked when she slapped my bottom, hard. I burst into tears. It was not just the pain, but also the sheer terror of the whole day.

"I want to go home!" I wailed. "Let me go. I want to go back to Mother."

For answer, Auntie crouched down so that her face was close to mine. She bared her teeth at me and it was like being snarled at by a fox. Instantly, I was sure she was going to eat me and I screamed at the top of my voice.

"Be quiet." Her voice was so cold, it was worse than the smack she had given me. I was so terrified that I stopped bawling and held my breath to keep the sobs inside. "Forget about your mother, and your family. I am your family now. I am your Auntie. And when you speak to me, you will call me Auntie. Now, we shall try again. Are you hungry?"

I gawped at her. She raised her eyebrows and stared at me silently. Finally, I understood what she wanted.

"Yes, Auntie. I am hungry." I gulped the words on a breath before I could cry again.

"So am I. We will break our journey now, eat, and spend the night here."

She took my hand again and I walked alongside her toward the most beautiful building I had ever seen. Even in my utter bewilderment, I worried that the people who owned the house would allow me to enter. Auntie was very richly dressed. I thought that her kimono alone must have cost more than I could count. My own kimono was patched and darned. Naturally, any money for clothes went to my brothers. I glanced down at my dusty bare feet and then back up at Auntie, beseeching her to tell me to wait outside. Perhaps, if I promised not to run away, she might allow it? Surprisingly, she seemed to understand my unvoiced concerns.

"Child, do something with your face. Smile, for the gods' sakes! You have no idea how the fates have favored you today. And for the rest of your life, if you do as I tell you. Listen to me. This is the most important thing you will ever learn. Hold your head up high. Look as if you are important. It doesn't matter how you are dressed. Do you understand?"

I glanced down at my ragged clothes and tears welled in my eyes again. Auntie snatched a breath, but before her hand could descend on me, I looked up quickly. I had always been very timid, and I had learned years ago that I didn't need to actually look grown-ups right in the eye, which they always seemed to expect. Instead, if I looked between their eyebrows, it seemed to make them think that I was really looking at them, and it was enough to hide my shyness. I did that now.

"Yes, Auntie."

I had no idea what she was talking about, but my answer and my raised face seemed to please her.

"Good. It doesn't matter how much you play-act, people only see what you let them see. They cannot look into your thoughts or your heart, child. Always remember that."

I turned her words over in my mind and found them oddly reassuring. Was Auntie clever at hiding her own worries, I wondered. A glance at her face told me not to be so silly. Nothing could ever scare Auntie. She wouldn't let it.

We walked into the building with my hand clasped firmly in Auntie's hand, and I kept my head up and my eyes wide.

True to her words, Auntie stared around as if the place disappointed her.

"A room. For tonight, for myself and my maid," she said crisply when a man came in answer to her call. I was to be her maid, then. I turned the thought over in my mind. It seemed odd that she had come to our tiny village to choose me as her maid. The knowledge was greatly comforting. At least I now knew what my future was.

Ah, the innocence of childhood!

The man bowed deeply and ushered us into a room so grand it stopped the breath in my throat. Futons were already laid on the polished wood floor and there were flowers beautifully displayed in front of a small shrine. It smelled sweet and clean. I tried not to gawp too obviously.

We ate in the room, but I cannot remember what the food was. Memory insists that it was delicious, but what passed my lips that evening I could not tell you. Soon after the dishes were cleared away, Auntie declared that she was exhausted and we would sleep.

"We will leave early in the morning. I have instructed the innkeeper to have a palanquin ready for us at first light."

And that was it. She rolled herself in her bedding and within minutes her breathing was the regular rhythm of sleep. I, however, could not sleep. Curiosity beat about my head like birds' wings, and no matter how tightly I shut my eyes, sleep would not come. We were in a *ryokan*. An inn. We must have walked very far from home, as I had never even seen a *ryokan* before. And we must have far to go still, as tomorrow we were to travel in a palanquin rather than walking.

Even above the mystery of it, one thing above all else kept me awake. I had never slept on my own before. Normally, my futon was shared and crowded with two of my brothers. I always slept between them, snug and safe. Whichever way I turned, there was a warm body by my side. On this strangest of nights, my futon stretched forever. No matter where my anxious fingers crept to, there was nothing but emptiness. And it was a cold night.

Tears blurred my eyes and crept down my cheeks. I was chilled and frightened and lonely. Only one thought gave me a little comfort. Mother had said that if I went with Auntie, then the whole family would eat well for a long time. That pleased me greatly and made me proud. But still, I was cold and getting colder by the minute.

I eased out of bed and walked across to Auntie's futon as quietly as a moth. I slid beside her and cuddled against her, stealing her warmth.

"If you have lice, and give them to me, then tomorrow you will wish you had never been born," she said.

"I do not have lice, Auntie," I whispered.

She said nothing else, and I slept next to her as close to contentment as was possible for a little girl who had just lost her old life.

TWO

Snakes must shed their old
Skins to find comfort. All I
Must do is change clothes.

*T*here were mirrors in the Green Tea House.

It was the first time I had really seen my own reflection—apart from a blurred outline glimpsed in the village pond when I took water from it—and the sight of my face looking back at me was startling.

I was so fascinated, I turned this way and that, viewing first one profile and then the other. I stuck my tongue out and watched with enchantment as the stranger in the mirror did the same thing. Would wonders never cease! Now, when I have mirrors made of glass all around the house and I can look at myself whenever I choose, I smile as I remember how easy I was to delight in those early days in the Green Tea House. The mirror that intrigued me wasn't even a particularly good one, as they were made of copper in those days, and my reflection was actually slightly misty.

My smile of pleasure didn't last long anyway.

There was far more in the tea house to terrify me than please me.

I shared my room with two other girls. My companions were called Aki—which means "Autumn" in English, and Ren, which translates to "Lotus." Both girls were about the same age as me, Aki being a few months older than Ren. Both of them had been in the Green Tea House for many months. Aki had arrived first. She had been there nearly a year already, and she let me know in no uncertain terms that she was my superior in every way.

"Finished with the mirror, have you?" she demanded.

I put it down quickly, embarrassed. I would have liked to explain that I was fascinated by it not from vanity, but because I had never seen myself properly before. But Aki was having none of it.

"Think you're worth looking at, do you?"

Ren giggled dutifully, as she did at most of Aki's words.

"Not at all, Aki," I said politely. I was about to explain, but Aki had no time to wait.

"Good. Because you're not. Where do you come from?"

Before I could give her the name of my village, she was speaking again.

"Doesn't matter. I don't suppose I would ever have heard of it anyway. I wonder how Auntie came to find you, out there in the sticks. Got some special talents, have you?"

I thought about it, and then shook my head. To my amazement, Aki seemed to find this amusing.

"You will have when Auntie's finished with you. I suppose that's what she sees in you. She likes raw clay so she can model it how she wants."

I glanced at Aki curiously, wondering if she realized what she had said. Tongue in cheek, I asked, "Can I expect to be as talented as you and Ren when she has finished with me?"

The sarcasm when straight over Aki's head. She raised her chin and almost smiled.

"You have much to learn, of course. Can you dance? Play the *samisen*? Sing? Perform the tea ceremony?"

I thought about it. I knew Aki would mock me whatever I said, but I spoke anyway. After all, however deficient I was in talents, Auntie *had* chosen me to be her maid, so she must have seen something in me.

"I can't do any of that. But does it matter if I'm going to be a maid?"

Both girls looked at me, and then Ren began to laugh. Aki followed a second later. I watched them both in bewilderment, deeply hurt that they should find me so funny. Finally, Aki's laughter was reduced to giggles.

"Is that why you think she's brought you here? To be a maid?"

"That's what Auntie told the innkeeper near my village," I protested.

"Well, she would, wouldn't she? It wouldn't be respectable for her to be roaming the countryside on her own." She wiped her streaming eyes and grinned widely. I sensed she wouldn't tell me any more until I asked, but Ren jumped in.

"Don't you know what this place is?"

"It's a tea house."

"No, it's not." Aki again, glaring at Ren to be quiet. "Well, it is. But tea houses are on every corner here in the Floating World. This isn't just any old tea house, it's *the* Green Tea House. It's famous throughout Edo. In fact, it's famous throughout Japan. Men travel for many days just to come here."

I stared at each of them in turn, totally bewildered. Edo I had heard of. It was the capital of Japan, the most important city in the whole of the country, which meant it was the most important city in the whole world. But if I was in Edo, how could I be somewhere called the "Floating World" at the same time? And why should anybody go out of their way just to get tea? My mother made excellent tea—when she could afford to buy it—but nobody came to take tea with us.

My expression set Aki and Ren off again. I watched both girls shake with laughter, clinging to each other for support. I had had enough. I stood and was ready to leave the room, in spite of the fact that I had no idea where I was going to go.

"Oh, let flow the water." Aki was smiling broadly. I was still suspicious, but these two girls—apart from Auntie— were the only people I knew in my new world, so I sat down again and spoke humbly.

"Please, Aki. I am only a simple village girl. Until Auntie brought me here, I had never been farther than the fields around my own village. If you would be so kind, please explain to me about the Floating World. And this place. And why I am here."

Aki preened at my words. "You are in the Floating World." I frowned, wanting to protest again that she had said I was in Edo, but she raised her finger and I was silent. "The Floating World is part of Edo. It is very famous. It is the place where men come to be entertained, to enjoy themselves." I nodded, although I still had no idea what she was talking about. "You are in the most exclusive tea house in the whole of Edo, which really means in the whole of Japan. Auntie allows only the richest and most powerful men to enter our doors, which is why we all have to be so talented. See?"

"No," I said simply. "If I'm going to be a maid, why do I have to be able to sing and dance, like you said?"

Aki closed her eyes and shook her head wearily. "I told you. You're not really going to be a maid at all. You're a maiko, like we are. When you've learned everything you need to know, you'll have your *mizuage* ceremony and then you'll be a geisha. If you're good enough. Are you with me now?"

Maiko? Geisha? *Mizuage*? The words chased around my brain. I knew of geisha. Everybody did. They were beautiful, talented women who used their many skills to entertain rich men. But I had never actually seen one. In fact, to me they were as far away from my life as the spirits that inhabited the unseen world all around us. And I had heard the word maiko. It had enchanted me, as it literally meant "dancing child." And now Aki was telling me that I was a maiko? But *mizuage*. Now that was a complete unknown.

I was so puzzled and surprised that I blurted the first words that came into my head. "What's a *mizuage*?"

I had expected more laughter, but instead, Aki and Ren turned their heads to stare at each other in an elaborate mime of amazement.

"You have to have your *mizuage* before you can be a geisha," Aki said slowly. "Have you never heard of it?"

"No. Is it some special kind of ceremony?"

Aki licked her lips. "Sort of." Ren giggled again, and Aki dug her in the ribs with her elbow. "The easiest thing will be to show you. Come on."

I followed both girls obediently and waited when Aki paused outside a screen door much like the one that led into our room.

"Tamayu-san." I glanced at Aki in surprise. The strident voice she used in front of me was suddenly soft and very humble. She waited a beat and then repeated the words again. When she was met by silence, she turned to us.

"She's not here. I thought I heard her go out earlier. Come on, we can slip in and she'll never know we've been here." In spite of her words, Aki slid the screen door open very slowly and carefully. "Nice, isn't it?"

The room was as large as the one we shared, but had more furniture and the screen walls were bright with prints. One in particular enchanted me at first glance. It showed a towering wave about to break over the top of a boat. I had never seen the sea, and I wondered if it was really as beautiful and fierce as this picture.

"Stop gawking and come over here," Aki called over her shoulder. She was on her knees in front of a large trunk and was sliding her hands through the contents. "Got it!"

I kneeled at her side, watching as she pulled out a fat book, beautifully bound in bright red leather. The characters on the front cover were embossed in gold.

"I can't read," I said reluctantly, even as my fingers itched to feel the leather and trace the gold characters.

"Doesn't matter." I was leaning against Aki, and I could feel her vibrating with excitement. "This is for looking at, not reading. It's Tamayu's pillow book. One of her lovers bought it for her. Must have cost him a fortune, and I don't know why he bothered. I bet there's nothing in here that she hasn't tried already."

She opened the front cover and held the book out to me on her splayed palms.

I stared at the full page illustration curiously. My first thought was that the drawing was quite beautiful. It showed a young couple—the man handsome, the woman beautiful, and their expressions rather serious—both very richly dressed. My eyes wandered down the page, and I gasped, feeling the blood tingle in my cheeks.

"No!"

Aki nodded seriously. "Oh, yes. That's what men and women do. Didn't you know?"

"Of course I do. I have five brothers. I've seen their trees of flesh often. But they didn't look like that! And they'd never dream of putting them there, I'm sure!" I finished lamely.

I expected Aki to laugh at me again, but instead she was serious. "Well, I expect where you come from they wouldn't even imagine doing things like this. But you're in the Floating World now and it's different here. Look."

She turned the page carefully, jabbing her finger at the new illustration without quite touching the paper.

"Look." Ren was so close to me that I could feel her breath on my cheek and in spite of my intense reluctance, I knew she would know at once if I tried to turn my head away, so I looked.

The illustration spanned both pages. The woman was on the right-hand side, the man on the left. But there were few clothes. The man's robe was flung back and beneath it, he was clad in a simple loincloth, folded in much the way sumo wrestlers wore their far bulkier versions. The woman had a kimono draped loosely around her, but it was pushed well away from her body. So life-like was the drawing that I could imagine her clawing at the cloth, frantic to push it away from her skin as it got in her way. I tried to focus on the kimono, but it was no good. My eyes were drawn to the middle of the two pages, where—just as the fine parchment met—both of the figures also joined.

I guessed that Ren was excited by the book. Her breath

was hot where it brushed my skin, and I was sure she was leaning more fiercely against me. I was deeply embarrassed. I would have given anything to be allowed to close the book, put it back in the chest, and try and forget I had ever seen it. And yet, at the same time, it held a dreadful fascination. I could not take my eyes off the couple, caught in their most intimate of moments.

The woman was lying on her back, with her widely splayed legs inviting the man, who was leaning toward her. My gaze was drawn to her black moss, and I was immediately terrified. My own private parts had a fluff of down, as misty as a dandelion head in seed. This woman's black moss unfurled like a chrysanthemum in full bloom, rioting on the page in its glory. My black moss would never look this! Was I doomed to failure right from the start?

Ren nudged me slyly. "See what he's doing?"

I glanced at the man. For a moment, I was confused. He was about to lean against the woman, I thought. Then I looked again and my eyes widened in disbelief. He had his tree of flesh in his hand, but it was like no tree I had ever seen on my brothers or even on my father. It reared from his body, stiff and straight. My eyes widened as I saw that the tip of his tree was already nuzzling between the woman's legs, aiming straight and true into her black moss.

I shook my head, lost for words.

Ren and Aki nudged each other and giggled. Ren pushed her face into mine, rubbing against me like a friendly cat. Her cheek was wet with sweat and the touch was unpleasant.

"Ever seen anything like that, have you?"

I shook my head. And yet at the same moment, I knew I was lying.

Long before—at least a year before Auntie had come to

our village and claimed me—I had been driving our ducks to a new pond. It had been a dry summer, and the pond in our own field was nothing but a nasty sheen of green slime.

"Take them down along the riverbed," Mother instructed. "Follow the track of the river down past the willow stand and you will come to a pond that should still have some water. Go later today, after the evening meal. And try and make sure nobody sees you. If there is water still there, it is better that nobody knows about it except you and our ducks."

She laughed, and I joined in dutifully, even though it seemed to me to be wrong that our ducks could drink and other ducks in the village had to go thirsty. I would do as she asked. Apart from anything else, if the ducks went thirsty for long, they would start to get thin, and that meant they would be killed and eaten. Not by us, of course. We had the occasional duck egg on special occasions, but that was all. The poor things would be sold to those who had money and inclination enough to eat flesh. Mother wrung their necks, but I was expected to pluck the sad little corpses, and I hated it. So, mindful of her words, I waited until dusk and then led our small flock alongside the river, hissing at them to be quiet whenever I was near a house.

Mother was right. I had to walk quite a long way along the riverbed, but eventually I came to a dip in the dry course and there was water. Not a great deal, to be sure, but the ducks piled in happily, drinking and throwing the water over their feathers in fine style. I watched them for a while, but the evening was hot and humid and eventually I took myself into the deep shade of a stand of camphor trees. The leaves smelled bitter, like medicine, but I was so grateful for the shade I barely noticed. My walk with the ducks had been long, and I was hot and tired. I knew I was falling asleep, but the ducks would not leave the water and I thought they would be safe.

A strange noise woke me up. I jerked upright, terrified that a fox had got amongst my flock. What Mother would say if I had to admit that I had allowed some of our precious ducks to be taken by a fox did not bear thinking about. I scrambled to my feet, staring around wildly. The ducks quacked softly and—I thought—looked at me curiously.

I was so relieved my flock was safe that it took me a while to realize the sound that had woken me was not coming from them at all. Intrigued, I walked to the end of the camphor trees and parted the low shrubs that grew in front of them carefully. I had no fear of real foxes, but full darkness had almost fallen and it was the time of day when fox spirits might be about. I was very careful to make no noise. I peered through the hole I had made with my hands and my mouth gaped in astonishment.

There were two bodies lying on the beaten earth of the clearing behind the shrubs. Two bodies that were so entangled that it took me seconds to work out that they were a man and woman. Or at least, a man and a girl. I thought the man must be hurting the girl. He was hitting her with his whole body, and she was uttering small, piercing cries. I almost ran forward, feeling I had to do something to stop this big, powerful man from hurting the far smaller, obviously helpless woman. But I did not. I knew who she was. And I knew the man, also.

The girl was called Chieko. It wasn't her real name, but was the name everybody in the village called her. It was what passed for wit in a village as small as ours. Chieko means "Wise Child," and poor Chieko was far from wise. She was actually simple. I had never even heard her speak. In fact, this was the most noise I had ever heard her make.

She was the despair of her mother, a nice woman whose husband had left her when it became obvious that Chieko was never going to be of any use and his wife hadn't gone on to produce any male children.

"I don't know why I don't sell her for a slave," she told my mother. "Well, I do. I can't think of anybody who would even take her for free."

My mother nodded sympathetically, although I could tell she was thinking proudly of her own fine male children.

But it appeared that her mother was wrong. Chieko did have a use after all.

The man who was enjoying her body was our neighbor, but much higher caste than we were. He owned much of the village next to us, and many of the fields surrounding our own village. Mother had always instructed us to look down modestly whenever he passed, but for some reason, I caught his eye once, and he paused and lifted my face with his finger under my chin.

"Well now." He hunkered down, but his face was still looking down at me. I was so terrified I could not even blink. "Surely, this is a pretty flower to be growing wild in the field." Mother shuffled up to us quickly, bobbing and bowing to him manically. "Your child?"

"Indeed, lord. Indeed, she is. A poor girl child, nothing more. Yet if she pleases you, lord, then I am truly blessed."

He pinched my chin, hard enough to hurt. I wanted to bite him, but I could feel the anxiety flowing from Mother, so I stayed still.

"What's your name, child?"

"Junko."

I heard Mother moan, and I wondered what I had done. The man had asked my name and I had told him. What was wrong with that?

"Pure child, eh? And does the name suit you, little one?"

I nodded. He laughed. His breath stunk of sake and garlic, and it took all my willpower not to turn my head away.

"Well then, Mother, I suggest you keep this one as pure as her name. I may come back for her one day."

He released my chin and slid a small coin into my hand, curling my fingers around it. He walked off whistling and I watched him go until Mother clouted me around the head and took the coin away from me.

Now, I watched as he reared away from Chieko. No matter how far he leaned back, it seemed to me that he was joined to her by his tree of flesh. Had he somehow hooked it into her so he could not let go? Was that why she was making such distressed noises? Fascinated, my gaze wandered up to Chieko's face. As I watched, her eyes flew open and her eyeballs bulged so hard I thought they were going to fly out. At the same time, her legs arched wide apart in a bow, and her toes curled so far under her feet that they disappeared. She cried out loud and the man lying between her legs laughed.

He fell toward her, his entire tree of flesh disappearing into her black moss. Black moss that was every bit as thick and lush as that in the pillow book. For a moment, I could not see Chieko at all. Then he rolled off her and lay on the hard ground, panting. I could see his chest heaving. Chieko was still. Then a curious thing happened.

Chieko's partner hooked together his robe with both hands, sitting up to fasten the sash. He rose to his feet and shuffled into his sandals. Threw a handful of coins on Chieko's body and walked away as if he could no longer even see her. I was about to dart forward, to ask if she was all right, but there was no need. She stood and stretched, tugging her own kimono tight and stooping to pick up the coins with greedy fingers. She walked away as if nothing had happened, just as the man had.

I herded my ducks together and walked home. I would have liked to have asked my mother about what I had seen, but caution laid a finger on my lips. I remembered how mother had seemed very pleased when Chieko's friend had paid attention to me. The coin he had given to me vanished into her obi instantly and we ate fish that night, and for many nights afterward. The fear that it could have been me, instead of Chieko, lying beneath him trembled in my thoughts. I mentioned casually to my older brother that I had seen Chieko with the man and he laughed out loud, then looked at me suspiciously.

"And what were they doing, little sister?" he asked.

I shrugged innocently. "Nothing. Just walking along the riverbank together."

"Aye? Well, you just keep away from that Chieko. She's..." He paused for thought and then shrugged. "She's not right in the head. I don't want you catching her silliness."

Why in that case did I see, with the good sight of my own two eyes, my brother and Chieko walking out of the village together not a week later after the evening meal?

Aki's elbow nudged me out of my reverie.

"See? That's what men and women do together. That's what's going to happen to you at your *mizuage* ceremony. A very rich man will pay Auntie a fortune for the privilege of taking your maidenhood. After that, you will become a geisha. Understand now?"

"I can't do things like that. My black moss isn't a bit like theirs," I said helplessly.

Both girls looked at me in astonishment and then

howled with laughter. Aki leaned on Ren for support, and I saw that tears of amusement were pouring down her cheeks. Ren started to say something, but laughter swallowed the words and she could do nothing but gasp for breath.

"And what is causing you so much amusement, my dear children?"

The man's voice was as smooth as fine silk, but it stopped Ren and Aki's laughter dead. Aki snapped the pillow book shut and slid it to the *tatami* matting, elbowing the folds of her kimono over it. Both girls were instantly quiet, their gaze fixed on the floor, their heads bowed courteously.

"Nothing, Big. Nothing at all." Aki's voice was as high and breathless as it had been when she had first tapped at the screen door. "This is the new girl. She knows nothing at all, so we thought we would show her how beautiful the Green Tea House is."

"Did you now?" The man's voice was cynical. I stared at him with frank interest. He was tall and slim with smooth skin the color of a tea rose in full bloom. His beautifully arched eyebrows were raised in an expression of disbelief, his rather full mouth pursed. He did not look like my brothers at all. Perhaps it was his expression that reminded me of them. Whatever it was, I decided instantly that I liked him.

"Aki and Ren have been very kind to me," I said shyly. Both girls nodded their heads in agreement. They were staring at me from beneath their lowered eyes and I could not interpret their expressions.

"And who are you then?"

I stared up at the young man and smiled. "My name is

Junko. Auntie bought me here from my village. Who are you?"

I thought I heard a whisper, soft as paper turning, from Ren. I glanced at her. Her eyes were fixed on the floor as if it held some strange fascination for her and her face had turned the color of tofu.

The young man laughed. It was a rich, deep sound, not at all like Aki and Ren's mocking amusement. I tilted my head back to see him better, and my smile widened. I did like him, I decided.

"My name is Big, Junko." He bowed deeply to me. "And if you are Junko, then it is you I am looking for. Auntie sent me to find you. To make sure you were being well cared for."

His eyes ran over Aki and Ren. Both girls spoke at once, their voices the gabble of birds flocking at twilight.

"We are surely looking after our little sister. Surely, Big."

"So you tell me. Now, both of you, out. Before Tamayu returns and finds you looking amongst her things."

Aki and Ren were on their feet in seconds. Aki glanced at the exposed pillow book and then looked at Big. Her expression was one of stark terror.

"Will you tell her, Big?" she whispered. "We meant no harm. We were just looking. Junko knows nothing about anything, and we thought...we thought it might be best to explain things to her."

"How old are you, Junko?" The curiously-named stranger ignored the other girls and spoke directly to me.

I thought about it for a moment. My youngest brother was about to celebrate his thirteenth birthday. I was just over a year younger than him and had been close to celebrating my own birthday when Auntie took me, so I would be not quite twelve.

"I'm nearly twelve," I told Big seriously.

"It seems to me that Junko has plenty of time to learn all she needs to know."

Neither Big's voice nor his smooth, pleasant expression wavered for an instant. Why, then, did Aki and Ren's eyes widen and their heads nod repeatedly, as if they had the palsy? I stared from them to Big with interest. He jerked his head over his shoulder and the girls jostled each other in their haste to get through the screen door.

I watched as he picked up the pillow book and returned it to the chest. It occurred to me to wonder that he knew exactly where it belonged, but in the midst of all the rest of the strangeness, it was nothing. His hands smoothed the layers carefully in place. I noticed his fingers were very long and the flesh of his hands a shade or two lighter than his face. I had never seen a man's hands that were so well kept, so elegant in their movements. In fact, I had never seen a man so clean, so well-groomed. Even the gentleman who had thrown me the coin had skin that was roughened by the sun. I remembered his fingertips had been calloused. They had rubbed against my skin when he pinched my chin.

"Why do they call you Big?" I asked. "It's a funny name for a man."

His grin split his face like a slice of melon. He had excellent teeth, very white and even.

"Don't you know? Didn't Ren and Aki tell you?"

I shook my head. I had no idea what he was talking about. He laughed, and I smiled with him, delighted that I was amusing this elegant young man.

"They told me nothing," I said simply. And then, encouraged by his laughter, and the fact that he reminded me a little of my brothers, I asked shyly, "Big, will you be my friend?"

The smile stayed in place, but I sensed that suddenly he was serious. I liked that. It was much better than being mocked by Aki and Ren.

"Yes, little Junko. I will be your friend. Does that please you?"

I had no need to think about it. "Yes," I said. I held my hands out so he could help me to my feet. His touch was both strong and gentle as he pulled me up.

THREE

When the moon is full,
Only then does the earth miss
Her lover's embrace

*M*y hand trembled so much I almost spilled the tea.

"Be careful." Just two words, and Tamayu's tone was indulgent, but I knew that later, when we were alone, she would shout at me. Tell me I was clumsy. That I would never be a geisha. That I had no talents at all. If she worked herself into a real rage, she would reach for the bamboo stick that was always left behind her door. If she did that, I would hold my hands out quickly, palms upward. I knew from past experience that it was better to offer my hands. If she had to tell me, then there would be more strokes added.

"Ah, the poor child is nervous." Tamayu's patron smiled at me. "She's a remarkably pretty little girl, Tamayu-chan. Not had her *mizuage* yet, of course?"

Tamayu bared her teeth in what looked like a smile and shook her head.

"Oh no. Most certainly not. She isn't thirteen yet. And she has much to learn before she can even think about becoming a real geisha." She leaned forward, tapping her patron flirtatiously on the hand with her fan, obviously determined to divert his attention from me. "Truth to tell, she's just a raw country girl. I sometimes wonder where Auntie finds them." She sighed deeply and shook her head.

It would, I thought, be very bad for me when Tamayu and I were alone.

Tamayu was my elder sister. Auntie had given me to her so that I could learn all the arts of a geisha from her.

"Think yourself lucky, child." Auntie poked me with her stick to remind me it was not sufficient just to listen to her. It had to be clear that I was paying her my full attention. "Tamayu is one of the most respected geisha in the whole of the flower and willow world. She will teach you to sing and dance. To play the *samisen*. To perform the tea ceremony sublimely. And above all, she will teach you how to entrance your patrons with your wit, to make any room you grace with your presence light up."

I wanted to say that I could not do all that! I was nothing, a nobody from the provinces. Tamayu was beautiful and sophisticated and talented. She was everything I was not. She could even look at her pillow book without blushing! Instead, I simply lowered my head as if I agreed with Auntie. I had not been in the Green Tea House for long, but it was long enough to know my place in this new and strangest of worlds. Aki had explained this to me a few days after I first met Big.

"You are the newest maiko. That means you are less than the rest of us, and must do as you are told. By all of us." That was fine by me. As long as I was given instructions, then I would follow them. It was not knowing what I should do that worried me. "And don't be thinking you're special just because Big has taken a fancy to you."

"Why is he called Big?" I asked innocently. Aki tittered.

"You've met Bigger," she said. I had, and he had terrified me to my very bones. He had drifted into the room where I was learning to play mahjong with Aki and Ren. As soon as his shadow fell over them, both girls put their tiles down and kowtowed to him, their heads striking the *tatami* matting. Not knowing any better, I simply stared at him. He glanced at me and then looked away.

"This is the new maiko, is it? Big told me she'd arrived." He was a friend of Big's, then? My spirits rose. Big liked me, so perhaps this handsome young man might also like me. I smiled at him shyly. He stared at me as if I weren't there. "What's she called?"

"Junko, Bigger-san," Ren and Aki spoke together.

"Junko. An ugly name. Suits her." Both girls giggled dutifully. "Tamayu is going to knock her into shape, is she? Looks as if she's going to have her work cut out for her with this one." He leaned down suddenly, his face so close to mine that I could see the pores on his nose. "Well, Junko. If you're going to be with us for some time, there's a couple of things you need to know. Do as Auntie tells you. Keep out of my way. And if I have to see you, don't make me angry with you. Understand?"

He reached out. His hand was so big it spanned my face and his fingers nipped my cheekbones painfully. He pinched harder. I held my breath and met his eyes.

"Pity she isn't quite ugly enough for Auntie to put her in the other place."

He let go of my face abruptly and stood. I wanted to rub the pain away from my face, but I was determined he not see that he had hurt me. He walked out without a backward glance, and only when I could no longer hear his footsteps on the polished wood of the hall did I put my hands to my face.

"You'll probably bruise," Ren said conversationally. "Did he really hurt you?"

"Not really," I lied. "But why did he want to hurt me? He's never even seen me before."

"Because Big likes you," Aki said simply.

I thought about this for a moment. I was pleased that Big liked me, but I couldn't see what that had to do with Bigger not liking me, and I said so.

"Because Bigger's jealous of you, of course." Aki rolled her eyes as if it was the most obvious thing in the world. "You don't know anything at all, do you?"

I shrugged my shoulders. "Not really," I said humbly. "I don't even know what Big and Bigger are doing here. They're not geisha and they're not patrons."

Aki and Ren exchanged glances. I thought they were going to laugh at me again, but they did not.

"They look after us," Aki said seriously. "If the patrons take a little too much sake and get a bit silly, the boys sort them out. If one of the geisha gets a bit above herself, then Auntie tells the boys to sort her out as well. And..." Aki glanced around as if making sure we were still alone, then lowered her voice. "They look after things in the other place as well. You do whatever the boys tell you, that's the important thing."

I nodded. But she still hadn't answered my original question.

"They work for Auntie, then. I see. But I still don't understand why Bigger doesn't like me. If he thinks I'm ugly and useless, why is he jealous of me?"

"Because Big likes you," Aki said again. She looked at

my face and sighed. "Bigger hates anybody Big likes. That's the way of it. They're friends. Very good friends, if you get my meaning."

I thought about. Of course, that made perfect sense. My oldest brother had always been very close to our neighbor's son, and they both made it very clear that I was not at all welcome when I tried to join them. And also, I now knew where the boys got their names from. It was obvious. Both men were tall, but Bigger was perhaps a couple of inches higher than Big. I was glad I had not asked. Ren and Aki already thought I was stupid. Asking such an obvious question would have made things even worse.

I decided it was best to keep out of Bigger's way. But Tamayu was my elder sister, and I could not avoid her.

She was perfect. And she hated me.

"She's very beautiful, isn't she?" I said to Aki.

"Very," Aki agreed. "And talented. She's teaching me to play the *samisen*, and sing and dance. She says I have natural talent and a perfect sense of harmony."

I did my best to look impressed, even though I was deeply puzzled.

It seemed to me that Aki had very little talent. I was made to sit and listen as Tamayu instructed her in the musical arts. I could see—and hear—that Tamayu was exceptionally talented. Her singing voice was beautiful, and to watch her dance was to feel tears of joy come to one's eyes. But Aki seemed clumsy at the side of her. And while she was perfectly competent as she plucked the strings of the *samisen*, there was no life in her music. And even I could hear that Aki could not sing. Her voice was flat and cracked. I knew if I mentioned it to Ren, it would get straight back to Aki. So I turned to my only friend in the tea house. I asked Big.

"Aki's her favorite," he said simply. "It's because Aki's never going to be any competition to her. Aki's all right, but she's never going to shine. That's why Tamayu hates you."

I frowned, even more puzzled, and he grinned.

"Sing for me, Junko."

I thought about it for a while and then smiled. I liked Big. If singing for him would make him happy, then I would sing. I had an excellent memory, and I could recall the words of a song that was a favorite of Tamayu's. I hesitated over the first verse, but then got into my stride and the words flowed out without me having to even think about it. When I came to the end of the song, Big said nothing, but simply sat and looked at me silently.

"Take a little advice from me, Junko," he said softly. "If you can help it, never sing in front of Tamayu. And when you learn to play the *samisen*—and she will teach you, for Auntie will insist on it—make sure you do not play extremely well when she is there. And when you learn to dance, pretend that you are wearing heavy shoes and it is difficult for you to lift your feet. In front of Tamayu, at least. When you perform the tea ceremony, be clumsy for her."

He wasn't smiling when he spoke, and I wondered if my singing had displeased him.

"If it pleases you, Big, then I will do it. But I think Tamayu will be angry with me."

And I was right. No matter how hard I tried, I could not please the beautiful geisha. I had no need at all to remember what Big had said. I was so terrified of Tamayu that as soon as I was near her, I was clumsy.

I watched Aki brushing out her elder sister's hair. Tamayu's hair fell almost to her waist, thick and straight and glossy. Aki caught the brush in a snag, and Tamayu—almost casually—raised her hand and struck Aki hard across the face with her knuckles. I winced, thinking if she could do this to her favorite, what could I hope for?

Aki's lips trembled.

"You're nearly as clumsy as she is." Tamayu jerked her head in my direction. "Get out, both of you. I'm expecting my *danna*. I don't want him to find the place full of idiots."

We almost ran down the corridor to our own room.

Aki shouted for the maid and we sat down on the *tatami*, waiting for our tea to arrive. I would have liked to put my arms around Aki to offer her comfort, but I could sense her anger and knew she would hate me touching her.

"She'll see," Aki blurted suddenly. "She thinks she's the only one that matters in this place. But she's wrong. I'll show her. Her and Auntie both."

She sipped at her tea, and I sat silently, my eyes on the matting. I had no idea what she was talking about, but I soon found out.

*P*erhaps a month or so later, all hell was let loose in the Green Tea House.

All we maiko slept together. As the newest girl, it was my task to rise first and call for the maid to bring us tea. I often thought of the days—already seeming a lifetime away —when my first task of the day had been to light the fire and prepare food and tea for my parents and my brothers. I only ate after they had had enough. If there was no food left, then I went hungry. When I remembered my empty belly, I gave thanks that Auntie had chosen me.

That morning, I was still half in sleep as I shrugged myself into my robe. I was nearly at the door before I realized that Aki was missing. I looked and looked, as if she might suddenly appear out of nowhere. Perhaps she had felt the need to go to the toilet urgently and had slipped out without disturbing either Ren or me. But if that was the case, why were her kimono and obi not hanging on their usual hooks on the wall? I bit my thumbnail anxiously, knowing instinctively that trouble was heading my way.

"Ren." Ren was a heavy sleeper, and I had to shake her hard to wake her up. "Ren, Aki's not here."

She peered at me blearily and yawned. "What are you talking about, Junko? Where's she gone?"

"I don't know," I almost wailed. "I don't know where she is. But she's not here. Look!"

Ren raised herself on her elbow and glanced about the room. The sleep fled from her eyes and she sat up.

"Go and wake Auntie up, quickly. Tell her Aki must have run away."

I did as I was told. As I pattered down the corridor in bare feet, my sleeping robe clutched around me, I said the words to myself over and over again. Aki's gone. Aki's gone. I'm sorry Auntie, but Aki's gone. It wasn't my fault. Honestly, it wasn't.

Auntie had no need to be woken up. She was already sipping tea when I tapped softly on her screen door. It was the first time I had seen her without makeup and her wig and I barely recognized her. She looked so much younger with a naked face and her hair plaited into thick ropes. Was she even as old as my own mother? I doubted it. She was, I realized, a pretty woman. She heard my words in silence, a silence that terrified me more than a shout could ever have done. I stood, twisting my fingers in my robe, waiting for her to tell me what to do.

"What time did she go?"

"I don't know, Auntie." My tongue was trying to stick to the roof of my mouth and I could barely get the words out. "We all went to bed at the same time last night and it was only just now, when I woke up to ask for tea, that I found she was gone."

Auntie stared through me. I trembled as I waited for her anger.

"She could have been gone for hours." I realized she was talking to herself, so I stayed silent. "Well, she will be found. And when she is found, it will be the last she will ever see of the Green Tea House. Go get my maid for me."

I scuttled off as fast as my trembling knees could carry me. There had been such a quiet menace in Auntie's voice, I felt sorry for Aki.

Tamayu was rousted from her sleep by Auntie's shout. We heard Auntie demanding to know if she had any idea where Aki had gone.

"How would I know?" she said sulkily. "The wretched child didn't confide in me at all. How could she do this to me? I always treated her well."

Auntie's voice cut across her whine like a sword slash. "You were too soft with her. I told you that." We didn't hear Tamayu's reply, but my heart sank as I guessed that in the future, Tamayu would be even harder on me. "Never mind for the moment. You can't coax spilled water back into the tray. What's done is done. I'll send one of the maids to rouse Big and Bigger. They must find Aki and bring her back. It might not be too late, even now. The Floating World never sleeps. Somebody will have seen her."

I felt sure Ren thought it was my fault that Aki had disappeared. She drank her tea in sulky silence and refused to speak to me. When I persisted, wondering out loud where Aki could possibly have gone, she turned her back on me. Deeply unhappy, I wandered out into the garden. I sat on a stone bench in the farthest corner, huddled into the wall. It had turned cold, and I shivered in my thin kimono. I was so lost in my thoughts that I did not notice the storm clouds that were gathering. When I did, it was far too late. Before I could think about moving, the rain was coming down so fast that I could not even see the door of the Green Tea House. A slash of lightning cut the garden in two, leaving my eyes almost blind with the dazzle. Thunder followed, so close on the heels of the lighting that I knew the storm was right overhead. I whimpered. I have always been terrified of thunder and lightning. But there was nobody to hear my distress.

Between the vicious crackle of lightning and the boom of the thunder, I lost all sense of direction. In any event, the rain cut off anything more than a hand space in front of me. I stood and darted back and forward, perhaps half a body length in each direction. For a brief moment, a gust of wind parted the torrent and I saw a wooden door set in the far end of the wall I had been leaning against. It was weathered almost to the color of the stone that surrounded it and it had only darkened enough to be seen by means of the drenching rain that beat against it. I had no idea where it led. I was so terrified, I didn't care.

My kimono was sodden, plastered to my body. In the moment it took me to reach the doorway, I was blind as well —the rain battered into my eyes and left me sightless. I hammered on the door, whimpering. I thought nobody was going to answer. In a moment of clarity, I realized I was probably trying to get through a door that led to the street, a door that would always be locked, unless Auntie had decided to use the garden for a party. Irrelevantly, I had a sudden memory of Tamayu talking about just such a party, where all the greatest men in Edo had been moved almost to tears by her singing and dancing one warm summer evening.

"I was superb," she said. Aki and Ren and I all nodded in agreement. Of course she had been. Who would dare doubt it? Not us!

I rested my head on the door in despair. I was about to turn, to grope my way back across the garden, find the tea house entrance somehow, when the door was flung open. Unbalanced, I literally fell across the threshold.

"Hora! What's this that the gods have thrown at us?"

The woman's voice was amused. I scrabbled to get to my feet, but my *geta* slid from under me and I fell back to the floor.

"*Sumimasen deshita,*" I babbled. "I am so sorry. I have brought the rain onto your floor."

"It doesn't matter, little one. Not at all. One of the maids will see to it. But what does matter is that you are soaking wet. You're from the Green Tea House, I suppose. We heard that Auntie had taken a new maiko. Is that you?"

Her hands were under my arms as she spoke, supporting me gently. I kept my gaze humbly on the floor, as politeness dictated, and used it to hide my puzzlement. Where was I? How did this woman know about me?

"What's your name, child?"

"Junko, *sama.*"

"Ah. You are the one we heard about, then."

As she spoke, she tugged my obi undone and pried my soaking kimono away from me. She shouted over her shoulder, and a moment later a plump maid was at her side, carrying a warm robe.

"Now, I wonder what's happened that's lured you out into this terrible weather, Junko-chan? Here, put this on. I was on my way to the bath when I heard you hammering. Would you like to bathe with us? It will warm you through, and we can all have a nice chat."

I was shaking so hard with cold that no words could escape through my lips. She didn't seem to mind. My savior took me by the hand, at the same time calling over her shoulder to the maid to ensure that my kimono and obi were dried.

I trotted at her side and with every step, I became more bewildered. I had thought the Green Tea House must be the most beautiful house in the whole of Edo. Every wall—even the roof beams—were richly gilded, and each wall was hung with exquisite scrolls. Even the *tatami* matting on the floor was of the highest quality. There was little furniture—except in Tamayu's room, which was crammed with chests and boxes all bearing precious ornaments that she told us smugly had been presents from her many admirers—but what was there was the very best. I had seen nothing like it in my village, had never imagined that such luxury could exist outside of the fabled riches of the shogun's palace.

Every time my eyes darted right or left, it seemed to me that this place was even richer, even more beautiful than the Green Tea House. The floor that was not covered by *tatami* was glowing wood block, each piece fitted so tightly to its neighbor that a sheet of rice paper could not have been coaxed between them. The walls were largely bare and seemed to my dazzled gaze to consist mainly of windows, each one screened with silk shades so very sheer that they barely stopped the grey daylight from entering. Fat, scented candles were strewn artfully about, almost works of art themselves in their beautifully wrought bronze holders. And it smelled delicious. Incense mingled with the scent of food cooking. I had taken nothing but tea since rising and realized I was hungry as my belly rolled, loud as the thunder. I bit my lip in distress, but my companion seemed not to notice.

"A bath first, little Junko," she said cheerfully. "And then I really think I am quite hungry. Would you care for some tea and *daifuku* cakes?"

My mouth watered at the thought. I had never even tasted *daifuku* cakes until Auntie brought me to the tea house. Now I loved them. Not that we maiko tasted them often, but occasionally Tamayu was given them as a present, and if she had too many to eat herself it amused her to scatter them to us maiko, rather as another woman might have scattered crumbs to the birds.

"Yes, please, *sama*," I said politely. My new friend laughed.

"Oh, how very formal! I see Auntie is teaching you well, Junko. But my name is Nami. Will it please you to call me by it?"

Such exquisite courtesy to an insignificant young girl! I nearly choked in my eagerness to agree.

"Yes, please, Nami."

She laughed as she pushed open a door. Instantly, a maid was at our side, helping us out of our robes and then pouring hot water over us. To me, this was perhaps the most miraculous part of my new life. In my village, we had bathed in the river, no matter what the weather. When the river ran dry, I had drawn water from the well and poured it from a huge pottery jug over first my parents, and then my brothers. Nobody had bothered to do it for me, and so I had struggled with the heavy pot myself. It slipped once and I gave myself a black eye. My brothers had howled with laughter at me. In the tea house, I bathed every day—in hot water!—with a maid to pour the water for me and then soap and rinse me before I climbed into the steaming bath with the other girls. Yes, the bath was the best thing—better even than *daifuku* cakes and not having to herd the ducks.

I followed Nami so closely into the steaming water that I might have been her shadow.

"Look, girls. This is Junko, the new maiko we have heard so much about. Isn't she precious?"

There were two women already in the steaming water. The steam was thick and I had tucked my head so politely far down, I could barely make them out. I slid into the hot water quickly, murmuring greetings.

"So, Junko. It's taken you long enough to find us."

The voice was kind and I dared to glance up. The woman who had spoken to me had no more substance than the steam that was curling around her. Her hair was tucked up out of the way of the water, but it seemed to me that it was as white as her skin, and her skin in its turn had no more color than the snow that fell in our village every winter. I stared rudely, unable to take my glance from her face. Could she see me, I wondered? Her eyes were beautiful, the perfect almond shape that Tamayu piled makeup on to achieve, but such a pale grey that the pupils seemed shockingly *there*, like a single brushstroke painted on a blank sheet of paper.

She was as beautiful as water spirits were said to be, the spirits that my mother warned me haunted the river, ready to snatch away any child that took their fancy. And she was smiling at me. For a moment, I was utterly confused. Had I somehow wandered well away from the tea house's garden?

Perhaps missed my way in the sound and fury of the storm and fetched up by the river?

"Don't be afraid of me, Junko," she said kindly. "My name is Gin. I am a geisha, like you will be soon. My friends here are also geisha, so we are all sisters together. This is the Hidden House. No doubt you've heard it spoken of?"

Gin. The name meant "Silver," and it described this beautiful spirit perfectly. It was the rest of her words that reassured me. I knew where I was. I was in the house that Aki and Ren called "the other place." The place that Bigger had said I would have suited if only I were uglier. I frowned at the thought and Gin's lips trembled with amusement.

"Go on, child. Ask. There should be no secrets between us."

"Bigger said I would do well here if I were a little bit uglier. But none of you are ugly at all. I don't understand."

There was a moment's silence, and then all three women erupted into laughter. I stared from one to the other, wondering what I had said that had amused them so. Finally, the one who had not yet spoken took a deep breath and tapped me on the arm to claim my attention.

"Dear Junko. You must remember that Bigger does not like any of us geisha. He is not a man that likes women very much." She paused and I nodded seriously. I understood that. He and my friend Big were very close. Bigger was a serious sort of man. He obviously did not have time for a woman's idle chatter.

"I know," I said proudly. "He is a very good friend of my friend Big. My brother back in the village had a best friend he would not share with anybody. I understand that."

The laughter died abruptly. All three women sucked in their breath sharply. Gin glanced from Nami to the woman whose name I did not know and then back at me.

"Big is your friend?"

"Oh yes," I said firmly, pleased to be able to own to at least one friend in my new world. "He caught Ren and Aki and me looking at Tamayu's pillow book. He was angry with them and sent them away, but when I asked him, he said that he would like to be my friend."

"Truly, Junko?"

"Yes. And I understand perfectly that Bigger doesn't like me because Big does." I beamed happily, delighted that I was appearing to be more than a foolish child.

"And what else did Bigger say about this place?"

"Nothing at all. Aki and Ren called it 'the other place,' and that is all I know. But I don't understand why he said that I would have to be ugly to belong here. You geisha are all very beautiful."

Nami smiled.

"You think Gin is beautiful? Even though she looks more like a spirit than a woman?"

I nodded. Of course she was beautiful.

"And me? In spite of this?"

Nami held her hands up in front of me and spread her fingers. I stared in fascination. Each finger was webbed from nail to base, exactly like a frog's foot. "My toes are just the same. Doesn't that make me ugly and strange?"

"No. Of course not. Everybody thinks Tamayu is beautiful, but I have seen her in the bath and she has bandy legs. But that doesn't make her any less lovely."

Nami's lips twitched.

"Auntie tells the patrons that I am a diving girl from Uminchu, and that my hands and feet are webbed because my mother mated with a water spirit. It's all nonsense of course. I can't even swim. But the patrons love to think it's so."

"And me, Junko?" The last of the women stood slowly, the water falling off her shoulders like silver rain. "Am I also beautiful in your eyes?"

As she rose, her breasts jutted out before her like boulders. I wondered if she would even be able to balance herself out of the water, they were so huge. Her nipples were dark brown, and stuck out like Tamayu's fingernails. Still she rose out of the water. Her waist was narrow, much more narrow than mine and I had always been proud of my slim waist. On either side, her hips swelled dramatically, balancing out her huge breasts. She turned, and her bottom stuck out so far it almost appeared as a mirror image of her huge breasts. I stared at her with interest. She wasn't fat, the slender waist saw to that, but she was certainly built like no Japanese woman I had ever seen before. But her skin was like silk and her face was lovely. I said so.

There was a long pause and I wondered if I had said something wrong. Tamayu was forever telling me I was a country bumpkin with no manners and less wit. Had she been here, she would no doubt have taken pleasure in telling me exactly what I had done wrong. I bit my lip anxiously. I would have done anything not to upset these kind, lovely geisha, these women who had told me they were my sisters.

"Her standing figure looks like a Chinese peony, her sitting figure looks like a tree peony, and her walking figure looks like a lily." Nami spoke softly, and the other geisha nodded their approval. "Not only are you very beautiful, Junko, but you are a bright and shining spirit. We are glad you have found us."

After the upsets of the day, the kindness of these lovely creatures was too much and my tears brimmed over.

"Please, can I come and live here with you?" I begged. "I

hate the Green Tea House and don't want to go back there. I'll be good. I'll do anything that you ask of me. Please, if you are my sisters, can I stay here?"

Gin shook her head, her expression serious.

"No, Junko-chan. You cannot stay with us. We would love to have you here. There are only the three of us at the moment in the house, and we would love to have a maiko like you to train. But it cannot be. You don't know about the Hidden House?"

I choked back my tears and was about to shake my head when a memory came to me. Tamayu and her fellow geisha Saki had been entertaining patrons. For some reason, Auntie had said that I was to be allowed to attend. Tamayu had decided that she was not in the mood for playing the *samisen* and had handed it to me with a smirk.

"Make yourself useful, Junko. The moon hides himself and makes us melancholy. Play us some music to suit our mood."

I took the lovely instrument carefully and began to pluck out a tune. It was one that I had heard one of the other geisha play and I had liked it, and it didn't seem at all odd to me that I should be able to play it from memory. Tamayu listened to me for a short time and then poked me hard with her foot.

"Enough! You pluck the strings as if they had done you some injury. Be quiet in case you offend these gentlemen's ears." She glanced around at the patrons, inviting them to applaud her wit. But they did not.

"Perhaps the sake has dulled your senses, Tamayu." One of the older men smiled at me. I smiled back shyly and he blinked. "The maiko plays beautifully. Finish your song, child."

I felt the hatred smoldering off Tamayu, but carried on

playing anyway. I loved the sound of the *samisen* and could barely believe that it was my fingers that were summoning this lovely music into existence.

"Auntie found her in the provinces somewhere," Tamayu said sulkily when I finally finished. "If you ask me, she would be more suited to the Hidden House than here."

She leaned forward and filled the sake cup of the man who had praised my playing. She had to nudge him to get his attention, and I knew I would be in trouble next day.

But as I thought about her words, I was bewildered. Tamayu and Bigger both obviously considered the Hidden House to be far inferior to the Green Tea House, yet to me it seemed a place of enchantment. And these three exceptionally beautiful geisha who were my new friends were even lovelier than Tamayu and Saki.

"Tamayu mentioned it once. She made it sound as if being sent here was some sort of punishment, but I would love to be able to stay here. With you all."

Gin smiled.

"We thank you for your kind words, Junko. But the Hidden House is not for you. You are perfect; we are not. And besides, we geisha here are special in ways that you could not be expected to understand." She glanced at the other women and they nodded encouragingly. "But for all that, we are truly geisha, and you must never let the likes of Tamayu tell you that we are not. Are you hungry, child?"

"Yes," I said simply.

"Good. Hiromi, will you call the maids to dry us?"

Wrapped in a warm robe and sitting next to a charcoal burner, I nibbled my *daifuku* cakes slowly. I would have loved to have gulped them down, but even more did I want my new sisters to think I had some manners.

As I ate, the geisha questioned me. Where was I from?

How long had I been at the Green Tea House? The maids had said there was some sort of commotion in the tea house earlier. What had happened? I answered quickly, explaining about Aki running away. Gin shook her head.

"Stupid child. Does she really think Auntie will let her go, after she has already spent a fortune buying her? Not to mention what she will have spent on her clothes and feeding her."

The question that had been lurking in my own mind popped up and I spoke carefully.

"Auntie gave my mother money for me as well. And I already have two kimonos. I don't eat a great deal, but I suppose it has to be paid for. But I don't understand why Auntie does it. I'm not kin to her, and she has no obligation to my family."

I peered hopefully at the faces surrounding me, and I was puzzled to see that each of the geisha was frowning. Finally, Hiromi spoke.

"Auntie owes you nothing, Junko. But with every meal you eat, with every kimono she buys for you, *your* debt to *her* becomes greater."

"I don't understand."

"In the fullness of time, you will have your *mizuage*. Your *danna* will pay Auntie a huge amount of money for the ceremony, but it will not be enough to pay her back for what she paid for you and for all she has invested in you. So you will work in the Green Tea House as a geisha, singing and dancing for rich men and entrancing them with your wit. They will pay well for the privilege, but it will never be enough for Auntie to let you go."

She paused and I saw that Gin and Nami were nodding in agreement. Clearly, I should understand all this. I did

not. But I smiled and nodded as well, as if everything had
been explained.

Tamayu had taught me well. Politeness was almost
everything in my new world. The geisha smiled with me, so
I thought that Tamayu was right.

As she always insisted she was.

FOUR

Time is a river.
It is fruitless to try and
Fight against the flow.

*A*s soon as the rain slowed a little, my new friends said I must return to the Green Tea House. If Auntie found me with them, then there would be trouble for all of us.

"Can I come back?" I asked hopefully.

"Surely." Nami smiled. "But only at a time when Auntie will not miss you. And remember, the Green Tea House may only open its doors in the evening, but here in the Hidden House, we also welcome patrons in the afternoon, so we will be busy then."

"I'll remember," I promised. But Nami had not finished with her instructions.

"Have you noticed that Auntie is not always in the Green Tea House? That often her bedroom is not slept in?"

I had not thought about it, but now Nami mentioned it, I realized that sometimes Auntie was not there, and at those times Tamayu in particular did not venture out of her own room, although, oddly, I often heard a man's voice coming from in there.

"When Auntie is not in the Green Tea House, then she is here," Nami explained. "And if she is here, then the boys are here as well. It would not be good for either Auntie or the boys to find you here with us."

"Ah!" I said with satisfaction. Now that, I understood. Given Tamayu and Bigger's disdainful comments about the Hidden House, I decided that it must attract a lower class of client than the Green Tea House.

That explained a great deal. It did not seem to me that the boys had a lot to occupy them in the Green Tea House. Our patrons were mainly older, very dignified men, who seemed to want to do little other than sit around and chat amongst themselves as they were entertained by the geisha. Perhaps that was why the Hidden House was different, I thought. Perhaps the patrons there were less cultured than ours and more in need of the boys to keep an eye on them. Probably that was why Auntie would not like me to be here, young and silly as I knew myself to be.

I slid back into the Green Tea House unnoticed. All the bedroom screens were pulled firmly closed. As if a flimsy screen could shield anybody from Auntie's anger! Ren was napping, curled up on her sleeping mat and snoring gently. But not for long.

I shook her awake as soon as I heard the clatter of wooden *geta* on the hall floor. We peeped out of our room timidly and then hurried into the main room at Auntie's shout.

The boys had found Aki.

She drooped in their grip. She looked very small, shrunken somehow, and I felt a flash of intense pity for her.

Each one of us had felt the sharp sting of Auntie's tongue when she was annoyed with us. That and the even sharper smack of her cane on the back of our legs when we had been particularly stupid. Aki, I thought, was probably in line for not just a telling off but, a beating as well.

Auntie stared at Aki. She stared for so long that all of us —except Aki, who simply stared at the floor—began to fidget.

"Where was she?" Auntie didn't even sound angry, and I sighed with relief. Perhaps Aki was going to escape punishment after all. I had always thought she was Auntie's favorite out of the three of us. Now I was sure of it.

"In the merchant's quarter, Auntie," Bigger grinned. "She was trying to hide in Jun-san's storeroom."

"And what were you hoping to find there, Aki?" Auntie said.

"His son loves me." Aki raised her head and stared defiantly at Auntie. "He's going to marry me. He promised."

Auntie's face changed. It was as if a sudden thundercloud had passed over the tranquil face of the moon. I felt, rather than heard, Ren moan softly.

"Really? You are even more stupid than I thought you were, child. And how did you make the acquaintance of this merchant's son? I know his father has never been here." She flared her nostrils in obvious contempt. "I would never let a man of his class into my tea house."

"We spoke to the young man." Bigger's tone was expressionless. "And we also spoke to his father. At first, Jun-san was inclined to be amused by his son's adventures. But when we explained to him that Aki had come from this tea house, he immediately realized what grave error his son had fallen into. He apologized on his knees."

"Is she still whole?" Auntie snapped.

Bigger shrugged. "I don't know. We spoke at some length with the son, and he swore that he had done no more than put his arm around her. It was all a mistake, he said. He had met her when she came to his father's shop on an errand, and she had taken a fancy to him. It was all her fault, he said. Every time she left the tea house to buy something from the shops, she hung about until she saw him. She lured him, he said. He had never promised to marry her, not at all."

"Did you punish him anyway?"

"No." Auntie raised her eyebrows and Bigger spoke quickly. "There was no need for us to spend time on him. He was terrified half out of whatever wits he possessed anyway, and Jun-san assured us that he would make sure that his stupid son would be suitably chastised. Now that, I do believe."

Aki whimpered, and I saw that fat tears were running down her face.

"Well, child? Is this tale of the boys the truth?" Auntie said.

"No! He loves me. He said he did. He wants to marry me."

Auntie closed her eyes as if she was in pain. "I don't care what the stupid puppy promised you," she snapped. "You've been here long enough to know that you can trust not a word that any man says to you. Ever. For that alone, you deserve to be punished. But you have also brought dishonor on yourself and on my house. That I will not tolerate. Take her to Kaede's house. Let Kaede examine her to make sure she's still intact. I can't be bothered to waste my time on her. Whether she's whole or she isn't, get whatever price for her you can."

Aki fell to her knees. She banged her head so hard on

the *tatami* that I thought her skull must have cracked. I was going to run forward and try to lift her up when Ren grabbed my arm and held on tightly. I turned to protest, but Ren simply shook her head and mouthed *no*. The look of stark terror on her face stopped me more surely than her grip on my arm.

"Auntie, no!" Aki raised her head and I gasped. I hardly recognized her, her face was so contorted with fear. "Please, let me stay here. I don't care if I stay as a maiko forever. But please, let me stay."

Auntie stared at her and then got to her feet. I thought perhaps she was going to hit Aki with her cane, but instead she simply leaned on it and clacked briskly toward the door. Big and Bigger hoisted Aki from the floor with their hands under her arms and walked with her as if she weighed nothing. It seemed to me that all the fight had gone out of Aki. She hung in their grip as if she was a dead thing.

Auntie paused at the screen door and turned. For a moment, I thought she had changed her mind and I was pleased for Aki. But I was wrong.

"Tamayu. I almost forgot." She smiled, but there was no humor in it. I glanced at Tamayu. Her face was a blank, beautiful mask. It did not change as Auntie went on. "I think that Junko has learned all she needs to know from you. As from this moment, you are no longer her elder sister. You may keep Ren. Her *mizuage* is arranged. But Junko will go to Saki. She will be her elder sister from this moment on."

I risked a swift glance at Tamayu. I expected that she would be as delighted as I was by Auntie's words. Tamayu had never liked me, I knew. And for my part, every moment I had spent in her company had been misery. Surely, if she had found fault with everything I did, she would be only too pleased to get rid of me!

But I was wrong. As it was afternoon, and we were expecting no patrons, Tamayu's face was naked of makeup. I watched as a bright, red spot flamed over each of her cheekbones. Her mouth tightened to a thin, hard line. Suddenly, she was ugly.

"As you wish, Auntie. Is she to sleep with Ren still?"

Auntie pursed her lips in thought. Oddly, I knew instinctively that she had no need to think, but was just stretching the moment to make Tamayu uncomfortable. I was torn between confusion and delight. I had no idea what Tamayu had done to make Auntie so angry with her, but at the same time I felt nothing but relief that she was no longer my elder sister.

"No. Ren can move in with you, until her *mizuage* is over. Then she will have a room of her own, of course."

I thought Tamayu was going to argue. Her eyes opened wide and I swear I could hear her teeth grinding. Auntie looked at her, her face pleasant and open, and Tamayu bowed her head.

"As you wish, Auntie. I will instruct the maids to move Ren's things into my room."

"No. They are very busy at the moment. Do it yourself."

Auntie threw the last words over her shoulder, clicking her fingers for the boys—with Aki still hanging between them like so much washing straight from the tub—to follow her. Only when their footsteps died away did Tamayu stand and walk out of the room. I thought for a moment she was going to speak to me. I was deeply relieved when she did not.

FIVE

Who can count the grains
Of sand on a beach? Surely
Only a fool tries

"Do kneel down, Junko." Saki patted the cushion at her side. "Now, do you think you might pour some tea for me? In fact, shall we make a game of it? Pretend I'm an honored patron and you're performing the tea ceremony for me."

I giggled happily. Saki was a plump, tolerant young woman, perhaps four or five years older than me. Nothing seemed to upset her. Whenever one saw her, it seemed she was about to smile. Everything in her life seemed to please her, from her patrons down to each mouthful of food she ate. She admitted that she was greedy.

"Life is far too short not to enjoy it," she instructed me cheerfully. "If I have one word of advice for you, Junko, it is this. Never do anything that you do not want to do. Never put a morsel of food into your mouth that you will not enjoy. If it is raining, do not sigh for the sunshine. Regret nothing."

She beamed at me. A demon of mischief made me want to point out that she had said far more than one word, but I did not. I liked Saki far too much to disagree with anything she said. Besides, her words seemed very wise to me.

I bowed low and passed her the brimming tea bowl.

"Very gracefully done," she said approvingly. "Now pour some tea for yourself and pass me one of those cakes. We'll have a little chat."

I made myself comfortable at her side, alert for anything this kind new elder sister might want from me.

"You've been with Tamayu for some time." She licked the remains of the *daifuku* cake off her fingers with huge enjoyment. "I can see she's taught you the tea ceremony very well. And I know that you can sing and play the *samisen*, for I've heard you. Can you dance as well?"

"Oh yes. Tamayu taught me to dance very well." As I said it, the shadow of Tamayu telling me I danced with all the grace of a lame donkey passed across my mind. "At least, I think she did," I added doubtfully.

"I'm sure she did. I cannot imagine Tamayu tolerating a maiko who couldn't dance. She herself is very proud of her dancing skills."

There was something in her voice that made me glance at Saki doubtfully, but she was smiling sweetly.

"And the patrons are delighted with you already. I've seen the way they look at you when we have a party of them." Saki made up her mind and darted her hand out for the last cake. A fraction away from it, she paused and looked at me hopefully. "Unless you would like it, dear?"

I would have loved it, but depriving Saki of cake would

be too much like denying a child her treat, so I shook my head.

"I will take far more pleasure from watching you eat it, Saki-san," I said honestly.

"There now!" Saki beamed at me. "What a sweet child she is! I'm so glad Auntie decided I'm going to be your elder sister. It's ages since I had a maiko to look after, and I know we'll make a huge success of you. You'll be the talk of Edo, I'm sure. I've nothing against Tamayu, you understand. She's one of the most sought-after geisha in the Floating World. Her patrons are many and distinguished. But I find she can be...Now how can I put this? A little prickly?"

I nodded. Prickly. Yes, that was a very good word to describe Tamayu. I imagined hugging her would be exactly the same as trying to hug a hungry wolf. "But just between us two, Junko-chan, I've heard that since she lost you as her maiko, Tamayu has decided that she's had enough of the Green Tea House. She's talking sweetly to her *danna* and is doing her best to persuade him to buy her out."

It was a moment before I understood what Saki was telling me. I put my hand in front of my mouth with shock. Appreciative of my obvious surprise, Saki nodded wisely.

"But Tamayu hated me," I said. "She always told me I was useless. That I would never be good enough to be a geisha here in the Green Tea House. Why should she want to leave now that she's gotten rid of me?"

Saki pulled a face. Then she shrugged, smiling again. "You must understand, when Tamayu lost you as her maiko, it was a huge loss of face for her. Everybody knows that you're going to be very special, very popular. Tamayu was going to take credit for that, of course. She was already telling all the patrons that she had taught you everything, that all your talents were only the same as hers, but secondhand. And what does she say to the patrons now when they ask about you? She can hardly tell them the truth, so she has to say that it was your fault. That you got above yourself because you're so beautiful and were cheeky to her, so she had to ask Auntie to give you to me. The patrons know it's all lies, of course, but they smile and nod to her face and then laugh at her behind her back."

I sat silently, trying to make sense of her words. Me? Special? Tamayu, of all people, was telling the patrons that I was talented and beautiful? I shook my head.

"Saki-san, I am afraid that none of that can be true. I am nothing but a country girl, a provincial nobody. I have no talents at all and still less beauty." I was suddenly seized with a fear so huge it made me tremble. "I will disappoint the patrons. Auntie will be angry with me and send me home. Or to Kaede's house to be with Aki."

Saki goggled at me. The sight of her sweet, calm face looking so worried almost made me forget my own fears.

"Nonsense, dear." She pulled a mirror toward her. It was a real mirror, one with glass in it, and very expensive. I knew one of her patrons had gifted it to her. Tamayu had been jealous and had nagged her *danna* to buy her a better one. "Now, just look at yourself and tell me what you see."

I peered in the mirror. This was really me. I saw a small face. Even features. Good skin. I put my finger on my reflection, expecting to feel warmth and was surprised when the surface was cold. But was I beautiful? No, of course not. I was what I had always been—just me. I shrugged and handed the mirror back to Saki carefully.

"I look like everybody else, Saki-san," I said simply. She bit her lip and then laughed.

"You just carry on thinking that, dear. Do you know, I

think that's part of your charm. You have no idea of the effect you have on the patrons, do you?"

I didn't know what Saki was talking about. Both Ren and I were called upon to attend the patrons often. We served tea and occasionally were called upon to dance or play the *samisen*. More often than not, we were expected to do no more than sit and be alert for whatever the patrons wanted. We made sure their sake cups were never empty. That the cushions they sat on were arranged for their comfort. If one of them said something witty, we laughed behind our fans and looked adoring. Most of the patrons were old men—*rich* old men. Often, they patted our arms or pinched our cheeks. I hated that.

Saki was smiling at me fondly, and I decided she was simply being nice to me. I blessed her for it. Tamayu had never been nice. Saki yawned and stretched, looking longingly at her futon.

"Would you like to go and sit in the garden for a while, dear? I have one of my favorite patrons coming to see me tonight and I really would like a little nap now."

Obediently, I jumped to my feet and left her snuggling down in her bedding. Normally, I loved sitting in the garden. It was sparse, a tranquil area of carefully selected shrubs and raked gravel, adhering strictly to Zen principles. It was a soothing, pleasant place. Yet today, it did not attract me at all. I was fidgety and wandered through the tea house, hoping to find somebody to talk to me. But there was no one. Tamayu was out. As Ren was also missing, I assumed that she was with Tamayu. Auntie's screen door was wide open, her room empty. The day was overcast and close. Even the maids were taking the chance to doze.

I paused outside Tamayu's room, biting my thumbnail. I knew what I wanted to do, but did I dare? I darted inside before fear could stop me and stood listening, sure that Tamayu would pop out from somewhere and clout me around the head for daring to go into her room.

"Well, if you don't enter the tiger's cave, you will not catch its cub," I said out loud. It had been one of my mother's favorite sayings, and hearing the words gave me courage. Even so, I walked toward the cedarwood chest on tiptoe and paused, listening, before I dared to lift the lid.

The pillow book was right on top, as if it was waiting for me. I ran my fingers over the smooth leather, as warm as skin. Amongst much else, in my time in the Green Tea House I had learned to read and write—nothing fancy, but better than nothing. Now, I knew the gold characters said "Tamayu's Book." I reached in and lifted the book out carefully, carrying it to the *tatami* matting where I sat with it opened in front of me.

The pictures held me spellbound, even as they frightened me out of my wits. I turned page after page, staring with my mouth dropping open. Couples entwined in ways I would not have thought possible. Men with men, women with women. One woman with two men. One illustration was so complex that I tilted my head to one side, trying to make sense of it.

"I see Tamayu's *shunga* is intriguing you, Junko."

I thought my heart had stopped. I dropped the pillow book as if it had suddenly become unbearably hot.

"Big!"

He stared at me and then walked in, sliding the screen door shut behind him. "Tamayu's gone to a *bunraku* performance. She's taken a fancy to one of the puppet masters. She's not going to be back for hours. Don't worry."

I smiled at my friend, and then glanced down at the

pillow book in embarrassment. It had fallen face open at my side.

"I don't know why I wanted to look at it. Aki thought it was fascinating, but I don't think I like it at all."

"Do you miss Aki?"

"Yes," I said simply. "I do miss her. Ren never seems to have time to chat with me these days. Saki's lovely, but she's older than me and I don't always know what to talk to her about. I get lonely."

"You can always talk to me, little one," Big said softly. He turned the pillow book to a new page and stared at it.

"But you're not always here. And you're not a girl," I pointed out. He laughed, and impulsively, I decided to take the risk of annoying him.

"Why was Auntie so angry with Aki, Big? You and Bigger brought her back, so where was the harm in it? I'm sure she would never do anything so silly again."

Big frowned and shook his head. "Aki did a very foolish thing, running away like that. It caused Auntie a great deal of distress. If it became known that a maiko from Auntie's house had dared to run away to chase a boy, then people would have laughed at Auntie. Her patrons would not have approved at all. Besides, Aki lied. She had lain with her boy. Not just once, either. I think a number of times."

I goggled at him. The memory of the man pounding at Chieko's body came vividly to my mind. Aki had done that? Not just once, but often?

"How did you know?"

Bigger laughed silently, his head thrown back. I reddened, feeling that I had said something very stupid. He wiped his hands over his face and smiled at me.

"When Auntie took you from your village, did she examine you?"

I stared at the floor, flooded with embarrassment. Before she had taken me from my parents' house, Auntie had sat me down on the floor and instructed me to open my legs. Wide. Without ceremony, she had slid her fingers into my private place and had fiddled around, finally pinching me so hard I had gasped with the pain.

"Yes," I whispered.

"That's what Kaede did to Aki when we took her to her house. Did it hurt when Auntie probed you, before she brought you here?" I nodded, unable to speak for embarrassment. "Well, it didn't hurt Aki at all. That's how Kaede and Auntie knew what she'd been up to. And that was another reason why Auntie was so furious with her. Because she'd been with a man, she couldn't have her *mizuage* ceremony. That means Auntie will lose a lot of money and even more face as her *danna* had already been arranged. And Kaede gave us barely anything for the stupid girl."

"Why was Aki so afraid of going to Kaede's house? Couldn't Aki be a geisha there, just the same as here?"

"No. Kaede's house is a common brothel," Big said bluntly. "The men who go there don't want the girls to sing and dance for them. They're only interested in taking their pleasure out of the girls' bodies. After what Aki had done, Auntie had no choice. Do you understand, little one?"

"No," I said helplessly.

He was silent for so long I thought he must be angry with me for my stupidity. Finally, he smoothed the pages of Tamayu's pillow book and held it out to me.

"Look."

I shook my head obstinately. I would be ashamed to look at the *shunga* with Big at my side. He stretched out his hand and pushed my face so that I was looking straight at the pillow book. I longed to close my eyes, but did not dare.

"This is what Aki did. She was a fool. She gave her body and her future to a boy who only wanted to boast about his conquest. She should have kept herself whole for her *danna*. She knew that. A girl cannot have her *mizuage* if she is not a virgin. And if she does not have her *mizuage*, she can never become a geisha."

I stared at the illustration, my face burning. A couple was entwined on a futon. The man's robe was thrown back from his body. The woman's kimono lay beneath her. The woman's legs were splayed wide. Even so, it seemed she was not satisfied with her posture, as her hands rested on the inside of her thighs, obviously tugging her legs still wider. Her back was arched, her small breasts thrusting toward her partner. The man was rearing over her, just the very tip of his jutting tree of flesh finding the entrance to her black moss. One of his hands was beneath her moss, lifting her toward him and the other was parting her secret place. I swallowed, so embarrassed I wished that Tamayu would come back and disturb us. Anything would be better than having to look at this with Big at my side.

Big spoke to me gently.

"This is what men and women do together, Junko. This is what you will do with your *danna*, during your *mizuage* ceremony. Afterward, you will be a woman as well as a geisha."

Big's voice was throaty. I glanced away from the book to his face. His upper lip was beaded with sweat and the pupils of his eyes were enormous. I thought that the *shunga* picture had excited him. My gaze went down to his lap. His robe was tented out as if a tree truly was growing there.

I giggled out of sheer nervousness.

"Do not laugh at me, child. Have you never wondered where my name came from?"

I shook my head. Both of the boys were tall. I had simply assumed that their names referred to their unusual height. It seemed I was wrong. Without taking his glance off my face, Big pushed his robe apart and reached his hand inside. His tree of flesh reared unfettered, seeming to bob at me with a life of its own. I stared at it, hypnotized.

The man I had seen laying with Chieko had possessed nothing like this. Not even the *shunga* pictures in Tamayu's pillow book could compare with it. Fascinated, I put my finger on the swollen tip and bounced it.

Big's reaction astonished me. He gasped loudly, and I was about to ask if I had hurt him when he grabbed my hand and wrapped it around his tree. How very small my hand looked, trying and failing to meet around that fleshy thickness! His flesh was smooth and warm. Veins made shapes like little worms. I wondered if they would wriggle away if I touched them, and ran my fingernail down one that was longer than the rest to find out. Nothing happened except that Big made a strange noise deep in his throat.

Wonder engulfed me. Surely, no woman could take this inside her? And yet, all the women in the *shunga* appeared to be enjoying their men's trees. Was this was what I could expect from my *mizuage*? A thought came to me suddenly. Surely, if I had to ride the dragon, at least it could be a dragon of my own choosing!

"Big, you are my friend." I stared at him earnestly and he nodded. To emphasize the importance of my words, I gripped his tree tighter. "Please, I know you. I like you. Will you be my *danna* for my *mizuage*? I know you'll take care of me and be very gentle. I can't bear to think a strange man, somebody I don't even know or like is going to pay to put his tree in me."

For answer, Big leaned forward and loosed the sash on my robe. He took one of my breasts in his hand and held it gently as he bent his head and put his lips around my nipple, sucking gently. It was quite shockingly pleasant and I sighed out loud with delight. Big raised his head and looked at me, a thread of saliva glinting between his teeth. He closed his eyes as if something was causing him pain and shook his head.

I was deeply hurt when he sat back, prying my fingers away from his tree. He drew his robe tightly back in place and then—with huge gentleness—pulled my own robe together and tied my sash.

"There is nothing I would like better, Junko. And you do me great honor by asking me. But it cannot be. Your *danna* for your *mizuage* will be a rich, important man. Already, many of Auntie's patrons have expressed an interest in you. You should be delighted."

I was not. All of the men who came to the Green Tea House were old. Many of them were much older than my own father. I hated it when they touched me, patted my hand, or put their cheek against my face. How could Big insist that one of them was going to be allowed to put his tree inside me! He was my friend. Surely he could persuade Auntie that he should be the one.

"If you won't help me, I'll run away," I said. "I'll go somewhere where you'll never find me."

"There is nowhere we wouldn't find you," he said simply. "Auntie has much influence in the Floating World. There's nobody who would shelter you, Junko. They would be too frightened."

"The geisha in the Hidden House will help me," I said defiantly. "They are my friends. Better friends than you are."

Big stared at me as if I had struck him. "The Hidden House, little one? And how have you come to make friends with the geisha there?"

I thought about lying, but I am a terrible liar and I knew Big would never believe me. So I told him the truth.

"The day Aki ran away I was in the garden. There was a terrible storm and I lost my bearings. I banged on the only door I could find and Nami opened it and let me in. The geisha were very kind to me," I said simply.

"They should have sent you straight back here," he said harshly. "The Hidden House is not for you."

Anger made me stubborn. I shook my head. "The geisha there are more beautiful than even Tamayu. And they are kind. Why should I not go to see them? They're my friends. My sisters."

"They are freaks," Big snapped. "That's why the patrons are willing to pay and pay and pay to go there. They attract the men who have a fancy for something strange, something different. They have no choice who lies with them. They're little better than the whores who are kept behind the lattice in the lowest sort of brothels. The Hidden House's door is closed to you, Junko. From this moment on. You will not go there again, ever."

He was so angry I dared not defy him to his face. But he was telling me lies, I knew he was. Nami and Gin and Hiromi were the most beautiful women I had ever seen. And they had been so very kind to me. I *would* go back to the Hidden House. And I would make sure that nobody saw me. Especially Big.

SIX

Without rain, there can
Be no life. My tears bring forth
Not life but sorrow.

I listened to Ren absently. Since her *mizuage*, she
had moved out of Tamayu's room and now had
her own quarters. But she still visited me often, and I was
glad of the company

"I don't really see why you're coming." I had drifted
away on the tide of my own thoughts. I had no idea what
Ren was talking about. "I mean, after all, you're only a
maiko. It should just be us geisha who go to an important
event like this."

I nodded, picking up the thread of the conversation
quickly. That evening, Tamayu, Ren, Saki, and I were all
going out of the Green Tea House. We had been hired to
entertain a powerful noble. Ito-san, a *daimyo*. Only the
shogun himself was higher caste than the *daimyo*. It was a
very great honor for the tea house.

"Of course *I* shouldn't be there," I agreed readily. The

thought of an evening all by myself was delightful. I might even be able to go over to the Hidden House, see if any of my friends there were free. "Perhaps if you mentioned to Auntie that you geisha didn't think I should go, she would change her mind."

Ren preened under the flattery, but shook her head.

"Tamayu says Auntie's determined you're going." She pulled a face. "She's even gotten you a new kimono for the occasion. More than I have."

I shrugged. What could I say? Ren poked at her hair and then brightened.

"Have you seen my new combs?" I had no need to reply as she rattled on happily. "One of my patrons gave them to me. You know, now that I'm a geisha myself, I often think what a fool Aki was."

"She was in love," I pointed out mildly.

Ren laughed. "So what? If the stupid girl had put her boy off for just a month or two, until she'd had her *mizuage*, she would still be here. And once she was a geisha, there would be nothing to stop her from taking as many lovers as she wanted, providing she was discreet about it. Instead, she's a prisoner in Kaede's house, at the beck and call of any peasant who has her price in his purse."

I felt a flash of anger so fierce I could not hold my tongue.

"And is she so different from us, then? We're just as much prisoners as she is. We're Auntie's slaves, instead of Kaede's."

"At least we don't have to whore ourselves for anybody who fancies us," Ren snapped back. She glared at me angrily. "And who are you to be so fussy anyway? Just what do you think would have happened to you if Auntie hadn't brought you here?"

My anger vanished as quickly as it had come. I stared at the *tatami* matting and said nothing. I knew what Ren was going to say, and she was right.

"You would probably have been sold as a slave. If you were lucky, your father might have found somebody who wanted to marry you. If he could scrape up a dowry, that is."

I shrugged my shoulders miserably. Our scrap of land produced hardly enough food to feed my parents and my brothers. Often, I went hungry. There would have been no dowry for me, I knew that.

"It was the same for me." Ren's voice was gentle suddenly, and I stared at her in surprise. "We're all the same. Tamayu and Saki and me—all of us. We all come from poor families. If Auntie hadn't seen something worth having in us, we'd all probably have ended up as a slave in a rich man's house. After I had my *mizuage*, Tamayu told me how it is.

"Auntie will take every penny the patrons pay for you," she said. "But if you're sensible, you can make the old idiots think they're gods. And if you do that, they'll give you nice presents. If you're lucky, you might be able to save enough to buy yourself out of here. If you're luckier still, you can use the talents the gods gave you to beguile one of them enough so that they want to buy you out and keep you for himself.

"That's what Tamayu's going for. The man who was her *danna* for her *mizuage* is besotted with her. He already has a wife, and a man of his class isn't going to set a high-born lady aside for a geisha. But she's sure he'll take her as his concubine, and she's happy enough about that."

"But there's no love in it," I blurted.

Ren sighed in exasperation. "Love? Since when did a Japanese man think about loving a woman? Oh, I suppose some of them that have been married for years and years are fond of their wives, but that still doesn't stop them visiting the like of Kaede's, or taking a concubine if they can afford it. And no matter how much they care about their wife, if she was barren or just produced girl children, there's not one of them who wouldn't put her aside like a worn-out shoe. That's the way life is. Make the most of what you've got, Junko. That's my advice."

She was right, of course. But I still didn't have to like it.

I sat very still while Saki put on my makeup. She had already dressed me carefully in my new kimono and obi, first patting my layers of chemises in place so that just a touch of silk peeked coyly through the neckline of the kimono.

"Your kimono is exquisite," she said enviously. "Auntie has a good eye. That pastel color would be all wrong on me, but it makes you look like a flower. Now keep still."

Her hand hovered over an exquisite jade pot, and then passed on to a small bottle.

"I don't think your lovely young skin needs any of that."

"What is it?"

"It's a very special skin cream." Saki looked smug. "One of my favorite patrons bought it for me. It's made from nightingale dung and is the most wonderful thing for keeping the skin bright."

I managed a smile, all the time thanking the gods that Saki had decided not to waste any of her precious potions on me. The thought of smearing my skin with bird shit made me feel sick. She tipped the bottle and slid golden oil onto the palm of her hand, massaging it carefully into my face with her fingertips.

"Camellia oil. Just a very little, so we can get your makeup on properly."

I nodded and she tapped my nose in mock anger.

"Be still, child."

I watched her hands busy themselves amongst a variety of pots.

"Now listen carefully. I will do this for you this time, and then you must do it yourself, under my instruction. I'll lend you my mirror," she said magnanimously.

As she spoke, she worked water into a white powder. When it was to her satisfaction, she raised her finger at me.

"Put your head back."

The paste slid on easily over the top of the oil. Saki's skillful fingers smoothed it quickly over my entire face and neck, working it down just past the neck of my kimono.

"Head forward," she instructed. "Now this part, you will always need help with. When you're a geisha, either your own maiko or a maid will do it for you."

Her fingers busied themselves on the nape of my neck, reaching down almost between my shoulder blades.

"For Japanese men, the nape of the neck is the most erotic part of the body."

Is it? I thought, startled. None of the men in Tamayu's *shunga* book had seemed very interested in the back of their partner's necks!

"I've left a W of bare skin for you. When you're a full geisha, it will be a V shape. There. Now, we'll finish your face. Open your eyes wide." She tipped a drop of very thick, cold liquid in each eye. It stung and I blinked. A second later, everything was slightly blurred, as if I were looking through gauze. "Don't worry, it's a flower distillate. It will make your pupils look huge. Keep very still for a moment."

Saki selected a fine brush, and I felt her dabbing at my eyebrows and then the corner of my eyes. Another stroke and my eyebrows were smoothed over.

"Pout," she instructed as she placed a quick dab in the

center of my bottom lip. Saki sat back and inspected me. "You'll do."

I could tell from her voice that she was pleased. She held her mirror up for me and I stared at my image, slightly fuzzy from the effect of the eye drops. My face was white. The outer corners of my eyes were red, as was the center of my bottom lip. I was so shocked, I put my finger on the glass, half expecting the strange person in the mirror to draw back from my touch.

"You are truly beautiful, Junko-chan."

I smiled, pleased that Saki was pleased.

"Thank you." I wanted to hug my elder sister, but I didn't dare, in case I disturbed anything.

"Junko." Something in Saki's voice made me pause. I stared at her, wishing I could see her expression properly. Between her thick makeup and the flower distillate that blurred my vision, it was impossible. "You do understand that tonight is important, don't you?"

"Of course I do." I was indignant. Did Saki think I was a fool? I had learned much since I had come to the Floating World. No longer did I think the man I had seen taking Chieko was an important noble. Now, I understood that he was nothing more than a man who owned more land than my own parents. A man who could afford to keep a couple of servants and fling some small coins at the peasant girl he had taken for his pleasure. In the Floating World, he would have been nothing at all.

And I knew that the man who had asked for all of us to entertain him tonight *was* a noble. I did not know him, but I knew of him. He was a *daimyo*, truly an aristocrat, and he was bestowing a great honor on the Green Tea House by patronizing us.

"I mean, you understand it's important for *you*?"

I was about to bite my lip when I remembered it had been painted, so I nodded instead. Cautiously.

"I'm only a maiko, Saki," I pointed out. "Nobody is going to be interested in me."

It seemed to me that Saki looked shocked beneath her paint. But then she smiled and I guessed I was wrong.

"You are a dear child, Junko. Has Auntie told you what your name is going to be after your *mizuage*?"

I shook my head. Auntie rarely spoke to me, and I was grateful for it.

"You are to be called Terue. It means 'Shining Blessing.' Isn't that a lovely name?"

I turned the words over in my mind. Shining Blessing. Saki was right, it was a lovely name. I smiled doubtfully.

"I hope I'll bring honor to it."

"You will, dear. I know you will." She hesitated, and then spoke gently. "I know that you find things very strange here in the Floating World, even now. I see you sometimes, looking uncomfortable. Isn't that so?"

It was as if a dam had been breached. Suddenly, all my fears and worries rose to my mouth, the words choking to get out.

"Yes. I just don't feel as if I belong here, Saki-san. As if I never will. I'm sure I'm not good enough to be a geisha. I'm just a simple country girl, not like the rest of you. I know I'm going to make a fool of myself and bring dishonor on Auntie's house."

I was almost panting with relief. I would have hugged Saki if I hadn't been afraid of disturbing our lovely clothes and makeup. There! It was out. Perhaps Saki would tell Auntie and she would send me home. At that moment, I would have welcomed it.

"Not like the rest of us?" Saki echoed. "And you think

we're in some way better than you, Junko-chan? I tell you, all of us geisha here should spend hours each day on our knees in front of the house shrine, thanking the gods for what they have chosen to bless us with." She paused, listening, and hearing nothing but silence continued. "You think Tamayu is in some way better than you?"

I nodded. Of course she was. Tamayu was beautiful and elegant and confident. She had lovers who showered her with presents. Her patrons—as she had reminded me every day that she had been my elder sister—were from the highest ranks of society.

"Tamayu's the daughter of a whore," Saki said brutally. "A whore who did not even amount to enough to be in the like of Kaede's house. Her mother was kept in a lattice brothel, and Tamayu was born there. You've heard of them, Junko?"

I felt as if my heart was in the grip of the first frost of winter, but I found a small voice.

"I have. Ren and Aki told me about them. They said that was where I would end up if I didn't behave myself and do as I was told."

"They lied, of course." Saki smiled indulgently. "I can't think of anything that you could do that would make Auntie sell you to such a place. Apart from anything else, they would pay hardly anything for you and Auntie has a hard head for business. The lattice brothels are truly terrible places, child. The women within them must flaunt themselves to all the men who pass by. They're expected to push their arms through the lattice and clutch at passing men. To blow kisses and tell their would-be customers how much they'll charge and what the men can do to them. To reveal their breasts openly. The men in their turn can chat with the women. Touch their breasts if they want to, or even feel their private places before they make up their mind which one to take for the pleasure of the moment and a few coins. The women have no choice in which man has them. Or how they take them."

"How did Tamayu get here, then?" I asked, intrigued.

"Tamayu is the luckiest one of all of us," Saki said seriously. "She should not have been conceived in the first place. If their courses are so much as a day late, the girls in such places are given a special drink by their Auntie, and any baby that has taken root is washed away. But it didn't work for Tamayu's mother. She hid her baby from her Auntie until it became obvious, and by then it was too late to do anything about it." She paused and cleared her throat. "I understand that Tamayu's mother suddenly became very popular with a few of the brothel's patrons. There are some men who find a heavily pregnant woman extremely erotic."

I grimaced. I couldn't help myself. I found the idea of a pregnant woman making love disgusting. Saki grinned at my expression.

"In any event, she was popular enough she was allowed to stay at the brothel until her baby arrived. It—I mean Tamayu—was left with her as long as she had milk to nurse her with." I stared at Saki in horror, and she nodded briskly. "Oh yes. There are also many men who enjoy pretending they are babies themselves and enjoy suckling at the breast."

I felt sick. But Saki wasn't finished.

"As soon as Tamayu was weaned, that was it. She was sold off. You see how lucky she was, once again? She should have been exposed and left to die. But no, a woman who had lost her own baby took a fancy to her and paid her mother's Auntie a few coins for her."

"How do you know?" I asked curiously.

"Tamayu told me all about it herself. One day when it was raining and she was feeling very down, she told me all about her life. I was supposed to sympathize with her and agree what a terrible time she'd had. I didn't. I told her she was truly lucky and should be grateful. She didn't speak to me for days afterward, but it was no great loss to me."

Thinking Saki had forgotten my question, I asked her again. "How did she end up here?"

"The gods smiled on her yet again. The woman who had taken her had more babies, but none of them lived for more than a few weeks until Tamayu was around five years old. The woman finally gave birth to a boy child, and healthy, so of course the woman had no interest in Tamayu anymore. She sold her on as a slave to a wealthy merchant. This man was a widower who had grown children. According to Tamayu, he made something of a pet of her. In any event, he eventually decided to remarry, and his new wife didn't like having Tamayu around at all, so she was sold again, but this time to Auntie. And that's how she ended up here."

"She's very beautiful," I said. "And talented. I suppose it's understandable that she should think she's special."

"She's all right." Saki shrugged. "But she isn't any more talented than any other geisha in the Floating World, and not as beautiful as some. And she's no longer young. That terrifies her. She knows that if the patrons begin to lose interest in her, then the best she can expect is that Auntie will sell her on to a less exclusive tea house. But you can learn a lesson from her, Junko. Because she acts as if she's special, then everybody believes that she is. Never forget, people cannot see inside your head. They see only what you allow them to see."

Echoes of Auntie!

"Is that why she keeps saying her favorite patron is

going to buy her out? So Auntie will think she's still very popular?"

"It is. The only thing is, Auntie *can* see inside your head. She knows what we're all thinking, and she's not taken in by Tamayu's show. If Tamayu can persuade her lover to buy her out, then Auntie will drive a hard deal, but she won't stop her from going."

I thought about this for a moment and then said shyly, "And you, Saki-san? How did you come to be here?"

"Oh, my tale is easily told. I came from a large family. We lived on the outskirts of Edo, in a poor village. I was the youngest. I had an older sister who married, but after that my father had no money to provide me with a dowry, so marriage was out of the question for me. One day, Auntie came to our village. She looked at many girls, but chose me. Father was delighted and said I was to go with her and not to be any trouble, so I did. Auntie brought me here and made me a maiko. I knew nothing at all at first. I couldn't sing or dance. I had even rarely tasted tea, so had no idea about the tea ceremony. She taught me everything I needed to know, and I shall be eternally grateful to her for that."

"Wouldn't you have liked to have been married? Had a family of your own?"

"And would that have made me any happier?" Saki stared at me. "We're all slaves here, child. We owe everything we have to Auntie. But is it so different from being married? If we had a husband, we would do exactly as he told us. If our prayers were answered and we had boy children, then they too would treat us as their slave. No, believe me. We're all better off here. We have good lives. And if you're sensible, as I am, then you save the flower money that your patrons give you. At the moment, I'm too valuable for Auntie to consider allowing me to buy my way out. But I'm under no illusions. The day will come when I wake up and find I have wrinkles on my face and my legs have become too stiff to allow me to dance gracefully. When that happens, I'll take my store of cash and I will go and talk to Auntie and I think we will deal very well together."

"And what will you do then?"

"I shall go out of the Floating World. I will buy myself a little house with a garden and every day that the weather is fine I'll sit in the open air and give thanks for the life I have had and the life that is still to come."

Saki laughed, gathering her kimono skirts around her.

"Come along, child. It sounds as if our palanquins have arrived. We've been serious long enough for one evening."

And thinking on her wise words, I stood tall and followed her proudly.

SEVEN

The tallest tree must
Start as no more than a seed.
So are dreams made true.

I stared down at my *tabi*. The evening was cool and normally I would have been grateful for the warmth of my *tabi* socks, comfortable as they were with their divided big toe. But geisha do not wear *tabi*. When they went out, their feet were bare inside their *geta*. I felt that my *tabi* marked me out as a mere maiko, and I wiggled my toes resentfully.

As well as that minor annoyance, the *daimyo's* house came as a huge disappointment to me. I had expected luxury, a palace, but the house—although big—was very simple, almost to the point of being bare. Even the guests— all men, of course—seemed to me to be very plainly dressed, although even I could detect the aura of power they carried with them.

Ren nudged me with her elbow. "See that one?" she whispered through a fixed smile. I glanced at an elderly man who was leaning toward Saki and smiling at her. "They say he's the richest man in Edo."

I peeped out from behind my fan. Why, I wondered, if he was so rich did he dress so carelessly? He wore no jewels at all. What was the point of wealth if one did not enjoy it?

"And that one..." Ren nodded fractionally toward an even older man and lowered her voice to an awed whisper. "He is said to be very powerful. He has the friendship of the shogun himself."

I was not greatly impressed. Tamayu and Saki had danced and sung and Ren had played on the *samisen*. I thought our patrons were extremely rude. They talked amongst themselves all the time and barely spared a glance for the geisha, working so hard for their pleasure. I saw Auntie walking toward to me and quickly straightened to attention.

"Junko. Please, circulate amongst the noble gentleman." Her voice was so pleasant, I almost glanced behind me to make sure she wasn't talking to somebody else. "Pour sake where it is needed. If all the gentlemen's cups are full, then make sure you are there when you are needed."

She waved her hand airily, and I obeyed quickly. Flasks of sake in their warming vessels were scattered about the room. I took the nearest one, and began to walk carefully amongst the scattered cushions. I felt terribly self-conscious, and was very grateful when one of the men raised his cup to be filled.

"You are very graceful, child." He smiled and I lowered my head, smiling in response as far as my makeup would allow. A much younger man—barely more than a child— sat next to him. I sensed he was as uncomfortable as I was and bowed to him.

"May I fill your cup, lord?" He held his cup out to me.

His hand was trembling so hard the sake would have slopped out if I had not gripped his wrist to steady it.

"My son, you do me great honor." The older man was smiling. "It is only right that any man should tremble in the face of such beauty."

I laughed. I couldn't help it. I heard this sort of polite nonsense every day in the Green Tea House. It meant nothing.

"My lord, the honor is entirely mine," I said. Still, I was pleased when both the son and the father looked at me approvingly.

"You are Terue, child?"

"No, lord." He raised his eyebrows in surprise and I hurried to explain. "When I become a geisha, my name will be Terue. But at the moment, I am plain Junko."

He laughed so loudly that Auntie hurried across, her face a frozen mask.

"My lord." She bowed low. "Has my silly maiko done something wrong? Please forgive her. She is an innocent child and has much to learn."

"Indeed, no. She is a great credit to you, Hana. It is many years since I have met with such a refreshing blend of beauty and charm. Perhaps Junko would like to dance for us, if that one—" he flicked a finger at Ren "—will play for her."

I needed no urging. I had watched longingly as the other girls danced. I loved every moment of the classic movements Saki had drilled into my head. I stared at Auntie hopefully, and she nodded.

So I danced. It was the first time I had danced in front of patrons, and for a moment, I was nervous. But it passed as the music captured my feet and the flow of the dance moved my heart. I was sorry when the music stopped and astonished when the patrons clapped. The old man who had been kind to me earlier called me over and patted the cushion at his side. I folded to my knees carefully, half an eye on his sake cup in case it needed filling. He leaned across to speak to me, smiling.

"Ah. I see our guest of honor has arrived. What a pity he missed your dancing, Junko. He would have enjoyed it."

He patted my shoulder, quite tenderly. I was certain I could feel his bones through the sparse flesh. I was even more certain that his touch had left the dust of years on my sleeve. I watched him rise with relief. He was a very old man. His bones creaked. I did not like him touching me.

"Now, you just stay there, Junko-chan. I shall not be a moment, and then we can have a nice little chat."

I was sure that nobody was watching me, and I stared around with interest. Most of the patrons had risen and were moving toward the newcomer. Only Lord Ito—the noble that Ren had said was a friend of the shogun—remained seated, obviously expecting that the visitor would be brought to him. I glanced up and the breath hitched in my throat.

The newcomer was a *gaijin*. I had never seen a foreign barbarian before. Even in Edo, there was only a handful of them and they rarely ventured into the streets. To find a *gaijin* here, treated as an honored guest by some of the most powerful men in Japan, was shocking. It was rude beyond belief, I knew, but I stared openly at him, wide-eyed with amazement.

Even stranger, I saw he was *talking* to the men who were ushering him forward. As he came closer, I realized he was speaking perfect, rapid Japanese. It was so odd, the familiar words pouring out of his *gaijin* mouth, that I laughed. Although he was across the room from me and could not possibly have heard me, the *gaijin* turned his head and looked at me.

I was frozen. Although neither I nor anybody else from my village had ever seen a *gaijin*, we had heard about them. Some said they were demons in human form. Others disagreed. They might be people, they said judiciously, but they were not the same as Japanese. It was whispered that the men had tails they kept hidden, very carefully. Their women, it was said, had their sex the wrong way around—across instead of down. Everybody agreed about one thing. They were so ugly it hurt the eyes to look at them.

They were all wrong. I had no idea about the tail, of course. It was remotely possible that he might have a tail, tucked away inside his robe, although I could not believe it. But for sure he was not ugly. Oh no!

I thought he nodded at me before he turned away, and I came to my wits quickly. *Gaijin* or no, this man was an honored guest of our patrons. We must honor him also. Perhaps I might be introduced to him later. I hoped so. Just as intensely as I had been repelled when the *daimyo* had touched me earlier, so now did I want to run my finger down this *gaijin's* face. His skin was the whitest I had ever seen, but it was not at all repulsive. Rather, it had the sheen of the best silk, and I longed to find out for myself if it was as smooth.

And then my patron came back and sat at my side. True to my training, I leaned toward him and pretended that I had missed his company. Aware of Auntie's eyes on me, I smiled and played the *samisen* and laughed softly at the witticisms that our patrons threw out like scraps scattered for koi carp to fight over. The sake cups were filled again and again. Perhaps it was the fumes from the sake that made me lightheaded, for my smiles seemed to come more smoothly as the evening wore to a close.

I knew I was supposed to remember each and every name of all the men, but I could not. It didn't seem to matter greatly. I called them all lord and bowed my head before them, and they seemed happy. I found time to speak a little more to the very young man, and that I did enjoy. But I was never allowed to get close to the *gaijin*. Nor, I noticed, were any of the geisha beckoned over to entertain him.

Finally, Lord Ito inclined his head at Auntie, and she gathered us girls together with the same brisk efficiency I had used to herd my ducks. We were out of the reception in moments. I glanced back over my shoulder to see if I could take a last glimpse of the *gaijin*. I had hoped he might be looking after me, but he was not.

EIGHT

A stone falls into
Water. When it is taken
Out, there is no trace.

*A*ll our gossip was about the *gaijin*.

We had each been given a little silken purse as we left the *daimyo*'s mansion. Of course, politeness had dictated that nobody would open it until we arrived back at the Green Tea House. I was astounded by the number of silver coins that mine contained, and the geisha agreed absently that it was a generous amount of flower money, as befitted the occasion, but unusually, they didn't bother to discuss it. Not even to ensure that no one had been given more than any another!

"Who was he?" Tamayu demanded, as if one of us, surely, would have had the wit to find out. Saki shrugged.

"No idea," she said. "But he spoke Japanese! I heard him! I could hardly believe it. If you weren't looking at him when he spoke, you would never have known he was a foreign barbarian."

We all murmured our agreement. Nobody had ever heard of a *gaijin* who could speak fluent Japanese. It seemed as if their foreign tongues simply couldn't wrap themselves around the syllables of our beautiful language.

"I don't think he's a foreign barbarian at all." Tamayu nodded her head wisely. "Did you see the color of his hair? Red as a fox, it was. And he had green eyes. I got a good look when I was pouring sake for another of the patrons. I think he's really a fox spirit, and he's laid some sort of enchantment on all of them. That was why none of us were allowed to get near him. Being women, and more intuitive than the men, we would have seen through his disguise in a second."

Saki and I took deep breaths, amazed at Tamayu's perception. But Ren was having none of it.

"He's not a fox spirit," she said smugly. "He really is a *gaijin*, a foreign barbarian. But I think he must be a very important one."

We all stared at her hungrily, and she smiled, pretending to look at her fingernails to prolong the moment.

"And how do you know? Lord Ito confided in you, did he?" Tamayu sneered.

"No. I asked one of the maids," Ren said simply.

"Well done, Ren," Saki said. "Now why didn't I think of doing that? Of course, the maids always know everything. So, who is he? What was he doing at a gathering like that?" She paused, and then added quietly, "Do you think he really does have a tail?"

Ren was preening again, and I waited impatiently for her answers.

"I asked the maid that," she said importantly. We hung on her words, eyes wide as we waited for the answer. "The girl I spoke to was full of it. She couldn't wait to tell me all about him. She said he hasn't got a tail at all. Or at least, not one that she had seen. And she said she should know—she'd seen him in the bathhouse many times."

"No!" Tamayu spoke for all of us. "A foreign barbarian, trusted enough to share the bath with a *daimyo*? Who is he?"

"She didn't know." The anti-climax was so disappointing, we all sighed as one. "Well, she knew his name because she's heard the *daimyo* call him by it. She says it's Seemon-san."

We thought about it.

"Funny sort of name." Saki sipped her tea daintily. "Although I suppose it fits with him being foreign. And the maid had no idea what he is?"

She meant, of course, why was he important. And surely, he was a most important man for him to claim a place at the side of Lord Ito.

"She had no idea, really. But she wondered if he might be a very rich foreign merchant."

We all laughed. The idea was so ridiculous that even I, the maiko, was not reproved for laughing out loud instead of giggling politely behind my hands.

"That's maids for you," Tamayu said. "Stupid to the core. How would a mere merchant come to be welcomed in Lord Ito's house? He might just as well invite a beggar to his table."

"Whatever he is, he has money," Ren said slyly. "She told me that he tips her so generously, she might as well be a geisha herself."

Tamayu shrugged. "Ignorant foreign barbarian probably has no idea how much he's giving her."

The geisha sipped their tea and yawned and the fascinating *gaijin* was forgotten for the time. But not by me. He had lodged in my mind and refused to go away.

Having nobody else to turn to, in the end, I asked Big's opinion.

He sprawled on my *tatami*, watching me practice the *samisen*. "So, did you enjoy your first venture outside the Floating World, little one?"

I broke off playing to answer him, laying the *samisen* carefully aside. "It was interesting," I said carefully. "Did Lord Ito pay a great deal to have all the geisha there?"

"He will have paid a huge amount. Auntie will have over-charged him grossly just so he could brag to his friends about how much the evening was costing him. Why?"

"The geisha worked very hard to entertain Lord Ito and his friends. But none of them seemed to even notice them. As long as their sake cups were full, they seemed happy."

"Yes? And who was filling the sake cups?"

"Why, me, of course. I was the only maiko there."

Big grinned and looked at me as if he had answered my question. I thought I would take advantage of his good mood and blurted out my thoughts.

"Big, there was a *gaijin* there. I've never even seen a foreign barbarian before, but this one seemed to be an honored guest. None of us could understand it."

"Looked like a fox spirit? Skin as white as the clouds? Red hair? A proper red-haired barbarian?"

I nodded, amazed.

"I've seen him a couple of times, strutting about Edo as though he owns the place. And Bigger says he's seen him at the kabuki and in a couple of the opium houses as well. Not the sort of place you would ever expect to find a foreign barbarian at all. Especially not on their own. The funny thing is, nobody challenges him. It's as if he's protected by some sort of spell. He's an odd one, no doubt about that. Speaks perfect Japanese, and even dresses properly. The only other *gaijin* I've ever seen wore some peculiar things around their legs that looked like tree bark. I couldn't work out how they even walked in them!" Big laughed loudly, and I joined in dutifully.

"Do you know what he's doing here, then?"

"No." Big shook his head. "Nobody seems to know why he's here or what his real business is. Bigger thinks he's something to do with the opium trade, which would explain why he's been seen in the opium houses, but I don't believe that either. If he's a guest of Lord Ito, then I think it must be something political. Best not ask, Junko-chan. If it's that important, then we don't want to know."

But I do! I thought silently. I wanted to know everything about him. What he is. Who he is. Why he's here.

"Anyway, never mind about the foreign barbarian. How was the evening for *you*?" He put a curious emphasis on the word you. I was bewildered, not understanding his question at all. I had served sake. Smiled at the patrons' witticisms. Suffered in silence when they touched me. What else was there to say? I shrugged and watched as Big's smile widened.

"You do understand why you were there, don't you?"

"To serve sake. To watch the geisha and see what they did."

"Auntie didn't say anything to you, then?"

"She told me to do exactly what the noble lords asked me to do. To listen carefully to them and make sure I pleased them. And that's what I did."

Big grinned so widely, I could see most of his teeth. But I still had no idea what was amusing him so much. I sat up straight and lifted my chin. I would not ask him. I would wait for spring to come around before I demanded to know why he was laughing at me.

"Dear Junko-chan. I think Auntie was very wise when she chose you. Now, tell me. How many lords were at the gathering?"

I thought about it, counting the faces carefully.

"Five."

"Five nobles. Five of the richest, most important men in Edo. All of them *daimyo*. All gathered together, enjoying an evening of music and song and pleasant company. At a huge price. And you say you didn't think they were paying a great deal of attention to the geisha?"

"I thought they were rude," I said bluntly. "I mean, I've never been to anything like that before, but I've seen the geisha entertain patrons in the Green Tea House and the men all seem to be entranced by them. Did these men think they were so important they couldn't be seen to be enjoying themselves?"

"No. It's not that at all. I think the *daimyo* were all there for one thing, and that it occupied their thoughts to the exclusion of all else."

"The foreign barbarian?" I asked.

Big shook his head, clearly annoyed. "Forget about him. He is nothing to us. No, they were all there to see you, Junko. Nothing else."

I laughed out loud. It was terribly rude of me, but I couldn't help it. I laughed so much, I had to wipe tears from my face. When I could see properly again, I looked at Big's face and all amusement died as I saw his expression.

"I'm sorry, Big," I apologized quickly. "I didn't mean to be impolite, but I thought you were joking with me. Why would such important men want to see me? I am nothing. Not even a geisha yet."

"You will be, when you have had your *mizuage*." Big stared at me, leaning forward slightly as if to emphasize his words. "And that is exactly why you went to that gathering. Auntie has told me that she has already had competing bids for your *mizuage*. Word has gotten out that there's a new jewel in the Floating World. The patrons you saw last night want only the very best. They want you."

I thought about those old hands. The wrinkled faces and balding heads. The tobacco pipe breath. Tried to imagine what their bodies must be like. I felt sick.

"But they hadn't even seen me before! Why would they be interested in me, a nothing from a tiny village?" I protested. "I don't understand."

"The men who have already bid for you are minor nobles. The men you saw are far more important. Now that they've seen you, they'll fight amongst themselves, bid any amount of money, just to ensure that they're the one who wins. It's a matter of face." He hesitated, and added, "You think Tamayu is more beautiful than you, Junko? That Saki and Ren are more talented than you? I tell you, even Bigger has said that you are the most precious thing that Auntie has ever found. And I know myself that to hear you sing and play is enough to bring tears of joy to the eyes. And even more important than your talents, you have a quality of innocence and purity that is beyond any price."

I shook my head. This was nonsense. I was Junko, the girl who was good for nothing but herding ducks and cleaning the house.

"Please, Big. Don't mock me," I whispered. "I'm nothing at all. I don't deserve the attention of such men as these. I'll make a fool of myself and bring dishonor to Auntie's house. She'll sell me to Kaede to keep Aki company. I know she will."

"No. You'll bring great honor to Auntie's House." Big smiled. "Don't worry, Junko. You won't do anything wrong." He patted my shoulder gently. "Don't worry about it. Soon, you'll be a geisha. And I promise you, then you'll have the whole of Edo at your feet."

I thought of those old, old men. Smiling at me. Touching me. *Taking me.* I thought about the pictures in Tamayu's pillow book and seriously considered taking poison.

NINE

The sweetest peach may
Harbor a worm within it.
Take care when you bite!

Of course, I didn't take the honorable way out and kill myself. Youth is easily injured, but forgets just as quickly. So it was with me.

As the passing days rolled into weeks and then months, I began to think that Big had been wrong. Or perhaps he had misunderstood something Auntie had said. In any event, as winter approached—and my thirteenth birthday, the traditional date for a maiko's *mizuage*—came and went, and nothing was said, I relaxed. I even laughed at my own silliness. How could I have taken poison when I hadn't the faintest idea even where to buy it?

Anyway, I was happy enough. Most of the time, at least. Saki was good to me, but in an indolent, lazy, just-doing-my-job sort of way. Tamayu ignored me, for which I was grateful. Ren had taken a lover and was so entranced with him that he was all she could talk about. I realized slowly that in the midst of people, I was lonely. I longed to cross the garden and visit the geisha in the Hidden House. It had been months since my first visit to the "other place," as Big had called it. I worried that perhaps they would no longer welcome me. Even worse, maybe they had forgotten all about me.

Finally, I took my courage in my hands and decided I would venture across the garden and take my chances.

The door leading to the Hidden House was unlocked, and I pushed it open carefully, marveling at the solidness of the wood. I had never seen a door before that was not made of thin strips of wood and almost transparent screens, and I paused to consider this strangest of doors for a moment. Was it made to keep the geisha in, or unwanted guests out? I had never even considered it on my last visit, and I was pleased with my new perception.

Even if I had not remembered the turns, the sound of voices—chattering, laughing—would have guided me. I tapped softly on the closed screen door and then pushed the flimsy barrier aside before my courage could fail me.

There was a second of surprised silence, and then three voices welcomed me in.

"Junko! Dear child! It's been so long!" Nami was climbing to her feet, her hands held out in welcome.

"Have you eaten, Junko?" Hiromi put aside her own rice bowl and gestured with her chopsticks to the food spread out on the *tatami*. "Shall I ask the maid to bring you a bowl? Tea, at least."

I had eaten earlier, but I accepted the offer of tea with gratitude.

"You forget, Hiromi," Gin reproved gently. "The Green

Tea House rarely keeps the late hours that we do. Once their patrons have taken their pleasure in the geisha's talents, they move on to other houses for different pleasures. They do not linger, as do our patrons. Junko no doubt broke her fast hours ago."

A certain sadness in her voice made me hesitate, but she was smiling and gesturing with her beautiful hands that I should sit down, so I did. The geisha huddled around me, pouring me tea and peering at me as if I had honored them with my presence. They were delightful, and I relaxed with a huge sigh of sheer pleasure.

"It's safe for you to be here?" Nami asked anxiously.

"It is. The boys have gone to the kabuki theater. Tamayu and Saki are out together. Ren is waiting for her lover, and will be blind and deaf to anything until he has been and gone. And Auntie has gone into the country. Big says she has heard of a girl who might make a suitable maiko. I hope Auntie likes her. I'll have somebody to talk to, to be my friend."

Gin smiled, but her amazing eyes were troubled.

"Yes. We heard Auntie had gone on a fishing expedition. But I don't think you quite understand. The new maiko isn't going to be company for you. She's going to take your place."

My spirits sank like a stone thrown into still water. My mouth was suddenly too dry to speak. I sipped tea and cleared my throat and forced words out.

"But I haven't had my *mizuage* yet. How can she be my replacement?"

The geisha looked at each other. Gin shrugged.

"It's not really our place to tell you," she said finally. "But if Auntie hasn't spoken to you, then somebody should. You know your *mizuage* is already late?" I nodded miserably. "Didn't you wonder why?"

"Big told me that Lord Ito's interested in being my *danna*, and so are some of his friends. But I didn't really believe him. I thought he was just being kind to me, and that really Auntie couldn't find a *danna* for me. Or perhaps I was too useful as a maiko."

"Big is right, Junko-chan." Nami took my hand gently. "We don't go out into the Floating World, we who live in the Hidden House. But we hear everything. Our patrons talk as if we were not there. As if we don't matter. And there has been much gossip about you. All five of the *daimyo* you saw in Lord Ito's house want the kudos of being your *danna* for your *mizuage*. None of them will give way. Auntie has taken bids on you, time and time again. And each time, the losers have come back and increased their bids."

I was appalled and spoke vehemently. "I'm not a prize animal to be auctioned off to the highest bidder! And never to one of those horrible old men. I'm not going to do it. Auntie can't make me!"

Gin shook her head. "Of course she can," she said crisply. "And does it matter so very much?"

I stared at her in horror. I had thought she was my friend, that—surely!—of all people the geisha in the Hidden House would understand how I felt.

"It matters to me! I'll run away," I said wildly. "Find my way back to my own village. If it's going to stop one of those horrible old men from taking me, I'll give myself to the first nice young man I can find."

"Don't be such a fool, Junko." Nami looked angry with me. "All geisha have to have a *mizuage*. We all had ours. And it wasn't so bad, was it, geisha?"

"Were your *danna* nasty old men? Men who were old

enough to be your grandfather? Men who made you shudder to even think of them touching you?"

"Yes," Nami said simply. "Of course they were. Young men don't have the money to pay for a *mizuage*. Or enough status to satisfy Auntie. You're really being very silly, Junko. What do you think would have happened to you if Auntie hadn't bought you?"

The geisha obviously expected an answer. So I considered my response carefully.

"Father would have done his best to find me a husband," I said dubiously. Would he? With five male children to feed and clothe, where would the dowry have come from?

"Perhaps," Hiromi said briskly. "And if your father had found you a husband, why would that have been so less terrible than enduring your *mizuage*? Your *mizuage* lasts for one night, Junko. Your *danna* will be a cultured, experienced man who knows how to treat a woman who has cost him a fortune. If you're very lucky indeed, he might be so enchanted with you that he wants to remain as your patron. So tell me, how is any of that worse than being married to a village boy? Somebody whose idea of charming his bride would probably be getting a sluice down at the village pump before the wedding?"

"And even worse, if there had been no money for a dowry for you, what then?" Nami took over, squeezing my hand tightly for emphasis. "When the crops failed, and your family was hungry, what do you think your father would have done? He would have sold you off for a slave, that's what. He would have had no option. You would have been just another mouth to feed, and a useless one at that."

I stared around at my friends, at their serious expressions. They only wanted the best for me, I knew. An idea came to me suddenly, and I grasped it eagerly.

"Gin, could you not ask Auntie if I could join you here, in the Hidden House? If I knew I was going to be amongst friends, here with you all, I could stand almost anything."

Nami let go of my hand as if it was suddenly red hot. I heard the hiss of breath from each geisha and my face burned. I had made a mistake, clearly. Yet I had no idea what I had said to upset them.

"Are you mocking us, Junko? This is no place for you." Gin's voice was ice. Her pale grey eyes were suddenly dominated by her black pupils. Her lips trembled with fury. She looked like an angry goddess, and I was very afraid. "You are normal. We—all of us here—are freaks. Listen to me. I was born like this. I never knew my father. Mother always said he took one look at me and ran away. Mother kept me—not because she loved me, you understand, but because she thought she could make a little cash out of me. She put it about that before I was born, she had dreamed that a river spirit, a *kappa*, had come to her and ravished her. I was the result, she said. Some of my first memories are of curious strangers peering at me and touching my eyes, to see if the color was real. I hated it. I thought I would have done anything to get away, but just like you, I didn't know when I was well off. Perhaps the supply of gullible visitors dried up, I don't know, but one day a man came from the great house in the next village, and my mother said I was to go with him. I did as I was told. What else could I do? At first, I thought my new life was wonderful. I was the same age as the daughter of the house, and I was dressed in a kimono and obi just like hers, except the colors were reversed. Her kimono was cream with dark blue branches; mine was dark blue with a cream pattern. I soon found that I had been bought as a gift for Yukiko-san. I was her slave, and she treated me like a toy. I had to trail around behind her, picking up things she discarded, taking her dog for a walk. I even had to feed her. If I displeased her in any way, she slapped me. At first, I thought it was much better than being in my village, poked and prodded by strangers. Hungry and cold. Here, I was fed and I had nice clothes. Yukiko was to be obeyed, and that was all there was to it. But gradually, things got much worse. Yukiko was very spoiled. She had her father wound in her obi, and as far as he was concerned, she could no wrong. If she tormented her puppy so it squealed, it wasn't her. The *kappa* had done it. So I was smacked instead of Yukiko. If she was bored and brushed ink all over her father's important documents, it was the *kappa*. That time, I remember, I was beaten so severely that every movement was agony for over a week. Things got so bad that I thought about running away, although I had no idea where I was going to go.

"Yukiko had a brother. Much older than she was. When I first went to the great house, he was away at university and I had been there nearly a year before he came home. He was very courteous to me, and I was so grateful, I would have done anything he asked. I soon found that Yukiko was deeply jealous of the small attentions her brother paid to me. She became nastier and nastier to me, telling tales to her father at every opportunity. Soon, not a day passed when I wasn't beaten, often badly. I had a tiny hole of a room, next to the kitchen. I didn't mind it. It was warm, and if I was denied food for some wrong—and that happened frequently—I could usually manage to steal something from the kitchen. And then the brother began to visit me in my little room.

"The brother—Toru-san—told me he was not happy with how I was being treated in his house. He would, he said, speak to his father about it. I kneeled at his feet in gratitude. He raised me up and put his arms around me, resting his head on my breasts. I was very beautiful, he said. He had never seen a girl like me. Now that, I believed!

"I didn't know what to do. His hand was sliding up my kimono, and I could feel his breath on my neck. I was panic-stricken. If he wanted to take me, then what could I do about it? And for that matter, did I want to do anything about it? I never got the chance to find out. Yukiko's puppy chose that moment to decide he needed to go out. For some reason, he hated Toru. The dog pawed my door open, saw Toru and began to bark. Loudly. The gods were against me that day. Yukiko followed the dog. She took one look at her brother, holding me in his arms, and screamed the place down.

"Of course, Toru-san said it was all my fault. Yukiko insisted she had seen me slipping a potion in his food. I was truly a *kappa*. I had bewitched her dear brother. Toru agreed with her. He had been having frequent bad dreams, he said. Dreams where he had been drowning in the river, entangled in the embrace of a *kappa* with my face.

"The father slapped me, very hard, and had me locked in the storeroom where the winter wood was kept. I think he would have beaten me very badly if he wasn't beginning to be afraid of me. It was dark and cold, and I could hear rats. They left me there without food or water for three days. By the time the door opened, I would have admitted to being a *kappa* if it meant I wasn't put back in there. As it was, I expected I was going to be executed. I was so hungry and cold and miserable, I didn't even find the idea of death greatly upsetting. I was resigned. If that was to be my fate, then so be it. Perhaps the next life would be better."

Gin paused, her thoughts long ago. She stared into

space, and eventually focused on me. I was hugely relieved to see the anger had left her face.

"The master didn't have me killed. He told me—standing so far away he had to almost shout at me to be heard—that he had received an offer for my worthless carcass. I was to go to Edo. He had sold me, he said. And he just hoped that I would not bring dishonor on his house. But before I went, I was to take the spell off his poor son, or he would reconsider and have the magistrates take my head off my shoulders for witchcraft. I had no idea where I was going, what my future life was going to be, but I didn't care. Anything had to be better than staying here. I waved my hands and muttered a few words, and that was it. He asked if the curse had been lifted. I nodded. 'Good,' he said. In that case, I was to leave his house. Now.

"I stood waiting, and after a minute or so, two handsome young men walked up to me. They smiled at me and seemed to be very pleased. The taller of the two tossed a fat purse to my master, and then they took one of my arms each and marched me off. I am quite tall, but I had to almost run to keep up with their longer stride. We spent the night at an inn—I slept on the bare *tatami* between their futons—and in the morning we walked again. By the time we arrived here, in the Floating World, my feet were blistered and dripping blood. I had never walked for such a long time in my entire life. I thought that the two men must have wanted me for themselves, but I was wrong, of course. As soon as we entered the doors of this place—" Gin paused and glanced around the room—"They let me go and simply stood, waiting. The woman I now know is Auntie came in then and dismissed the men with a nod. She walked around me and finally thrust her face so close to mine I could feel her breath on my cheek. I had no fear left. I just sat where the boys had dropped me and stared back at her.

"Auntie started to smile, and then she laughed out loud. She demanded to know how old I was. Did I have any family? Had I always looked like this or had something happened to me? Had I ever lain with a man? I answered all her questions as best I could, and when I had finished she told me to lay back on the *tatami* with my legs wide apart. She slid her fingers into my black moss and I felt her nails scrabbling inside me. Finally satisfied, she told me to sit up.

"'Forget your past life,' she told me. 'It is over for you. I have bought you. You will be taught how to play the *samisen* and sing and dance. You will perform the tea ceremony with grace. You will smile at my patrons and make them think that they are truly being beguiled by a *kappa*. You will service their every need and be pleased to do it. And in return, I will feed you. I will give you beautiful clothes. You will be given a bed and protection. No one will be allowed to hurt you. Except me, should you disobey me. Understand?'

"I was bewildered, and could do no more than nod. That obviously displeased Auntie, as she hit me hard across my breasts with her cane. I whimpered, and she grinned. Then she went out and two maids came in. They took my old clothes away and led me to the bath.

"And I've been here ever since. I do as Auntie said I would. I smile at the patrons. I sing and dance for them. I make them feel as if they're great men whose every stupid remark is the most profound wit. And I please them with my body in ways you wouldn't be able to even imagine, Junko. We all do. And I—all of us—are pleased to do it."

"Why are you telling me all this?" I asked wildly. "I don't understand. What's it got to do with me? With my *mizuage*?"

"To make you grateful. To make you understand what you're trying to throw away," Nami answered, instead of Gin. "All our stories are much the same, here in the Hidden House. And if we're grateful to Auntie for rescuing us, then you should be a thousand times more grateful. She's taken you from a lifetime of slaving from dawn to dusk for nothing at all to a life that's going to be pure delight."

"Think," Gin interrupted. "You have a golden future ahead of you. You're being sought by some of the wealthiest men in Edo. These men are nobles, Junko. They only have to click their fingers to be showered with whatever they want. And they want you. If they wished, they could simply tell Auntie that they were taking you, give her some gold, and tell her to be content. But they're not doing that. They're arguing amongst themselves, offering more and more money for the privilege of being your *danna*. Can't you see the honor this is bringing to you? Nothing like it has ever been known before. It's the gossip of the whole of the Floating World. And all you can do is moan about it and say you're not going to do it? Honestly, Junko. You should be on your knees, giving thanks for your good fortune."

I felt a hard knot form between my breasts. I was deeply sorry I had angered my friends. Suddenly, a new fear possessed me.

"But what if I'm not good enough?" I whispered. "What if I can't please my *danna*? What will Auntie do with me then?"

Gin smiled.

"That's simply not going to happen. Your *danna* will have paid an impossibly large sum for the pleasure and privilege of taking your virginity. He will be looking forward to teaching you about the arts of love. *Your* role is to be innocent and entirely without knowledge of a man. If your *mizuage* were to be a failure, then it would be wholly your *danna*'s fault, not yours."

The geisha were looking at me indulgently. I felt as if I were a very small child who had confided some silly worry to them. I took a deep breath and managed a smile.

They were right, I supposed. I would do my best to be grateful for my good fortune.

TEN

Every blossom
May hang secure on the branch
Only for a time

The feast was sumptuous. Not only was the food of the very best, it had been prepared so that it was an enticement for the eyes as well as the tongue. And so much! I thought that far more would be wasted than was eaten.

Delicious as it all was, I found it difficult to choke more than a few mouthfuls down. I knew Auntie was watching me as an eagle watches a rabbit, so I hid my lack of appetite by fussing around my *danna*. As soon as he took a sip of his sake, I was at his side to refill his cup. I held his plate for him. Finally, in desperation, I picked up his chopsticks and fed him myself. He ate and drank so much, I hoped he might fall asleep, but he did not.

It seemed no time at all before Auntie was clapping her hands and the maids were taking the remains of the feast away. They would eat well tomorrow, I thought. Although I had seen no signal pass between Auntie and Lord Dai, suddenly the geisha were getting to their feet and bowing deeply to my *danna*. I watched them file out of the room. If my legs had not been trembling so much that they would not obey me, I would have thrown caution to the wind and followed them, no matter what unimaginable horrors Auntie found to punish me with.

As soon as the geisha had gone, the maids returned, their arms full of futons and bedding. They paused, waiting for Auntie's signal to transform the reception room into a bedroom.

"My dear Hana." Lord Dai smiled his old man's smile, revealing stumps of teeth browned by many years of tobacco pipes. His breath stank of tobacco as well. "I thank you for the hospitality of this house. The feast was wonderful, a delight to the senses, and I know that there are even more heavenly delights awaiting me very shortly." Auntie smiled at his politeness, bowing repeatedly. She froze into stillness as Lord Dai continued. "But, could I ask you that Terue-chan and I may spend our first night together somewhere a little more intimate? I have a fancy for somewhere, shall I say, a little more private?"

I kept my face blank, but I knew what Lord Dai really meant. Amidst the rest of her careful instructions, Saki had told me bluntly that I could expect Auntie to watch my *mizuage*.

"She has spy holes almost everywhere in the tea house. And she changes them now and then so one is never sure if she is watching or not. It's to be expected. She does it to make sure we all perform to her standards."

"She's going to watch me and my *danna*?" I was appalled.

"Without doubt. She'll watch you very carefully, I

promise you. She won't sleep until your *danna* leaves you." She paused, smoothing her already creaseless kimono carefully. "Junko-chan, you won't do anything silly, will you? I know you're worried about your *mizuage*, we all were. It's only natural. But if you upset your *danna*, then Auntie will say it's my fault. That I haven't trained you properly. And she'll be even more angry with me than she is with you."

I could take Auntie punishing me, but the idea of Saki taking the pain in my place was intolerable. I remembered dear Gin telling me how she had been hurt in the place of her young mistress. I had winced for her, so how could I even contemplate doing the same thing to poor Saki, who had always been kind to me?

"I'll do my best not to disappoint Auntie. And to be a credit to you," I promised.

Saki was smiling instantly.

I had my bath. Alone. Once I was dried, I was carefully dressed by Saki in the new clothes my *danna* had purchased for me.

"You really are the most fortunate of girls," Saki said. "It's not unusual for a *danna* to buy his choice of maiko a kimono for her *mizuage*, but Lord Dai has even given you an obi and new underclothes as well. I'm sure your chemise has been dyed in the traditional manner, by being rubbed with rose petals. It's just beautiful. And look at these combs for your hair! All so very lovely. It must have cost him a fortune."

Auntie fussed around, staring at me from every angle. Saki watched us, her expression fretful.

"No makeup at all, Auntie? And no wig?"

Auntie shook her head. "Lord Dai has commanded that she should be brought to him in the flesh. If that is his wish, then it shall be so."

"I have failed little Junko as her elder sister!" Saki wailed theatrically, her head bowed to her breasts. "I haven't presented her correctly."

"You have not been allowed to present her correctly," Auntie corrected her firmly. "She's prepared? You're sure she's ready?"

My head swiveled between them. I felt that I was invisible, no more than a piece of fish lying on a market stall as the merchant and the housewife argued about its price. The idea made me feel as if my skin had suddenly grown scales and I longed to scratch at myself.

"She's ready." Saki smiled at me fondly. "I've instructed her in the protocol of the evening. She knows what to expect, and she's truly humble and grateful that an important man such as Lord Dai wishes to be her *danna*."

"Is she?" Auntie glanced at me and I felt that my flesh—or scales!—had been stripped away and she could read my very thoughts. She leaned toward me, as if she were about to pinch my face—something she did often when she thought I was not paying her due attention—but instead, she tweaked the neckline of my beautiful new kimono. "She'll do."

And now, I was about to find out exactly what I would "do" for.

For a moment, I expected Auntie to refuse my *danna*'s request. To make some excuse that another room was not available. But Lord Dai held her gaze and suddenly she was bowing and smiling.

"My lord, of course," she said smoothly. "There is a room prepared for Terue. It will not, of course, be sufficient for the honor you have done to my house, but perhaps it will suffice for tonight?"

Lord Dai stood and stretched. I could have sworn I

heard his old bones creak with the effort. With exquisite courtesy, he bent stiffly from the waist and offered me his hand to help me to my feet.

"You are kind, Hana. I assure you the room will be sufficient. As long as this beautiful flower is at my side, then the bare riverbed would be a luxurious resting place."

My legs were wobbly, both from trepidation and sitting for too long. I rose shakily. Lord Dai led me from the reception room, with Auntie pattering in front of us. From habit, I almost paused at the door of the room I shared with Saki, but a raised finger from Auntie led me onward.

This was my new room, then. As Auntie had said, it was small, perhaps six mats in size. But I could see the shadows of bats flitting past the window screen and guessed it must look out on to the garden. There was a futon laid out on the floor, ready. Hooks on the wall, for my kimono and obi. Even a chest with a flat top, so it would double as a table. I had never had a space of my own in my whole life. I was so overwhelmed, I nearly cried. My elation lasted as long as it took for my *danna* to slide the screen door shut and turn toward me. Auntie had lit a lamp, and its light cast cruelly on Lord Dai's wrinkled face. I thought he looked like a demon, come to drag me off to hell. I was turned to stone where I stood.

He rubbed his hands together. Then he fumbled in his wide sleeve and produced something, which he held as if it were precious. He took the couple of steps needed to bring him to my side and sat down. At his signal, I sat beside him, staring at the *tatami* as though it fascinated me.

"My dear Terue-chan." His voice was fluttery and dry, like moths beating their wings. "You are nervous, of course."

He stroked my arm through my kimono, and I managed

a smile. For a moment, I wondered if he had forgotten my name, and then I remembered that I was no longer Junko.

"Lord," I whispered.

"Perhaps we could look at this? Together? I will leave it with you as a present. Afterward."

He nudged me with his elbow and obediently I looked at his hands. At the pillow book that he was holding open for me.

I suppose it was meant to be an enticement. To arouse me. I stared at the illustration and almost gagged with repulsion. Not at the picture, which was beautifully done, but at the knowledge that—very shortly—it would be me who was beneath my *danna*. Me whose face was a tiny distance from his breath. That it would be his tree of flesh that was searching for my black moss with the insistence of a cat that has cornered a mouse.

"Exciting, isn't it?" Lord Dai turned the fresh, crisp page carefully. His long fingernail traced the outline of the woman in the next picture. "Look, Terue-chan. Look at the pleasure she is giving her man!"

I looked and wished it was a day, a month, a year from now. That tonight was so far away that I could look back without shuddering. And then I remembered Saki's anxious face, pleading with me to do my best, and I found a smile.

"It is a very beautiful book, lord," I whispered. He seemed pleased with my response.

"Stand up, Terue." I climbed to my feet with no grace at all and simply stood, waiting for his command. "Take your clothes off for me."

I reached for my obi and tugged at the knots. My *danna* held up his hand and I stopped, bewildered.

"No, not like that. Slowly. My thoughts wish to have time to see your glories before my eyes do so."

His eyes were shining. His lips parted and I saw a thread of saliva joining the stumps of his teeth. I had to fight the urge to tear off my clothes as quickly as I could, to get the moment of my taking over as soon as possible. My searching fingers found the crease of the knot in my obi. I worked at it carefully, pulling and tugging with a slowness that was not deceitful. It had taken Saki and a maid both to dress me. Now, I understood why. Eventually, I got the knot apart. The obi dangled from my hand, the silk feeling like water in my fingers. Absurdly, I could not bring myself to simply drop the beautiful thing to the floor. Gathering my courage, I took the few steps to the wall, and hung it carefully from a hook.

Lord Dai cackled and clapped his hands.

"Excellent. I do so hate to see a careless woman. And now the kimono."

After the obi, that was nothing. I unwrapped the under sash and the kimono simply slipped off my shoulders at a shrug. I lifted it in my arms and let it flow over the chest.

The night was cool and I shivered, with cold and fear. I looked anywhere except at my *danna*.

"Come here." His voice was hoarse, and he cleared his throat with a rasp. My legs moved like wood as I jerked toward him. He said, "Sit," and I plumped down onto the futon bonelessly.

For the longest time, Lord Dai did nothing at all. He looked at me without so much as moving his head. In spite of what Nami and Gin had told me, suddenly I was sure that I would be clumsy and inept. That he would find me a disappointment. He would tell Auntie, and she would punish both me and poor Saki, who had done her best. The memory of Aki being sent to Kaede's house rose in my mind. Was that my fate tomorrow? I moaned out loud and instinctively reached out my hand and stroked Lord Dai's robe where it nestled in folds in his lap.

I heard him gasp, and then his hand was on my wrist, gripping it tightly. For an old man, his strength was surprising. He wagged the index finger of his free hand at me, and I was so relieved to see he was smiling that I could have cried.

"My lord," I whispered. "I am nothing but an ignorant girl. I know nothing about how to please a man, other than what I have seen in your pillow book. I am deeply afraid that I will not make you happy."

He did not speak, but I could tell from his expression that he was delighted. He leaned forward and put his finger beneath the under sash that held my flimsy underclothes in place. He tugged until the sash came apart, and the silken layers fell open. He paused for a while, clearly relishing my nakedness, and I was reminded of the greedy way he had inspected the food at the feast earlier.

"May I dance for you, lord? Sing, perhaps? Would you like me to call for the maid to bring you some more sake?" Anything to put off the moment I had been hurrying along a short while before!

He ran his long, yellow fingernail down between my breasts and I yelped.

"No man has ever touched you before." It was a statement rather than a question, and I simply bowed my head in agreement. "You are very beautiful, Terue-chan. And you have a beauty within you that is even greater."

As he spoke, he pushed my underclothes off my shoulders, prodding them fully away from my body. His glance ran down from my breasts to my black moss. It took every scrap of willpower I possessed to stop myself shielding my body with my arms. Apparently satisfied at last, he leaned forward and took one of my nipples between his lips, suckling it as if he was a hungry child. Hidden from his vision, I closed my eyes and swallowed nausea.

His lips were very dry. And his stumpy teeth very rough. I moaned, both with pain and agony of spirit.

"Ah, you like that!" Lord Dai mumbled his words against my breast.

"I'm at your command, lord," I whispered. I was wood, as unyielding as a tree branch. From somewhere, I remembered the words Saki had drilled into me and repeated them. "Anything my lord wishes will give me great pleasure."

He sat back, looking at me approvingly. I grimaced and he must have taken it for a smile, as he smiled back happily. I stared over his shoulder, concentrating on the patterns the shadows of the bats made on the window screen.

He was still fully dressed. Abruptly, he undid the sash that held his robe together and lay back on the *tatami*. He waved his hands at his own body, holding his palms open in a gesture of invitation.

This was it, then. Finally. I sent up a fervent prayer to Benzaiten, goddess of all geisha, that she would help me to survive somehow and pulled apart the folds of his robe gingerly. I stared at my *danna*'s tree of flesh in shock. Or rather, I stared at where it should have been.

There was nothing. I was bewildered. Big's tree had reared in such glory that it had astonished me. All the men in the pillow books had trees that—even if they did not match Big's fleshy rod—were, at least to my innocent eyes, truly awe-inspiring. My *danna* appeared to have nothing there at all. In my surprise, I leaned forward for a better look.

Immediately, Lord Dai grabbed the back of my neck in

an iron grip. Before I had time to draw breath, he was pulling my head down to his groin. He mashed my mouth against his flesh, writhing against me like a hooked fish. I heard him groan, although whether it was with pleasure or disappointment, I had no idea. I parted my lips to try and breathe, and he pushed hard against me. And I found his tree.

Compared to Big's tree, it was no more than a bud. Saki had explained to me very carefully that many patrons liked nothing better than to put their tree in a woman's mouth. I pulled a face, but she had been firm.

"If your *danna* wants that, and he probably will, then you must pretend it is the most delightful thing in the world, and you are enjoying it above anything." She saw my expression and smiled. "He will be fresh from the bath and clean. Did you suck your thumb when you were a child? Look on it in the same way."

Lord Dai's tree was barely as big as my own thumb, and I have small hands. As well as that, it was as limp and soft as a pile of fresh dog's turds. I was horrified. Thoughts of Kaede's house rose to haunt me. I parted my lips and ran the tip of my tongue over the lump of soft flesh. When nothing happened, in desperation I nipped it gently.

My *danna* sighed deeply. He fastened his hands in my hair and my combs flew everywhere as he tugged, my hair cascading down past my hips. He held me away from him with my hair, the burning pain making my eyes water.

"You are truly beautiful, Terue-chan," he panted. I was bewildered. How could he compliment me when I was obviously failing miserably to arouse him? But he was smiling, so I smiled back tremulously and winced as he wound his fingers in my hair, tugging at my scalp unmercifully. He took the hanks of my hair and wound them around his wilting tree. Tugged them so tight that his flesh bulged through, bright red and shiny. Still not content, he sawed at himself until I was terrified his skin might split.

His tree began to grow beneath his hands and I saw it start to pulse through my hair. This time, when he pressed my lips reluctantly against it, it jerked back at me. I kissed it dubiously, and Lord Dai shrieked like a woman.

"Bite!" he shouted. "Hard."

I fastened my teeth into his half-erect tree and bit down on it, grinding my teeth together until I was sure I could feel them meet through his flesh. And the harder I bit, the more my *danna* shrieked with pleasure.

Suddenly, he was all movement. He yanked my hair from around his tree violently and grabbed me by the shoulders, manipulating me until my mouth was over the very tip of his tree. Then he thrust himself between my reluctant lips.

I gagged, my lips wide, fighting for air. Even though his tree still seemed limp in comparison to Big's rearing erection, it filled my entire mouth. Tears flowed down my cheeks and I retched. Lord Dai was shouting, but there were no words in the noise. Suddenly, his whole body was rigid. For one terrible moment, I thought his old heart had given up on him and he had died in my mouth. The idea was so awful, I screamed and bit down hard on his tree.

He burst his fruit in my innocent mouth, his seed cascading down my throat, the excess running out from between my lips. I choked, almost vomiting as the warm, sticky mess filled my mouth. Yet still it came until I would have welcomed the relief of death.

Lord Dai fell out of my mouth as suddenly as he had thrust himself into it. He collapsed onto the futon and lay panting violently. I sat beside him with my mouth full of his seed and realized with overwhelming horror that I had no choice but to swallow it. He had closed his eyes, and I took advantage of the moment to pinch my nose closed, hard. I could still feel the warm, slimy texture as it slithered down my throat like glue, but at least I couldn't taste it.

I longed for a drink of tea to take away the nastiness. Normally I did not drink alcohol, but at that moment I would have given a year of my life for a flask of strong sake. But I knew I could not shout for the maid—still less leave the room myself—until my *danna* left me. Instead, I waited silently.

"Terue-chan." Even in the two words, I understood that he was pleased. "You have no idea what I have done to win you. But it was worth it. There shall be no secrets between us now."

I managed a deep breath, wondering with repulsion what new horrors he was going to suggest. But I was entirely wrong.

"You have mended me, child. You have given life where before there was only the deepest of sleep." I was so surprised, I dared to look up at him. He was nodding and smiling. "When I was a young man, my tree would have delighted any woman. But in recent years, my strength has left me."

"My lord has honored me with his presence. I can ask no more," I murmured dutifully. Truly, I had learned my lessons well!

"Ah, when I was younger..." His voice trailed off and he was silent for so long, I began to hope he had fallen asleep. But he had not. "But now I am an old man, Terue. My wife died some years ago. I have had no heart to replace her. I have many concubines, but none of them please me like they used to. None of them have ever pleased me as you have tonight."

He took my hand and began to stroke it. I cringed as he put my little finger in his mouth and sucked on it gently. Knowing I was supposed to be delighted by his tenderness, I managed a sigh that might, if he chose, be taken for pleasure. He pulled my finger from his mouth. It came out with a small pop.

"I will tell you the truth, Terue-chan. From the moment I saw you at Lord Ito's, I hoped that I'd found the one woman who would be able to rouse me again. It's many years since my tree has taken any interest in a woman. I've consulted the best doctors. Been given medicine that tasted so bitter, I almost wondered if the cure was worth it. In any event, it was useless. I've visited acupuncture masters without number. Given gifts to the gods that would have raised a temple. And nothing did any good at all. I even stopped visiting my concubines, I was so ashamed of my lack."

He stopped speaking and stared at me.

"My lord, I'm sorry," I mumbled. What else was I expected to say? He rested his head on my shoulder, his chin digging in to my bones. He had a mole on his temple that sprouted sharp hairs. They scratched infuriatingly. When he spoke again, I knew instinctively that he did not want me to see his face. And I knew why. I could feel his tears gathering in the hollow of my shoulder bones.

Suddenly, I knew him for what he really was. An old, lonely man who missed his wife and longed for the return of the youth that had left him forever. No matter that he was rich and powerful. I felt almost sorry for him.

"I visited a witch," he whispered, as if it was something to be ashamed of. "One of my friends confided to me that he had consulted her over the matter of whether he should take a particular woman as his wife. She had given him very good advice, he said, and he was delighted with his choice of bride. I dithered about it for weeks, and finally decided to go to see her when I spent the night with my favorite concubines and neither of them could give me any pleasure. They were greatly distressed, and of course I let them think it was they who were lacking, all the time knowing it was my fault. Anyway, I tried to tell the witch that I'd come on a similar errand to my friend. I was thinking of remarrying I said, and was unsure whether it was right for me. I had gone in my plainest robes, of course, and alone except for one servant, so she would have no idea I was a noble."

I cleared my throat, choking back hysterical laughter. The witch would have known in a second that my *danna* was a rich man. She would have read it in his bearing, his attitude. How, I wondered, could such an important, and I supposed very wise, man be so very innocent?

"My lord was very prudent," I murmured. His chin was sharp, and I wished he would move, but he did not.

"I thought so. But she saw through me in a moment. She listened to me, and then told me to send my servant away. As soon as he was gone, she took my palm in her hand and spat on it. She rubbed both my hands together, and then grinned at me. She said that she knew what I was really there for. That I had come to recover that which I had lost. My hand told her that I was not a happy man, she said. That I had lost the most precious gift of any man."

I sat still, fascinated despite myself. Lord Dai blew a hot breath on my skin and nodded to himself before he went on.

"I knew there was no point in lying to her. I just shrugged and waited for her to tell me my future. I had been to the wise men, she asked? And given opulently to the gods? I said I had. In that case, there was only one cure for my problem. My hopes soared. Nobody else had offered me the hint of a cure. She held out her hand, and I put a purse full of silver in her fingers. She didn't even bother to count it, just put it on the floor as if it was no more than she expected. She leaned forward and poked me in the chest with her finger.

"'You're an old man,' she said. My hopes began to fade at once. Did I need a witch to tell me that? But she was smiling, so I listened. 'Only youth and beauty and purity can cure what ails you. You'll know the girl as soon as your eyes fasten on her. Once you see her, you must take her, no matter what the opposition. She's the only one who will be able to give life to your tree of flesh. If you allow her to slip through your fingers, then the curse of lack will be with you until your dying day.'

"And that was that. She sat back and began to fill a pipe, puffing away on it as if I were not there. I was angry, but with myself, not her. I thought myself a fool for going to her. And I carried on thinking that way until I saw you, Terue-chan. And at that moment, I knew that the witch was right. If the other *daimyo* had gone on raising the bidding for you, I would have continued even if it meant losing every scrap of my fortune. I felt sure that the gods had sent you to me. I was even more certain of it when Lord Ito proposed that it was time to call a halt. He said that we could go on until eternity, bidding and counter-bidding, and that still at the end of the day only one of us could be your *danna*. I agreed at once when he proposed that we should draw lots for you, and accept whoever the gods smiled upon. And I was the fortunate one, as I had known I would be all along. And now I know that truly the curse will be lifted from me."

He took a deep, contented breath. He was falling asleep, with his head snuggled on my breasts. He stirred a little, and his hand found my arm and clutched me tightly. His grip was fierce, the gesture deeply possessive. I sat very still, unwilling to disturb him as my thoughts flitted like bats, swooping at twilight.

My friends in the Hidden House had been mistaken when they had assured me that I could do nothing wrong. I was still whole. My *mizuage* had been a failure. Auntie would be furious with me. And not just me, poor Saki would also feel the lash of her anger. I had let us both down.

It was worse than anything I had imagined.

My *danna* snuffled in his sleep like a contented child. He didn't awaken even when my tears splashed on his face.

ELEVEN

Butterflies are so
Beautiful. Why then do moths
Cause me to shudder?

*L*ord Dai slipped away from my room just before dawn.

I had not slept all night, but now I feigned the deepest of sleep. He leaned over me and stroked my face gently. I felt him pause and knew he hoped I would awaken. I kept very still and finally heard him leave. Only then did I pull on my sleeping robe and sit up, my knees drawn to my breasts, staring at the wall.

I was still sitting like that when Big visited me. He came to my room even before the maids were stirring. I marveled at his confidence that I would not only be alone, but would welcome him. He sat on my *tatami*, as comfortable as if he were an invited and honored guest.

He smiled at me slyly. "Well, little one? Was it as terrible as you expected?" He didn't wait for my reply, but carried on. "I suppose he gave you that, did he?"

He poked his finger at my pillow book. I nodded dully and watched as he flipped open the pages.

"And where did he begin, I wonder? At the first page and work his way through it all?"

He grinned at me, and I had an almost overwhelming urge to confide in him that I was still whole. But caution laid a hold on my tongue and I lowered my head shyly. Apart from anything else, I was too embarrassed to speak of it. I knew I was blushing, but Big seemed to think it was modesty and his smile widened.

"So now you know, Terue. You survived, after all?" I glanced up at him. I could not read his expression. He kissed his fingertip and placed it against my lips. The gesture was very tender, but it made me feel no better.

"My *danna* was very thoughtful," I said cautiously.

"Yes? And was his kindness so great that it made up for having an old man inside you? Did he give you pleasure, Terue?"

Big's voice had changed. Suddenly, it was harsh, and I jerked back, stung by his tone as much as his words.

"I took no pleasure from him," I said. I was deeply hurt. Why was Big, my friend, speaking to me like this?

"Ah. So you say. But now that you're a geisha, perhaps you're like all the rest of them. So full of deception and deceit you don't even know you're lying."

He was angry. And I had no idea why. After the horror of my night with Lord Dai, it was too much to bear. I put my hand on the sleeve of his robe and tugged at the material, forcing him to look at me.

"Big. What is it? What have I done to upset you?"

I saw his anger collapse. He put his hand on the back of my neck and pulled me toward him. His voice buzzed softly against my ear.

"I'm sorry, Terue-chan. I didn't sleep at all last night. The thought of you being taken by that old man haunted me. Did he hurt you?"

"No, not at all," I said truthfully. I was relieved. Dear Big! He had only spoken harshly because he had been worried. For a second, I thought again about telling him the truth, but I was too ashamed. "He was very kind."

"Did you enjoy it, then?"

"No!" I had no need to say more. Big read the truth in my voice and smiled.

"Do you remember, little one? Do you remember begging me to be the one who took you for the first time?"

I nodded, even more deeply embarrassed. I looked down at the *tatami*, wishing that Big would go away and leave me alone with my thoughts.

"Do you understand now why I could not be the one? Auntie would never have tolerated it. But things are very different now. You are no longer a maiko. You are a geisha, and you're free to take anybody you please for your lover."

It was a moment before I understood what Big was saying. And when I did, I froze in disbelief. He was asking me if I wanted him as my lover. But even if I desired him, how could I agree? I was still whole. Besides, I didn't want *anybody* as my lover. If the previous night were anything to go by, I would be very happy if I was never so much as touched by a man ever again.

"You do me great honor, Big," I muttered. "But it's too soon. I don't want to. I mean, I couldn't."

My words trailed off miserably. I liked Big a great deal, and I didn't want to offend him.

"I understand." I glanced at him from beneath my eyelashes. His expression was serious. "It's too soon for you. I know how you worried about your *mizuage*, and I suppose it wasn't very pleasant for you, being taken by that old man. But I promise you, with me, it will be very different." He stood elegantly, like a cat stretching. At the door, he turned and spoke softly. "I'll make you very happy, I promise you. But don't expect me to wait too long. I'm not a patient man."

Big's presumption took my breath away. Surely, he must know that I had had no idea what I was asking when I had begged him to take the place of my *danna*. Did he really think that now he could simply walk into my room and demand me? It seemed he did. His visit distracted me, but not for long. I expected Auntie at any moment, demanding to know how things had gone. Deciding to take the tiger by the tail, I went and tapped on her door. There was no answer, not even when I tapped harder. I poked my head timidly around the door to be sure, but the room was empty, the futon unruffled.

She wasn't there. By the look of her futon, it hadn't been slept in. I was limp with relief, but I knew that Auntie might come back at any moment. I decided quickly that I would seize the chance to go and talk to the geisha in the Hidden House before she appeared. Ask the advice of my true friends.

The geisha surrounded me, patting my arms and smiling, welcoming me. The smiles faded into horror as I spoke.

"Lord Dai was unable. I'm still whole," I blurted miserably.

The indrawn breath from all the geisha sounded like the wind rushing through reeds.

"He didn't like you?" Hiromi asked dubiously.

I shook my head. "No, it wasn't that." I explained about my *danna*'s problems, and how he had been instructed to wait for the right woman by the witch. And that he was convinced that I was the one. I blushed ripely as I told them that Lord Dai had been aroused enough to burst his fruit in my mouth.

"Many of the very old men are like that," Nami said simply. "Their trees can rise so far, but not far enough to match the bird to the nest. Still, you think he was happy with you?"

"Yes." I nodded. "I'm sure he was. He still seems to think I'm the one he's been waiting for."

Their faces lightened.

"Well, that's not too bad, then," Gin said. "I daresay your *danna* wasn't the first one who couldn't manage to get what he paid for."

She sounded relieved. But her smile faded quickly as I told them about Big's visit. A cloud of unease seemed to settle on the girls at the mention of his name. I had learned much in my time in the Green Tea House, particularly in the months before my *mizuage*. Before then, I had been kept at arms' length by the geisha. I was with them, yet not of them. As my *mizuage* approached, they relaxed, and even Tamayu spoke freely in front of me. And one thing I had learned was that the boys were feared by all the geisha. Nothing was actually said in plain words, and I was intrigued. Eventually my curiosity was too great to be contained. I asked Saki quite bluntly why everybody was afraid of them. We were sitting in the garden, taking the early sun. Saki had her head thrown back, basking in the warmth, and she answered me without moving her head, her voice very low.

"You think Big is your friend, don't you?"

I was surprised. I had never confided my friendship with Big to anybody in the Green Tea House. But I should have known. Sneeze twice in the comfort of your own room and next day somebody was bound to ask if you had caught a cold. Even our courses all started within a day of each other, our rhythms were so bound together.

"He is my friend. He's always been very kind to me."

"Perhaps so. But be careful, child." Saki spoke quietly. "You understand what Big and Bigger do here? And in the other place." She nodded very slightly toward the Hidden House.

"They keep the patrons in order, don't they?"

"That they do. Nobody causes trouble if the boys are about the place. But they do more than that, child. They make sure none of the geisha cause trouble as well. You remember Aki?"

Of course I did. Poor Aki, who had tried to find her freedom and instead had found herself a prisoner in Kaede's house.

"The boys found her easily because nobody in the Floating World would dare to lie to them. And before she went to Kaede's house, they punished her for her stupidity. Not just to teach her a lesson, you understand. But to remind the rest of us what would happen if we tried to be as foolish as Aki. That's what they do. They are enforcers. They keep the patrons in order, and us as well. And always remember, they're Auntie's eyes and ears. Whatever they hear, Auntie hears."

She set her lips firmly together then, and I knew I would have to be satisfied with what she had said already. I sensed it was only half a tale, but at that time—with all the confidence of youth and innocence—I was convinced it didn't matter to me anyway. She didn't understand that Big really was my friend. Now, looking at the geisha's serious faces, I understood they were more worried about Big than Lord Dai's failure.

"You can't let Big take you," Nami said bluntly. "Does he know that you're still a virgin?"

"No. I couldn't bring myself to tell him. I was too ashamed."

"You should have done. He would have known immediately that you couldn't take him as your lover when you were still whole."

"I suppose he's going to be angry I didn't tell him straight away, isn't he? And even angrier that I can't take him as my lover now that he's asked me." A glance at the geisha's faces assured me I was right. "But not half as angry as Auntie's going to be with me when she finds out how I failed Lord Dai. It's hopeless, isn't it? Perhaps I should just run away. Get as far as I can before Auntie gets back."

"And sign yourself into Kaede's, next to Aki?" Nami looked at me pityingly. "That's what would happen, you know. You'd make Auntie and Lord Dai both lose so much face, they'd never be able to live it down. And I promise you, she'd set the boys on to you first, to let us all know nobody was above being punished."

"But Big is my friend. He wants to be my lover. He wouldn't hurt me, and I'm sure he wouldn't let Bigger hurt me either."

Nami, Gin, and Hiromi were all staring at me, their faces full of pity. Gin shook her head slowly.

"Terue-chan, listen to me. If Big was really your friend, wouldn't he want you to come to him freely? Not barge into your room and tell you he was going to take you as his lover, whether you liked it or not."

"I hadn't thought about it like that," I said reluctantly. I found a smile from somewhere and added Tamayu's favorite phrase when it came to discussing the opposite sex. "But he's only a man, isn't he? They never think."

But Gin was having none of it. She shook her head, her face tight with worry. "Terue. You do know about Big and Bigger, don't you?"

"Of course I do. They're friends. I know that."

"They're more than friends. They're lovers," Gin said brutally. My mouth fell open, but no words came out. "They came to the tea house together. They were lovers right from the start. As far as Bigger is concerned, women are an abomination. He hates all of us, mainly because we can distract Big from him from time to time, just as he's distracted by you now. That's why Bigger hates you so much. If Big is dangerous, then Bigger is terrifying. Don't put your trust in Big, Terue. Bigger will get him back, no matter what he has to do. It's happened before. And when he does, Bigger will teach him to hate you as well, to punish you for daring to steal Big from him."

I rubbed my hands over my face, to hide my expression. I was so choked with emotions, I could hardly breathe. I felt deep disappointment and something that was almost sorrow for Big, the man I had thought my true friend. And also did I feel naïve, and incredibly stupid. Everyone knew about the boys. Everybody except me. How very foolish the Hidden House geisha must think me!

"I didn't realize," I whispered. Thoughts of Lord Dai's pillow book made me blush like a ripe plum. There had been pictures in there, of men pleasuring men. Men who lay together, their trees secure in each other's mouths. That was what the boys did for each other?

I closed my eyes in embarrassment so I couldn't see my friends' expressions.

"Then what can I do? Auntie's going to punish me, no matter what. And I can't even turn to Big for help. Oh, it's all such a mess! There's no way out of it for me."

"There is." Gin's voice was firm. "You're forgetting. Auntie must know what happened—or rather, what didn't happen—already. She always watches everybody's *mizuage* through one of her peep-holes. I can't understand why she hasn't demanded to see you already this morning."

"She doesn't know yet. She couldn't watch us. Lord Dai said he wanted to be private with me, so we spent the night in my new room. Anyway, she's not in the tea house. I went to see her as soon as Big left me, and her futon hasn't been slept in."

"Ah." Gin raised her eyebrows. "If she couldn't keep an eye on you, that explains why she isn't there. I can guess where she is."

The geisha exchanged sly glances. I stared at them, deeply puzzled.

"I imagine that her lover wanted her and she decided she had earned her own pleasure." Gin smiled.

"Auntie? Auntie has a lover?" I shook my head in disbelief. Yet something else I knew nothing about! "But she's too old! And she's...she's Auntie!"

I saw that the geisha were hiding laughter politely behind their hands. Nami gathered her manners first.

"You are very young, Terue-chan. Auntie may appear old to you, but trust me, she is not. Not so many years ago, she was the most beautiful woman in the Floating World. She is still a pretty woman, even now. There have been other lovers, but none as special as this one. He has Auntie under his spell. But none of that matters at the moment. We must solve your dilemma. Listen to me. You must go back to the tea house, now. As soon as Auntie comes back, go and see her. Kneel and kowtow to her and tell her everything. Just as you've told us."

"But I can't do that!" I protested. "I told you, she'll be so furious with me, she'll put me aside at once. She really will sell me to Kaede's house, to keep Aki company."

"No, she won't," Nami said firmly. "Tell her all about Lord Dai being unable. Tell her about the witch's prophecy. That's important. Auntie isn't going to be angry with you, I promise. But you must tell her everything, straight away."

I was bewildered. It seemed to me that confessing my failure to Auntie could only make things worse—if that was possible. And it would still leave me the problem of Big. The geisha waited for me to speak, and for the first time, I noticed that Hiromi and Nami were fully made up. Gin was not, but I guessed that she would never try and hide her amazing skin and eyes with paint. Were they expecting patrons, I wondered? If they were, I should not be here.

Even as the thought came to me, Gin raised her head and looked alarmed.

"Quick! Over by the shrine. Kneel down and keep your eyes fixed on the floor. Keep silent. Don't move."

Her fear was contagious, and I responded automatically. I was kneeling as close to the shrine as I could get when I heard the sound of men's voices in the outer hall of the Hidden House. I had been right, the geisha were expecting patrons. In listening to me, they had lost track of the time. There was only one entrance to the reception room. I had no way of escaping.

"My lords!" Gin was on her feet, bowing repeatedly. I could not see the men, but I guessed from the different voices that there were four of them. "Welcome. May I send for sake for you? Or if you have not bathed yet, perhaps you would like to visit the bathhouse?"

"Ah, Gin-chan!" I thought that the man who spoke had already taken too much sake. His voice was very loud, and his words slightly slurred. "Sake, yes! Lots of it. But we have no need of the bath. Perhaps later, but not now. And a pipe for each of us, as well as the sake."

The screen door had been left open, and two maids bustled in with cups and sake flasks in charcoal burners. They put them down and at a quiet word from Gin returned quickly with more trays.

"May I prepare a pipe for you, lord?"

"Yes, in a moment. Who's that?" Even with my eyes fixed on the *tatami*, I felt the man stab his finger toward me. The gesture was so rude, I guessed he was already drunk. "Have you a new treasure in the Hidden House, Gin? Is she a surprise for us? What secret does the delicious little morsel hide, I wonder?"

"Ah, lord. No." Gin's voice was high and breathy, almost girlish, and so unlike her normal speaking voice I understood deep in my gut that I was in danger. "I am so sorry. This is...this is Junko. She is a maiko from the Green Tea House. Auntie sent her to us with an urgent message, and I'm afraid she didn't have time to leave before you arrived. I'll dismiss her now, if it pleases you."

"No. No, it doesn't please me at all. Make me a pipe, Gin. You, Junko. Stand up and come over here."

I obeyed, but stood as far away from him as I dared.

"Maiko, are you? Why aren't you wearing *tabi*, then?"

I swallowed. It had delighted me that morning to put on my *geta* without *tabi*, the divided-toe sock that I had worn as a maiko. Geisha never wore *tabi* outside the house. As I now considered myself to be a geisha, neither would I wear them. Now, I wished devoutly that I had.

"I think you're not telling me the whole truth, Gin." Gin was rolling the bowl of the opium pipe over the flame. Already, the fumes were beginning to float sleepily on the air. "What do you think, gentlemen? Fancy a bit of variety?

Looks to me as if we might have something new to play with."

Gin leaned across and pushed the pipe between her patron's lips. He inhaled, holding the aromatic smoke in his lungs for a long time. Perhaps it was not the first pipe he had taken that day, for it seemed to have little effect on him.

"Aye, Ikko. She's a beauty, all right," said one of the other patrons sitting next to Nami. He also had a fuming pipe, but his other hand was fumbling deep inside the neck of Nami's kimono. She stared straight ahead, her smile looking as if it had been painted on her lips. "Got some special talents, has she?"

"I promise you, gentlemen. She's just a maiko from the Green Tea House. Auntie sent her across urgently, so no doubt she had no time to put her *tabi* on." Gin widened her eyes urgently at me, and I bowed deeply to her patron.

"I am so sorry, Ikko-san," I murmured. "I have no right to be here, disturbing the honorable gentlemen. I will go now."

Ikko wagged his finger at me. "Not so soon, little one. Stay awhile. Don't worry about Auntie. I'll have a word with her."

All of the men laughed. Ikko took his pipe from Gin and pushed the stem between my lips.

"Suck in the smoke. Take a deep breath, and hold it." I started to choke, and he grinned. "Again. That's it."

The smoke tasted like flowers, releasing their perfume after rain. But it was very hot, and I coughed most of it out. But suddenly, I was no longer afraid. I smiled at Ikko-san, trying not to laugh as his face swayed in and out of focus.

"Ikko-san." Gin's voice was so loud it startled me. Why couldn't she just be quiet and let me float off gently? "Ikko-san. Junko is Auntie's favorite. The man who is to be her *danna* is one of the most important men in Edo. I cannot tell you his name, but he's very powerful. Auntie really will not be pleased if anything should happen to Junko before her *mizuage*."

"In that case, Auntie should take greater care of her treasure, shouldn't she?" He held out the opium pipe to me and I sucked in the smoke. I held his wrist to keep the stem steady, and Ikko licked his lips. "Joji, what do you think? Between the four of us, we should be able to scrape up enough to make Auntie forget this one's *mizuage* is going to be a bit irregular."

He laughed and I giggled with him. After all, if he did but know it, my *mizuage* had already been far more irregular than he could ever imagine!

I glanced around the room lazily. My lips formed into an "ooh" of amazement as I saw that somewhere along the way Hiromi had lost her kimono and underclothes. She was completely naked, lying on her side on the *tatami* with a man full length on each side of her. I nodded wisely to myself. I had seen this before. She had become an illustration from my pillow book. As I watched, one of the men took his rigid tree of flesh in his hand, and pushed it deep in her black moss. As if the other patron had been waiting for the signal, he thrust hard at Hiromi from the back. I remembered vaguely that Lord Dai had shown me this in my pillow book and said it was called "splitting the melon" and that it was very pleasant. I had assumed bitterly he meant it was pleasant for the man, as I could not believe that a woman would enjoy it. Looking at Hiromi, I decided I had been wrong. She was grunting, and her face wore exactly the same expression of rapture as the woman in my pillow book.

The man Ikko had called Joji had his head in Nami's lap.

She was still fully clothed, but her kimono was thrown aside. I was astonished to see she was wearing nothing beneath it. I glanced at her face. It seemed to be contorted in agony. Surely, that couldn't be right.

"You see, Junko? My friends are pleasuring themselves at the same time as they pleasure dear Hiromi. And Joji has given not a thought to his own desires. Instead, he's seeking the seed with our lovely diving girl. See how she rejoices in his attentions? Perhaps you might like it if I did something similar for you?"

Gin made a strangled sound deep in her throat. If Ikko heard her, he gave no sign. He put the pipe down carefully and leaned toward me, putting his hand on the nape of my neck and pulling me toward him. His fingers slid down the front of my kimono and found my breasts.

"After all, there are many ways in which a woman can be pleasured and give pleasure to a man in return and still remain whole. Isn't that so, Gin-chan? And that being the case, there's no need at all for Auntie to know what's gone on here this afternoon. Junko's *danna* can still have her and never be any the wiser that we've been there before him."

His fingernail was ragged and it caught on my nipple. The pain was surprisingly great, and I tried to wriggle back. Ikko clutched my breast harder so that it really did hurt.

"It seems to me that you're not quite as innocent as a maiko should be, Junko-chan. None of this appears to astonish you at all." He licked his lips and I wanted to explain to him that I had seen it all before. But only in my pillow book. Before I got the chance to speak, he was whispering to me again. "Would you like it if I sought the seed with you, Junko? Or perhaps I could split the melon for you. I would like that. Or you could lick and kiss my tree until I burst my fruit in your mouth." Memories of Lord Dai doing just that made me shudder. I saw at once that Ikko had mistaken my horror for the tremble of desire. He grinned widely. "Or perhaps all of those. But first, I think it would entice my appetite to see Gin here play with you." He smiled at Gin. "It's always exciting for a man to see two women pleasuring each other."

"Ikko-san, I cannot," Gin whispered. I stared at her, wondering why she was so obviously horrified. All of the geisha in the Hidden House had brushed my hair, kissed me, and stroked my face. It would be odd that her patron was watching us, but if that was all he wanted, I would be happy to do it.

I held my arms out to Gin and smiled encouragingly at her. But I froze as I saw Ikko-san reach into his robe and pull out his tree of flesh. To my innocent eyes, it was huge. Not as astonishingly large as Big's tree, but most certainly a river monster compared with Lord Dai's wilting stick. The sight of it blew away the opium fumes that had made my head swim. He ran his hand up and down the length of his tree and wagged the nasty thing at me.

"Later on, but not too much later," he said hoarsely. "When I've seen Gin seek the seed with you and watched you give her pleasure in return, then I shall have you, little one. I shall take great delight in splitting the melon with you."

"I'm afraid, dear Ikko-san, that you're going to have to take your fun elsewhere. This child is not for you. She's spoken for."

I had not heard the screen slide open. Neither had Ikko. His mouth dropped in surprise and suddenly he was thrusting his tree of flesh back in his robe hastily.

"You're her *danna*? This foolish creature never said. I'm so sorry, Seemon-san. Had I known, of course, I would never have presumed..." Ikko's voice choked off into silence. He cleared his throat and tried again. "Do run along, child. Gin was quite right, you have no place here in the Hidden House."

I scrambled to my feet, almost falling over my own feet in my eagerness. The newcomer held out his hand to me and I took it gratefully.

"I would not disturb you gentlemen in your pleasures," my savior said politely. "I'll take this child back to the tea house myself. And perhaps take a little tea there before I return. I hope you will have taken your delights and we will be able to discuss our business by then."

He bowed politely to Ikko-san. His skin was as white as silk and the hair falling onto the collar of his kimono was as red and thick as the winter coat of a fox, strong and lustrous to protect it from the cold.

I knew him. I had seen him before—just once, when I had gone with the geisha to entertain the nobles. But that was not how I knew him. I knew him in my flesh and my bones and my private places. In my head and in my heart. And also did I know that was why the gods had made my *danna* unable, so as to save me for this man. It all made perfect sense now.

The fact that he was a foreign barbarian mattered not at all.

He took my hand and tucked it into the crook of his arm as if it was the most natural thing in the world. It should have been unforgivably rude of him, to touch me so intimately when we had not even been formally introduced. But it was not. His touch was as familiar to me as if he were an old friend. Or already my lover.

He was silent as we crossed the garden, and he opened the door of the Green Tea House for me. My arm felt naked when he released me. I stood staring at his face, hypnotized by his exotic beauty.

"I knew we would meet again. You were called Junko when we met before. I asked Lord Ito who you were. Has your name changed since then?"

"Yes. I'm Terue now."

"A lovely name. I'm called Seemon, Terue-chan. I must go now. I'm sorry, but I have no choice. But I'll come back to you. Would you like that?" I nodded, finding no words. "Good. We shall talk then, amongst other things. But it may be some time. Will you wait for me?"

I longed to ask him when. To tell him that no matter how short the time, it would be too long. But the door was ajar, and I feared somebody would hear us.

"Yes. Yes, please."

"I'll come back as soon as it's safe for us. We must tread very carefully, little Terue. Remember that, and tell nobody that we have met. Now go, before I forget myself and start gossip before there's anything to gossip about."

He smiled at me with his young man's smile and put his hand very gently in the small of my back to urge me through the door. When I turned to look at him, he was already halfway across the garden, but I saw his head turn toward me as if it had been drawn by a magnet, and I was certain I saw both amazement and joy in his expression. And then the Hidden House swallowed him completely.

I went and sat on my *tatami*, my thoughts whirling. How strange that only hours before the thought of welcoming a man into my body repulsed me. Now, all I could think of was Seemon's touch on my skin, his lips on my body, and I shuddered with pleasure.

And then I remembered I still had to face Auntie, and my pleasure died stillborn.

TWELVE

This life or the next
Life. Truly there is nothing
New under the sun.

J kneeled before Auntie quickly, and then thought better of it and prostrated myself. I gabbled my story, my words muffled by the *tatami* as I blurted out everything as soon as I could.

When I had finished, I lay still, waiting for her fury to whip me unmercifully.

"Lord Dai was gone before I got back this morning. But he left a very handsome present for me. Very generous indeed." I was amazed. Auntie sounded thoughtful rather than angry. "He left a message with the maid to say that he would return very soon and that he looked forward to talking with me when he did. Tell me again, what the witch said to him. And sit up. I can barely hear you, muttering into the *tatami* like that."

I rose to my knees, and—watching her expression carefully—told her again what Lord Dai had confided in me.

"Ah. That explains a great deal." I risked a glance at her face. She was smiling broadly. "There was much at stake amongst the nobles who bid for you, child. Not just the money for your *mizuage*—for such men as them, it was next to nothing. But more than anything, it was also a matter of face. Now I understand why Lord Dai was willing to risk so much to get you."

I saw that she was truly pleased and thanked Nami and Gin silently for their good advice.

"I often wondered why Lord Dai didn't take another wife after his first wife died. Especially as he has no children, not even by his concubines. And now I know. Well, I think we may say that things have turned out even better than one could have hoped."

I could hardly believe her words. Auntie was clutching at reeds. Surely, she must understand, as I did, that I had been Lord Dai's last hope. And I had failed him.

"But Auntie," I said cautiously. "That's all wrong. He couldn't manage to take me. I'm still whole."

"You are foolish, child," Auntie said impatiently. "It doesn't matter. He has it in his head that you're the cure for what ails him. He may not have succeeded completely straight away, but you aroused him more than any other woman has been able to for years. He'll come back to you, often. And you will please him more and more each time."

I kept my face blank with an effort that hurt the muscles in my cheeks. Lord Dai would come back to me? And if—when—he finally took me, would I then find Big waiting on my futon for me?

Auntie leaned forward and patted my cheek almost fondly. "Ah, I knew you would be special, right from the start. Once word gets out that Lord Dai's your patron, I'll be able to name my own price for anybody else who wants your services." For a moment, my confused thoughts conjured up memories of my friends in the Hidden House. Was Auntie going to sell my body, just as she did with theirs? I sighed with relief when she went on. "Everybody in the Floating World who matters will come to the tea house to be entertained by the geisha who has the great Lord Dai at her feet. It's essential, of course, that you keep yourself pure for when he's finally ready for you. There will be no lovers for you, Terue. No matter how long it takes. In case you think you can sneak a man in behind my back, I'll instruct the boys that they must ensure that doesn't happen. That nobody lays as much as a finger on you."

Auntie smiled, and I smiled with her. I thought she gave me a strange look, but then, she had not heard my conversation with Big. At that moment—if I had dared—I would have embraced her in my thankfulness that she had unwittingly kept Big away from me.

"Yes, Auntie," I murmured.

THIRTEEN

Each snowflake that falls
To earth is unique. Such a
Pity they must melt.

he other geisha were all of a flutter. I thought
they resembled butterflies in the grace of their
motions and the movements of their colorful kimonos.

No matter how important the patrons, normally they
moved fluidly, as if they were playing a game where everybody knew the rules and it was essential that each moment
was played accordingly. This evening, it was as if a stone
had been thrown into a quiet pond, casting ripples as far as
the land. They giggled behind their fans, opened their eyes
wide, tilted their heads to one side flirtatiously.

And the guest of honor—seated as was only proper in
front of the *tokonoma*, the alcove that was bare except for a
single silk scroll and a beautifully arranged *ikebana* spray of
flowers in an elegant vase—smiled at each of them in turn.
He inclined his head and appeared delighted with their
attentions.

I hated all of them. Tamayu. Ren. Even my elder sister Saki. How dare they throw themselves at Seemon like this? Even worse, how dare he appear to enjoy their attentions? Well, two could play that game.

"Kita-san." I leaned slightly nearer to my companion. "May I be of service to you? Perhaps some sake? Or could I play or dance for you?"

"Terue-chan, thank you. A cup of sake would be most welcome. It is hot this evening and I would welcome the refreshment."

Hot? I had thought it cool earlier and had hurried to climb into my clothes after the bath. I glanced at Kita's face and was surprised to see he had beads of sweat on his forehead. I leaned forward and fanned him tenderly at the same time as I waved my hand to the maid to bring sake.

"Terue." Auntie's voice was honeyed. "Tamayu will entertain Kita-san. Come over here. I wish to introduce you to our guest of honor."

I bowed politely to Kita-san. He pouted like a child deprived of a promised treat as I rose to my feet and I hid a smile behind my fan. Tamayu would need all her talents to keep him happy.

"Seemon-san." Auntie's hand was resting on my shoulder. I wondered if she could feel the blood pulsing through my veins. I schooled my expression to be no more than politely interested. "This worthless girl is Terue, our youngest geisha. You haven't seen her before as she's been greatly occupied with her *danna*, Lord Dai. I am, of course, delighted that such a great man has seen fit to honor a humble child from my house."

"Indeed, Hana." I was amazed all over again at his command of Japanese. He spoke like a native of Edo. "I had heard the gossip, of course. And now that I've seen Terue-san, I can quite understand how she came to enchant such a great noble."

His voice was warm. I risked a quick look at his face. He was smiling, inclining his head slightly as though the conversation was deeply important to him.

"Don't make her feel important, Seemon." Auntie smirked. "It's bad enough having Lord Dai at her feet without you telling her how lovely she is as well."

"My dear Hana, all your geisha are exceptional. If they were not, they would have no place in your tea house. And anyway, you know perfectly well that none of the geisha are as lovely as their mistress."

Auntie smiled. It was like watching a butterfly hatching from a pupae. She looked years younger suddenly. It crossed my mind that she looked a little flustered, and that she only turned to reach for a flask of sake to hide her face. Seemon glanced at her quickly and then stared straight at me, opening his eyes very wide and parting his lips, almost in a kiss. The expression was gone in a flash, but it was enough.

The rest of the evening was a strange journey. I watched the other geisha cluster around Seemon at every opportunity. He charmed them, just as he had charmed Auntie. At least I had the consolation of seeing that he seemed to favor all of us equally. All, that was, except me. To me, he was simply polite.

Kita-san tired quickly of Tamayu's attentions and claimed me back to his side.

"You find our *gaijin* fascinating, Terue-chan?"

I jumped with surprise. I thought I had treated Seemon like every other patron.

"He is the first *gaijin* I have ever seen properly," I said quickly. "I did not mean to be rude."

"Ah!" He wagged his finger at me roguishly. "I have noticed that all the ladies find him fascinating. Is it his hair? So different from us Japanese men, of course. Or..." He leaned forward and spoke softly. "Or is it the stories that we have all heard about the *gaijin* men? Do you think he really does have a tail?"

"I have no idea, Kita-san." I was deeply grateful for my makeup. I could feel my cheeks glowing. "I suppose he is an attractive man, in a strange sort of way."

"You don't sound too sure about it." He seemed pleased. "Quite right. Stick to what you know, that's what I say."

I watched Seemon covertly as I fawned on my patron, doing my best to make him feel he was the sole object of my attention. He pressed sake on me, and although I rarely drank, I took several cups simply to be polite. After a while, I realized that Kita-san had been right. The room seemed to me to be unbearably hot and I was forced to use my fan in earnest.

"I thank you for your hospitality, Hana." I blinked. Seemon was rising to his feet and bowing deeply to Auntie. "But it's late, and I think it's time we left you."

I glanced at the oil lamps. The wicks needed trimming, and the level of the oil had sunk by half. I was astonished. Where had the evening vanished to? All the patrons were rising at Seemon's words, stretching and yawning and easing the cricks out of their necks. Kita-san was alone in seeming to wish to linger, but Seemon caught his attention and he rose instantly, a dog obedient to his master.

"Perhaps I could arrange a little further entertainment for you all?" Auntie smiled knowingly. I froze. I knew only too well what she meant.

It was perfectly normal, of course. These men had been entertained by us all evening. They had been served sake and tea. They had listened to us sing and dance, raised their heads high as we had flattered them endlessly. Now, it was time for other entertainment entirely. They were no doubt ready to move on to one of the less reputable houses in the flower and willow world, where they would spend the night with high-class courtesans. And if the house in question was recommended by Auntie—as was usually the case—tomorrow, she would instruct one of the boys to go round and collect her flower money for the introduction. Who knew? It might even be that they would simply move across the courtyard to the Hidden House. The very thought filled me with intense jealousy.

Seemon was leaving me to go and enjoy himself with another woman. Perhaps even a woman who was my friend.

"I thank you, Hana." He smiled at Auntie and shrugged his shoulders. "But I, at least, have business early tomorrow and my thoughts are already fully occupied. I doubt I would be able to do justice to any other woman this evening. Of course, my friends may have more stamina than I do."

The other patrons grinned and nodded enthusiastically. Even Kita-san appeared pleased by the idea. I had to keep my fan unfurled in front of my face to hide my delight at Seemon's words.

We bowed the patrons out. Cash chinked in our hands. These were generous men. Kita-san wrapped my fingers around my flower money, leaning toward me confidentially.

"I doubt that Lord Dai could ever tire of you, child. But if that day ever came..." His voice tailed off and he raised his eyebrows suggestively.

I smiled and did my best to look flattered, even as I remembered that he was on his way to pleasure himself with another woman. What high opinions these men had of themselves!

The patrons crowded out together, in high spirits, the geisha following in their shadows. Seemon hung back as Auntie hurried to the hall to bid farewell to her other guests. Suddenly the room was empty of everybody but us two.

He took the few steps to my side quickly and spoke softly and urgently.

"Tomorrow, as early as you can slip away without being seen, come to the garden door of the Hidden House."

We both heard the sound of slipper-clad footsteps in the corridor and suddenly Seemon was speaking in a normal tone, his voice seeming very loud in the empty, echoing room.

"Good night, Terue-san. When I next see Lord Dai, I shall compliment him on his luck in winning you."

Auntie smiled and stood back from the open door to usher him out.

FOURTEEN

Even the echo
Of the moon in a puddle
Is magnificent

*O*nce all the patrons had gone, I waited impatiently. I longed for the geisha to yawn and complain they were tired. That they thought the patrons would never leave. That sitting on their heels for so long had made them stiff and they needed the maids to massage their legs before they could crawl into their futons and sleep.

But the gods turned a deaf ear to my hopes.

"Well, wasn't that the strangest thing!" Saki darted a glance around at each of us, her face alight with interest.

I yawned, feigning boredom. "What was so strange about it?" I asked lazily. "The patrons are always just the same."

"I know one that isn't!" Tamayu said, her tone eager. "Isn't Seemon-san amazing? Do you know, he even made up a haiku to praise the flower in my hair?"

Ren and Saki murmured appreciatively. I managed a

smile. Oh, why couldn't they all go to bed and leave me with my thoughts?

"He's delicious." Saki nodded. "I don't care if he has got a tail, the rest of the men could learn a thing or two from him about what it takes to please a woman. I actually felt as if he was listening to what I was saying!"

"Did you notice, he even had Auntie hanging on his words?" Ren giggled.

"I should think so," I said casually. "He was the guest of honor, after all."

The geisha nodded seriously at my words.

"And don't you find that very strange?" Tamayu's forehead was furrowed, as though she was finding it difficult to put her thoughts into words. "I mean, charming as he is, he's only a *gaijin*. Yet he seems to know everybody. Or at least all the important people."

"That's true," Ren agreed eagerly. "And nobody really knows anything much about him. The only gossip I've heard is the same as Lord Ito's maid told me. He's said to be a very important trader, come to see if he can persuade our merchants to do business with his country. But if he were just a low caste merchant, the nobles would never welcome him into their company, would they?"

We all shook our heads. Not that it mattered greatly to me. If Seemon had been nothing more than a tradesman come to do some work on the tea house, I would still have been attracted to him. Although even as I told myself that, I wondered. He was an attractive man, for sure, but part of that allure was the aura of mystery around him.

"Who were the other patrons tonight?" I asked. "Auntie was very nice to them, but I didn't know any of them. They were neither nobles nor merchants, even I could see that."

Saki and Tamayu exchanged knowing glances.

"Of course," Tamayu said smugly. "You new girls wouldn't have seen them before. Saki and I have, but never together like they were tonight."

"Are they important men?" Ren asked. "They weren't superior caste, were they?"

"Not nobles, no." Tamayu frowned, clearly ordering her thoughts. "But not merchants either. I've heard it said that they are the men who really hold the power in Japan. They're civil servants. Salarymen."

"Oh, is that all?" Ren was clearly unimpressed.

"They might not appear to be rich, but they are. And far more importantly, they hold real power in their hands." Saki nodded seriously. "They don't get paid much, but anybody who wants anything done at the highest level goes to them. And the more important the favor, then the more it costs. These men are very high ranking civil servants. They matter, trust me. I noticed Kita-san was very interested in you, Terue."

"He seemed to be." I nodded.

"Be nice to him," she suggested. "If something should happen to Lord Dai, and at his age, you never know what his health's like, it would be good for you to have somebody else in line to be your patron."

I blinked in surprise. Saki was seriously suggesting that Kita-san could take my *daimyo's* place? I suddenly understood how very important tonight's patrons had been.

"And the *gaijin* is their friend?" Ren, too, had obviously made the connection.

"Exactly," Tamayu said crisply. "It's very strange. All the other *gaijin* in Edo are largely confined to Dejima. With it being an island, the authorities think they're safe there. And anyway, all the *gaijin* I've ever seen have been Dutch, and he isn't."

She spoke the strange word carefully, preening at her skill in a foreign language.

"How do you know Seemon-san isn't Dutch?" I asked innocently.

"Because when we were at Lord Ito's house, I heard one of the patrons ask Seemon-san if he spoke Dutch, and he laughed and said he did, but not as well as he spoke Japanese."

"But if he isn't Dutch, where does he come from? We know he must be important or the great men wouldn't even bother to notice him. So what is he here for?"

Silence met my questions.

"Don't know," Tamayu said finally. "Nobody does. Some say he's taking an interest in the opium trade. He'd better watch out if he is as the yakuza aren't going to be pleased about a *gaijin* interfering in their business. He goes to the kabuki a lot, but I can't believe he wants to buy a share in the theater. The men who own it would never let a *gaijin* buy into the kabuki anyway. And there's already enough Dutch *gaijin* merchants who want to export our silk and porcelain. They've got that market to themselves."

"I think it's something to do with politics," Ren said. "It can't be anything else, can it? I mean, everybody knows that Japan is the most important country in the whole world and that every other country envies our wealth and culture, so perhaps Seemon-san has been sent to take a look at us. So he can go back home eventually and explain to his nobles how great we are and how they should be afraid of us. To warn them not to try and tamper with us."

"Do you know, she might even be right?" Saki said slowly. "It would make sense. At least that would explain why all the nobles and important civil servants are being so courteous to him."

"But where has he come from?" I persisted.

Saki shrugged. "No idea. If he's not Dutch, what other countries are out there?"

That silenced all of us. We knew there was a world outside Japan, but what it was, what the countries called themselves, we had no idea. It didn't matter to us. We had never given it a thought. Why should we? Every Japanese person knew that Japan was the greatest, most superior country that had ever existed. Compared to our own culture, the rest of the world was inhabited by savages who had to be kept at bay lest they contaminate our purity.

The idea that even one *gaijin*—special as he appeared to be—might be able to infiltrate our sealed world was deeply disturbing.

Tamayu yawned suddenly. "It doesn't matter." She shrugged. "I don't expect he'll be here for much longer anyway. I suppose the nobles are treating him like some sort of new toy. When they get bored with the novelty of him, they'll forget all about him and he'll just go back to wherever he came from."

My stomach clenched at the thought. Seemon was going to leave? Soon? Ah, no! I would not let that happen.

Perhaps some of my thoughts showed on my face because Saki smiled at me.

"Oh, I don't know. He seems to be quite well established here. Perhaps he'll stay with us long enough for at least one of us to find out if he really has got a tail!"

We all laughed, but Saki put her hand on my shoulder when we reached her door, holding me back until the others had gone.

"Take care, younger sister," she said softly. "Tamayu's right, for once. He's a *gaijin*, and eventually he'll go back to wherever he came from. Make sure he doesn't take your essential being with him when he goes."

I smiled and shook my head. What nonsense! I barely knew him.

Yet.

FIFTEEN

Catch a tiger by
The tail if you must. But be
Quite sure you are quick!

I was tired, but sleep eluded me, so I got up very early, before even the maids had risen to light the fires and prepare tea. I heard them, after a while. Listened to them laugh and chat amongst themselves. Sometime later, I heard voices in the hall and understood that Auntie and the boys were leaving the tea house.

Last night, it had seemed the simplest thing in the world. All I had to do was slip into the garden, stroll across the short space that separated the Green Tea House from the Hidden House, tap on the door, and step into Seemon's arms. But as night fell into my room, my doubts and fears had grown along with the shadows.

What if one of the other geisha decided to come into the garden with me, to sit in the sun? What if Big—or the gods save me, Bigger—noticed me going into the Hidden House? What if Auntie saw me and wanted to know what I was doing, where I was going? Oh, it was all impossible. I couldn't do it. I didn't dare. My hopes curled and died before they could even see the light of day.

The knowledge that Auntie and the boys had gone out made me feel a little better. I got up and dressed, wandering around the tea house in bare feet like a silent ghost.

All the other geisha were still deeply asleep. Tamayu was snoring; she always denied that she snored, but she did. Ren was silent. I dared to slide her door open a fraction and sighed with relief as I saw she was curled up in her futon, deep in her dreams. I hovered outside Saki's door for a long time, listening carefully. Eventually, I heard the whisper of her breath and relaxed.

"Do not wake the other geisha." I caught one of the maids hovering in the corridor, obviously wondering if she should take tea in or wait awhile. "We were very late to bed last night. Let them sleep."

And that was it. I had nothing left to fear.

Still, I hesitated.

I opened the door into the garden and stared across at the Hidden House door. Just like the tea house, the other place presented a closed face to the early sun. The shadows told me that the morning was barely awake. Was Seemon waiting for me behind that closed door? Waiting and wondering why I didn't go to him?

A bird—a dowdy little thing with nothing to recommend it—landed at my feet. I glanced at it and then caught my breath as it began to sing. The liquid notes flowed out effortlessly, soaring in their beauty. I glanced around, expecting to find that it was singing to attract a mate, but there was nothing. The bird finished its song abruptly, ruffled its feathers, and then flew off, only to land on a shrub halfway across the garden. I was sure it was glancing back at me.

Whether it was or not, I made my mind up.

I stepped cautiously into the garden, not daring to look behind me. Another step, and then another, and I was next to the bird. I raised my eyebrows at him. In response, he took flight and soared over the garden wall. Very well. If he could fly, then so could I! I covered the rest of the garden at a swift trot. I tapped on the Hidden House door before I could think about hesitating.

The door opened at once. Seemon stepped aside, inviting me in silently. I moved so quickly I knocked into him in my hurry.

"You came. I was beginning to worry."

"Close the door, please!" I was hopping from foot to foot. "Are any of the geisha up yet? Did anybody see you come in here? Where are we going?"

Seemon smiled and laid his fingers on my lips. "Shush, little one. Nobody will see us. Come."

He turned and walked down the corridor, away from the room I had already seen. The layout was similar to the tea house, so I guessed we were going toward the kitchen. Were we going to slide out through a back door? I was very pleased and urged him silently to hurry.

But I was wrong.

Instead of going into the kitchen, he pulled a screen aside and led me into a large, very richly furnished room. A futon was laid on the floor but had clearly not been slept on. I was appalled. We were going to stay here, in what was obviously somebody's room?

"Here?"

He shook his head and tugged me across the room. He halted at the wall and pushed a strut in the screen. A section of the wall slid aside and he pulled me through, immediately closing the door behind him.

"We're safe here, I promise," Seemon reassured me.

But fear had me in its grip and I shook my head fiercely. "Anybody could come in and find us! We can't stay here."

He put his arms around me and held me tightly against him. I could feel his chest moving with each breath and it calmed me.

"No. Nobody will find us here. Nobody else in the Hidden House knows about this room, not even the geisha here."

"Nobody?" I wanted to be reassured. Feeling his arms wrapped around me was enough to quell my concerns.

"Nobody except me and Hana."

I almost shrieked aloud. Of course Auntie would know about it. And if she came back and found us in her secret place? I fought in his arms, terror making me strong. But Seemon was far stronger still.

"No," he said firmly. "Terue, do you really think I would expose you to danger? I will not. Hana has gone out of Edo. She's had word about a girl that might be promising for the Hidden House and she's gone to look her over. She took the boys with her as the area she's headed for is not safe. It will be late tonight before she gets back."

"How do you know?" I demanded.

"Because Hana mentioned it last night," he said simply. "Trust me. The Hidden House has many secrets. This room is one of them. Now and then, a very important man might have need to disappear for a while. When that happens, Hana is pleased to let him stay here for a day or two until it is safe to slip away. That door—" He nodded toward what looked like another wall— "leads straight into the garden, and from there into the street."

"How do you know?" I asked suspiciously.

"It was whispered to me by one of the greatest yakuza in Edo. He had taken a great deal of opium at the time, and I think his desire to impress me took over his discretion. He himself had used the room a couple of times, when rival yakuza were after his blood and he needed a safe place for a while. He assured me if things ever became difficult for me in Edo, then Hana would be able to get me out safely."

I stared at him in bewilderment. Who was this man who could call both nobles and yakuza his friends? And why might he need to get out of Edo secretly?

"Don't worry," he said soothingly. "None of it matters, Terue-chan. Not to us. Do you trust me?"

"Yes," I said simply.

He nodded, clearly pleased. "Then truly nothing else matters."

He kissed me gently on my forehead. I trembled at his touch, just as I had trembled when Lord Dai had touched me. But what a world of difference lay between the two experiences!

Seemon stepped back and looked at me, his gaze taking me in from head to *geta*. I waited, taking pleasure in his obvious delight in my presence.

"Seemon." I whispered his name and understood that it was already precious to me.

"Terue. Shining blessing. Dear one."

He held his arms out wide, and I simply folded into him, content for the moment to feel him against me. He kissed my ear and I giggled as it tickled. His breath huffed in amusement and his mouth moved across my face, finally finding my lips. I froze. What was I supposed to do?

He moved his face away slightly.

"Have you never been kissed, Terue?"

I almost laughed aloud. "Japanese men do not kiss. Or at least, they do not kiss on the lips."

"Then I shall teach you something new today."

His lips moved back to my mouth. His tongue flicked my lips and I shivered with pleasure, even more so when his tongue parted my lips and forced itself lightly into my mouth. I had no idea how to respond, so I stayed with my mouth ajar as his tongue ran over my teeth, finally flirting with the tip of my own tongue. The sensation was so pleasurable that I gasped and unintentionally bit his lips.

"Ah, but that is delicious."

Seemon's voice was throaty with pleasure and I closed my eyes in relief. Lord Dai seemed happy for me to bestow small hurts on him. Perhaps all men were the same? He slid to the futon, taking me willingly with him. I felt his hands running down my robe, his fingers tugging at the knot of my obi. I was about to reach down and help with the intricate tie when I realized there was no need—he had already loosened it. The thought skipped through my mind that he must have had practice undoing a Japanese woman's intricate clothing. I pushed it aside deliberately. I would let nothing disturb this moment.

He slid my kimono and undergarments aside. I felt his gaze on my body. I longed to open my eyes, to see if he liked what he saw, but I dared not. What if I saw an expression of disappointment on his face?

"The joints of thy thighs are like jewels, the work of the hands of a cunning workman. Thy navel is like a round goblet, which wanteth not liquor. Thy belly is like a heap of wheat, set about with lilies. Thy neck is as a tower of ivory. How fair and pleasant art thou, oh love, for delights!"

He crooned the words softly. It barely meant anything to me at all, but the words themselves were lovely, and I understood with infinite delight that he was complimenting me. He leaned forward and flicked his tongue into my belly button. His voice buzzed against my empty stomach.

"Those words were written many hundreds of years ago, by the wisest king the world has ever known. They are from my people's holy book." I approved of that. I had no idea what the *gaijin* religion was, but surely it couldn't be so very wrong if it contained such beautiful words. "They are the words of a king, when his queen from a foreign land came to him for the first time. Do they please you?"

I nodded. I had no words. Certainly none that could hope to match the poetry of those Seemon had just spoken to me. He smiled at me and then dipped his head again so that his tongue trailed down the slight bowl of my belly and dipped into my black moss. I hissed with pleasure.

His tongue lingered for a moment and then he sat back, watching me. I realized he was expecting a response, but I had no idea at all what he wanted, what I should do. Oh, I had seen the *shunga* in the pillow books. And I had pleased Lord Dai, somehow. I wanted nothing more than to pleasure Seemon, but I had no idea what I was supposed to do. I felt gauche and very, very young.

To my profound relief, he solved the problem for me.

He pried the knot of his sash undone and then shrugged off his robe entirely. Another unknown to add to the strange wonders of this strangest day! Japanese men did not appear naked in front of women, not even their wives and concubines. I had noticed it in the *shunga* and had asked the other geisha how it came about that the women were nearly always naked and the men fully clothed, with their robes flung open at the most? They had stared at me as if I were asking a stupid question and I had felt very silly. Tamayu answered grudgingly.

"That's just the way it is. When you finally acquire a lover, you'll find it doesn't matter at all."

I had thought at the time it seemed unfair, that the men should be able to see the whole of their woman's body whilst their partner had a peek and nothing more. But it seemed Tamayu did not, after all, know everything! I stared at Seemon's nakedness hungrily.

His chest was deeply muscled and had a light down of hair on it, slightly darker than the hair on his head. The contrast to his white skin was exciting and I shuddered with pleasure. The line of hair continued down in an arrow to his navel, and my eyes followed it down quite naturally. Down, and further down, to his black moss. To my amazement, his black moss was almost black. I thought that the further away from the sun his body was hidden, the darker his hair became. The idea pleased me greatly and I smiled widely.

"Ah, Terue. My poor body amuses you. I am deeply sad."

"Oh no! Not at all!"

I was horrified until I realized he was teasing me. I placed my hand flat on his chest and gave him a little shove. Immediately, he caught hold of my hand and raised it to his mouth, taking each finger in turn and sucking the tip very gently.

"Ah."

I closed my eyes with pleasure and his tongue trailed into my palm, licking and nibbling. The pleasure was so great I felt goosebumps erupt all over my skin.

Finished with my fingers, he released my hand and leaned forward to lick each nipple in turn. When he removed his head, the early morning cool made them stand erect. Suddenly, I understood the very fine line between pain and pleasure.

I could take no more. Forgetting everything that Auntie and Saki had instilled into me, I lurched forward with no grace at all and leaned into him, rubbing my head on his chest and wrapping my arms around him. I didn't care. I knew nothing except the need to have him as close to as much of me as possible.

He patted kisses on the top of my head. Took my ear in his mouth and bit it gently. Trailed his tongue down my neck to suckle at my breasts. By the time his mouth had reached my navel, I was on fire for him. I felt that if he took a moment more to enter me, then I would explode.

"What do you like?" I heard him whisper, his voice hoarse. "What can I do for you that will give you great pleasure?"

"Touch me. Please." I was trembling. I wanted to tell him that I needed him to slide his fingers in my black moss. To rub them up and down until I was ready for his tree. But the words stuck in my throat, and all I could do was to whisper "please" again.

He understood what I wanted better than I knew myself. His head slid down my stomach and his teeth plucked at my black moss. I reared against him, moaning deep in my throat. He waited for a heartbeat and then his nose and lips were sliding into my sex, rubbing up and down. His face seemed cold to me, until I understood that it was my internal heat that was the greater. I arched my back to find more of him and wailed out loud when he moved away from me.

"There are many games we can play, Terue," he whispered. I wriggled impatiently. I had no time for words. I threw myself back on the futon, my arms flung out and my legs as wide apart as I could force them. My muscles complained at the violent movement, but I didn't care. I watched Seemon's face and saw the fire in his eyes and knew that my moment had come.

"Wait," he said again, but I could not. Instead of speaking, I launched myself off the futon, wrapping my arms and legs around him, dragging him back down with me.

"Lie still," he commanded. I could feel his tree sliding down my belly, and in spite of his instruction, I reared up to him. I couldn't help it. I was on fire for him. For a single second, I thought of how it had been with Lord Dai. His old man's body and withered tree.

Seemon was watching my face intently. He spoke very softly. "Dear Terue. I will never hurt you. I will never do anything you do not want me to do. Does that please you?"

"Yes. Oh yes." And truly, I was delighted by his words. Not just what he said, but with the promise that he would be there for me again and again and again.

And then he was sliding his erect tree into my moss. Probing for my hidden place. I held my breath, tense with fear and excitement. There was a flash of pain, so intense it made me squeal out loud, and then Seemon filled me and I gave way to a pleasure so great I would not have believed it could exist a moment before. I felt him hesitate.

"Seemon. Do not stop. No." Even as I spoke, I thrust myself against him and wrapped my legs around his waist, imprisoning him in me. I felt a moment of curious resistance, and then it was too late for both of us.

He thrust at me, his rhythm quickly becoming more urgent. I understood instinctively that he was close to bursting the fruit. I wanted to scream out loud, to tell him it was too early for me, but I doubted he would hear me in the midst of his passion. Instead, instinct came to my aid.

I loosened my grip on him and wriggled away, until only the very tip of his tree remained in my secret place. My flesh felt very cold without him, but I was determined. I saw the confusion in his expression and almost laughed at the thought that I could control his passion so easily. Very, very slowly I allowed us to come together again. I knew instantly that I was right. I had broken his rhythm and slowed him down.

Taking advantage of my moment, I rolled over so that Seemon was lying beneath me. I understood at once that I was in charge. Slow, fast. Gentle, hard. It was all up to me to dictate how I wanted him to make love to me.

The knowledge was hugely exciting.

His eyes were closed, his lips parted. I watched his face as I rode him, saw the pleasure my every movement was giving to him. Felt my own heat rise and rise until the fire in my belly consumed me entirely and I understood why the word for orgasm—*yonaki*—meant cries in the night. I was moaning out loud, unable to stop the feeling taking over everything.

And to my joy, Seemon burst the fruit with me. He did not cry out loud as I did, but his lips peeled back in a rictus that mimicked pain. His hips ground against me and I laughed out loud as I felt his hot seed gush into my body.

We slowed together. Finally satiated, I slid off him and lay on the futon at his side. Seemon propped himself on his elbow and pulled the bedclothes over my body tenderly. I snuggled into his shoulder.

"Terue."

I waited for him to say more, and when he did not, I raised my head to look at him. I put my head on one side, smiling encouragement.

"I was the first." It was a statement, not a question.

I nodded. "Yes. Lord Dai is unable," I said simply.

His face crumpled, and for a terrible second, I thought

he was going to cry. I was horribly hurt and confused. I had expected him to be pleased that he had taken the gift of my maidenhood. What was wrong? Suddenly, I felt like crying myself.

"You didn't like me? I did something wrong?" I pleaded with him to answer me.

Seemon raised his fingers to my face and traced the line of my cheekbone. "I like you too much, Terue." His voice shook. "Oh my God. What have I done?"

SIXTEEN

It is said that one
Should always look forward with
Anticipation

*M*y pleasure crumbled to hurt.

I had expected Seemon would be delighted to find he had been the first man who had ever entered me, and I was bewildered and terribly hurt that he seemed to be—not angry exactly—but deeply worried. Nor would he explain to me. Far too soon, he insisted that we had to go. I stiffened, keeping my face calm. I would not let him see my pain.

"This way leads into the garden, in the far corner. Wait a moment, until you're sure nobody is watching, and then slip across to the tea house."

As I put my hand out to slide the screen aside, he put his own hand on my shoulder, stopping me.

"Terue-chan. Forgive me. I had no idea that you were still untouched. I'm deeply honored that you gave yourself to me." I took a deep breath. That was better, but not what I wanted to hear. "Now is not the time for us to talk. Not the place either. Will you come to my home? Give me the chance to explain?"

Would I? For a moment, I was unsure. Then he leaned against me and said "Please" so intently that my doubts fled and I was suddenly aflame with excitement.

"I've rented a house on the Street of the Goldsmiths, just outside the walls of the Floating World. The fourth house along on your right. You can't mistake it—it's the only house in the whole street that isn't a merchants' shop. Do you know how to get there?"

"I've been there," I said cautiously. Lord Dai had taken me to buy trinkets. I wished I hadn't thought of my *danna* at that precise moment.

"Will you come and see me tomorrow? Please?"

I wanted to say yes. But how could I? Auntie would be back tomorrow. So would the boys. Of course, now that I was a geisha, I was at liberty to go out at any time I was free, but whenever I ventured outside the tea house, I was expected to take a maid with me, and I was never certain that one of the boys wasn't my shadow.

"I can't," I said reluctantly. "I couldn't go out without a maid. And one of the boys could follow me."

He nodded. "The maid we can deal with. Choose the oldest girl—I think she's called Aimi."

I was amazed that he had bothered to learn the maids' names. Half the time, I was sure the patrons had difficulty in telling us geisha apart, especially after a few flasks of Auntie's superb sake.

"Why her?"

"Because she's old and plain. She gets fewer presents from the patrons than the other maids, and she's bitter because of it. I feel sorry for her, and I've always made a point of thanking her for her services and made sure she gets a decent amount of flower money." He smiled wryly. "Because of that, Aimi will do anything to please me, poor woman. Get her on her own and explain to her frankly that you're going to visit your lover, but that you don't want anybody to know, especially the boys. Tell her I will reward her very well for her discretion."

I barely heard his last words. He had said I was his lover! My emotions had been at the bottom of the well a moment ago. Now, they soared with the birds.

"But what about the boys?" I murmured.

"Don't worry about them. The kabuki has a new production tomorrow. Bigger loves the theater. I'll send a message to the tea house tonight to tell him that he's been invited to be the honored guest of Ichikawa Danjuro, the lead actor. And of course, should he wish to take a friend with him, the kabuki would be delighted to welcome them both. Bigger would never miss a chance like that, and, naturally, he'll want Big to share the honor of going with him. The play starts around mid-morning and will go on until the light fades. They'll be out of the way all day. Hana will either be delighted with the success of her expedition, in which case she'll be too busy making plans for the new girl to notice that you're missing for a few hours, or if it was a failure, she'll be angry and not stir from her room all day."

I stared at him, wonderingly. It seemed my *gaijin* was well enough acquainted with the lead actor in the kabuki to ask him a favor and get it. And how well he knew the workings of the tea house and all of us who lived in it! What other mysteries did he hide? I shivered with pleasure at the knowledge that I would find out. Soon.

"Tomorrow," he said. His hand was gentle on my shoulder, urging me forward. "Wait until you're sure that the boys have gone. And until then, take very great care."

I could feel the warmth of his hand lingering as I slipped across the garden. I couldn't resist taking a single look back. The door was closed, but I thought I saw movement behind one of the screens. For a moment, I was worried I had been seen. I shrugged the thought aside. This was the Hidden House, and my friends there would be discreet, I knew.

*In spite of Seemon's confidence, I was nervous as I passed through the gate of the Floating World. He had been right about Aimi. I explained to her frankly where I was going, and it was clear that she was delighted for me. For the first time, I wondered what it must be like being a lowly maid somewhere like the Green Tea House, working all hours, constantly at everybody's beck and call. But better, surely, than herding ducks and slaving for my large family! At least the maids were well fed and had somewhere warm and comfortable to live. But then I looked at Aimi's beaming face and realized that even living in poverty in my village I had something that she had lost long ago.

Hope.

The tea house would be her life until she was so old she could no longer perform her work. And what then?

I hoped that Seemon's present would be very generous indeed.

Aimi and I slipped down the goldsmiths' street with many a cautious backward glance in my case. If Big or Bigger really had been following me, they would have known at once that I was up to something. Aimi's sturdy common sense comforted me.

"Don't worry, mistress. I saw them both go off to the kabuki earlier. They were in fine spirits. I doubt they'll be back before evening. And don't forget, we're outside the Floating World now, and the kabuki is well inside it."

I stopped as we came to Seemon's house, suddenly awkward as I wondered how I should ask Aimi to leave me without sounding rude. Aimi solved the dilemma for me.

"There is a tea house just in the next street. I have a cousin who works there. If you would permit it, mistress, I would like to go to see her and drink tea with her."

I slipped a coin into her hand and she was gone in a second.

Seemon was waiting for me. His door slid back at my timid knock.

I stepped inside and he embraced me. I slid my *geta* off in the hall and moved into a large room. My eyes opened wide as I stared around.

Was I still in Edo? Still in Japan for that matter? Or had some stray spirit delighted in taking over my senses as I stood wrapped in his arms and transported me to somewhere very strange? Seemon smiled at my confusion.

"Does it seem odd to you?" I nodded. "I imagine if a Japanese person went to my country, then they would try and recreate Japan in their house. I suppose that's what I've done here. Would you like to sit on a chair, or would you prefer the floor?"

I had no idea. Neither option seemed at all right. The floor was not covered in *tatami*, but instead had a large, thick covering thrown on top of wood blocks. It looked so precious that I hesitated to even stand on it, let alone sit! Seemon was indicating a piece of furniture with four legs, like a small table, but this was a table with a high, straight back to it. It looked horribly uncomfortable to me. Bewildered, I simply stood, staring around this strangest of rooms.

Every spare inch of space was crowded. There were more of the strange table-like things. Several real tables, but even they were covered in thick cloths that hung almost to the floor. There was a chest of sorts against one of the walls, a large, rectangular wooden construction with two doors. And—strangest of all!—something that looked to my bewildered eyes like an impossibly thick futon, raised up off the floor and bounded at the head and foot by metal struts. An open chest in the corner, crammed with books. And every surface was covered in things. Open books, unrolled scrolls, and other things I couldn't even name.

But there was no shrine. No scrolls on the walls, anywhere. Not even so much as a vase with a carefully arranged *ikebana* flower display, the simplicity of the end result giving no indication of the time it had taken an attentive geisha to get it just so.

Perhaps it was the strangeness of the place that Seemon called home, but suddenly I was shy and awkward in his presence.

"I would prefer the floor. If it's all right to sit on the tapestry?"

"Of course. It's called a carpet, and it's made to sit and walk on."

I folded to my knees carefully, taking care not to ruffle the surface.

Seemon sank down beside me and we both sat in strained silence for a moment.

"Terue-chan." He paused and I stared at the carpet shyly, tracing the outline of a rose so carefully done that I could hardly believe it wasn't real. "I'm sorry. About yesterday."

I raised my head and stared at him in disbelief. He was apologizing for taking me? But why? Hadn't we both given and taken great pleasure in each other? If he had regretted it, why had he asked me back here today? My dismay must have shown on my face.

"I'm not sorry about making love to you. Never that. But I had no idea that you were still whole. I thought that Lord Dai was your *danna*. I had no right to be the first, none at all."

I spoke urgently. "You don't understand. His tree can't rise. He told me he's been like that for years. He went to a witch to seek advice, and she told him there was only one woman who could make his tree live again. He thinks I'm the one, even though it's obvious I'm not." A vision of my *danna*'s wrinkled face and dry, bony hands rose in front of me and I blurted. "I hate him. Every second he's with me, I feel sick."

Seemon was quiet for so long, I began to feel deeply uncomfortable.

"I'm truly honored that you chose me as your lover, Terue-chan," he said finally. "And I will never regret that. But Lord Dai is a very powerful man. He has friends who are more powerful still. I may have put us both in very great danger by being unable to resist you. For that, I am sorry, and for that alone."

"What danger? What are you talking about? Are you frightened of Lord Dai? He could never tell anybody he failed me, you know. He would be too ashamed."

"I can't begin to explain things to you. You wouldn't understand."

I shrugged and stared around the room, looking

anywhere but at his face. A Japanese man would have understood instantly that I was insulted by his words and was punishing him by my inattention. But Seemon, of course, was a *gaijin*. And in spite of his grasp of our language and much of our culture, this passed him by. I understood when he spoke that he was obviously pleased to change the subject.

"I suppose everything here is strange to you. Are you uncomfortable in my home?"

"It's so very different from a Japanese house," I admitted. "There's so much furniture. So many *things*. And what is that ugly decoration?" I rose to my feet and edged my way to the wall. I fingered a strange sculpture hanging there that seemed to represent a tortured man. "It's horrible. Why would you want such a nasty thing in your home? Is it somebody you know? Are you honoring their spirit by having it on view?"

I traced the outline of the body hanging from a wooden crosspiece with my fingertip and shuddered. The sculpture was very skilled, every detail of the agony the man was suffering had been carved in meticulous detail. I glanced at his face and closed my eyes in sympathy at his pain.

"I suppose I'm honoring His spirit." Seemon was close behind me. "That is a representation of the son of my God. His own people turned on him and nailed him to a cross to die. But my religion says that he came back from the dead and now lives on in spirit to save all our souls."

This seemed to me to be the greatest nonsense, and I said so.

"How can a god have a son of flesh? And if he was put to death, how could he come back to life? And everything that lives has a soul. Does he also want to save the souls of dogs and cats and rats? And why? What's he going to do with them?"

I paused, suddenly realizing that I had just insulted his religion beyond any redemption. I was relieved when I saw he was smiling.

"Everybody thinks the other person's religion is nonsense," he said cheerfully. "When I was younger, I took my own religion so very seriously that I considered becoming a priest."

I giggled. Seemon? A priest?

"Truly. My mother is a very religious woman. Our priest came to the house often, and she was always honored by his presence."

"And your father? Did he love the priest as well?"

"What a clever girl you are, Terue-chan. No, my father was not in the least interested in religion. But it kept my mother happy, so he didn't complain. Or at least, not until it seemed that the priests were going to claim me for their own."

"Why did you want to be a priest? I understand that it would have pleased your mother, but if your father was unhappy about it, surely you must have respected his wishes?"

Seemon smiled. He took my hand and led me back to the strange floor covering. I was very pleased to be out of sight of the tortured man—the tortured god. The ornament made me deeply uncomfortable and I wondered again how Seemon could ever have thought of entering the service of such a strange religion.

"I think it was the theatricality of it all, more than anything. The cross you were looking at is just a symbol," he explained. "Something to remind us of how He gave his life for us poor mortals. My mother's religion is called Catholicism."

I mouthed the difficult syllables silently, and Seemon smiled at me.

"The priests in her religion wear gorgeous robes. They sing during ceremonies. Prepare speeches and deliver them to temples that are full of people. They are honored whenever they go amongst those who believe in their God."

Ah, now all that I could follow perfectly. It sounded very much like a kabuki play to me.

"You wanted to be an actor!" I said, delighted that I understood at last.

Seemon laughed until he had to wipe the tears away from his face. "Oh, dear child. I'm not in the least surprised that Lord Dai risked everything for you. You are truly wonderful."

"He paid a large amount for the pleasure of taking me. But the gods—*my* gods—didn't favor him. He paid for almost nothing. But the money doesn't matter greatly to him. He's a very rich man."

"It's not just the money he risked." Seemon's laughter died. "You must understand why I was so worried when I found out about Lord Dai. I assumed that he was your lover. That your *mizuage* had been a great success. Now that you were no longer a maiko, I thought you were free to take a lover. I was overjoyed that it should be me that you chose. You filled my every waking thought from the moment I first saw you. I was obsessed with you."

Ah, now that was what I had wanted to hear!

"Then nothing else matters," I said happily. But Seemon shook his head.

"Terue, Lord Dai is a very important man. He moves in

circles where he has friends who are even more important and powerful than he is."

"What of it? The fault lies with him. And he can hardly tell his important friends about his failure, can he?"

"No, of course he can't." Seemon let go of my hand and cupped my face in his fingers, forcing me to look straight at him. "But there's something you don't know about. I tell you, Lord Dai will never let you go. There's too much at stake for him. It's not just his pride. It's far more even than just the witch's prophecy."

"No. You're wrong. He can't force me to like him. Eventually, he'll realize how much he disgusts me and that I'm never going to change my mind. He's not a fool. He'll come to understand that I can't be the one he's looking for."

Seemon hesitated and then spoke slowly and carefully. As if he was talking to a child. "Terue, listen to me. Please. You know Lord Dai and four other nobles drew lots to see who would win you for your *mizuage*?"

"Yes. Auntie told me that. But what difference does that make?"

"Lord Dai cheated. He paid Hana a huge amount of money to make sure he got the slip of parchment with your name on it. If anybody ever found out he had done that, he would be disgraced. He would have to leave Edo. Nobody in society would so much as speak to him again. His life would be over. So he is bound to you not just by his belief in the witch's prophesy, but also as a matter of his own honor. He risked everything for you. And now that he has you, he isn't going to let you go."

Tears blurred my vision. I had no idea I was crying until the salt stung my eyes. I wiped them away angrily. He was right, of course. For such a great noble to have cheated in a matter of honor—and cheated his closest friends, at that—

was unthinkable. But he had done it. And now it was I who had to live with the consequences of his actions.

"You can't save me from him?" I pleaded. "You know many important people. They respect you. If you told them the truth, perhaps he would be so ashamed he would walk away from me."

"I can't," he said simply. "I'm sorry, but I can't do that. Not even for you. Not even for us."

I spoke softly, determined to hide my hurt. "Then I'm sorry, Seemon-san, to have caused you distress. I will leave now. I did not understand that you were so much in fear of Lord Dai and his friends."

I began to stand, but Seemon was quicker than I was. His hands were on my shoulders and he pushed me down gently but very firmly.

"Terue, please." I looked up at him and saw pain in his eyes. "I was wrong to say I couldn't explain to you. You deserve that much at least. Please, stay. Give me a chance to tell you as much as I can."

He crossed the room and returned quickly with a large, brightly colored sphere in his hands. I looked at it stonily.

"Do you know what this is?"

I shook my head stubbornly. A pretty thing, to be sure, but what did it have to do with us?

"It's a globe of the world. The patterns represent each country and show where they are relative to each other."

I shrugged, wondering why he was showing it to me. I touched the sphere and it spun beneath my finger. Reluctantly, I found myself becoming intrigued. Everybody knew that there were countries outside Japan, of course. I knew that China was close to us, and that our huge neighbor was both feared and hated. The kingdom of Chosun was somewhere nearby. One occasionally saw Chosun people in Edo, but they were very much disliked. The Dutch came from far away, but I had no idea where. But there were so many colors on Seemon's globe, so many shapes. Could it possibly be true that there was so much outside Japan?

"Where is your home?" I asked curiously.

"Here." He moved the sphere and then stopped it with a touch, placing his finger on a large shape. "That's where I come from. It's called America."

I repeated the word silently to myself. America. I had never heard of it.

"And Dutch?" I asked. "Where's that?"

Seemon smiled. "That's the name of the people. The country is called Holland." He traced an area within a much larger pattern. It seemed to me to be very far away from America.

"Where's Japan?"

"Where do you think it is?"

I stared at the globe, fascinated in spite of my deep hurt. Japan was the center of the world, of course. Nowhere else was as splendid. Nowhere else had our wealth or culture. So Japan must surely be in the very middle of the world. I poked my finger at a huge outline that dominated the center of the globe.

"There."

"No. That's Africa. Japan is half a world away from there." He took my finger away and spun the globe again. When it stopped, he pointed at a long sliver of islands. "There. That's Japan. Next to China."

I shook my head. This could not be! We were tiny. Compared to the bulk of China, we were nothing at all. Even Seemon's homeland was far, far bigger than we were, and I had never even heard of it. Was he mocking me?

"I promise you, that is Japan."

"If we're that tiny and that unimportant, why have you bothered to come here?" I said angrily. And then, as the thought struck me, "And what's all this got to do with Lord Dai?"

"Listen." I was about to speak again, but Seemon put his finger on my lips, silencing me. "It will be difficult for you to understand, but I'll do my best. Will you give me a few moments? If you're still angry with me at the end of it, then I'll take you back to the tea house and I promise I'll never trouble you again."

He looked so serious, I decided I would listen. I nodded.

"I told you I was considering becoming a priest."

"What's that got to do with it?" I was impatient. This was nothing new.

"It matters, I promise. You need to know everything to understand why I'm here and why Lord Dai is so dangerous. If my father hadn't been so horrified at the thought of losing his only son to the church, then I would probably have spent the rest of my life in America, following in his footsteps. We have a large plantation—that's a sort of farm—in southern America. It has made us very wealthy for generations. My father wanted me to get married and have a family. Settle down and take over the land when he died."

I nodded. Of course he did, as was only natural.

"But he realized that I wanted more than that. Oh, my thoughts of being a priest would probably have died anyway when I realized what was truly involved. But my father was so worried he arranged to get me well away from the plantation. To see life, as he put it. My uncle is an important man in my country's government. My father arranged for me to go stay with him. I loved Washington— that's the town in America that's the same as Edo is here— but I loved it even more when my uncle was asked by the government to move to England. I insisted I should go with him. Nothing on earth would have stopped me."

"Where's England?" I interrupted. Seemon pointed to it on the globe and I laughed. It was even smaller than Japan!

"It may be small, but it's a very important country in the world. And it has a new queen. A woman who is greatly respected everywhere."

"Is she young? Pretty? Did you see her?"

"Yes, she's very young and very beautiful. And extremely intelligent. I was fortunate to meet with her a number of times."

Instantly, I was jealous. Was she prettier than me? Did he like her better than me? Seemon appeared not to notice and continued to speak.

"I was deeply flattered that Queen Victoria seemed to take an interest in me. At first, I couldn't understand it, but I soon realized that something was going on behind my back. I was introduced to some of her important men who questioned me closely. Did I speak any foreign languages, they asked. French, I said. I had learned that from my grandmother who came from Louisiana where French was spoken as much as English. Apart from that, just Latin, but I had found that very easy to learn. That seemed to surprise them.

"'Latin is a difficult language.' The man who was talking to me suddenly ceased speaking in English and switched to Latin. I did likewise out of politeness. Before we could talk for much longer, my uncle interrupted.

"'My nephew is not doing himself justice,' he said. 'When he was in Washington, he was very friendly with a number of Italian and German diplomats. He taught himself to speak both languages.'

"'But I don't speak them very well,' I pointed out. It did no good. The queen's man was obviously pleased.

"'Do you think you could learn to speak Japanese?' he asked me. 'And not just well, but as though you were born there.'

"I was beginning to be extremely interested. I had heard of Japan, of course. It was a mystery to all of us in the Western world, and intriguing as a result. But why would I ever need to speak the language?"

Seemon paused and smiled at me, his eyebrows raised as if he was asking me if I had followed everything he had told me so far. I was so excited, I could barely keep still. I wriggled my toes on the carpet and sneezed as the fibers it was made from went up my nose.

"Is that why you're here? Because the young queen sent you to us?" I frowned, understanding even as I spoke that it was a stupid question. For sure, if this important queen had sent him to us, then Seemon would have been seated at the side of the shogun and never allowed to mingle freely with us common people. But he surprised me yet again.

"Sort of. Of course, I asked the politician why he wanted me to learn Japanese. He glanced at my uncle, who nodded, and then he explained.

"'Both England and America are very interested in Japan. It's essential to us that we find new places we can trade with. We are both growing nations. We must find somewhere to sell the goods we produce or we will no longer flourish. Besides, it's generally considered that the Dutch have had Japan to themselves for far too long. They tantalize us with stories of the immense wealth of the country, but they refuse to let anybody else anywhere near. We've both had enough of that. We want to open Japan to the world. But in particular to our two countries.'

"I understood him at once," Seemon went on. "While I had been in Washington, I had heard rumors about the political situation. But what was I supposed to do? What could one man possibly be expected to do on his own? I pointed this out, although by then I was on fire to try whatever was asked of me. Japan! The politician might well have been talking about sending me to the moon, the idea was so exotic. Yet the ideas he was raising were tantalizing.

"'What do you want me to do?' I asked bluntly.

"'We want you to learn to read and write Japanese so that it becomes as familiar to you as your own language. We want you to immerse yourself in Japanese culture. If you agree, we will ship you to Japan. There are a couple of Dutch merchants who have been in Japan for many years. They want to go home, but don't have enough money. In return for that money, they will let you live with them on the island of Dijima, which is just outside Edo. They will find somebody to teach you to read and write Japanese. They will immerse you in the culture of the country. When you are ready, they will introduce you safely into Edo itself. You will have letters of introduction to what they have assured us are amongst the most important men in Edo. You will have unlimited money. We want you to make yourself known to the men whose names we give you. Apart from them, you will mingle with Japanese society at all levels. Learn how to understand the people's lives, what makes them work. You will find out how strong their army is, whether they have any sort of navy. What weapons they use, how they fight. You will learn their strengths and weaknesses. When you are sure there is nothing important to us that you have missed, the Dutch will get a message out to us and we will bring you back here. I don't have to tell you that there are huge risks involved. If you are discovered by the Japanese, you may well be executed.'

"'I understand that,' I said with a nod. Already my thoughts were far away, here in a country I had never yet seen. I was deeply excited, but still had a flicker of caution. 'But I think you're forgetting one thing. The mission is doomed to failure from the start.'

"Even my uncle looked startled. I shrugged and pointed at my hair.

"'I could never pass as Japanese. There may be red-haired Dutch, but surely I'll be strange to Japanese eyes, looking like this?'

"'Nobody is asking you to pass as Japanese. That would be foolish in the extreme.' He wagged his finger at me, and I was reminded of a school teacher reproving an inattentive scholar. 'You will be what you seem to be. A cultured young man who is used to moving in the correct society. A man who is so interested in Japan and all things Japanese that he has taken the time and trouble to learn the language. And above all, you will have letters of introduction from Queen Victoria herself. They will say that she has heard much of the great and glorious land of Japan. That she is deeply interested in your wonderful country and would take it as a personal favor if the Japanese nobles would show you the kindness of allowing you to live amongst them. We know from our Dutch friends that the Japanese government is aware that Victoria is on the throne, just as they are aware of the progress that is being made so very quickly in America. We hope that they will accept you as a gift from the gods, that they will think we are very naïve in sending you, and that you can be used to give them information about the world outside Japan. Information they need.'

"'Is that likely?' I asked, wanting to be persuaded, desperately.

"'Our Dutch contacts think so, as long as your Japanese is good enough, and you learn enough about the culture to respect it properly. And don't forget, you will have a very deep purse. It wouldn't do at all for them to think we've sent a pauper. We hope the nobles will be flattered enough to allow you to live amongst them. After all, you are only one man. What harm can a single, apparently innocent, man do?'

"'Then I'll do it,' I said at once.

"We shook hands, and a week later I was on board a ship bound for Japan. I spent nearly a year with the Dutch on Dijima, learning as much as I possibly could about all things Japanese. Even though I normally found learning languages an easy thing, it took me a long time before I was confident in your beautiful language. Eventually, my merchant friends decided I was ready, and they got word to Lord Ito, who was intrigued enough to grant me an interview. My government had been right. The letters from Queen Victoria opened his door for me, and before I knew it, I was being introduced to everybody in society in Edo."

"I see," I said, although in all honesty I was still bewildered. What did all this have to do with Seemon and me? With Lord Dai? "Or at least I understand that you must take great care. But why is it so very terrible that we're lovers?"

"Because I believe that out of all the nobles only Lord Dai is suspicious of me. He's always polite to my face, but I've heard that he has been asking questions about me, sowing the seeds of doubt in the other nobles' minds. If he found out that we were lovers, he would never forgive either of us. He wouldn't rest until he had hard evidence against me. There would be no escape for me, and I'm afraid that you would probably go with me to the grave, dear one."

"I would rather die with you than lose you and be bound to Lord Dai forever," I said simply.

Seemon stared at me seriously. "You understand that I can't stay here forever, no matter what happens?"

I nodded, even as my heart fractured at the thought of losing him. "May both our gods grant us as much time as possible," I said softly and held out my arms for the comfort only he could give.

SEVENTEEN

The wind sighing through
Pine branches to my ears is
The noise of dry bones

I thought that as long as I had Seemon as my lover, I could stand Lord Dai, if only to keep Seemon safe. But it wasn't long before I understood that I was deluding myself. My *danna*'s attentions quickly became less kind, and far more demanding.

Perhaps if I had not known of the danger I had unwittingly lured Seemon into, I might have found the courage to refuse Lord Dai. But how could I when my beloved's very life was in my hands? Instead, every time he came to me, I felt I had to try and find ways to please him. Anything to distract him from Seemon.

And worse, he grew in confidence with every visit. And so did his tree of flesh. At first, he had been content—more than content, clearly delighted—when I pleasured him with my mouth. But I knew there would come a time when it would no longer be enough. And to add to my woes, increasingly I worried about Seemon's safety. Lord Dai mentioned him occasionally. Commented with a sneer that Auntie was making a fool of herself by fussing over the ugly foreign barbarian. Did Lord Dai seem a little too casual when he asked if I spoke to Seemon often? Did I know anything about him? I shrugged and said I was merely polite to him, even as my heart thumped with fear. I didn't mention it to Seemon. I had no wish to add to his burden of worry.

The more Seemon made love to me, the more did my repulsion of my *danna* grow, until the mere thought of him touching me made my gorge rise. When I had been a small child in my village, my brothers had caught small birds to sell as table delicacies. The way of catching them was simple. They snared one bird, and then tied a thread around its leg. They bound it to a branch, where it sang its distress loud and clear. Other birds fluttered close to see what was causing it to sing so loudly and were easily caught in their turn. I had always felt sorry for the tethered bird, and now, I was just as much a captive.

There was no way out that I could see. All paths led to Lord Dai.

Even though I knew what a terribly dangerous game we were playing, Seemon was in my very soul and I could not let him go. I told myself time and time again that it would be better to put him away from me now, before it was truly impossible. Yet I could not. With each meeting, we became closer and closer. Our thoughts entwined, as well as our bodies.

I loved him. There was no escape from that, just as there was no escape from Lord Dai.

It was foolish of me, of course, to tempt fate. I should have known that the gods are easily angered when they are taken for granted, but I was smugly delighted to find it was surprisingly easy to carry out my longed-for assignations with Seemon. With *my lover*. Even to think of him in that way gave me a thrill of pleasure.

Because of my high status as Lord Dai's favorite, I was sought after by only the very richest men in Edo. And Auntie was very fussy about who she would accept. Wealth was not enough on its own. My patrons had to be important men. Men who would further enhance the reputation of the Green Tea House. Consequently, I had fewer appointments than the other geisha in the tea house and more time to myself. Of course, the boys still watched over me. But they could not be in two places at once. Because the Hidden House welcomed patrons in the afternoon as well as the evening, often they were fully occupied there. And I was the soul of caution. Whenever I went to Seemon's house, I took a different route, pausing often to pretend to glance into the shops as I passed by to make sure one or the other of the boys was not following behind me.

Although I was relieved to have time to myself, I was puzzled why Auntie was so pleased by my lack of patrons. Saki seemed amused when I mentioned it to her.

"Have you any idea how much Auntie is charging the patrons for the pleasure of your company?" I shook my head and she smiled. "As much as she charges for all three of us combined, and more besides."

I was shocked. Why? Why would anybody pay that much just to chat with me or watch me dance or listen to me sing? The other girls were just as talented as I was. In fact, I often thought that Saki herself had by far the most beautiful voice out of any of us.

"I don't understand. Why?"

"Part of it is because of Lord Dai," Saki explained

patiently. "He is a great noble and a very important man. If he favors you, then the rest of Edo society must follow. And of course, the other nobles who were not successful in becoming your *danna* have to be seen to be gracious enough in defeat to still wish you to entertain them." I winced inwardly, thinking how Lord Dai had cheated these men to get me. "But apart from all that, you are very beautiful. And very talented. And you have something else that the rest of us lack. You sit at the side of your patron and look as if he has done you the greatest favor in the world just by seeking your company. You have the knack of laughing in exactly the right place and making your patron feel as if he is the wittiest of men. Oh, I know. We can all do that, but you have something more. Something unique. Don't ever take your-self too seriously, Terue-chan, or you will lose your charm."

I laughed and changed the subject. Tamayu came in then and claimed Saki's attention and I was glad. I slipped away and sat quietly in the garden, watching the closed door of the Hidden House longingly. It was well into the afternoon. No doubt my friends were entertaining patrons. I sighed as I thought that I would have liked nothing better at that moment than to have gone to them and taken tea and talked to them about nothing at all.

As I could not do that, I thought about Seemon instead. Mindful of the danger I might bring on him, and fearing the boys' watchful eyes, we were simply courteous to each other whenever he came to the Green Tea House. Nor, after that first time, did we meet in the Hidden House. Seemon said it was too dangerous, that there was a chance that Auntie would find us, and I agreed wholeheartedly with him. Besides that, I felt that I would be betraying the trust of the geisha in the Hidden House if I met my lover there without them knowing. And I could not tell even them about him.

Not that I thought they would betray my trust. I knew they would not. But I feared for them. If Seemon's secret was ever discovered, it was better they knew nothing at all.

So when I knew it was safe—and only then—I sauntered casually out of the tea house and made my way to the Street of the Goldsmiths. Occasionally, Seemon was not there and I would go back to the tea house with a heavy heart.

Today, he was at home and I was happy. But it is a rare day in winter that does not have a cloud in the sky, and Seemon had news that made me miserable.

He had to go out of Edo. Lord Ito had invited him to his country residence to hunt. It was a great honor and he could not refuse. The journey alone would take nearly a week and he expected to stay away for some time.

"Take care you don't find consolation in some other geisha's arms." I pretended to be sulky.

"And who is there who could take me from your side?" Seemon kissed me and put his arms around me, holding me tightly. I relaxed against him. Oddly, I detected that he was stiff, his muscles tense. There was something wrong, I sensed it. I raised my head and peered at his face.

"What is it?"

He was silent for so long I began to be afraid. I clutched his robe as if my foolish hands could be enough to make all well.

"Terue-chan. Do you remember me saying that my time here was limited? That one day I would have to go back to my own home? When I come back from my visit with Lord Ito, that time has come."

I shook my head wildly, denying his words. "No. No, you can't go. Why now? What's happened that's changed things? Aren't you happy here?"

"I must leave." I saw tears shining in his lovely eyes and I kissed them away.

"No." I spoke firmly, as if my denial could make it so.

"I don't want to go, Terue. I promise you that. But I've already stayed much longer than I intended in the first place. I've had messages from my government, demanding to know how much longer I need to stay. They're getting impatient with me. I've sent messages back, lying to them. Saying I need more time. But they're demanding that I return. I have no option. They're already threatening to cut off my funds. If that happens, all at once I'll go from appearing as a rich man to being a pauper. The nobles will know at once that I've lived a lie. I'll be a dead man."

"You must go, then," I said somberly. "Better to have you a world away and alive than here only in spirit."

"My dear, dear Terue. Don't you want to know why I stayed here so long? Because of you, my own love. I couldn't leave you. If I have to go, and I think I must, will you come with me?"

Could I leave behind everything I knew, my whole world? For what? An uncertain but at worst exciting future with the man I loved? In spite of the seriousness of it all, I almost laughed out loud.

"Yes. Oh yes. I wouldn't want to live without you anyway."

He held me tightly in his arms for a long time. I was exhausted by the violent storm of my emotions and I was almost asleep when he spoke softly, his words muffled by my hair.

"It will be dangerous, for both of us. You understand that?"

"Of course I do. But life can't be lived without risk. They

say that a frog in a well can never know the great sea. I don't wish to be that frog."

"Very well. As soon as I come back, I'll get in touch with my Dutch friends and ask them to arrange transport for both of us."

"Promise? You won't go without me?"

"I promise. I will not leave Japan unless you are with me."

"Must you spend time with Lord Ito? Away from me?"

"I'm sorry, I have to go. If I refuse such an honor, it will be asking for trouble. Don't worry. As soon as I get back, I'll make plans to get us both away."

My senses knew Seemon had left the moment he passed through of the walls of the Floating World. I was restless. Nothing pleased me. I practiced on my *samisen*, but put my beloved instrument away when the music sounded dead and unlovely. I picked up a book and tried to read, but found it had no interest for me. I chatted to Saki and Ren and found I had little to say to them. Even the gossip that Tamayu had taken a new lover left me uninterested.

The only real consolation I had was the absence of Lord Dai from my futon. The girls teased me about it, demanding to know what I had done to my *danna* to drive him away from me.

Tamayu smirked at me. "Perhaps he's finally gotten tired of you being cold to him." I gasped in surprise and she sniggered. "Did you think we hadn't noticed? The silly old fool must truly be mad for you to put up with your disdain for so long."

"Leave her alone," Saki said calmly. "Whatever she's doing—or not doing—for him, she has him dangling on a piece of silk. Anyway, I know why he's not here. I heard one of my patrons saying that he's gone on a religious retreat to the temple at Sensoji. He'll be gone for at least a week."

Released from anticipation of my *danna*'s presence, I fell asleep easily that night. As soon as I lay on my futon, I concentrated on Seemon. I recalled his image to my mind and tried to hear his voice. I put out my hand, hoping to feel the illusion of his warmth on my futon. I had found in the past that if I focused hard enough like this, then I dreamed of him. Tonight, I did not.

Instead, in my dreams, I was alone. I walked in a beautiful garden. Tall, dark green pines whispered around me. Somewhere in the distance, the sea foamed and fell on a beach, the waves whispering amongst themselves. Even in my sleep, I was mildly astonished. I had never seen the sea. How could I know its sound? I sat on a stone bench and the warm sun caressed my face tenderly. Suddenly, I was filled with a glow of such intense content that I felt golden. My whole body was relaxed. Peace was within me and I was so happy I felt I could have soared with the birds.

When I awoke, the joy lingered. I lay on my futon utterly happy and utterly relaxed. I felt as if I had eaten the sun and it glowed within me. I stretched and yawned, running my hands over my belly and breasts, simply for the pleasure of feeling my own skin.

And stopped abruptly.

My breasts were tender beneath my touch. I probed a little harder and winced at the pain my touch aroused. There was no pain in my belly, but my fingers told me that my stomach was rounded. I had always envied Saki her flat belly. Compared to hers, mine was a hill. Now, that hill was higher than it had been. I probed and prodded myself in disbelief.

Sat up and shook my head. Counted on my fingers, and then did it again.

It could not be true. The more I denied it to myself, the more certain I became. My last courses had been more than five months ago.

There had been no bitter drink for me. Even if Lord Dai's tree had reared for me, there would still have been no drink. Had I become pregnant by him, Auntie would have rejoiced.

I stared into space, unable to believe I had been so foolish. How could I not have noticed my missed courses? The answer made me flinch. I had been so taken up with Seemon, nothing else had mattered. The morning was cool and I wrapped my arms around myself, hugging my breasts tightly and shivering at the pain I caused myself. For the longest time, my mind was blank. I knew neither joy nor fear. With a huge effort, I made myself think.

The baby could be gotten rid of without much problem. Any apothecary—if I bribed him well enough—would give me a draught that would do the job. If I was...what? Five, perhaps six months gone? It would not be pleasant, but it was not too late. I jerked to my feet suddenly and reached for the large glass hand mirror that had been one of the many presents from Lord Dai. I turned to and fro, inspecting my body in the glass. First my breasts, then my belly. I had always been—apart from that mounded stomach—very slim. Now it seemed obvious to me that I was fatter. I probed my belly gently with my fingertips and gasped as I was sure that I felt something move in response to my touch.

I knew instantly that no matter what, I could not bring

myself to murder my baby. The baby Seemon had created with me.

"No." I whispered the word out loud. "No. Whatever happens, I will not lose you. I will not let anybody take you from me. You have moved. You are part of me."

I sat down abruptly and stayed on the *tatami* for a long time, waiting for my babe to move again. When she did—and I was sure it was going to be a girl child—I felt such love as I had never known existed in the world.

EIGHTEEN

One cannot touch the
Past. Yet who would deny that
It was once our joy?

*T*hings were very difficult for me with Seemon gone. It would have been bad had I not known that I was carrying his child. As it was, so great was my misery I went and shopped in the Street of the Goldsmiths just so I could have a reason to linger outside his house. It did no good. Without his presence, the house was just a house, with neither soul nor heart.

I had to pretend that all was well in my world. I had nobody I could confide in about my baby. And still I had patrons who demanded to be entertained. Patrons who were paying very well indeed for my smiles and whispered compliments. I began to hate myself and wonder if I was turning into Tamayo, who could charm her patrons even when she had had a bitter argument with her own lover and refused to so much as talk to the rest of us.

And worst of all was Lord Dai.

He did not linger long at his retreat. A few days after Seemon left Edo, he was back at the tea house. Auntie was clearly delighted, which was all for the good. She had been grumpy lately and had taken to slapping us all with her cane or lashing us with her acid tongue for no reason at all.

Tamayu said it was because of her time of life, that it was only to be expected at her age. Ren insisted it was because she was having problems with her lover. I agreed with Ren. I had noticed that Auntie was with us in the tea house more frequently these days, and was far more likely to be frowning than smiling. But the thought of Auntie having a lover was distasteful and I pulled a face. Ren laughed.

"She's not so old that she couldn't still enchant a man, you know."

"Ren's right," Saki agreed languidly. "Don't forget, Japanese men tend to be sensible about that sort of thing. The older woman has learned many ways to please her man. And even when she is too old to actually employ the arts of love, she can still capture a man with her wit." She glanced meaningfully at Tamayu, who shrugged sulkily. "And anyway, Auntie is still young enough and pretty enough to catch any man who takes her fancy."

"I suppose you're right. Auntie hasn't gotten around to having to rely on her wits, yet," Tamayu said spitefully, and in spite of my own worries, I laughed at her acid comment and then was ashamed. I found it in my heart to feel sorry for Auntie and hoped that she would make up her quarrels with her lover. Apart from anything else, if she were happy with her own man it would surely stop her doting on Seemon.

In any event, Auntie's watchful presence meant that I dared find no excuse to avoid Lord Dai.

My patron stroked my hair, smiling his pleasure at my company. I thought I knew what he wanted. Of late, he had come to demand that I stand in front of him naked while he called orders to me. He wanted to watch me stroke my breasts. Part my black moss and rub my private places. It took me a while to understand that he also wanted to think I was taking great pleasure out of the performance. As it appeared to please him greatly when I did, I soon learned to moan and close my eyes and push out my breasts in a parody of delight. He never seemed to realize that my mind was absent from my body, that I was putting on a performance worthy of anything he might see at the kabuki. And as for me, if it made him burst his fruit quickly without him actually touching me, it was well worth it.

I was actually beginning to undo my robe in anticipation of his request when he stopped me.

"No, my dear Terue. The moon is full tonight, have you noticed?" I had. It was so bright it put the scented lamp in my room to shame. "And the face of the moon god is plain to see in it. I have been waiting for such a night. I went back to my witch a few weeks ago, and she told me that the gods had decided to reward my patience. That on the first night when the moon shone like this, I would finally be healed. That is why I went to Sensoji, to make an offering and to pray that she was right."

I tried to take a deep breath, but no air reached my panting lungs. I made a sound like a very young kitten mewing, and Lord Dai seemed delighted. My baby. Oh, my baby. Nobody but your father should ever touch me. And now this nasty old man was ready to take me at last. I felt sickness rise in my throat and swallowed convulsively.

My patron was so pleased with himself he didn't even notice my expression.

"Ah, you have been so very patient. I knew all along that I was right, that you really were the one. And tonight, we will both be rewarded for our long wait."

"I am truly delighted, my lord," I lied. "Would you care for some sake?" Anything to put off the final moment.

"Later, perhaps. But now, look what I have for you!"

He leaned back, flicking his robe aside. I shuddered as I saw his tree of flesh rearing with all the vigor of a young man. It wasn't exceptionally large. And, oddly, it wasn't as wrinkled as the rest of his ugly, old man's body. But still I stared at it and felt sick. He intended to put that into me, into the place that only Seemon had a right to be. Where my baby had been safe—until now.

He wagged his tree at me and I froze. I could think of nothing that would stop him. Suddenly, I remembered how he loved it when I took him in my mouth. I shuddered at the thought of his seed flowing hot and thick down my throat, but even that was better than taking him inside me.

I kept my eyes closed as my lips closed around his tree. Even blind, I knew it was not going to be as easy as I had hoped. Normally, when I took him in my mouth, my *danna* moaned and bucked his hips in ecstasy. Tonight, he lay supine and relaxed. I heard him sigh with pleasure, but that was all. I was barely surprised when his hands fastened in my hair and he pulled my lips away from him.

"It is good that you should think of my pleasure rather than your own, Terue-chan," he said tenderly. "But the time for waiting is over. And our time has finally come."

I stared at him, transfixed as the rabbit that cowers in the shadow of the soaring eagle. He leaned forward and undid my sash, allowing my robe to fall away. Hope rose in my mind. Surely, he would notice my swollen breasts? My rounded belly? Notice and question? And if he did that, I would be saved. I would confess to him at once that I had taken a lover, and he would be so angry he would turn his face from me. Auntie would be incandescent with rage, but it didn't matter. As soon as Seemon returned, we would leave Japan together. Forever.

My hope died almost as soon as it came. My patron simply didn't see what was before his eyes. He lowered his head and suckled at my breasts. The pain was exquisite and I moaned. Lord Dai seemed to find my response pleasing. He raised his head and smiled at me, his brown stumps of teeth exposed. He gestured that I should lie back on the futon. I could not, would not, move. When my frozen limbs refused to obey his command, he shook his head at me, smiling, and put his hands on my shoulders. I pushed against him, but his strength was amazing. He seemed to move me effortlessly, as if I were no more than a child's cloth doll. I stared at him in disbelief and saw his eyes were not just shining, but the pupils were unnaturally huge. I knew, instantly, that the witch had given him more than good news. What potion had she offered that gave him such bodily strength and made his tree rear with all the vigor of a young man?

Still, I tried. I wriggled like a fish beneath his hands, desperately trying to get away. He was having none of it. His grip on my shoulders was iron. I swung my legs sideways, and in response, he loosed one hand and grabbed my knee and forced my legs wide apart. I tried to resist, but his strength was astounding. In the past, had he been a younger man, or even a man I was fond of, I would have described him as a tender would-be lover. But tonight, all was different.

He shoved his leg between my thighs and put his hand back on my shoulder, forcing me to be still. His other hand delved into my black moss, his fingernails ripping and tearing at my dry flesh. I shrieked with dread and pain but immediately wished I had stayed silent. Lord Dai seemed to delight in my terror. His tree of flesh followed his probing hand. A moment later, he was pounding at me, pinning me flat with his own body.

His mouth smothered my lips. I couldn't move. Could barely breathe. Could think of nothing but my baby, so cruelly violated by this hideous old man. My own pain was nothing compared to that.

I thought he would never finish. No matter how I tried to get away, his body kept me prisoner beneath him. I scratched and bit at any part of him I could reach, only stopping when I realized my actions were arousing him even more. In the end, I did the only thing I could. I stayed still and silent, simply enduring until he had finished. Bitterly, I realized that at least he would have no reason to believe I was not whole. I was so very dry and rigid that he had to fight to push his tree into me, and every movement was agony for me.

Just as I thought I was going to scream out loud with the pain and the horror of it, Lord Dai finally slowed. I felt him burst his fruit, his seed hot and copious as he jetted into me. He lurched off me and lay on his back, gasping for air. I hoped with the fury of shame that perhaps it had been too much for his old heart and that he would trouble me no more, but I was denied even that sour comfort.

After a moment, he rolled over and my skin crawled as he thrust my legs apart again and inspected my black moss carefully. Finally, he grunted with apparent satisfaction and stood, gathering his robe around his shoulders.

"I shall leave you to your sleep, Terue-chan," he murmured. "I hope that you will sleep as well as I know I shall, and that your dreams are very beautiful. We will speak again very soon."

He bowed deeply and respectfully before he turned and walked away.

My tears came as soon as the screen door slid closed. I cried silently, my tears more silver than the light of the full moon. He had hurt me, badly, but I didn't care about that. I would heal. I supposed that in time the memory of my violation at his hands might even lessen. But my baby, what about her? I recalled Lord Dai staring at my black moss and appearing to be very pleased. Fear gripped me tightly. I forced my hand down to touch my private parts. I was sticky —of course—but when I raised my hand to the moonlight I saw that my fingers were black with the blood that smeared them.

My baby. Oh, my baby. I moaned, my fist balled into my mouth. I prayed out loud that the blood was from where Lord Dai had forced himself into my dryness. But I couldn't be sure.

Instinct ruled me, forcing me to my feet. I needed my friends. The tea house was silent around me as I staggered down the corridor and out into the garden. Gravel bit into my feet as I crossed to the Hidden House. Later, I would find that my feet had been cut badly, but at the time I didn't notice at all. I banged on the door with my fists and my head and fell into the hall when it was jerked open. I lay on the floor and stared wildly up at the shocked faces of the geisha from the Hidden House.

Nami gathered her wits first. She bent down and tried to lift me up, but she was not strong enough on her own. Gin took one arm and Hiromi the other, and with Nami's hands gripping my waist, the girls hauled me up between them and Gin kicked the door shut with her foot.

My friends walked me down the corridor, supporting me tenderly. It was only when we arrived at the reception room I had seen before that they allowed me to slip to the *tatami* and began to ask questions.

"What is it? You're hurt. What happened?" Nami rubbed my frozen hands anxiously. "Oh, your poor feet! You walked across without *geta*?"

"They don't matter," I said dully. "Lord Dai. He went to the temple and prayed and the gods heard him. He took me. His witch must have given him something to enhance his tree. He was so strong, I couldn't fight him. I tried, but it was no good." The tears came again, and I could find no words.

"Shush, dear." Gin put her arms around me and rocked me to and fro as if I were a child who had fallen and injured herself. "I know, it's very bad. But you knew it would happen eventually. At least neither he nor anybody else will ever be able to hurt you like this again."

"It's not me. I don't care about me." I stared at them, their outlines blurred by my tears. "I don't matter. It's my baby. I think he must have hurt her."

The hiss of indrawn breath was like a shout in the silence. I wiped my eyes and wished I hadn't as I saw their shocked faces.

"Baby?" Nami put her hands on each side of my face and made me look at her. "You're sure?"

I nodded.

The geisha looked at each other, and to my intense relief asked no more questions. Gin told me briskly to get to my feet and the girls walked me down to the bath. Once I was up to my neck in the steaming water, I felt some of my pain leave me.

The geisha stared at each other until finally Gin shrugged and took charge.

"How far gone are you?"

"About five months. Perhaps nearly six."

They stared at my body, distorted by the scalding hot water.

"One would never know," Hiromi commented, and I managed a smile, grateful that they were neither disapproving nor, it seemed, even surprised.

"We always thought Auntie had been very foolish, forbidding you a lover. Who is he? Big after all?"

I shook my head so hard the water rippled across the entire bath.

"No. Never him. Seemon."

Their silence was more eloquent than words. I saw their silent, appalled glances, and thought they were disappointed that I had chosen a *gaijin* as a lover. I wanted to cry all over again.

"Does he know?" Hiromi asked quietly.

"No. I only realized myself a couple of days ago, and he'd already gone out of Edo, to hunt with Lord Ito." I paused and my fear rose again. "It doesn't matter. Lord Dai hurt me, and I'm sure he's made me lose my baby."

"It would be better for you if he has," Gin said grimly.

I stared at her in horror. These women were my friends. If they felt like that about my poor baby, what chance did I have amongst those who did not love me so well?

"Listen to me, child." Gin spoke softly, but her tone was firm. "I may sound unfeeling, and for that I'm sorry, but do you understand the danger you're in? You were supposed to keep yourself intact for Lord Dai. It would have been bad enough if you'd become pregnant by a Japanese man. If that had happened, from what I hear, Dai is so besotted with you he may even have been willing to accept the child as his own. But Seemon is a *gaijin*. If the babe is born, it will be obvious to everybody that it couldn't be Lord Dai's child. He would be a laughing stock. The loss of face would be unbearable for him. He will insist that the child be exposed at once before anybody could even see it. It's likely he'll tell Auntie to give you poison, and she wouldn't dare refuse."

I shook my head, my eyes downcast. "Seemon is leaving Japan very soon," I said softly. "I am to go with him, back to his own country. Lord Dai will never be able to find us."

"Dear Terue, do you truly realize the danger you're all in? You and Seemon-san and your baby?" Nami's voice trembled with the effort of making me understand. "You've been fortunate so far. Nobody would know you're pregnant yet. But before too long everybody will be able to see. If your baby is still alive, that is. First things first. Would you allow me to examine you? I'm the eldest of seven children, and I helped my mother birth most of my siblings. She lost another two, so I know what I'm looking for."

We climbed out of the bath and bundled into thick, warm robes. When I was dry, Nami led me to her own bedroom and told me to lie down on the *tatami*. Gin and Hiromi clustered around us, but I didn't mind in the least. These were my friends, and they meant me no hurt.

Nami put the lamp close to us, and her fingers ran over my belly, stopping now and then to prod and feel. Eventually, she laid her head on my stomach and gestured to the other girls to be silent. Finally, she sat back on her heels.

"May I feel inside you?" she asked courteously. I nodded and stared at the ceiling as she probed gently and carefully. The hot bath water had soothed my poor flesh, and her examination was uncomfortable rather than painful.

"Your baby is alive. And as far as I can tell, healthy."

Hiromi shook her head, her face grave. "Gin was right. It would have been better if you had lost it," she said bluntly.

"Safer for you. Safer for your baby, and for Seemon-san. How soon does he intend to leave Japan?"

I forced myself to think. Seemon had said he would not be back in the Floating World for weeks. And it would take time after that for him to arrange to get us both out of Japan.

"Probably a month or so after he gets back to Edo."

"At best, you'll be seven months gone by then," Hiromi said. "You might be able to hide it if you tie your obi very tightly, but if anybody sees you naked..." She shrugged. I knew they were all thinking of Lord Dai.

"Perhaps if I ate very little?" I said hopefully. The geisha looked at me with pity in their eyes and I slumped. "Then what can I do?"

"If you think Auntie or Lord Dai are becoming suspicious, come here," Gin said firmly. "Don't stop and think about it, just come, no matter what time the day or night. If you can get to us unseen, we'll manage to get you out of Edo until Seemon-san can make his arrangements."

"Thank you. But I'm not going to bring danger to my friends."

And it would be terribly dangerous for them. If Lord Dai found out the truth, and that I had gone to them, then the geisha in the Hidden House would share my fate. I could not do that to them, no matter what.

"I'll manage somehow. Whatever happens, it can't be any worse than it was this time. If he finally notices anything, I'll lie to him. Tell him I have a problem with my stomach. Perhaps if I tell him I'm horribly constipated and that's why it's swollen it might disenchant him!" I joked weakly.

The girls helped me back into my kimono, and Hiromi

insisted I take a pair of her *geta* to get me back across the gravel.

"I'll return them as soon as I can," I promised.

"Make sure you do!" she said firmly and then smiled. "Anything that brings you back to us is worth its weight in pearls. Take care, little Terue. And next time we see you, I hope it is in happiness."

NINETEEN

The nail that sits the
Proudest invites the hammer
To knock it down flat

I thought I would never sleep the rest of that
night, but I was so exhausted and distressed that
before I knew it, the light on my face woke me up and I realized that it was actually much later in the morning than
when I usually awoke. And I was barely dressed before
Aimi came to say that Auntie wanted to see me.

I kneeled in front of her, trying not to show my deep
fear. No summons from Auntie was ever to be treated
lightly. Were yet more troubles to be heaped on my
shoulders?

"So, Terue. It has been how long since your *mizuage*?" I
remained silent. Auntie knew perfectly well it had been well
over half a year ago. "A long time, I think. And there has
been nobody but Lord Dai for you, in all that time?"

"No, Auntie," I lied woodenly. She knew. She was

playing with me. I waited silently for the executioner's axe to fall.

"Excellent. Well, child. I must tell you a message from Lord Dai was waiting for me as soon as I woke this morning. I'm amazed that you didn't come and wake me to tell me the good news yourself. But I daresay that you were too shy to mention it to me." I nodded silently, wishing she would just get on with it. "Or perhaps you were on your way to talk to me about it now. But no matter. I have to tell you that you are the most fortunate geisha in the whole of the Floating World. Lord Dai has made an offer for you." She was smiling widely at me, nodding her head and raising her eyebrows, obviously expecting me to be delighted. Her words were so far away from what I had expected, I was struck dumb.

Auntie prodded me playfully in the shoulder with her cane.

"And—from your point of view—it is even better than one might expect. He hasn't offered to make you his concubine. You've enchanted him to such an extent, he wants to marry you. He's got everything arranged. You are to be formally adopted by Lord Ito's family. Once that is in place, you will take the Ito family name and Lord Dai will marry you. I hope, child, that you realize how the gods have smiled on you."

Her words penetrated my mind slowly. Before I could manage to speak, I was shaking my head.

"No." I raised my head and looked at Auntie. For one insane moment, I contemplated telling her the whole truth. But the moment died and I told her only part of it. "I will not marry him, Auntie. I cringe every time he touches me. I would spend the whole of the time I was with him in hell."

To my astonishment, I could see clearly that Auntie was not surprised. She raised her eyes to heaven and sighed.

"You are a stupid child, Terue. Go on, tell me. Do you think yourself in love with some poor student or other? Or is it that you have fallen for the charms of a handsome kabuki actor? I knew you would be difficult. It doesn't matter, anyway. Lord Dai wants you, and that's the end of it. Are you really surprised? After all, you've finally proved the witch's prophecy." I shook my head, my expression tight with disgust, and Auntie prodded me again with her cane. Hard, this time. "And as for this nonsense about living the rest of your life in hell, that's up to you, isn't it? If you put your womanly talents to good use, you could kill him in a few months. If he's tougher than I think he is, within a year at the most. And then you will be a rich, free woman from a good family. What else could you want?"

She meant it. I stared at her in abject horror. It was all such a mess, and I could see no way out of it. I wanted to weep. For myself. For Seemon. And above all for our baby. I stared straight ahead, listening to Auntie's gloating voice. My thoughts tumbled like butterflies in the sun.

At that moment, my babe chose to turn. The movement was so unexpected, I gasped out loud. Auntie glanced at me and I somehow had the presence of mind to turn the noise into a laugh.

"I hear you, Auntie. But no. My answer is the same. I will not marry Lord Dai. In fact, I don't want him near me ever again. I hate him."

I was rigid with panic. But I forced my stiff lips to smile, all the same.

"You are beyond my belief, Terue." Obviously convinced at last, Auntie got to her feet. She towered over me as I knelt before her. "That's your last word?"

"It is."

"Then we must take measures to break that willful mind of yours."

I could have pushed past her, I supposed. Ran for the door and escaped into the Floating World. But even as I thought it, I knew there was no point. I wouldn't have gotten to the end of the street before the boys caught me, and they would not be gentle. For my baby's sake, I couldn't risk it.

Auntie was staring at me as if she still couldn't believe I was defying her.

"You will go to Lord Dai in the end," she said quietly. "And before long you will be glad to go to him, I promise you. His message said he was going out of Edo. No doubt the poor fool is making preparations for your marriage. While he is gone, you will stay in your room. Nobody will see you. Nobody will even speak to you. I will take away your *samisen* and your books. I don't want you to be distracted from your thoughts about your future. I will feed you, but you're only going to get plain rice and water. You may go to the bath, but you will go alone. You will not leave your room, not unless the tea house is on fire. One or other of the boys will guard your door day and night. When you come to your senses, you may ask the boys to bring you to see me. Until then, you are dead to me."

Bigger escorted me to my room and went away with armfuls of my possessions. He paused in the doorway and shook his head at me, his expression amused. He waited for me to speak, but when I did not, he shrugged and turned away. For the longest time after he had gone, I simply sat on the *tatami* and stared into space.

And then my baby turned. I put my hand on my belly and gave thanks.

TWENTY

The tallest tree is
Surely grown to be climbed by
The very smallest!

*I*f I had I really been alone, then I don't doubt I would have given in quickly. I had never been on my own in my entire life. When I was a child in the village, I was always surrounded by my brothers and my parents. Here in the tea house, the other geisha were always close by.

To be truly alone, day after day after day, was something I could not even begin to comprehend.

But of course, I was not alone. I had my dear daughter with me constantly. Even though I could not speak aloud to her, for fear one of the boys would hear me, I could chatter away happily to her in my own mind.

And in one way, Auntie had done me a very great favor. There was nobody to notice my thickening waistline. I saw only the maid, Aimi, and she barely dared to exchange more than a whispered word to me when she brought me my rice or escorted me to the bath. She knew. I saw it in her anxious glances. I reassured her with a smile and a single finger placed against my lips. Even so, as she poured rinsing water over me in the bathhouse, she had the courage to whisper, "Seemon-san?"

I inclined my head in answer, not at all sure that Auntie wasn't watching us through one of her many peepholes.

"He's back in Edo," she murmured, leaning close to me as she helped me climb into the bath. I closed my eyes. How could I have lost count of the days that had passed since I had been imprisoned? My heart clenched with worry. How long had he been back? Did he wonder why I had disappeared? Did he think I had given in and gone to Lord Dai after all? My anxiety was so great, I risked a whisper to Aimi.

"When?"

"A few days ago. I'll get word to him."

She moved away and I stepped carefully into the steaming water.

I had always loved the bath. At first, it had been the simple joy of being thoroughly clean. Soon, it had grown beyond that as I came to understand that the bath was a place to gossip and linger and laugh in the company of the other geisha. The only time that the pleasure was absent was when Big and Bigger bathed with us. Even though they kept to their own side of the bath, we were inhibited by them. When the boys were present, the bath was a quiet, hurried affair.

Now, I soaked and climbed out with as little pleasure as if the boys had been with me.

But at least I had hope. Seemon was back. Aimi would get word to him. Somehow, he would come and release me. Us. And then I remembered that he had no idea that I was carrying his child and misery descended like persistent rain on a summer day. Would he be angry? Would he still want me to escape with him?

I sat in my room and for the first time since Auntie had locked me away, the tears flowed.

"Feeling sorry for yourself, are you?"

I smeared the tears away with the back of my hand and blinked and focused. "Big. I didn't hear you come in. Please." I waved my hand at my bare room. "Make yourself as comfortable as you can."

"Why couldn't you wait for me?"

I stared at him, not understanding. His face was set but his eyes betrayed his hurt.

"What? I don't know what you mean." I tried the effect of a smile, and for a moment I thought Big was about to strike me. I jerked away from him and he lowered his hand and stared at it as if it was strange to him.

"It's not Lord Dai's. I could understand it if it was. But we gathered from Auntie that he couldn't manage to pleasure you until recently. So who is your baby's father, Terue? Who managed to sneak in before your *danna*?"

He might just as well have hit me. I could do no more than shake my head.

"Don't bother denying it. The others must be blind." I put my hand on my belly defensively, but he shook his head. "You've put on a bit of fat, but that's easily explained by all the rice Auntie's making you eat. It's not that. It's you. You're glowing. I've watched you sitting there with a happy smile on your face. Sometimes you put your head on one side, as if you're talking to somebody. And you are, aren't you?"

"Yes," I said simply. What was the point in denying it?

"Who?" he persisted. "One of the other patrons? Somebody you met outside the tea house? Who?"

He stood and leaned over me. Placed his hands on my shoulders and thrust his face toward me. So close his pupils were enormous.

"Do you love him?"

"Yes." I saw the pain in his eyes and felt hugely sorry for him, this man the other girls thought so terrible. Even knowing that he and Bigger were lovers made no difference. Who was to say he couldn't love both of us? And suddenly, I was sure that he would never hurt me. No matter what.

"Big, will you help me escape?"

"Why should I? So you can run off with your lover?" He tried to sound amused, but his voice caught and grated.

"If you love me, then help me. If I stay here much longer, then Auntie will know. And if that happens, things will be very bad for me. And my baby. You don't want to see me hurt, probably killed."

"Who? If you want me to help you, then tell me. Who stole my place, Terue?"

I saw his pain shine through his attempts to keep a stone face. I could not lie to him.

"Seemon-san."

I expected him to be furious. I had taken a *gaijin* for my lover, dared to prefer a foreign barbarian to him. His reaction bewildered me.

He threw his head back and howled with laughter.

"Seemon-san? Really? By all the gods, that man must truly have something that the rest of us lack. Does he really have a tail? Or is it something even more mysterious?"

I put my head on one side, watching his face anxiously.

"I don't understand."

Big grinned into my bewildered face. "You do know he's

been Auntie's lover almost since he first appeared in the Floating World?"

His grin widened as he saw my appalled expression. I shook my head, mute with horror. Seemon, my lover, had pleasured himself with Auntie? I didn't want to believe Big, but in my heart, I knew he was right. Suddenly, so many small things that had puzzled me made perfect sense. Seemon, who had been Auntie's guest of honor so very often. Who always seemed to know her plans. How he knew that Lord Dai had cheated to win me. I remembered the way the geisha in the Hidden House had looked at each other when I had told them he was the father of my baby. At the time, I had thought it was just shock. But now I understood. Did everybody in the Floating World know Auntie was his lover? Everybody but me? My baby kicked, but for once I could take no pleasure in it.

Why hadn't he told me? I would have been hurt. Oh yes! But at least it would have been better than this humiliation.

"I didn't know," I said dully. Big stared at me. His grin faded, and I understood that he felt sorry for me. I hated him for it.

"He should have told you," he said angrily. "She pounced on him almost as soon as he appeared amongst us. I daresay he didn't stand much of a chance. What Auntie wants, she gets. I should have guessed he was your lover. Bigger was only saying the other day that Auntie's was a winter romance, and that come the spring her lover had lost all interest in her. Of course he had. What would he want with Auntie when he had you?"

My spirits rose the tiniest bit. Auntie had snared him before he had even seen me. And if Big was telling the truth, as soon as we had become lovers, he had lost interest in Auntie. But he should have told me, all the same!

"Don't blame him too much." Big must have read my thoughts. "He's a *gaijin*. They don't think in the same way as we Japanese. He probably thought you would be deeply hurt if you knew about Auntie, so he hid it from you."

A Japanese man would simply have told me as a matter of fact. The affair had happened. What was the point in denying it? Would I have been any happier if he had told me? Of course not. But in my present mood all I could think was that he should have told me!

"You do realize what trouble he's bought down on you?" Big's righteous anger was arrowed at Seemon. "If it had been anybody but him, Lord Dai might have been persuaded to own the baby as his own. But if it's born looking like a fox spirit, you're dead, all three of you."

I shuddered. His blunt words had finally made me wake from my dream.

"Will you help me then?"

"I can't. It doesn't matter where you—or he—go in Japan, you can't hide. Lord Dai will hunt you both down and have you executed. He has to. It would be too much loss of face to do anything else. As it is, I doubt his reputation will ever fully recover from the shame of it."

"Help me," I persisted. "Seemon is going back to his own country as soon as he can make arrangements. I'm going with him."

"Are you?" Big looked at me curiously. "Does he know about the baby?"

"No."

I stared at my hands, laced across my belly. Big had no need to say any more. What if Seemon was horrified about my—our—baby? What if he refused to allow me to go with him? Then I—and my precious baby—would die, and that was all there was to it. But that wasn't going to happen. I wouldn't let it happen.

"Help me," I said again. I threw caution to the wind and decided I had to trust Big. I had nobody else. "Aimi can get a message to Seemon for me. He can make the arrangements for us to get away from Japan quickly. If you help me get away from here, that is."

I watched Big's face working, understood the warring emotions that were going on behind it. I leaned forward and put my hand on his sleeve.

"I know I've hurt you, and I'm sorry for it. One cannot help who one loves. That's in the hands of the gods. But if you still love me, then help me. If you don't, then I'll die."

"And if you do, who's to say we won't meet again in another life?"

But he didn't believe his own words, I could see that. I waited and was rewarded for my patience. He stared over my shoulder, and I could see his mind was working.

"The wise men have forecast that the cherry blossoms will be at their best in about two weeks, so the *hanami* festival will be held then," he said finally. I stared at him in bewilderment, wondering why he was telling me this. My confusion must have shown on my face clearly as he raised his finger to silence me. "Auntie always takes her geisha out to stroll amongst the cherry trees when they're in full blossom on the first day of the festival. It's an ideal opportunity for her to show off her own precious flowers to the world. And of course, she goes with them. She's told Bigger that if you haven't come to your senses by then, she's going to dress you in your most expensive kimono and obi and take you with the rest of the geisha to eat and drink and enjoy yourself under the beauty of the cherry trees. She's sure that after so long alone, you'll realize what you're missing and give in."

"I don't understand. What difference does that make?"

"It's probably the only chance you'll have to get away unseen. Auntie will tell you about her plans the day before. Agree with her. Make her think she's right. Eat a good meal that night. Next day, tell her your stomach was so unused to rich food that you're very ill. On no account can you go outside the tea house. You need to be close to a chamber pot. She'll be furious with you, so bow your head and appear penitent. Her anger will pass when she thinks she's getting her own way. But I'm sure she'll be at least a little suspicious. She'll tell me to stay here and keep an eye on you."

"What if she tells Bigger to stay, not you?"

"She won't do that. Auntie knows I'm fond of you. Because of that, I promise you that I'll be the one selected to watch over you. It'll be a subtle warning that you're not for me, that I'm to guard you for Lord Dai."

He spoke so bitterly, I had to believe him. I put my fingers on his hand in an attempt to give him what comfort I could, but he shook me away angrily.

"Don't touch me. I'll do what I can for you, but for the gods' sake, don't remind me what I've lost."

TWENTY-ONE

Sometimes the soul is
The mirror of life. I do
Not love my image

I doubt that my sanity would have survived those last weeks without my baby's presence. But I did have her, and I spoke silently to her, constantly reassuring her that everything would be well and that soon we would be with her father.

But who was there to reassure me?

Big did not speak to me again. Perhaps Aimi felt it too dangerous to talk. The most she managed was a reassuring smile. With that, I had to be content. I lost track of the days and nights I spent alone. I had almost given up hope and I was shocked when Auntie visited me.

"Well, child? You appear none the worse for your ordeal. In fact, you're positively blooming. Solitude must be good for you."

I kept my eyes down. Had I not, I knew Auntie would have seen the hatred glowing in my eyes. This woman I had once feared had known my lover. Had taken him into her body in the same way as I had. And I had to pretend I knew nothing.

"I have been very lonely, Auntie." I was amazed. My voice was level and quiet, with not a hint of the fury that was raging through me.

"Serves you right," she said brutally. "And have you changed your mind yet? Or shall I leave you here for another month or two to think about it?"

I prayed as I have never prayed in my life that Big was right. I was almost too hasty. In my worry that she might change her mind, I was ready to blurt out that I would do anything she wanted. But I glanced at her face from beneath my lowered eyelids and saw the suspicion there. For a heartbeat, I was sure she knew everything. Then I realized it was my own calm answer that had made her wary.

"I...I don't know." I shrugged and did my best to look cowed. I heard Auntie tap her cane on the floor angrily and hunched my shoulders, staring down humbly.

"I'll say that for you, you're tougher than I gave you credit for. Very well, perhaps I can offer you something to make your mind up. Tomorrow is the first day of the *hanami* festival. It might do you good to see what you're missing. You can come with me and the rest of the geisha to see the blossoms. The wise men say the weather will be good. We will stroll amongst the people and when we are tired we will sit beneath the trees and eat and drink and watch the world go by. When we return, you can tell me if you want to come back into that world or if you are going to persist in this foolishness."

Even if I hadn't known that this was my only chance of escape, I was suddenly so hungry for life and laughter that I longed to agree. As it was, I remembered I had a part to play and did my best to look worried.

"Will Lord Dai be there?"

"He will not." I heard the anger vibrating in Auntie's voice and in my heart was glad of it. "He knows that you're reluctant to go to him, and the old fool has told me that he will wait until you're ready to come to him because you want to. He's deceiving himself, of course," she added with casual cruelty. "I'm amazed he's waited this long. By the end of the month, at the latest, he'll be banging on my door telling me he'll take you even if you have to be prodded with a sword to pant out your wedding vows."

She waited for me to speak, and when I remained silent, she turned on her heel with an exclamation of anger. At the door, she turned and said almost casually, "I'll leave your door open. The boys will no longer guard you. You can come out whenever you like. I daresay you'll want to eat supper with the rest of us."

I found the open door frightening. I had spent so long locked in my prison, the thought of freedom was intimidating. It wasn't until Saki came and told me firmly that I was to come to eat with everybody that I dared move.

Supper was delicious. The *tatami* was full of enticing dishes. Rice steamed and fried, fish, lotus root prepared with ginger, dishes and dishes of vegetables, miso soup, and noodles. My mouth watered as I accepted a bowl of steaming udon noodles and a dish of pickled vegetables. Strangely, when I came to eat I could barely swallow more than a mouthful or two, but under Auntie's watchful gaze I did my best. But the tea! That I couldn't get enough of and drank cup after cup without finding it anything but delicious.

I was grateful when the food was taken away and Auntie clapped her hands briskly.

"To bed, all of you. We will be up early to prepare for the festival."

As I got to my feet, I was suddenly tremendously hot. I wiped my forehead nervously and was surprised to find I was perspiring heavily. My stomach gave a sudden rolling lurch and I almost laughed hysterically. Surely, I couldn't really be ill?

I got little sleep that night. Every time I slipped into dreams, my belly woke me again. Toward morning, I could neither sit nor lie for the pain. I wanted to pass water constantly, but when I tried there was nothing but a trickle. I sat on the floor with my back to the wall and almost wailed with misery.

I was still sitting there when Auntie came to see if I was ready. She stared at me in disbelief.

"What is the matter with you, child?"

"I don't know," I whimpered. "My belly hurts dreadfully, and I keep needing to make water."

She put her hand on my forehead and snatched it away in distaste.

"You must have eaten too much last night," she said accusingly. "You certainly drank too much tea. Well, I hope you don't think the rest of us are going to miss our fun because of your stupidity. You can stay here. I'll leave one of the boys to keep an eye on you. Do you want some medicine for your stomach?" she added grudgingly.

I shook my head, trying desperately not to draw my legs up to my chest as a spasm of pain shook me. How could I dare take something that might hurt my baby?

"Very well. Big can stay with you. If you want anything, you can send for your maid."

She walked out without a second glance, and shortly afterward I heard Saki and Ren and Tamayu giggling their way down the corridor and out of the front door.

"They've all gone." Big lounged in my door. "Give them a few minutes and we'll go across to the Hidden House. *He's* waiting for you there. You can both slip out safely to the side road from there. What's the matter with you?"

"My stomach hurts," I said simply.

Big frowned and poked me with his toe. "You haven't really got a stomach upset, have you?"

A sharp wave of pain cut off any words I might have had. I cringed with embarrassment as I felt a flood of wetness between my legs and realized I had wet myself. Then I cried out loud as the pain came back, very fiercely.

"What is it, mistress?"

I knew things must be very bad when I saw Aimi simply pushing Big to one side. She kneeled beside me and put her hand on my belly. She glanced up at Big and shook her head.

"The baby's coming. Her waters have broken, so it's not going to be long. Help me get her to her feet. We have to get her over to the Hidden House now, before things go any further."

Big's face was appalled. Aimi flapped her hands at him urgently, and between the two of them, they managed to haul me to my feet and half dragged, half walked me across the garden.

I was in so much pain and distress, I barely realized that it was Seemon who opened the door to us.

As it happened, Aimi was wrong. My baby took much longer to arrive than she had predicted. Between the spasms of pain, I did my best to listen to her urgent instructions. Nothing else seemed to matter, not even Seemon's anxious face peering at me and then retreating as Aimi told him, firmly, to get out of the way. From time to time, I thought I saw one or other of my friends from the Hidden House leaning over me. I called out to them, but there was no reply.

"They're not here," Big's voice boomed at me from far away. "A couple of their wealthier patrons decided it would amuse them to take all the geisha from the Hidden House to see the *hanami*. They've gone in a couple of closed palanquins so they can see and not be seen. No use hankering for them."

I wept at the loss of my friends as much as the pain that seemed determined to tear me apart.

But even hell is not eternal, and just as the dusk began to chase the light away, my lovely baby slid into the world with a healthy bawl. Oh, but she was so tiny! And so very, very beautiful. Aimi cleaned her and wrapped her in a shawl and placed her in my arms. And I fell in love utterly and completely at that moment. Her lips sought for my breast and—uncaring whether Big was watching or not—I gave her my nipple and sighed in contentment as she sucked her life from me.

I could happily have stayed there forever. I knew where we were, in the secret room in the Hidden House. It was right, I thought, that things should have come full circle. This was where Seemon and I had first made love. Next door to Auntie's apartment. The irony of it pierced me. But it was the place where our baby had chosen to come into the world. It didn't matter. The only thing in the whole world was my dear daughter, snuggling deliciously in my arms.

"Her name is to be Kazhua." I smiled at Seemon. "Look. She has your hair, and your eyes, green as emeralds.

'Green Leaf.' A beautiful name for the most beautiful of babies."

I couldn't understand why Seemon was crying. Did he not already love his baby as much as I did? I held her up to him, and he took her off me and held her in such a way that I knew she was truly precious to him.

"She is very beautiful, dear one." His voice was choked with tears. "But we must leave her here, you understand that?"

I smiled at him. Silly man! What on earth was he talking about? Leave my baby here? What nonsense! He squatted down beside me and handed Kazhua back to me tenderly.

"We will come back for her as soon as we can. I promise you that."

Seemon felt in his sleeve and handed something to Aimi, speaking to her quietly.

"You can't be found here. Auntie will know you helped us and she'll take her anger out on you. Get away from the Floating World. Go now, and get as far as you can before morning. I don't know how to thank you enough for what you've done for Terue, but that money should be enough to get you well away from here and to keep you for a long time."

Aimi looked at me and I saw tears were streaming down her face. I smiled at her and gestured for her to go. Seemon was right. If Auntie found she had helped me, her life would literally not be worth living. She snatched the purse and walked away quickly, as if a slower pace would have been intolerable.

Kazhua grasped me with her tiny hands and I kissed her damp curls tenderly. A man groaned, but I was too taken up with my baby to know—or care—if it was Seemon or Big.

"You must both go. Now." Big's voice was relentless and

cruel, I thought. "Listen to reason, Terue. The baby must stay here. If you take her, she'll die. She's arrived too early. You have a terrible journey in front of you. She isn't strong enough to survive it. Do you want to kill her?"

His words pieced the tender cloak of love I had wrapped around myself. I shook my head slowly.

"I will not leave her. I can't."

"Then what are you going to do? If you stay, you will die. All three of you. Is that what you want?"

"Of course not."

"Listen to me, Terue. He's right. We must go." Seemon's voice was hoarse with unshed tears. I shook my head stubbornly.

"I'm not going to leave her, Seemon. I just can't. Go and save yourself. Leave both of us here, where we belong."

"You're blind." Distressed by the loud voice, Kazhua bawled loudly and Big had to shout to make himself heard. "Don't you understand? If you stay with the baby, all three of you will be dead by morning. Auntie will have all of you killed. She has no choice. If she doesn't dispose of you before Lord Dai finds out what's happened, he'll execute all three of you and Auntie as well. He has to. The loss of face would be too much for him to take."

"Big's right." I heard the pain in Seemon's voice and clutched Kazhua tightly. "Terue, we must both go. At once."

I shook my head defiantly. No. I would not go. How could I leave my precious baby here, a world away from me?

"You must go," Big repeated. "It's the only chance any of you have. There's a palanquin and bearers waiting for you both at the garden door. It can slip away from here through the back streets and take you to the docks unseen." He nodded at Seemon but did not look at him. "He says he's booked passage for you both on a *wasen* boat that's ready to sail for the East Indies. That will take you safely out of the reach of Auntie."

Seemon squatted down beside me and put his arms around me and Kazhua. Exhaustion filled me suddenly and I leaned against him, grateful for his warmth and strength.

"We are caught, dear one," he said softly. "I will not go without you. If we stay, all of us are going to die. If we take our baby with us, she will never survive. It is many, many weeks travel to my home in America from the East Indies, and it is a terrible journey. We must leave her here, with Big. We have no other option."

"No." My lips were numb. I could barely force the words out. "No. I will not leave her. Please, don't ask me. She is more than life itself to me."

"It will not be forever. We will come back for her as soon as we can. Will you look after our daughter, Big? For Terue's sake? Make sure she is safe?"

Big sighed and then nodded reluctantly. "If that's the only way I can make sure Terue is safe, I will do it. I will not let Auntie hurt her baby."

I stared at them and saw the pain in both their faces. Seemon held his arms out to me, and I understood finally that I had no choice. I handed him my precious baby and at once my breasts ached for loss of her.

"If Big will promise to care for her, then I suppose we must leave her." The words choked in my throat. "If it's the only way we have any chance of finding her again, at least in this world, I suppose we must do it. Wait, I must write to her. Explain to her that we had no choice."

There was a pile of paper, brushes, and ink on a table. I picked up the brush and began to write. I was not practiced in the art of calligraphy, and I was angry with myself that I found it so difficult. Finally, I folded the sheets and handed them to Big.

"You will give her that, Big?" I stared at him, desperate to make him understand. "If we cannot come back for her before then, give it to her when she is old enough to understand. But above all, you must tell her, time and time again, that we both love her. That we had no choice at all. Tell her that we will see her again, just as soon as we can. And remember her name is to be Kazhua. Green Leaf. For her beautiful eyes."

"I will tell her all she should know," he said woodenly.

"We must go," Seemon urged. I walked before him unsteadily, lost in the pain in my body and the pain in my heart. Seemon paused in the doorway and handed Big a small casket.

"There is thirty gold koban in there. Please, use it as you see fit to look after our daughter. If there is anything left, give it to her when she is old enough to make good use of it."

Seemon turned me away and pushed me gently toward the hidden door in the Hidden House before I could change my mind and rush back to my Kazhua.

"She will be all right, won't she?" I whispered. I felt Seemon sigh. "We will come back for her, promise me."

"We will see her again, dear one. I know it."

I was sure I heard Kazhua cry and I turned back, but Seemon closed the door firmly and the sound was cut off.

I wept with her.

TWENTY-TWO

> How can I describe
> Colors to you when you are
> Blind to all my words?

The only memory I still have of the first weeks of
our journey is the sound of wild geese.

Every waking moment, I heard them. I was very ill and I
thought they were flying alongside us to wish me well.
Seemon told me later that they were not geese at all, but
seagulls. I had never seen or heard a seagull, but I knew
perfectly well what a wild goose sounded like, so I knew he
was wrong.

I didn't bother to argue with him. What was the point?
What did the song of a bird—no matter which bird—
matter compared to the loss of my daughter? I sobbed so
long and so much I began to wonder how it was possible for
my head to contain so many tears.

Seemon cried with me, holding me in his arms and
telling me over and over again that we had no choice. That
we had to leave our daughter or we would all have died.

And—after a while—that there would be other children born to us.

I hated him for that. How could I love children as yet unborn when my own dear Kazhua was left far behind me? I pushed him away and for a long time refused the comfort of his arms. I had to give in when the ache in my breasts became too much for me to bear. Seemon held me tenderly and I offered him my nipple silently. I almost cried with relief as my milk was drawn out of me by his lips, and then I did cry, silently so he would not notice, as I thought that it should have been my baby, not my husband, who suckled there.

I began to think the gods were intent on tormenting me. As if the loss of my child wasn't terrible enough, as the days went by I began to dwell more and more on Auntie. Images of her lying in my lover's arms rose unbidden to my thoughts. Had she also gone to his house? Laid with him in his strange bed. Laughed—as I had laughed—when the feather softness of his mattress had closed around me? Had he taken her in the tea house when I was there and might have heard them?

Bitterness consumed me and I turned my face from Seemon.

"Terue, what is it? Is it Kazhua? I promise you, I miss her just as much as you do."

No, you don't, I thought silently. *You can't. You made her with me, but you didn't give birth to her. Never had her suckle at your breast. You are not her mother.* I glanced at him and saw the pain in his face and thought he had no right to be hurt and suddenly I was angry.

"I wasn't thinking about Kazhua," I lied. I thought about her almost every waking moment. At night I dreamed of her. "Why didn't you tell me that Auntie was your lover?"

He stared at me as if my words had been spoken in a language he didn't understand. For a heartbeat, I wondered if Big had lied to me. Then he closed his eyes and his face lowered and I knew Big had not lied.

"How long have you known?"

"Big told me. While I was locked in my room, waiting for you to return," I said bitterly. "I didn't want to believe him, but it's true, isn't it?"

"I'm sorry," he whispered. "Yes, it is true."

"Why? Why her?"

Ah, but that was the very heart of the thing! Why Auntie? Had it been a geisha from the Floating World, even a courtesan, my hurt would have been so much less. But Auntie!

"I couldn't help it," he said defensively, and I almost laughed. The age-old excuse of any man found out in wrong-doing. It wasn't my fault. I couldn't help it! I waited in silence. I would not help him. "I was introduced to Hana almost as soon as I came into Edo. She was very kind to me at first. Don't forget, I was in Japan to make the acquaintance of the greatest men. And she knew everybody. She introduced me to them all and eased my path because they trusted her. More than that, she corrected my language and manners in such an elegant way I hardly knew she was instructing me. She made me *feel* Japanese. I was very grateful to her."

"So grateful that you took her as your lover. How could you!"

Seemon rubbed his hands over his face. "Terue, if I had seen you first, there would have been nobody else for me. But I didn't know you even existed then. And Hana is a very attractive woman." I shook my head and he smiled ruefully. "She is. You only see her as your Auntie, not as a man would see her. She is a pretty woman, and very amusing company. I promise you, those of my new acquaintances who suspected about it envied me greatly."

My world turned around me. Auntie, attractive and sought after? The terrible woman who had beaten us all into submission with her cane and even more with her acid words? The woman who could terrify each of us geisha into obedience with no more than a single look? Then I remembered the geisha in the tea house gossiping about Auntie. Saying that in her younger days she had had the greatest yakuza on Edo at her feet. So much so that he had bought the tea house and the Hidden House for her so she would never want for money. What utter fools all these men were!

"Did she come to you in your house?" I had to know. "Did you make love to her in your bed?"

"No." He sounded so surprised by the question, I believed him. "Never. She always insisted that we go to the Hidden House. And even there, never to her apartment. Always to the secret room. I asked her once if she was ashamed of me, and she said not at all, but it was because she delighted in me being her secret joy. That she wanted to keep me to herself and that nobody in the whole of the world was to know about us."

I knew instinctively that Auntie had been deluding herself. The geisha in the Hidden House had known, but in their love of me had not told me. Did I wish they had? I supposed not. Then I remembered how we had first made love in the secret room and I was angry again.

"Why did you take me there? How could you make love to me in the same place that you had *her*?"

His jaw dropped in surprise. "I wanted you," he said simply. "I was so frantic, it was the first place I thought about. I knew we would be safe there, and once I got you alone, we would be able to make plans to meet again somewhere else. It never occurred to me that it mattered."

Tamayu had often sneered at her patrons. And her lovers, as well.

"Men are all the same," she insisted. "They just don't think like we do. In fact, when they're in lust, they don't think at all."

I had thought her harsh at the time, but now I understood that she was right. Seemon had not been thoughtless. Rather, he had simply not thought at all. I had thought him different. I was wrong.

"Forgive me, please?" He knelt on the floor at the side of our berth. "I can't undo the past. But I promise you, as soon as I found you, I had no interest at all in Hana."

"But you kept on seeing her," I said coldly. I needed to know the whole of the truth before I could begin to forgive.

"Yes. I felt I had to. She had been very kind to me and I knew that she was at least a little in love with me. How could I just tell her that it was over, that I had found somebody else and wasn't interested in her anymore?"

I stared at him incredulously. That was exactly what a Japanese man would have done. It was only what Auntie— Hana—would have expected. And how was keeping her hanging on, wondering what she had done wrong, any better than telling her the truth straight away? Seemon was staring at me imploringly and I shook my head.

"Seemon," I said wearily. "If the day ever comes when you tire of me, please tell me at once. Don't make excuses. Just tell me."

"That day will never come."

He raised himself on his elbows and lay beside me. He meant it, I knew.

My anger spent itself and drained away. He was right.

The past was over and done with. Nothing either of us could say had the power to change a single moment of it. He fell asleep in my arms and I lay beside him, wishing it was Kazhua who was snuggled up to me.

He was asleep almost immediately. I was exhausted from our confrontation, but sleep would not come to me and I lay awake for a long time, my thoughts whirling aimlessly.

As I finally dropped into sleep, I realized that for the first time I could no longer hear the song of the wild geese.

TWENTY-THREE

It is only when
The past is put in its place
One can move forward

I hung onto Seemon's arm for balance, bewildered as it seemed that the solid earth was still rocking beneath my feet. He held me tightly and spoke reassuringly.

"Don't worry. The motion of the sea has gotten into your legs. In an hour or two, you'll be fine."

We walked along the dock as unsteadily as a man who had drunk far too much sake. And Seemon was wrong. I was not fine. My legs, indeed, did recover their balance. But my head did not.

In spite of the fact that he told me again and again that he was just as much a stranger here as I was, I could not believe him. If that was true, why then did everybody in this small settlement on the American coast seem to find their way to our lodgings? Invitations were pressed on us. We were invited to parties, to dine, to go for meals in the countryside. Seemon said these were called "picnics" and assured me I would love them. He was right to a certain extent. At least they meant I could sit comfortably on my heels for a while.

I was bewildered and asked why these strangers were so interested in us? Had we been back in the Floating World— and how I longed for that to be so!—the best we could have hoped for would have been to be ignored. In the flower and willow world, *gaijin* were sneered at. People drew their robes back when a Dutch trader passed, concerned that they would be contaminated in some way by their touch. Out of all the *gaijin* in Edo, only Seemon, with his grasp of Japanese and his willingness to learn our way of life, had been accepted. I had fully expected to be treated as a foreign barbarian here in my new world. After all, wasn't that exactly what I was?

"They find you fascinating." Seemon smiled at my confusion. "The women look at you in envy, and the men envy me for having you with me. You are truly beautiful, Terue. No matter where you are."

I managed a smile at his words, but even Seemon confused me. I thought that he was a different man here in his own world. He seemed more comfortable than he had been in the Floating World. More relaxed. And above all, at home. Whereas I was now the stranger. Sometimes, he forgot I spoke hardly any English and began a sentence in Japanese only to change to English halfway through. At first, this angered me greatly and I snapped at him. He always apologized, but still constantly forgot. After a while, I stopped asking him to speak to me only in Japanese and instead listened carefully to his words. It made little sense to begin with, but gradually, I pieced together full sentences, and before we left the settlement of Yerba Buena, I could understand what the rest of the *gaijin* were saying if they spoke slowly and I concentrated very hard. I did not want to appear foolish by trying to speak English badly, so I simply pretended I didn't understand them. Besides, I soon found that if the *gaijin* thought I couldn't understand what they were saying, they spoke freely in front of me.

"She's supposed to be one of those exotic Japanese dancing girls. What do you call them? Geisha, isn't it?"

The older woman smiled at me and offered me food, a strange sort of cake that was far too sweet for my taste. Still, politeness insisted I take it and pretend to enjoy it as well. I nodded and smiled and swallowed the insult along with the food.

"I suppose she's quite pretty if you like really tiny women." Her companion shrugged. "My Sam thinks she's divine. Typical man. Just because she's so small and looks as if she's made from porcelain, he thinks she needs looking after."

"They're supposed to be married, aren't they? But I notice she doesn't wear a wedding band. Do you think maybe they went through some heathenish sort of wedding ceremony in Japan?"

"Maybe. Still, even if they did, it's not going to mean a thing here, is it?"

Both women laughed. I hid my face behind my fan and watched them watching me. I was very glad when Seemon asked me if I thought I was well enough to travel again.

"How do you feel about setting off soon? If you still feel unwell, we can stay here for as long as you feel you need to."

I still ached, although I knew that the feeling was more for the loss of Kazhua than anything physically wrong. And I wanted, more than anything, to get to Seemon's home. To begin my new life as his wife. Perhaps even, and I astonished myself with the thought, to make another baby. Not to take my darling Kazhua's place, never that. But my arms ached to cradle a child, and the love I had never been able to offer my lost child overflowed my senses.

"I'm ready to go," I said promptly. I was puzzled to find Seemon appeared less than eager.

"You're sure? It's a very long journey, and it's not going to be pleasant. And we're not going straight to my home." My spirits sank. Where else was there for us to go? Seemon saw my disappointment and put his arms around me tenderly. "I must go to Washington first. Report back to my taskmasters. Hand over my diary and answer their questions. As soon as I'm done there, we can go home."

"I suppose I must be grateful to them." I managed a smile. "After all, if they hadn't sent you to Japan, we would never have known the other existed. Tell me about your home. Will I like it there?"

I felt him tense and immediately I was worried.

"You're going to find things are very different in Virginia to what they are here." He hesitated and added quickly, "But I'm sure you'll be happy there."

He spoke in Japanese and I understood instinctively that he wanted to impress on me the importance of his words. The journey didn't worry me greatly. After all, I had already traveled halfway around the world and survived. And how could Virginia be so different to Yerba Buena? It was still in America, wasn't it?

"I want to go, of course. What's different about it?"

"Yerba Buena is a very small place. Oh, I know the people here are all very proud of their settlement, and they insist in a few years it will be a big town, but at the moment it's nothing more than an outpost. Virginia is a very old place. People have lived there for centuries." He paused for thought and I stared at him, silently urging him to go on. "I was born and brought up there. My family have been there for generations. Before I went to Washington with my uncle, I thought my hometown must be the grandest place in the whole of America. I soon found that it was actually only a small place, compared to Washington. But the people who live there are very proud of Virginia, and of their heritage. They are perhaps a little set in their ways and don't take kindly to anything new."

"Just like Edo," I said drily.

"No, not at all like Edo, dearest. I wish it were. But no matter. I know they'll love you, Terue-chan. Just as much as I do."

I shrugged off his words and waited impatiently while a strange man fiddled with an odd-looking machine that Seemon said was going to "take our photograph." A few days later, I stared in awe at a perfect picture of the two of us standing side by side. How tall and handsome Seemon was! I told him so and he laughed at me. It was strange. This photograph seemed to reflect me far more clearly than any mirror ever had. I stared at the photograph for a long time. This was what other people saw, then. My breath caught in my throat as I wished beyond anything that I could get a copy of it to my dear Kazhua, that she might know her mother next time I saw her.

We set off the next day. All our new friends in Yerba Buena came to wave us off and I was touched. I had been wrong about the women not liking me, I decided. After all, their words had been far kinder than anything the people of Edo had ever said about the *gaijin*! I rather thought I would like to come back here one day. But in a future that was far distant. First, I was going to Seemon's home. To meet his family.

The thought worried me. I was torn. Much as I wanted

to go to his home, to the place that was to become *my* home, I was deeply afraid his family may not be happy with his choice of wife. And if they hated me, what then? I would have liked to have shared my worries with Seemon, but I did not. It would have been too much like insulting the family I had not yet met. Finally, I admitted to myself that I was pleased we were going to Washington first, to postpone the inevitable for a while longer.

But getting to Washington was another thing entirely. The journey was long and difficult and dreary. Our carriage jolted and rattled until my poor bones shrieked for relief. When we did stop—for food and to spend the night—the food was dreadful and the beds were not only hard but full of bugs, which seemed to dote on me. I scratched and scratched until my poor skin was raw. They ignored Seemon entirely, and that annoyed me greatly.

"Will there be bedbugs in Virginia?" I asked, and wondered why he winced.

"No. I can assure you, you will find no bedbugs in our house."

There were no bedbugs in our hotel in Washington either. That pleased me greatly. In fact, the whole of Washington delighted me.

In Yerba Buena, the thing I had missed above all was the hustle and bustle of the Floating World. Although Washington was nothing like my old home, at least it was busy and noisy and full of people, and I loved it instantly.

Seemon took me around the city on our first day, and after an hour my mouth ached from the constant smile on my lips. I sensed that the *gaijin* here were different from the people in Yerba Buena. They were obviously curious about my kimono and *geta* and stared openly at me, but there was no malice at all in it. I overheard a few of the women whispering as we passed and was delighted when I understand they were saying they found me beautiful, "like a living doll" as one elderly lady murmured to her husband. I had no need to hear his reply to know he agreed with her. I could see it in his expression.

Only one thing terrified me in Washington.

We turned a corner, and I stopped dead. My hand flew to my mouth and I gasped in shock.

"Seemon, stop." I tugged at his sleeve and tried to back away. "Look, over there." I was so distressed I forgot my manners and pointed. "It's an *onryo*. Can't you see it? It's following close behind that man. Please, you must go and warn him he's in danger!"

Seemon's gaze followed my pointing finger. I was outraged when he laughed out loud. If I had dared, I would have dashed across myself and told the poor man about the vengeful spirit that was almost as close as his shadow.

"Terue-chan." Seemon took my hand and squeezed it gently. "I'm sorry I laughed at you. But you've no need to worry. He's not a spirit at all. I promise you, he's flesh and blood."

I shook my head, disbelieving. This was really a man then? Or did this strange new world have such powers that they could tame spirits and make them follow at their master's heels like a faithful dog?

"But his skin is black," I pointed out dubiously.

"There are many black people in America." Seemon shrugged, as if it was of no consequence. "When we get to Virginia, you'll find lots of them on my family's plantation. They work for us."

"All black people are servants, then?"

"In this part of America, yes. Don't worry your dear

head about it. You'll soon get used to seeing them about the place when we get home."

I was deeply suspicious, but as the *onryo* followed its master peaceably, I decided not to pursue my concerns. Apart from anything else, I had no desire to attract its attention. And I had something else to be anxious about. If Seemon's family was wealthy enough to have many servants, what would they think about him bringing a penniless geisha home for his bride?

Seemon was deeply unhappy when he discovered his uncle was not in Washington to greet him.

"I thought he would be back from England by now. He did get back, but he was sent on to Rome soon after," he told me glumly. I was unhappy as well. But for a different reason. I had hoped to get some clue from his uncle how I would be received in Virginia.

I soon found out.

TWENTY-FOUR

Moonlight lies on the
Path to enlightenment. My
Road is still too dark.

"You killed him, Simon. Just as surely as if you took a knife and slid it between his ribs. I knew no good would come of you going off to that heathenish country for years, but even I never believed it could be this bad."

Seemon's mother reminded me of Gin. She was as tall and slender as my friend, and her hair was as startlingly white. It was piled up on top of her head in an elaborate style that was very similar to Gin's. As she was dressed from head to foot in black, her hair appeared almost luminous in contrast. And she actually held a fan clenched in her hand, even though she used it with no grace at all, flailing at the air in front of her face as though she was intent on punishing it for being so fiery. I couldn't understand that at all. It was hot and humid, but it reminded me very much of summer in Edo and I was very comfortable. For the moment, at least.

Then I saw Seemon's rigid expression and understood that his mother's words—spoken very rapidly and with an accent that made them difficult for me to understand—were upsetting him deeply. Somebody had died, that was clear. I listened to Seemon's—or as it appeared I must now call him, "Simon"—reply and felt his anguish.

"Mother. This is not the time to discuss blame for Papa's death. I'm deeply sorry, but I had no way of knowing he had died. What happened?"

"His heart," she snapped. That, at least, I understood. But if his heart had failed him, how could Simon be to blame? I was not left in doubt for long. "The doctor told me he had to put heart failure on the death certificate, but he agreed with me. It was really grieving for the son who might as well have been dead that killed him." She finished on a note of triumph.

Simon was rigid, although whether with anger or grief I couldn't tell. I moved a step toward him and then paused, awkward. His mother glanced at me as if she had seen me for the first time. Odd, as I had seen her casting simmering, sideways glances at me from the second we had walked into the room.

"Very well. We'll talk later, when we're alone. What's this you've brought home with you? Thinking of using her for breeding, are you? Well, I suppose it would make an interesting combination. There's always a market for something novel in the way of slaves. Although she's such a scrap of a thing, I doubt she would be much good in that direction."

Simon's breath hissed between his clenched teeth. His hands were balled into fists, his body rigid. His mother had spoken casually, but I knew instinctively that her words were intended to wound him. And me.

"Terue is my fiancée, mother," he said evenly. "We are to be married as soon as it is proper. Although with Papa's death, I suppose that will be delayed until after a correct period of mourning."

She stared at Simon for as long as it took to draw a deep breath and then crumpled to the floor silently.

Simon rushed across and kneeled at her side, patting her hands and face gently. When she did not move, he placed his head on her breasts, listening for a heartbeat. His face was ashen, his lips moving soundlessly.

"Terue. I think she's dead," he called urgently. "The shock of me arriving home after so long away and just telling her we were to be married has been too much for her. Oh, God. It's all my fault. I've killed her as well as Papa."

He lifted one of her hands to her lips and kissed it repeatedly, moaning softly all the time. I hid a smile behind my hand. This was so like a kabuki performance, I was tempted to laugh out loud. Surely Simon could see his mother was play acting? But it appeared not.

He rocked back on his heels and shouted. "William. Quick, get in here. collapsed."

I wondered if the man had been listening outside the door. He had frightened me when we had first arrived at the house. He skin wasn't as black as the man I had seen in Washington, but he was much darker than anybody I had ever seen in Edo, and his tufty hair was a peculiar, rusty color that puzzled me. Simon had introduced me to him as soon as we got out of our carriage and he had smiled widely, bobbing his head in a gesture that was almost a bow. Simon had taken his hand and pumped it enthusiastically, which worried me. What if Simon was wrong and this really was a vengeful spirit out to steal our essential beings? But I supposed as Simon was still living and breathing, this strange creature must just be yet another sort of American.

Now, he pushed Simon aside gently.

"I think she just fainted, Master Simon." He walked briskly over to a gilded side table. I had thought when we entered the room that the huge amount of furniture in it was far too opulent for either comfort or taste, but remembering Simon's cluttered house in the Floating World, I had held my words in my mouth. William poured a large quantity of amber liquid into a very beautiful glass and came back quickly. "Your papa's death was a great shock to her. And I daresay you coming home so soon after was just too much for her. Could you lift her up for me, master?"

Simon put his arms beneath his mother's body clumsily. She tipped to one side like an overfilled sack. I caught William's glance and walked over quickly, taking the glass from his hand so he could help Simon lift his mother without causing her injury.

"Thank you, ma'am." William nodded his approval. "Could you just hold it to her mouth?"

I wasn't in the least surprised when she parted her lips at once. Whatever was in the glass smelled very pungent, but most of it went down her throat anyway. I wiped the dribble that ran down her chin carefully with my thumb, and I was certain that it was my touch rather than the contents of the glass that roused her to speech.

"Oh, what happened to me? I feel terrible. Simon, is that really you? Have you come home to me at long last?"

She stared around, her eyes rolling wildly. Simon sighed deeply with relief and spoke gently.

"Mama. Thank God you're all right. Of course it's me. You fainted, that's all. Nothing to worry about."

I saw the flash of anger that shot across her expression at Simon's last words. She was play acting again, and very badly. I sat back on my heels and regarded her with amusement. How Simon would laugh about it with me later, when we were alone.

"I fainted? You're sure that's all it was?" She placed her hand on her ribs. "My poor heart is racing. I shall go to bed at once. William, tell Suzanna to bring me up my cordial. And send a messenger for Dr. Andrew to come and see me tomorrow. That is, if you don't mind the upset, Simon?"

Her voice changed as she spoke to her son. It was soft, almost—and the thought made my skin crawl—girlish.

"Mama, of course not. All that matters is that you're well. Can you manage the stairs? Will you be all right?"

For a woman who appeared sure she was on the verge of death, she got to her feet surprisingly briskly.

"I must do my best. I'm so sorry, I can't think what came over me." She smiled pitifully. "Of course, you don't want me around, causing problems. Not when you've just got back. I daresay you and your...your fiancée have so much to talk about. I'll leave you to it, Simon, darling. I just know you'll want to sleep in your papa's room. It's just as he left it. After all, you're the master of High Grove now. William, see to it that *her* things are put in Simon's old bedroom. Goodnight, dear. I'll see you in the morning."

I watched her totter out with immense respect. Even Auntie could never have turned things to her own advantage with greater skill.

"She gonna to be fine, Master Simon," William said gently. "With all that brandy and a glass of her cordial as well, she'll sleep like a baby."

"Is she really ill, William?" Simon asked anxiously.

"She's just a bit over-excited." William scratched the

side of his nose and pulled a face. "She knew you was coming home sometime soon. Got your letter from Washington right enough. Maybe she just got a bit worked up, thinking about things."

Simon nodded and I felt him relax. I only wished that I could. My muscles were so tense I could feel my right leg jumping as it tried to go into a cramp. Everything was so very strange, so different from anything I had imagined. Out of all of it, the one thing I understood only too well was that my mother-in-law hated me on sight. That, I had expected. Had I married Lord Dai—or any other Japanese man for that matter—it would have been just the same. My mother-in-law would have spent her entire life until I arrived being bullied by her men-folk. First her father would have made it clear that as a female, she had no status in the family. Her brothers would have expected her to be at their command. And her husband would simply treat her as a servant, if she was lucky. Until her own sons married and brought their wives home to live in the family house, there would be no one of lower status than she was. Under the circumstances, of course, she would bully and demean her daughter-in-law. I had expected it, but that made me feel no better at all.

"I guess you're right. We'll all feel better in the morning. Are the bedrooms made up, William?"

"Sure are. Soon as she got your letter, the mistress gave orders to get the rooms put in order."

"Good. Come, dear. A good night's sleep is what we both need."

I slumped with relief. I was too wound up to even think about sleep, but the thought of lying next to Simon—and much more!—was enticing. I smiled at William and he bowed his head politely in return. I guessed that Simon liked him greatly, and I was pleased that he seemed to like me.

Simon helped me upstairs. Stairs still worried me a little. I had never even seen stairs inside a house in Edo, and my *geta*-clad feet still found them difficult to judge. This staircase was the grandest I had ever seen outside a temple. It was so wide we could both walk side by side up it, and it even had carpet running down the middle. My earlier worries about Simon being even richer than Lord Dai came back in a rush. Would I have to be adopted into a good family before Simon and I could marry correctly? I hoped not. I had no desire at all to wait for such lengthy formalities.

He paused outside a painted and gilded door and threw it open.

"There you are, Terue-chan. This is the bedroom I had as a boy. I'm sure you'll find it comfortable. You'll find the chamber pot under the bed, so no need to worry about finding your way about in the night. I'll show you over the house tomorrow, and if you feel up to it, we could go about the plantation a little so you can get the feel for things. I don't suppose we'll have any callers just yet."

He stood aside to let me enter. I turned, my arms half raised to welcome him to me. To my astonishment, he dropped a kiss on my forehead and walked away from me.

"Sleep well, dear one," he called. I poked my head out of the room and watched as he went through an identical door at least thirty steps down the corridor.

I was bewildered. Where was the pleasure I had anticipated? The delicious love-making that would go on until we were both exhausted? I tried to take comfort from the knowledge that this had been Simon's room for many years, but there was no trace of him that I could see. There was too much furniture. Well-polished solid pieces, each one crammed with vases—lacking flowers—and pieces of porcelain that seemed to me to have no purpose at all. There were prints on the wall, reproductions of scenery that was foreign to me and ships under full sail. The latter made me shudder. I had had enough of ships, thank you! My combs and brushes had been laid out on one of the few empty surfaces, and the doors of one of the tall pieces of furniture had been left open. I saw my kimonos and under things had been hung, ready for my use. But of Simon, there was nothing at all.

I made my mind up instantly. This room was not home to me. Without Simon, it could not hope to be. I slipped my *geta* off and walked softly down the carpeted corridor, counting my steps carefully until I was sure I was at the right door. I lifted my hand to knock politely and then laughed at myself. I was not a servant bringing tea! My lover was concealed behind this door. I had no need to ask to be allowed into his presence.

"Terue? Is that you?"

"Were you expecting somebody else?" I asked.

Simon was sitting up in the middle of an enormous bed. It was wider even than the one we had slept in in Washington. I blinked at it in surprise and then had to fight the urge to laugh.

"What are you wearing?" I asked, walking over to him. I took a fold of the material in my fingers and rubbed it with interest. Not a sleeping robe, more like a sack that enveloped Simon from his shoulders down to where he disappeared beneath the bedclothes.

"It's a nightshirt," he said defensively. "Terue-chan, what are you doing here? Didn't you like your bedroom?"

I threw off my own sleeping robe and climbed in beside

him. Fascinated, I discovered that his garment appeared to reach all the way to his ankles. No matter, that would soon be disposed of.

"My place is with you," I said simply and held my face up to be kissed. I sensed his reluctance and took matters into my own hands. Literally. I took his face in my fingers and held him tightly as I slid my lips over his mouth. I forced my tongue between his lips and knew whatever demon was haunting him had been vanquished as I felt him sigh and he kissed me back.

The terrible nightshirt entangled me dreadfully, but we were both laughing by the time I managed to drag it off his body. Simon slid his arms around my waist and lay against me, rubbing his face against my breasts like an affectionate cat. He needed to shave, and his infant beard tickled.

I had no time for preliminaries. Had we been in Japan, I would have subdued my desire somehow. I would have forced myself to wait through increasingly arousing caresses until I was sure we were both ready. But tonight— my first night in my new home—everything was different. I ran my hand down his belly and found his erect tree. I fingered it with immense pleasure, pulling his hood back and forth, sliding the silky skin between my fingertips until I heard him groan with pleasure. Still holding onto his tree tenderly, I guided his seeking fingers between my black moss, groaning in my turn as he reached into me, stroking and nipping my tender places.

I felt my fires building almost at once.

There had been little delight between us in Washington. At first, we had both been so drained from the terrible journey from Yerba Beuna that we fell into bed at night and slept the sleep of the dead. The only time I awoke before morning was when I dreamed of Kazhua, and even in the deepest sleep, I knew my dreams were illusions. Later, Simon had been taken from me day after day by the officials who had summoned him back, and when he returned he was so on edge that our love-making had been both quick and—for me at least—unsatisfying. Here it seemed that the joy we had had between us in Edo had returned, and I moaned out loud with pleasure and relief as his hands found my breasts.

I wasted no more time and simply slid myself across his waist, lowering my body on to his tree. I sensed him hesitate for a moment, and then it was too late for both of us. His rhythm increased at once, and I encouraged him with cries that were too urgent to form words.

My *yonaki* was upon me even more quickly than I had expected. I cried out loud with pleasure and was delighted when I realized that Simon was following close behind me. I felt his heat explode inside me and gripped him tightly until he was completely still. Only then did I slide off to lie contentedly at his side.

I was almost asleep when Simon spoke.

"Terue, you can't stay here. You must go back to your own room. But put your robe on first."

"Simon?" If it hadn't been for the sternness in his voice I would have thought he was joking. "Why? Why can't I stay here? With you, where I should be?"

"No. You can't." He sat up abruptly, as far away from me as he could manage in that horrible, soft mattress. "You can't stay here. It's not proper. You shouldn't have come to me at all. It's not right, with Papa barely cold in his grave. Anybody would think you were some sort of negro slave, rutting in lust."

My hand was about to run down his chest, but I

stopped, frozen in mid-air as I heard and understood what he was saying.

"I had thought I was no longer a slave, Simon," I said stiffly. "I thought I had left that behind me in Japan. But it appears that I was wrong. I'm sorry if I've offended you. I will go now."

I made to swing my legs out of the bed, but Simon grabbed my wrist and pulled me back.

"Terue, no. I'm sorry. I didn't mean it like that, not at all. You don't understand."

I lay beside him rigidly, his fierce grip holding me in place as my new world shattered into a thousand pieces around me.

"I was a slave in the Floating World. I understand that to you I am still a slave."

"No!" His voice was tormented. "You are not a slave here. You will never be a slave again. But you are my betrothed wife, and as such we must...we must behave ourselves. It's different here from how it was in Edo," he added lamely.

"Why?" I asked. "If I'm betrothed to you, why can't we lie together? And what does it matter if I'm a slave or not? I was a slave when I was a geisha. Auntie owned me. I could never pay her back for what she had spent on me and she would never have let me go to lead my own life. Lord Dai paid a fortune to deflower me. If I'd married him, I would have been his slave in turn."

I felt Simon shudder at my words. "You are not a slave here," he said slowly, emphasizing each word. "That is all in the past for you. This is your new life, and it's very important that you never tell anybody that you were treated as a slave in Edo. And especially you must never speak about being sold for your *mizuage* to Lord Dai."

"Why?" I was bewildered. None of that had mattered to us in Edo. What had changed?

"You remember the black-skinned man you saw in Washington? And you saw William and Suzanna here?" I nodded, lost. "They are all slaves. But not like you were in Edo, dear one. Most black people in America—certainly here in Virginia—are truly slaves. They are owned by whoever buys them. They can be sold again at the whim of their master. They must do as their master tells them or they will be punished. They cannot leave their home without getting a pass from their master. If they try to run away, they will be found and punished severely. If the master takes a fancy to a black woman, then she must go to him, no matter if she already has a husband. If the slaves have children, then they are also owned by their master. They have no hope of being free, ever. We have well over a hundred slaves here on the plantation. They're a measure of wealth. The more slaves a man owns, the more he can culti-vate his crops and the richer he is. That's just the way it is here. But you are going to be my wife, not a slave. Do you understand?"

I thought about it. I remembered poor Aki, sold to a brothel for daring to run away to her boy. I thought about my dear friends in the Hidden House, expected to give their bodies to any man who had enough money to buy them. I thought about Auntie keeping me a prisoner to force me to agree to marry Lord Dai. I thought about Simon telling me I was no longer a slave and wondered.

"Yes," I said finally. "I understand."

If Simon heard the doubt in my voice, he gave no sign of it. "Good." I felt him relax. "Dear Terue, you are free now and forever, and you are going to be my wife. That is all anybody here needs to know about you."

I closed my eyes tightly and took a deep breath before I asked the question that was uppermost in my mind.

"Then why I can't be with you?" I asked. "Must I wait until we are married to really be your wife? Why has that changed?"

"I told you." Simon sounded annoyed, but I had no idea why. "It's partly because I'm in mourning for Papa's death, but it's mainly because we're betrothed. In this country, a man does not lie with his fiancée—his betrothed—before they are married. It's unheard of. Except amongst the slaves, and nobody cares what they get up to," he added with unconscious cruelty.

I didn't want to look at his face. Instead, I stared at my hands. The hands that had caressed him to joy so many times. I heard his words, but I understood only one thing.

No matter how often he told me it wasn't so, here in his own world, Simon was ashamed that I had once been a slave.

TWENTY-FIVE

When you speak cruelly
To me your words fall like cold
Snowflakes on my face.

I sat uncomfortably at the table, concentrating on keeping my breakfast eggs on my fork long enough to get the food into my mouth. I was glad to have something to distract me.

Simon's words from the night before seemed a little less harsh in the morning light. Had I really expected this *gaijin* world to be like Edo? This was his home, not mine. It was natural that I should be the one who bent to his customs. Yet still, one thing astonished me.

Simon's mother appeared to have no recollection of her outburst at all. She smiled at Simon constantly. Told him how glad she was to have him home. Even said how proud his father had been of his adventures for the government. How he had known his heart condition was getting worse, but had tried desperately to hang onto life until Simon came back.

"I daresay she'll take a while to settle here." She nodded at me, showing a great many rather large teeth. I smiled back sweetly. "She needs to learn English, of course, to begin with. And no doubt everything will be very strange to her."

I stared at my cup silently, wondering how much of the vile liquid William had called "tea" courtesy compelled me to drink. It was horrible, and I knew I would never get used to it. I suppose I should have spoken then, told my new "Mama" that my English was quite good—not as good as Simon's Japanese, of course, but enough to get by—but I did not. I doubted she would speak directly to me even if she knew I understood her. It seemed to me that it would make her discourteous manner even worse if she continued to ignore me when she knew I understood her. One of us, at least, would be polite!

Simon turned to me, speaking in Japanese as he told me what his mother had said. I noticed that the words that had passed between them somehow seemed to have lost something in the translation. According to Simon, his mother had said that I would soon settle here and that she was delighted that he had brought me home as his bride.

Simon assured me that we would have time to ourselves that first day, and I had been anticipating it very much. But he was wrong.

We were barely out of the front door—his Mama had insisted I take a parasol as the sun was so hot. I thought she had seemed almost angry that I didn't find the weather at all oppressive—when a carriage came to a halt at the front door, dust billowing around its wheels.

"Damn it. The drums have sounded quickly." In spite of his angry words, Simon was smiling widely. He switched abruptly to Japanese. "Terue-chan, some of our neighbors have come to visit us already. I'm afraid our trip around the plantation must wait a little. No! Don't kowtow to them. Don't even bow. Just smile and lower your head a little."

I stiffened awkwardly, caught off balance. These appeared to be important people. I had automatically begun to lower myself to my knees to greet them with appropriate humbleness. But it seemed that was the wrong thing to do. And Simon was angry with me again, but I had no idea why.

I smiled at them as I had been told, hiding my hurt behind my smile.

"Mr. Sydney! Dear Mrs. Sydney! Johanna. How lovely to see you all again!"

"Simon!" A young girl sprang from behind the wide skirts of the woman Simon had called Mrs. Sydney. I thought she was perhaps twelve or thirteen. Almost a young woman in Japan, but here, still a child, something that was obvious from her behavior. I was thrust aside as she threw herself at Simon, wrapping her arms around his neck and squealing loudly with pleasure. "You've been gone forever! You look just the same, though. God, I expected to find you wearing a hat with a tassel on it and skirts instead of trousers, you've been amongst the celestials for so long!"

She smelled as if she had bathed in perfume. The scent was so strong I sneezed loudly and colored at my rudeness. I had noticed before that even the *gaijin* men seemed fond of wearing scent to mask the stink of the flesh they consumed and the fact that they had no idea how to wash properly. It was still strange to me. In Edo, even a crowd of Japanese would smell only of clean skin. Or at most of *jako*, the flower seeds that were folded into clothes in storage. *Jako* seeds smelled a little like musk geranium, and in such discreet amounts were very pleasant.

Simon was holding the girl at arms' length, but I could see he was pleased at her welcome. I tilted my parasol a fraction, and the movement caught his eye.

"Johanna, a very good day to you. May I present my fiancée, the lady Terue? And I was in Japan, not China."

I heard her parents gasp. Johanna glanced at them both and then burst out in hearty laughter.

"Oh, honestly, Simon! You are so naughty, teasing Mama and Papa like that. Why, she's just a high yellow negress! Pretty enough, but we got slave octoroons at home got as light skin as she has."

The silence fell around us like snow.

"Simon, take no notice of Johanna. Her mouth always did run away with her, and nothing's changed there." Mr. Sydney's booming voice broke the quiet abruptly. "Glad to have you back, that's for sure. And this lovely lady is your fiancée, you say? If all the Japanese gals are as beautiful as she is, I'm not at all surprised it's taken you so long to come back home."

I held my hand out to him and was confounded. He did not shake it, but instead raised it to his lips and gave the back a smacking kiss. Truly, Simon's mama had been right when she said I had much to learn.

Simon ushered us all back inside. I watched our visitors curiously. The man took out a large handkerchief and wiped his face and neck thoroughly. His wife immediately took out a pretty fan and wafted it in front of her face vigorously. Johanna was obviously deeply perplexed. She stared from Simon to me with the frank curiosity of innocence. Simon's mama came back in at the sound of their voices and greeted them with cries of delight before she, too, took out her fan and plied it briskly.

"Ain't it just too hot?" she demanded of nobody in

particular. I almost broke my silence to say this was nothing compared to Edo in the height of summer, but Mr. Sydney spoke first.

"It ain't the heat, it's the humidity that's the killer," he said firmly. "But look at this little lady here. Cool as a cucumber, even in that tight robe. Ain't she just something?"

His wife shot him an exasperated glance, but it was Johanna who spoke.

"Where did you find her, Simon? I never even seen a Japanese woman before. She ain't really a negro, then?"

Simon frowned and then shrugged resignedly. It was easy to see that Johanna was a favorite in this house, no matter how atrocious her manners. I simmered silently, waiting for his reply.

"Johanna, Terue is a Japanese lady of very high birth. She is as pure blooded as you or me, I can assure you. In fact, in Japan she was about to be forced into an arranged marriage with one of the highest nobles in the place until I rescued her and snatched her away from him."

"No!" Johanna's eyes were like saucers. She glanced at me and then rose, curtseying very prettily before she came across and stood in front of me.

"I sure am sorry," she apologized. "But I wasn't to know!"

Everybody laughed loudly at her contrite face, and I smiled myself.

"Well, ain't that really romantic!" Mrs. Sydney said. Even Simon's mama managed to look pleased. "I guess it will be a while before you can tie the knot, Simon? I mean, she's going to have to learn to speak English to start with. And of course, with your dear papa just passing away, it's not possible for you to even think about making arrangements until after the mourning period. I guess it'll be a year, at least, for you, Simone?"

For a moment, I thought she had spoken to Simon and glanced at him for his reaction. But it was his mama who spoke, and I was thoroughly confused. Simon had the same name as his mother?

"A year, at the very least," Mama Simone spoke firmly. "I think myself it will be a good deal longer. Of course, I shall never lose him in my heart." Mrs. Sydney nodded understandingly. "Of course, if Simon wishes it, he need only be in full mourning for the first year. But I'm sure he'll appreciate how much his mama feels her loss and he'll be happy to wait until I'm ready."

Simon murmured something I didn't catch and after a moment's respectful pause the chatter resumed. It seemed to me that the longer they talked the less I understood of the conversation. They all spoke so very quickly, and the words began to sound less and less like the language Simon had unwittingly taught me. And different still to how the Washington *gaijin* had spoken.

I was very pleased when they finally left. And horrified when Simon told me that they would be the first of many.

"Now the word is out that we're back, we can expect visitors every day." He shrugged. He saw my expression and spoke quickly. "Don't worry, you did well. Nobody expects you to be able to speak English, so it doesn't matter. Just look pleasant and you'll do fine. As we're in deep mourning, we won't be expected to return calls, and there's no question of us attending any parties or anything, so you'll have time to settle."

I was deeply curious about my new world, but Simon seemed to think I would be pleased to have some time to myself.

I supposed he was right.

TWENTY-SIX

My thoughts are as foam
On the sea. I try to grasp
Them and they are gone

"What is it, Terue?" Simon asked quietly. "You look unhappy."

I jumped guiltily, wondering if he had read my thoughts.

"Of course I'm not unhappy. As long as I am with you, I am content wherever I am. But I cannot stop my thoughts straying to our daughter. If she were here, then my happiness would be complete," I said honestly.

"I understand," Simon said quietly. "If only Kazhua were with us, our world would be perfect."

"Do you think she is well? That she is being cared for?" I spoke of my daughter longingly, immediately feeling the familiar, hellish ache in my body at the mention of her name.

"I think she must be well, and cared for," Simon said

quietly. "If it was otherwise, I'm sure that both of us would feel it in our hearts."

He put his arms around me and held me tightly, and I was very glad. I had longed for Simon's embrace when I awoke early that bright morning and had slid quietly into his bedroom before anybody except the house slaves was stirring.

"You still haven't made that clock show the right time," I said absently.

"It was stopped the moment Papa died, and it's not going to be set right until Mama comes out of mourning for him." He stroked my hair gently. "She takes these things very seriously."

I wondered how long she would mourn. As far as I was concerned, the sooner she put aside her black clothes and set the clocks right the better. The whole house seemed to sympathize with her loss.

"Will you be all right?" He grasped my hand and looked at me anxiously. "Mama insists I have to go with her into town, to see my godmother. Mama says she's been ill and has been asking for me. I think we'll be gone until this evening."

I would have laughed if he hadn't looked so worried. I had crossed an ocean without taking harm and he thought I might be in danger here, in his own home?

"Go," I said firmly. "I shall put on an old kimono and be comfortable and enjoy myself wandering about the house in peace."

"If you're sure?"

"Go!" I smiled at him. "Go visit your godmother, and don't worry about me."

I waited until the sound of the carriage wheels had died away before I slipped outside, delighting in the sunshine that caressed my face. The peaches on the lovely trees that arched the length of the drive outside the great house were beginning to ripen. I fingered those I could reach until I found one that gave beneath my touch and I plucked it and ate it greedily as I wandered through the garden. Slaves were working there, pulling up any weed that dared to show and clipping the bushes into shape. As I passed, they bowed their heads and shuffled their shoulders around their ears. I would have liked to have spoken to them, to ask them about their families, their lives, but none of them would meet my gaze, so I assumed it would not be courteous to question them and just smiled politely at them instead.

Oscar led me to William. The dog bounded up to me, huffing happily to himself as he capered around my legs. I patted his head and tickled behind his ears, pleased that he was so obviously delighted to see me. He dashed off again and then paused, looking back at me. I followed him. Why not? I was fond of the boisterous pup, and today my time was my own to do with as I liked.

"Missy Terue. I should have known it was you when Oscar dashed off and left me to fend for myself."

William got to his feet as I approached him. He had been sitting at the side of a small lake. Simon had brought me here and had warned me to be careful as the water was deeper than it seemed. William had a fishing rod pushed firmly into the soft earth at the side of the lake.

"There are fish in there?" I asked curiously. "Fish worth eating?"

"Sure are. Trout and bass. Both good for eating. Catfish as well, but the mistress don't like them so well. She says they taste muddy, but I get on well enough with the taste of them."

Oscar plonked himself down and I sat beside him more

cautiously, wriggling my toes happily in the sandy earth. William watched me and smiled. I was comfortable in his presence.

"William, are you a slave?"

He stared at me thoughtfully. He was so different from the slaves I had seen in the garden, and the men and women who worked in the house—none of them would even look at me, still less speak—that I wondered if I had made a mistake. But it seemed not.

"I am, Missy. Born a slave here at High Grove. Daresay I'll end my days as one as well. Just pray it's here and not somewhere I ain't comfortable."

"But you're not like the other slaves," I said. William tilted his head to one side and watched me as I pulled Oscar's silky ear through my fingers.

"Guess not," he said finally. "But why you interested?"

"I was as much a slave as you are, when I was in Japan," I said simply. "I was owned by somebody, just like you are. She was going to make me marry an old man. If Simon hadn't taken me away, I suppose I would have had to take him, in the end."

William stared at me. "Well, that may be so. But begging your pardon, missy, I guess you weren't in quite the same situation as slaves are here."

"I was," I protested. "I had no more freedom than you do, William."

William pursed his lips and stared at his rod. He seemed to make his mind up suddenly.

"I think maybe I'm a lot better off than the rest of the folk about the place. Nobody told you, I guess, that Master Simon and me had the same father?"

My mouth opened and closed, just like one of the fish in the lake. No words would come out. I hid my head in Oscar's silky coat to hide my dismay and confusion.

"I thought not." William smiled and shook his head. "Don't you worry about it, miss. Ain't nothing unusual in these parts. Nothing to be ashamed of neither."

I took courage from his kindness and looked at him questioningly.

"That's how I come to be favored." William smiled. "The old master took a real fancy to my mama. She was a truly good looking woman when she was young. I understand Mistress Simone was never what you could call a warm sort of lady, if you understand me?" I thought of Mama Simone's cool expression and colder words and guessed at once what William meant. I could not imagine Mama Simone ever taking pleasure in the delights of the futon. "The master took my mama to his bed soon as he saw her and she was his favorite for years. That'll seem odd to you, I guess?"

"No. Not at all. In Japan, it's normal for wealthy men to have a wife and concubines. Generally, they all live in the same house. The poorer men have to make do with visiting courtesans, but their wives still expect it."

I had surprised William, that was obvious.

"Well, I'll be damned. Maybe Japan is more like America than I would ever have thought. So my mama was the master's concubine, eh?" The thought seemed to amuse him as he laughed out loud, showing his teeth in a wide grin. "Anyway, that's how I come to be a house slave. I worked in the kitchen when I was a young 'un, fetching and carrying. When I got a bit older, master told me off to look after his horses and the carriages. And when the old house-steward died, the master put me in his place. I thought when my mama died, I was gonna be sent back to the fields, but Mistress Simone said no, I was to stay in the house."

That puzzled me greatly. "Why? I can't imagine that Mama Simone would be happy to have the son of her husband's concubine in the house. Begging your pardon, William," I added politely.

"No offense taken, missy," he said promptly. "You're right. Mistress was always picking fault with my mama. Whatever she did, it wasn't right. Mistress had her whipped time after time. Said she was a cheeky slave and was too fond of talking back."

"And Simon's father allowed it?" I was amazed. "But she was his concubine. She had his son. Why didn't he stop it?"

"Because mama was nothing more than a slave," William explained patiently. "He might have been fond of her, after a fashion, but she weren't nothing to him, and the mistress was his wife. Mama always said he was a good man and she was thankful he told the overseer not to lay it on too hard when she got a whipping."

I shook my head. The ways of men were truly strange!

"So why didn't she throw you out of the house when your mama died?"

"I thought a lot about that, missy." William nodded for so long I thought he had lost track of my question. But I was wrong. "In the end, I decided she done it to punish the master. While I was there in plain sight, she would never let him forget how he had doted on my mama. I saw her looking at me sometimes, and she was sort of gloating, if you know what I mean. I just knew that ever they had an argument, she would throw how he had been good to my mama in his face. How sweet she was, letting me stay in the house. That sound like nonsense to you, Missy?"

I shook my head. Not nonsense at all. It made perfect sense to me. William seemed pleased. We both sat in silence for a while. William watched his rod, and I stroked Oscar, thinking about all he had told me.

"You're a great deal older than Master Simon, aren't you?" I asked finally.

"That I am, Missy. That was another reason the mistress hated my mama so much. For the longest time, it looked like she wasn't going to have any children of her own. None that survived, anyway. She caught pregnant a couple of times, but always lost the babes before they had any chance of being born alive." I thought of my own, dear Kazhua and the pain was intense. "When she managed to hold on to Master Simon, the whole house was celebrating for weeks. That's how he came to be called Simon, after her. But there weren't no more babies after Master Simon. Not any sign of them."

I stared at the placid lake water. Time after time I had held my breath when my monthly courses had shown signs of being late, only to be disappointed when they arrived. Could it be that Simon was going to be like his father and that only one baby would be given to us?

I was in a very somber mood as I walked back to the big house.

TWENTY-SEVEN

Rain falls on my face
With the same pleasure as a
Much loved friend come home.

"*J* heard Samuel Jacobs lost more than a dozen slaves last week. Just spirited away into clean air. Seems like there's some folk around think they're above the law. Of course, old man Jacobs got the hounds out to hunt 'em down, but they found nothing at all. And further south, I understand it's even worse."

Simon was furious, I could tell from his voice. Mama Simone nodded sympathetically. I tried to look concerned, but it was difficult. My sympathy was with the slaves, and I wished them well. I had heard the hounds baying, night after night, and it was only too easy to think what it must feel like to know they were on your heels, intent on ripping your flesh with their hungry teeth. And I doubted that any of the planters would think there was anything at all wrong in allowing them to tear apart any slave who had been foolish and uppity enough to attempt to escape. Mama Simone obviously agreed.

"It's organized, Simon. I'm sure of it. Any slave who's stupid enough to try and make a run for it on their own would never get more than a mile or two. Any piece of white trash is going to ask them for their pass in hope of picking up a reward if they get a slave on the run. And none of them can swim, so no hope of getting across open water to put the hounds off the scent." She shook her head angrily. "Of course, if everybody treated their slaves as well as we do, they wouldn't want to run away in the first place."

I stared at her, barely able to believe she wasn't making a joke in the worst possible taste. The slaves on High Grove plantation were treated well? It was only a month or so ago that all of the slaves were summoned in from the fields to watch one of the young women being whipped for some misdemeanor. Mama Simone had suggested that I should witness it as well.

"After all, she's going to be mistress when I pass away. She needs to know how these things are done."

Simon pulled a face but agreed.

I watched in horror as the slave was stripped to her waist and hauled to the stocks, where her neck was forced into a large central hole, and the top wood slammed down to hold her fast. Why, I wondered, didn't she shout and scream and struggle? But she did not. Instead, she stared at the ground, her face blank.

"Ready, Master Simon?" The overseer, a man I saw rarely, raised a whip with a number of lashes dangling from the handle. "How many you want me to give her?"

"Start off with twenty. See how she takes it."

The girl started to scream after the first few lashes. I watched dumbly, praying to any god that was listening that the sound of my own heartbeat might drown out her agony. But the gods were elsewhere that day, and after a bare minute or two, I could stand it no longer.

"Simon, stop him. He's killing her."

"She has to be punished, dear." Simon patted my hand gently. "If we let Shula get away with it, the others will think they can do the same." He spoke loudly, to be heard over her howls.

"What did she do?" I asked, hoping that somehow her crime might be so bad that it deserved this terrible pain.

"She ran away. We sold her daughter to another plantation. When Tom caught her—" He nodded at the overseer. "—she told him she was trying to get to the child. Stupid bitch. She must have known she would have been sent back to us, even if she'd managed to reach her daughter."

I stared at my man in complete horror. Could he not understand Shula's pain? Had he not felt the same when we had left our own daughter far behind us? Perhaps he read my thought in my face. He shook his head and frowned.

"I know it might seem harsh to you, dear. But she's young and healthy. She'll have lots more children. In a few months' time, she'll have forgotten she ever lost this one."

"Simon, please. No more," I whispered hoarsely. He sighed and glanced at Tom. I guessed the first twenty lashes had been administered, as the overseer was standing with his whip raised, obviously waiting for instructions. Simon shrugged.

"Give her another ten, Tom. And then let her go. My lady here is tender-hearted, so I'll spare Shula for her sake." He raised his voice, so the entire crowd of slaves could hear him. "Let this be a lesson to all of you. I'm letting Shula off lightly because my lady here feels sorry for her. Not for any other reason. But if any one of you tries to run away, you'll get your own punishment and hers as well. Understand?"

The crowd murmured, stirring amongst themselves. I was amazed to find Mama Simone was looking at him approvingly.

"A nice touch, that. Well done, Simon. Makes you look merciful but at the same time gives the slaves a warning they're not going to forget for the future. Lets them know that none of them can get away with mischief, no matter what."

Shula's cries tailed off as Tom lowered his whip for the final time. He beckoned at one of the slaves and he ran forward at once with a bucket in each hand. Tom threw the contents on Shula and she screamed again.

"Saltwater," Simon explained. "Might sting a bit now, but at least her skin won't suppurate."

"You'll sell her on now, Simon?" It was barely a question. Mama Simone was obviously sure she already knew the answer.

"Soon as she heals," Simon said. "Always a market for a fertile slave down Carolina way. Should be far enough away."

Simon and his mother exchanged a glance I could not interpret. I walked back to the house between them, wondering if I would get home before I was sick.

TWENTY-EIGHT

All are born to die
The important thing is what
You do with your life

*N*o matter how I tried, I could not forget Shula's painful humiliation. Bewildered, I asked Simon time and again why running away to find her daughter had been such a crime that she had needed to have the skin whipped from her back. He shrugged my questions off impatiently, as if I was deliberately trying to annoy him by refusing to understand the obvious.

"It's just the way it is, Terue-chan," he snapped. "You can't be sentimental about slaves. If we're too lenient with them, they'll think they can get away with anything. Don't worry your head about it."

The sound of carriage wheels distracted him. I heard his voice exchanging pleasantries with Mama Sydney, and a moment later he left the house, calling that he was going to the drying sheds with Mr. Sydney. That pleased me greatly. Papa Sydney never said anything impolite to me, but then again, he had no need to. I could feel his lust lingering on me whenever he was in the same room as I was. He made me shudder. I didn't mind Mama Sydney, but I found Johanna very hard work. Now, Mama Sydney closeted herself with Mama Simone, and it was made clear with turned shoulders and lowered voices that I was not welcome.

I really didn't feel comfortable with Johanna at all, which was unfortunate as she had taken a great liking to me. But she was so very difficult to talk to! Ask her a question, and her answer was often simply "yes" or "no," after which she simply stayed silent, obviously waiting for me to take up the threads of the conversation again. Sometimes, I wondered if she might be a bit simple. For sure, whenever I was alone in her company I wished I had never let it be known that I had learned to speak English.

"Don't pull him about, Johanna," I said. She was fussing Oscar roughly, far beyond the bounds of his patience. "He's not some sort of doll."

She pouted and stared at me and tugged hard on Oscar's silky ears yet again.

"You can't tell me what to do." Her lower lip jutted stubbornly. "You're only a high-class black whore."

"Am I? And who told you that?" I blinked at the vicious words.

"Oh, nobody." She saw my expression and grinned. "Well, nobody actually told me. But I heard Papa say it to Mr. Withers."

"Really? And what else did Papa say?"

"He said much the same as I did the first time I saw you." Joanna smirked, suddenly talkative. "He said you were the best looking high yellow slave he'd ever seen, but that there was no way Mrs. Beaumont would ever let Simon marry a foreigner. Especially one who had been no better than a whore in her own country."

I managed a tight smile. "Is that so? Well, it's a good job Simon doesn't feel the same way, isn't it?"

"Papa says it's only a matter of time before Simon comes to his senses." She chirped, pulling at Oscar's ears again. He gave a warning growl, but this time I let her continue. "And when he does, he says there's going to be a queue a mile long at your door, competing to see who's next in line. What did he mean by that, Terue?"

"I have no idea. I told you not to do that," I added as Oscar snapped at her and Johanna snatched her fingers away.

Her unconscious cruelty blasted away the barriers I had erected around my own thoughts. Of course, I knew that Simon was in mourning for his father's death. He had explained that we would not be able to marry until the proper period of mourning had been observed. Even if he had not, I would have seen from the approval showered on Mama Simone by the good people of Virginia that the family was only doing what was expected. I had agreed willingly that we could not marry at once. But as the months dragged on, I had begun to question to myself: how long? Still, I pushed my concerns away, convincing myself that all would be well if only I had the patience to understand the way things were in my new world.

Johanna had shattered my illusions. I was bitterly ashamed of my own foolish naivety. Simon had no intention of marrying me. How could he, when I was just as low born as Shula and the rest of the slaves on the plantation? And not just a slave, but a whore as well. Of course, my place was as his concubine, not his wife. I cringed at the knowledge that everybody had understood that except me. I felt ill when I thought how they must have laughed at me behind my back.

When Simon came to my bed that night, as had become his habit, I was waiting for him impatiently. I could have taken him to one side earlier, told him I needed to speak to him in private. But it had seemed to me that the words that needed to be said had to be spoken here, in the place where he had deceived me for so long.

I had drawn the shrouding drapes fully back, allowing the cold, white moonlight to flood in. Simon paused on the threshold, his head on one side, like a dog sensing a strange scent.

"Good evening, Seemon-san," I said in Japanese, very politely.

His eyebrows shot up in surprise. "And good evening to you, Terue-chan. Why so formal all at once?" he replied in Japanese. Suddenly, he was the old Simon again, the man I loved. For a moment, I was tempted to back away. Then he was turning casually aside from me, loosening his tie, and I made my mind up. I had to know for sure.

"You saw Mr. Sydney today," I said. He paused with his jacket half off and frowned at me. "I wonder what you spoke about? Did you perhaps tell him how exotic we oriental women are? Did you discuss the details of what we do together?"

An image rose in my mind of Papa Sydney leaning forward to catch Simon's words. His eyes wide and sweat beading his forehead as Simon murmured about how Japanese women were skilled in the arts of love. How to *them*, things that would make an American woman faint were perfectly normal. I watched Simon's face intently, and I was certain he flinched, although when he spoke he simply sounded confused.

"What on earth are you talking about, Terue? I did see Sydney today, but it was only to discuss tobacco prices." His jacket finally removed, he sat on the bed at my side and smiled at me fondly. "Now, what nonsense have you got in your head all at once?"

"Do you think of me as one of your slaves, Simon?" I stared at his face as I spoke. "Is that why we haven't married?"

As soon as my words were out, I knew I was right. Fury contorted his face and made it ugly. There for a moment, and then gone. He laughed shortly.

"Terue. What is all this rubbish? Don't be so silly. Has Johanna been rattling some nonsense to you? She's so spoiled, I swear it's turned her brain. Take no notice of her. I love you. You know I do."

He sounded so sincere, I almost believed him.

"Do you really love me? All the other planters are happy enough to keep a pretty slave for their pleasure. Why should you be any different? Don't touch me!" I almost shouted the words as Simon reached out to me. He jerked back as if he had been stung. "When we left Japan, we were going to be married as soon as we came here. But that didn't happen."

"That was before I found out Papa had died." He drew back, frowning angrily. "I explained it all to you, Terue. How we couldn't be married until the mourning period was over. I thought you understood."

"Oh, yes. And how long is mourning going to last for, Simon? Another six months? Another year?"

He stared sulkily at the bedclothes. "You don't under-stand," he muttered. "Things have to be done properly."

I was so angry, I was shaking. Simon seemed not to have noticed.

"Oh, forget it. We'll talk about it later, dear." He threw the bedclothes back. "A lot later."

My fury erupted. Before I knew I was going to do it, my hand lashed out and struck Simon a ringing blow across his face. I am small, and my hands are tiny, but I put the full force of my anger and disgust in the slap. His head rocked back and he stared at me in amazement.

"Oh, now I see what all the nonsense is about." A smile stretched his lips. "You're playing a new game tonight, are you? Well, I guess two of us can play at that."

He lunged forward, his teeth meeting in my neck. Had I been aroused, the pain would have been exquisite. As it was, it was simply painful. I would have pushed him away, but Simon had both my hands imprisoned in his grip. I struggled furiously, wriggling and shoving with my shoulders, but the more I tried to get away the more excited Simon became. I could feel the heat of his body and his tree digging into my thigh. I wondered cynically how much of the passion was genuine and how much was designed to distract me. Suddenly, I knew how to stop him.

I stopped fighting. Went as limp as a dead animal. Allowed him to bite at my breasts and push his knee between my thighs without so much as moving. It took a few moments, but finally he raised his head and stared at me in confusion.

"What? Terue, what is it?" I detached myself from his grip and leaned away. "You don't really believe I don't love you, do you? Would you be here if I didn't?"

He sounded deeply hurt. I ignored it and spoke carefully.

"I believe that you thought you loved me in Japan. But I also believe that here things are different. That you made a mistake in thinking you wanted me as your wife. You would be happy to keep me as your concubine, and then you could marry an American girl. A white girl of your own class. I think you were happy to leave our daughter behind so you didn't have to own her as your child. And if that is the case, there is no future for us. I will go."

"You can't believe all that nonsense!" He was sitting bolt upright, staring at me and frowning. "Of course I love you. I would have given anything to be able to bring Kazhua with us, you must know that. How can you even think about leaving me? Anyway, where would you go? What would you do?"

I could tell from the indulgent tone of his voice that he thought I simply wanted to be reassured and then all would be well again.

He was wrong. I had spent the whole of the day thinking about my own future and I had a ready answer for him.

"Don't worry about that. I've noticed that the newspaper always carries advertisements for the big hotels. They always seem to want staff. I'll go to Richmond to one of the hotels there and get a job as a chambermaid. They all offer room and board, and a little bit of money besides. It might not be ideal, but at least I'll be able to support myself until something better comes along."

"Terue, no." Simon looked horrified. "You can't do that. The wages they pay is little better than slave labor. It would be degrading for you."

I almost laughed at his choice of words. "Really? Well, I suppose you ought to know about that, Simon." Suddenly, I was weary of this game. "You're right about one thing. Johanna did tell me what people thought about me. She heard her papa discussing me. It seems that most of the men around here are waiting for you to get tired of me so they can step in and take your place. Have you any idea at all how that makes me feel? I might just as well have stayed in the Floating World and accepted Lord Dai. At least he would have been overjoyed to make me his wife!"

"I love you." He repeated the words softly. I turned to face him and saw tears glistening in his eyes. "Please, Terue. Don't leave me. I can't live without you. I don't *want* to live a day without you. And you're wrong. I'm not ashamed of you. I love you just as much now as the day we left Japan. I always intended that we should be married. It's just that, when we got here, things were so difficult."

His voice tailed off and he stared into space miserably. I waited for him to finish silently. In spite of my brave words, I knew in my heart that I wanted him to convince me that I was wrong.

"It wasn't just father's death," he said eventually. "Although that was a terrible shock to me. It's Mama, as well. She relies on me. I'm all she's got left. And I soon found out that Papa let things slip badly on the plantation. I had no idea what was involved in running things. I had to learn all that. And quickly. I've felt as if I am being torn into pieces, as if there isn't enough of me to go around." He took a deep breath and nodded to himself, as if he had come to a decision. "You're right about one thing. All of the men round here think I'm the luckiest son of a gun on earth. I never talk about you—about us— ever. So they make it up. If I ever was stupid enough to let you slip away from me, they would fall over themselves to get you."

Simon reached out and took my hands, holding them gently in his fingers.

"Can you forgive me, dear one? I've caused you terrible hurt. I'm sorry." He paused, watching my face. "Terue-chan, will you let me make it up to you now? Will you do me the honor of becoming my wife? As soon as I can make the arrangements? Please?"

I thought about it and shook my head. Simon stared at me with his mouth ajar.

"No," I said simply. "I can't. I know you believe what you say at this moment. But how long would it be before you began to listen to the people around you? Before you began to realize you had made a terrible mistake? I can't live with that hanging over me. I'm leaving, Simon. As soon as I can."

I fixed my eyes on the floor rather than look at him. For a moment, he was quiet and very still. I risked a glance at him and drew a sharp breath as I saw the tears streaming down his face. He groped blindly for my hand and held it tightly.

"You're wrong. So very wrong. What can I say to convince you, Terue? If you leave me, I'll die."

I was about to shake my head, to tell him he was being silly when he spoke again.

"There's no point in me living without you. If you go, I'll kill myself."

His words were so flat, I believed him. I rubbed my thumb over his face, wiping away the tears.

"Don't leave me. Please," he whispered. I closed my eyes and he leaned against me and put his arms around me. His embrace was very tender, and after a while, I found I was crying with him.

"Please?" he said again. Even as I let him kiss me, I wondered if I was doing the right thing. Then Simon whispered again that I was his life. That if I left him, it would be the death of him. He pleaded with me to stay, to become his wife. Somehow, my foolish heart got the better of my senses and I gave in and returned his kisses. I returned them with far less enthusiasm than he had shown, but he seemed not to notice.

I had assumed that our wedding would be a very quiet affair. I was entirely wrong. It seemed that most of Virginia wanted to see us become man and wife before Simon's god. Even Mama Simone was almost gracious in defeat and told Johanna to shut up when she said she would never have believed it.

TWENTY-NINE

The blossom plucked too
Soon has no perfume. Nor can
The tree bear its fruit.

"*M*a'am?" Suzanna greeted me as soon as I walked through the door. She was wringing her hands in her apron and spoke so rapidly I could barely follow her words. "You been gone so long, I was worried! And there's a visitor for Master Simon, but he say he gonna sit and wait until somebody come back. I told him the master ain't gonna be back until tonight and he should come back tomorrow, but he won't go. Says he'll speak to you if the master's not here."

I raised my hands to calm the anxious gabble. "Is he somebody we know, Suzanna? A neighbor?"

"No, ma'am. He ain't. I don't know him at all. And he talks so funny, I can barely make out a word. But he's a gentleman, for sure. I done put him in the drawing room and given him coffee. Did I do right?"

"Quite right. Don't worry. I'll go see him and explain he

has to come back. Could you bring some fresh coffee for me, please?"

I had long gotten over trying to enjoy American tea. No matter how I tried to explain to the kitchen girls how I wanted it, my tea always came in a huge cup, dark brown, and stewed. At least coffee tasted as if it should be made strong and I could drink it without grimacing in pain.

My strange visitor stood as I entered the room. He was so tall, he blocked the little light that managed to filter through the black drapes. I blinked, trying to adjust my eyes from the fierce sunshine outside.

"Good morning, ma'am. I'm sorry to intrude, but I've come quite a long way and didn't want to have a wasted journey. I had hoped to speak to Mr. Beaumont, but the girl says he isn't here."

I understood what Suzanna meant at once. He spoke slowly, but his accent was the strangest I had heard in this country. He rolled his words as if tasting them before they left his lips. I found his deep voice and strange accent very attractive.

"I'm sorry, my husband has gone into town on business. He's unlikely to be back until late this evening. The overseer is here. Could he help you, perhaps?" Suzanna came in with my coffee and I took the cup from her. "Would you like some more coffee?"

I was vaguely alarmed when he said yes. Should I have turned him away? Told him to come back tomorrow? For once, I wished Mama Simone was here, that she had not gone with Simon. She would have known how to deal with this stranger's business so much better than I did.

Then I looked my visitor full in the face and I felt a deep ripple of pleasure. His eyes were the blue of ice on a shallow, frozen river that shines unblemished in the sunlight. I had never seen eyes that color before and they intrigued me. His hair was almost as black as mine. It should have seemed odd. He should have had brown eyes to match his hair, but he did not. He smiled and everything about him seemed right. I was absurdly disappointed when he spoke again.

"I think I need to speak to Mr. Beaumont. I heard he might have some useful slaves for sale, and I'm in the market to acquire some good men."

He was a slaver, then. Ah, but I was sorry about that.

"Yes. You must speak to my husband. I can't help you," I spoke coldly.

I had long ago learned to expect a flicker of amazed disbelief—occasionally disgust—in new acquaintances' eyes when Simon introduced me as his wife. I watched this man's face for any surprise, but saw none. I was pleased about that, at least.

"You must be Terue-san." He smiled and looked abashed. "What a silly thing to say. Of course you are. As if I would expect to find any other Japanese ladies here in Virginia. But I'm forgetting my manners, forgive me. I'm Callum Niaish. You don't know me, but I've heard a great deal about you."

He stood and bowed, very deeply. And correctly. I managed to conceal my astonishment by the time he straightened up.

"I speak a very little Japanese." He spoke in Japanese! His words were slow and careful, but it barely mattered. As soon as I had learned sufficient English, Simon had stopped speaking to me in Japanese. To hear my own beautiful language spoken again, and so unexpectedly, almost brought tears of pleasure to my eyes.

"I am honored to hear your words," I managed to say.

"But how do you come to speak Japanese? Nobody at all here speaks it. Except my husband, of course."

He replied courteously. "I must apologize. I'm afraid my Japanese is very bad. My Chinese is better, but I'll do my best."

I realized with mounting delight that his Japanese accent was pure Edo. How was this possible? I had no idea, but I was going to find out!

"Your Japanese is excellent, I assure you. But please, how do you come to speak my language?"

"My parents are missionaries in China. In Shanghai. Although it's a long way from Japan, my amah was Japanese. In fact, she was born in Edo and moved to Shanghai with her parents when she was a young girl." He gained in confidence as he spoke. I noticed there was no trace of the puzzling accent I had heard when he spoke English and I was intrigued.

"But you are not American," I said firmly. "Nor do you look Chinese! How do you come to be here?"

"It's rather a long story."

He sipped his coffee and I was aware he was watching me intently over the rim of the cup. I met his gaze firmly. He smiled at me and I bit my lip, trying not to smile widely in return. Where were my manners when I needed them? This man above all would appreciate genuine courtesy, and here I was, questioning him and staring at him boldly. Oh, well. If one has eaten poisoned food, one might as well eat the plate, as the saying went.

"Am I to get an answer then, Mr. Niaish?"

An American would immediately have told me to call him by his given name. Mr. Niaish's manners—unlike mine! —were much better. He did not.

"I'm Scottish, Terue-san," he said. "If that means anything to you."

I remembered Simon's globe of the world with a rush of gratitude. Remembered him spinning it for me and pointing at England, telling me how the tiny island was so amazingly important.

"Your country adjoins England," I said quickly. "And like England, you are ruled by the young Queen Victoria. But that is many miles from America, and even further from China. How come you to be in either place?"

"Indeed!" He was laughing at me with those strange blue eyes. How, I wondered, had I ever thought of them as cold? "As you say, our neighbor is England, and we are ruled by the same queen. I congratulate you. But I told you, my parents are missionaries, and the church sends them anywhere there are savage heathens who need to be converted." He was laughing at me again. Two could play at that game!

"Does that include America? Is that why you are here?"

He almost choked on his coffee as he glanced at my innocent expression.

"Indeed, no. I'm no missionary, Terue-san. I make my own way in this world." He leaned forward slightly, emphasizing his words. "My father had little to say in his own future. My grandfather was a traditional sort of gentleman. The first-born son inherited the title and the estates." Ah, my visitor was of noble birth then. Of course, any *daimyo* or samurai family would order itself that way. I nodded approvingly. "The second son was expected to go into the army and serve his country. That was what my uncle did. And very successfully. He's a high-ranking officer. That left my father. He had little choice in the matter, he was doomed for the church. Papa is nothing if not wholehearted. Not for him an easy living as a country parson, or even the trappings of a bishop should he be so fortunate as to find preferment. Instead, he married when he was a very young man and determined his life was to be that of a missionary. I was born in Scotland but my parents whisked me off to China when I was very young, when the church sent Papa there." He paused, a faraway look in his eyes. I knew instinctively he was thinking of his childhood home.

I spoke without thinking. "I wake in the mornings sometimes, and if there's a cool mist, I sometimes think it's autumn and I'm back in Edo again."

We were both silent for a long time. It was a companionable sort of quiet, and I was very sorry when Suzanna—obviously thinking my visitor had gone—came back to clear away the cups and then stood awkwardly, folding her hands in her apron.

Mr. Niaish climbed to his feet. Instead of holding out his hand to be shaken, he bowed. I responded with pleasure. Suzanna goggled at the pair of us.

"Please clear things away, Suzanna," I said firmly. "I will show Mr. Niaish out myself."

We stood on the veranda. I was unsure whether to hold my hand out to be shaken or to bow again. Oscar rescued me from awkwardness.

"Hello, boy."

Mr. Niaish bent and patted the dog's head. I watched in surprise as the labrador fawned around him, pushing against his legs and whimpering with pleasure. Oscar was a guard dog, and a very good one. In spite of the fact that he was infinitely gentle with me, Simon had whipped him once when he had shown his teeth and gone for a neighbor who had knocked on the door and entered before Suzanna could let him in.

At least the moment of awkwardness had passed.

"I'll come back tomorrow morning, Terue-san. If you could tell Mr. Beaumont to expect me, I would be grateful."

"Of course."

I smiled and went back into the house. But I couldn't resist peeping through the curtain until horse and rider had vanished around the turn in the drive.

THIRTY

> The bamboo that bends
> Before the wind is stronger
> Than the tree that breaks

*S*imon came back from town much later than I
expected, and in a terrible temper. I was
surprised. Simon rarely showed his anger. He barely spoke
at dinner and announced he would go to bed early. Even
Mama Simone appeared anxious and I was so chilled by the
atmosphere I put thoughts about my visitor aside. For the
moment, at least.

Mama Simone sat silently, plying her embroidery
needle with the cloth held close to her eyes in the gaslight. I
would have liked to have followed Simon to bed immediately, if nothing more than to shower him with questions
about his day. But Mama Simone would have gloated, I
knew, thinking that I had run to her son to comfort his bad
mood. So instead, I sat quietly, saying nothing until she
finally gave in and snapped that she was going to bed
herself. She added pointedly that she hoped I would turn

off the gas mantle before I went upstairs. She knew I would. It was just something to be angry about.

A minor triumph, but it made me smile to myself.

There was no light except the half-moon peeking through the gap in the bedroom drapes. But my eyes were accustomed to the darkness and I could see Simon's shape, humped in the bed like an animal curled in its den. I understood from his breathing that he was still awake, and I expected him to speak as I undressed and hung my clothes in the wardrobe. When he stayed silent, I knew something was very wrong.

I was irritated. No matter how badly Simon's meeting had gone, he had no right to sulk like a child. To exclude me as if it was none of my business. Besides, I wanted to give him my news, to discuss Callum Niaish's intriguing visit. The thought brought a vivid memory of blue eyes and a deep voice speaking beautiful Japanese and suddenly I was deeply excited. Of course I was. Niaish had been fascinating. I just knew that Simon would be as deeply interested as I was.

"Simon. Wake up."

I shook his shoulder when he ignored me.

He was wearing his nightgown. How I hated that ridiculous garment! But nothing I could say could persuade Simon to wear a light sleeping robe, so I supposed I had to put up with it. I kneeled up, almost rolling against him as the deep, feather mattress gave way beneath me. I giggled, fully expecting him to share my amusement, but he did not. I dug my elbow into his ribs and finally got a response.

"Terue, go to sleep. I've had a long day."

He shrugged the sheets around his ears. My mouth dropped open in disbelief. I lay still for a few seconds, running my hands over my belly and flanks. My skin tingled beneath my fingers and excitement built under my own touch. I slid my hand over Simon's hips and found his tree. I smiled to myself when I found he was already half erect. Tired? I doubted it! Sulking, more likely.

I slid my hand beneath the buttons on his nightgown and stroked slowly down to his tree. Finding it, I took it in my hand and stroked and rubbed tenderly. His erection strengthened a little, but it was still disappointing. Simon neither hindered nor helped. He simply lay still. I blinked with surprise. Had we been in Edo, I would have immediately concluded that he had been with a *yujo*, a woman of pleasure, and that she had exhausted him. But here? He had spent the day with Mama Simone, talking to the family's attorney. The idea was laughable.

But my own need was growing as I felt the heat of his body. I determined at once that I would bring him back to life. The ridiculous nightgown parted beneath my fingers as I tugged and pulled at the many buttons, finally pushing the garment completely away. Simon was trying to pretend to be asleep. If I hadn't been so annoyed with him, I would have laughed out loud at his antics. Instead, I trailed my tongue down his chest, pausing to tease his navel and finally taking his black moss between my teeth. I tugged gently, and then more fiercely.

"Terue."

Just my name, nothing more. But he had finally stopped ignoring me and I felt his tree bob against my cheek and I knew he had been unable to resist me. He thrust at me, and I took his flesh in my lips hungrily. He swelled and hardened at once and soon filled my mouth.

His hand found my breast, his fingers cupping it as if it were a ripe apple. His touch was exciting and I melted into arousal with the anticipation of delights to come. I was about to slide his tree from my lips when to my utter shock he burst his fruit in my mouth without warning.

Simon lay back into the mattress as soon as my mouth left him. I barely had time to lick my lips before I understood he was dozing already. Not fair. Not fair at all! My private places clenched on themselves in disappointment. I ran my hands over my body, trying to smooth away the longing and sighed as I found I was making matters worse for myself.

I was seething with frustration. I breathed in and out through my nose, taking deep breaths until I knew I was in control of my emotions, if not my body. I slid my hand over his belly and found his tree—although wilting—still had some life left in it. I moved quickly, throwing my leg over his hips and hauling myself on top of him, sliding my private parts up and down on his tree.

"Terue. Tomorrow, I promise. Please, let me sleep!"

"You're tired, husband, but I'm not."

I felt him snatch a breath, and knew I had won. His tree began to rise for me once again and I slowed my rhythm at once, determined to keep him waiting, just as he had tried to make me wait.

He put his hands on my hips, trying to lift me. I knew it was his intention to lift me bodily on to his tree, but I was having none of it. I fell forward on him, my lips finding his mouth. Could he taste his own seed on my lips? I found the idea intensely arousing and opened my mouth to allow my tongue to caress his teeth.

"Ah!" His breath was soft in my mouth.

"Are you still tired? Shall I stop?" I laughed, knowing I had neither intention nor will to stop. Simon laughed with me.

"Witch," he said softly. "Nobody could be tired when you don't want them to be."

His fingers slid down my belly and found my sex, sliding into me by feel. He caressed me slowly, tenderly, and in response, I rubbed against him fiercely. I pushed hard until he understood what I wanted, and finally slid his fingers inside me, pushing until I moaned with pleasure. I could wait no longer; I raised myself and slid onto his tree, riding him at my pleasure until I felt my *yonaki* building, building, building until it overwhelmed my world and I screamed with pleasure.

Simon's breathing was finally beginning to fall into the rhythm of true sleep when I remembered Callum Niaish. I shook him urgently.

"What? Not again, Terue-chan. I really am tired. Let me sleep."

"Simon, wake up. We had a visitor while you were gone."

I told him quickly about Niaish and was surprised to find he was suddenly very alert.

"I don't know him, but I've heard about him. Calls himself a slave trader, but he offers such low amounts for good breeding stock only the most desperate planters have sold him anything." He laughed abruptly. "Mind you, if he raises his prices a bit, I might be willing to sell him a few warm bodies."

This was not at all what I had expected and I was shocked. Simon took pride in never selling what he called "prime stock." He had explained to me earnestly that slaves were wealth. The more slaves a man had, then the richer he was and the higher his prestige. Slaves were only to be sold when they were past their best and could no longer be made to pick tobacco speedily or even process it well. That was the way it was here, and I wasn't to worry about it.

But I did.

Now, I understood with a feeling of dread that something was very wrong. I was wide awake and picked my words carefully.

"Did your meeting today go well?"

"Did it hell as like."

I flinched. Simon never cursed in front of me. Even worse, he appeared not to have even noticed his words. Truly, the appointment he had described as "just a bit of business" must have turned out to have been very bad indeed. "Seems Papa took out a loan on the plantation while I was in Japan. Or so Abe Olders says."

Abe Olders. I knew him, but not well. He wasn't a close neighbor. He owned a plantation on the other side of town. I had seen him at events, though. A big, beefy, red-faced man who shouted rather than spoke. I didn't care for him.

"What's it to do with him?"

"The attorney says that Papa was turned down for a loan from the bank. That year was a terrible crop for tobacco and cotton alike, and half the plantation owners in Virginia were asking the banks for money. Papa left it too late to apply for a mortgage at reasonable terms, so when Abe Olders let it be known he might be able to advance him some money, he had to crawl to him and pay his terms. The attorney says the interest on the loan has never been paid back, so the original debt is much more than what Papa borrowed. Mr. Olders is now after his money."

"Did Mama Simone know about it?"

Simon laughed without humor. "She knew about the original loan, but she doesn't take any interest in that sort of thing. Far as she's concerned, Papa looked after the money when he was alive, and now that he's gone it's down to me."

"Are we poor, then?"

"No, of course not. It's just come as a bit of a shock, that's all. Don't worry about it. The attorney's going to sort things out." Simon put his arm around me and I thought he was going to sleep. I jumped when he spoke again. "You said Niaish is coming tomorrow morning?"

I knew then that we were in trouble.

THIRTY-ONE

The tongue is but three
Inches long, yet it can fell
A man two yards high

"Good to meet you, Mr. Niaish."

Simon spoke pleasantly enough, but I knew at once he didn't like our visitor. I joined the conversation eagerly, and then wished I had not.

"Simon, Mr. Niaish speaks Japanese! Isn't that wonderful?"

Simon turned and looked at me as if I had made a joke in bad taste. I had spoken in Japanese, and he promptly replied with great formality, in my own language.

"Terue-chan, you must be in error. I hardly think an English gentleman will speak Japanese."

"I'm Scottish by birth, Mr. Beaumont, not English if you please." Niaish started in English and then switched calmly to Japanese. Simon's face reddened, although with anger or embarrassment I had no idea. "But I do speak Japanese, although my Chinese is much better. As I explained to

Terue-san yesterday, my parents are missionaries in Shanghai and my amah was from Edo. It's thanks to her that I speak a little Japanese."

"I see. Well, if we are to do business together, perhaps you would do me the courtesy of speaking American, Mr. Niaish? Terue-chan, I think you can leave us now."

I rose stiffly and bowed to Mr. Niaish, furious with Simon for dismissing me so rudely. I would have had words with Simon about it, but when our visitor left he was in such a temper even Mama Simone kept her eyes down and said little.

"If that man ever comes back when I'm not here, don't let him into the house, either of you!" Simon paced the carpet between us, finally throwing himself into an armchair and flinging his leg carelessly over the side.

"Your business with him didn't go well?" I asked cautiously.

Simon glared at me. "I wouldn't have believed that word could have got round so quickly that the plantation owed money, but it must have." His fingers tapped an irate tattoo on the chair arm. "Niaish wanted to buy slaves off me. Nothing but the best, he said. Prime stock, with plenty of years of labor left in them."

"We could have spared him a few, Simon," Mama Simone said hesitatingly. "Tom says the crop isn't anything special this year. A dozen or so hands wouldn't be missed and the money would be welcome."

I glanced at her strained face and thought about Simon insisting she had no idea about finance. If Mama Simone was worried, I figured I should be concerned as well.

"Money?" Simon stared at her incredulously. "The amount he offered was an insult. And he even knew which slaves he wanted to take off me. Nothing but the best for Mr.

Niaish. He'd done his homework all right. I sent him off with a flea in his ear. I doubt he'll dare to show his face around here again."

I was disappointed that I would not see Callum Niaish again. I had enjoyed speaking Japanese with him, and even more had I enjoyed his company. Such a great pity he was a slaver. That, I could never forgive.

*In Japan, we would say "misfortunes never come singly." For myself, I prefer the poetry of the English version: "When it rains it pours." For certainly, it seemed that misfortune had chosen to pay great attention to High Grove Plantation, and that the storm clouds had gathered above us with a vengeance.

Barely a week after Simon refused Callum Niaish's offer, Shula disappeared. And this time, there was no trace of her to be found.

Simon was beside himself with fury when the overseer came to break the news to him.

"What do you mean she's gone? What do I pay you for exactly, Tom?" The overseer stood like a cowed child, staring at his shoes. "When did she go?"

"I don't rightly know, Master Simon. Her back had healed, but she still kept on that it hurt real bad and she wasn't fit to work in the fields yet. Given the way things were, I thought maybe another few weeks wouldn't hurt for her to lay up." He turned his hat in his hands and glanced up at Simon miserably. "That being so, I didn't trouble myself when I didn't see her at muster for a few days. I went to see if she was fit this morning, and her cabin was empty. I asked the others where she was, but they said they didn't know. Said Shula had always thought herself above them and they didn't visit with her greatly."

Simon stood and prodded him in the chest with his finger.

"Anything at all left in the cabin?" he demanded.

Tom shook his head. "Picked clean, Master Simon. Not a shred of anything to give a scent."

"You whipped anybody since Shula?" Tom shook his head. "Then we do have something. Give the hounds the scent of the whip and let them loose. Wherever she's hiding, they'll find her. Bring her back, and then we'll see how uppity she is. Wait, I'll come with you."

I sat for a long time, staring at nothing. I was deeply sorry for the absent Shula and prayed silently that she might somehow escape. But my own grief was greater. How, I asked myself, had my gentle, caring husband changed so very much?

Consumed with pain both for myself and Shula, I wandered through the deserted, silent rooms of the big house. Mama Simone had taken to her bed, demanding Suzanna bring her tonic to her and then telling me firmly that she had a headache and was to be left alone. Why, I wondered, did she think I would have sought her company?

The wind had risen abruptly and sighed under the door to flirt around me like dead spirits. I shivered and walked outside, blinking against the dust that eddied up.

"Ma'am, it's going to rain."

I had gotten no further than the drive, yet still William sounded anxious. I was grateful for his concern.

"You should go back into the house before you go getting wet."

"Will you come in and sit with me, William?" I coaxed.

"Master Simon's gone after Shula and Mama Simone's taken to her bed. I've nobody to talk to at all."

He shook his head. "Can't do that, ma'am. Wouldn't do." But his face brightened as he added craftily, "Mind you, if there ain't nobody about, I daresay it would be all right if you came and sat down in the kitchen for a while."

I agreed happily. Oscar came with us and put his head on my knee with a sigh of pleasure.

"Do you think they'll catch Shula?" I asked.

William pursed his lips and made a "maybe" gesture, waggling his hand from side to side. "Bad thing for her if they do. Won't be no mercy this time, no matter what's gone by."

"Why should she get special treatment, William?" I asked curiously.

William patted his fingers on his lips, as if he was trying to force his words back in his mouth. I was intrigued immediately.

"William? Why is Shula different from the rest of the slaves? Why should she get special treatment?" I persisted.

William cleared his throat. Stared at Oscar. Shuffled his feet. "Ain't my place to talk about it, ma'am," he said finally.

"Very well. I'll ask Master Simon when he gets back."

His face was horrified. I pretended to stand up and he put his hand out at once, the fingers spread in a gesture that said "Stay!" as clearly as if he had spoken.

"You ask Master Simon and he's gonna want to know who been talking to you about Shula," he said unhappily. Picking up on the fear in his voice, Oscar whined softly. "Guess I ain't got no choice. But if I tell you, you gotta promise never to let on that you know."

"I don't know anything," I pointed out.

"You just keep it that way, ma'am." William blew out his

cheeks in a sigh. "Keep old William's skin in one piece if you do. Now you gotta remember, everything I going to tell you about happened when the old master was alive. Long before Master Simon went off and found you in foreign parts." He looked at me imploringly, and sickness rose like a living thing in my throat. I could not speak and simply nodded. "Shula's a mighty pretty girl. Bright skinned, as well. Not surprising, Master Simon took a fancy to her. He was a younger man then, and young men got appetites."

He broke off and glanced at me, his eyebrows raised as if he was wondering if I understood his meaning. I heard a rumble of thunder in the distance, but my body was ice in the intense heat before the storm. Shula who was a pretty woman. A woman who was uppity and considered herself above the other slaves. And Shula had had a daughter, and the child had been sold to another plantation without her mother. Sold by her master, Simon.

I made the connection instinctively.

"Shula's daughter? She was Master Simon's child?"

"Couldn't have been no other," William said softly. "Hair dark red, just like Master Simon's. Eyes greenish-brown and skin so light she might have been taken for white at first glance. A real beauty. Master Simon didn't never take no other slave. Just Shula," he added consolingly, as if it might make me feel better.

I stared at Oscar, running his ears through my fingers. Oddly, there was no pain. Only a cold, cold place where my heart should have been. My thoughts flew back to Simon and Auntie. He had not told me about her either.

But this was infinitely worse. Not only had Shula been his lover, but he had had a child with her. A daughter, just like my Kazhua. Simon and I had been forced to abandon our child. I had always been sure that Simon grieved for

Kazhua's loss as much as I did. Now, I knew I had been wrong about him. Why should a man who had already brutally sold his own child into slavery without a single regret care about his other bastard child? I was bewildered. Suddenly, I wondered if I knew my husband at all. If I had ever known him.

I nodded at William and spoke quietly, trying and failing to hide the pain in my voice.

"I hope Shula finds her baby. I had to leave my daughter —our daughter—in Japan when Master Simon helped me escape. Her name is Kazhua, and she has red hair and green eyes, just like her father. Just like Shula's daughter. I think about her every day. Don't worry, William. I'll never mention that I know about Shula to Master Simon. But I hope they don't catch her."

William stared at me for a long time. I stared into space, blinking back tears.

"I think Shula done got clean away, ma'am," he said finally. "And I just know you gonna find your own daughter, in the end."

Simon came back very late. So late, it was the early hours of next morning. He sank beside me and lay silently. I could barely hear his breathing for the sound of the rain pounding down on the roof and dripping from the veranda.

"You got her?"

"No. No trace at all, just like all the other slaves gone on the run lately."

His voice was even with no trace of anger. Was it possible he was pleased Shula had got away? Was it even more possible that he still felt something for the mother of his child? Oddly, I found it in my heart to hope that it might be so. His next words disillusioned me.

"Don't know how she's done it, but I'd lay odds she's

trying to get to her daughter again. I've sent word to let the child's owner know Shula might turn up and to get her back to me if she does."

"And if you get her back?"

"She gets whipped. Properly this time, no matter what you say about it. And as soon as she heals, Mr. Callum Niaish can have her for whatever he's willing to offer."

He turned over and very soon began to snore, quite softly.

The rain stopped after a few minutes. I lay still, sure I could hear the thirsty soil drinking the wetness down before it could evaporate into the hot, hot air. And I thought, over and over again, *What about our daughter, Simon? Did you mean it when you told me we would find her and bring her into safety, no matter how long it took? Did you really love her? Or even then did you resent her for being a bastard half-breed who should never have seen the light of day? Were you secretly pleased when we had to leave her in the Floating World?*

My thoughts wore me down and I slept eventually, only to dream of running over endless fields with the dreadful slave hounds baying just out of sight.

THIRTY-TWO

Who travels for love
Finds a thousand miles to be
As short as one mile

*J*ust as a rainbow lingers in the sky after rain did joy come back to us. Or more especially to Simon.

He never mentioned Shula, and I thought he had simply forgotten about her. I had not. I wondered every day if she had been reunited with her lost child.

When the unknown man was admitted to the great house, my heart sank. Was it news that Shula had been found at last? Was she perhaps on her way back to us? Then I realized the stranger was dressed as a gentleman, and that his accent was from Washington, not Virginia. Simon smiled politely at Mama Simone and me as he asked us to excuse him while he had conference with the stranger. I was not deceived. I read the excitement in his voice.

The men were closeted together for several hours. Simon showed him out himself. I heard them pause on the doorstep and the sound of polite laughter. Eager as I was to hear the news, Mama Simone was before me.

"Well, Simon?" She was almost coquettish, her head on one side and a simper on her lips. "Are you going to share the news with us? Something good, I hope?"

"The best possible news, Mama." He rubbed his hands together happily. His palms made a noise like paper turning. "The government has decided to act on my information at long last. They're mounting a naval expedition to Japan under the command of Captain James Biddle to try and force a trade deal. I met Biddle in Washington. He's a good man. I'm sure he'll be successful. I'm to go with them as interpreter and general factotum."

I had no idea what "factotum" meant. It didn't matter. Simon was going back to Japan. Back to find our daughter. I had been wrong. Hope came back to me at last. My whole body stiffened with joy.

"I am coming with you," I said at once. Simon paced the length of the room and back, his hands clasped behind his back. He stopped straight in front of me.

"You are not." He spaced the words, emphasizing each with a jerk of his head. "It's too dangerous for you. Do you think memories have grown short in the Floating World?"

"If it's too dangerous for me, what about you? As you say, the Floating World has a long memory. If the authorities find you, they'll execute you with great rejoicing, and your government isn't going to be able to help you when they're a world away. If either Auntie or Lord Dai find out you're back, somehow they'll have your skin. They're never going to forget the way you insulted them."

We were speaking rapid Japanese. Mama Simone's head swiveled between us, her face tight with anger. Finally, she could stand it no longer.

"For God's sake, speak English! Isn't it bad enough that you're going back to that heathenish place without you speaking in tongues so I can't understand you?"

Simon ignored her, his whole attention on me. Mama Simone stood, her hand clutched to her heart.

"Stop it! I feel faint. I'm going to die, I know I am."

She swayed theatrically, clutching her chair for support. When Simon said nothing, she straightened abruptly.

"You're killing me. Just as you killed your father! Is that what you want, Simon?"

"Go to your room, Mother." The silence following his command was so intense it could have been cut and served like tofu. "Go and lie down. Tell Suzanna to bring you your cordial. You'll feel better after a good sleep."

It hadn't taken me long to understand that Mama Simone's tonic was actually laudanum. I was shocked at first. I had seen the effects of taking opium too often in the Floating World. I assumed Simon had no idea that his mother was consuming it in large quantities, and I had broken the matter to him carefully.

"Laudanum? Yes, of course she has it. All the ladies take it for anything from a headache to sleeplessness."

"But it's opium!"

"Not like the opium you know," he said indulgently. "It's much weaker. Even babies are given laudanum to help them with teething. Don't worry about it."

But I did, until I realized that a good spoonful of her tonic not only put Mama Simone to sleep for hours, but also greatly improved her mood for the rest of the day.

Now, I could feel her shock. But still she did not go. Not until Simon shouted for Suzanna and told her the mistress was not well and was to be taken upstairs. I was astonished when she went—with a backward glance of pure hatred in my direction.

"You cannot come back to Japan with me," Simon said. "If it were possible, don't you think I would love to take you?"

A ripple of suspicion made me wonder. Take me back—and leave me there? I said nothing, trying to order my tumbling thoughts.

"Listen, Terue-chan." As if he had read my mind, Simon's voice was suddenly very gentle. "I know you want to come back with me. I understand you want to try and find Kazhua yourself. Even if I thought I could somehow persuade Biddle to bring you along, I wouldn't do it. You would be signing both our death warrants. If I'm in danger, with all the support of the American government behind me, what chance would you have? Auntie would hear you were back straight away. And she wouldn't rest until she got you. Is that what you want? To find yourself in the Hidden House for the rest of your days? Because that's what she'd do to punish you. She wouldn't kill you. That would be too easy. Instead, she'd make your life a living hell. You know she would."

I rubbed my hands across my cheeks and was astonished to find they were wet with tears. Simon was right. My head knew that, but my heart refused to listen.

"Kazhua? You will bring her back to me? You promise?"

Simon kneeled in front of me and lifted my hands to his mouth, kissing them gently. I stared at his bowed head, willing myself to believe.

"I will find her," he said softly. "I will find our daughter and I will bring her back with me. Here, where she belongs. I promise you that."

I nearly told him then that I knew about Shula. Knew

that she had borne his child. The child he had sold away from her mother. But I did not speak for fear of casting a shadow on my hopes about my own child.

I worried about Simon returning to Japan, but it was far worse for Mama Simone. For the first time, I realized she was an old woman. I had always thought of her as vigorous, as one who time would not dare touch. Now, she walked with a stoop. She took to her room—and no doubt her laudanum—far more frequently. I thought that her skin became almost transparent so one could see the blood coursing through her veins beneath. And she breathed so loudly her nose whistled with the effort.

Reluctantly, I mentioned it to Simon, but he shrugged off my concerns.

"We all get old, Terue-chan," he said. "But I doubt Mama will take any harm while I'm gone." He laughed shortly. "She would never dream of dying without me being there to see it."

How long had he seen through Mama Simone's play acting and not seen fit to tell me he knew? But this was not the time to argue about it. Instead, I said, "How long will you be gone, husband?"

Simon shrugged, but I was not deceived by the gesture. I waited with dread for his answer.

"I'll not try and fool you, dear one," he said brutally. "I have to go to Washington first. I'll be there for a few months, briefing Biddle and waiting for the final preparations. The journey will take months. Exactly how long will depend on the weather. I have no idea how long we'll stay in Japan. But all in all, I'm going to be gone for perhaps a year."

I had been apart from Kazhua for many times as long as that. If it took another year to bring her back to me, what was that to the time that had already passed us by?

"Come back to me, Simon," I said simply. "Bring our daughter back with you and bring yourself back safely. I'll pray for both of you every day until you're both back here."

I did not say which god would hear my prayers, and Simon did not ask. I was grateful for that.

Mama Simone refused to come to the railway station to see Simon off. I guessed she thought she was punishing him, but Simon was obviously too excited to care.

He leaned out of the carriage door, clutching my hands.

"Take care, dear one," he said earnestly. "I think Tom will be able to run things well enough in my absence. I've instructed the attorney to pay that vulture Olders enough to keep him off your back until I'm home again. I'll try and write, if I can. If not, don't worry. When I come back, I'll have Kazhua with me. I promise you that." He nodded at William, switching abruptly to English. "William, I'm leaving the mistress in your hands. You look after her well for me or I'll take it out of your hide when I get back."

William grinned as if he had made a joke. I wondered if he had. They were brothers, after all.

The train whistle shrilled and I stood back. Simon leaned out of the window, waving at me until he was just a blur in the distance. William waited for me and walked behind me to the carriage.

When we got back to the plantation, Mama Simone had taken to her bed.

Tom came to me daily for instructions, just as he had with Simon. At first, I thought he was just being polite, but before long, I came to understand that Simon had been wrong. He genuinely needed to be told what to do. He looked at me hopefully, his hat twisting in his hands. For myself, I was deeply torn. If it were in my power, I would have freed all of the slaves at once. Offered to pay them wages if they would stay with me. But how could I? I had promised Simon that I would take care of the plantation until he returned. I was tormented. I either betrayed myself or I betrayed my husband's trust.

Of the two, I preferred the pain of betraying myself.

So I listened to Tom carefully when he told me about yields and babies born and slaves past their best who needed to be retired to processing work. After a while, I understood enough to ask him if this year's crop was better or worse than last year's and frowned with him when he shrugged.

"The weather ain't been kind, ma'am. Too damp for the good of the cut tobacco. The harvest is going to be all right, but not as good as Master Simon hoped."

When the request for Mama Simone to go and see the attorney came, I didn't bother telling her. I went myself and listened to the lawyer's dry phrases with great attention and was shocked.

"My husband told me that Mr. Olders had been given enough money to keep him contented until he returned," I interrupted.

"Well, yes. That's what I advised, and I thought Mr. Olders would be happy, right enough." The attorney had a round, pouting mouth. He pursed his lips now and I almost laughed, it looked so like a button had been sown onto his face. "But it appears that Mr. Olders has heard your husband is going to be out of the country for a while, so I guess he's decided to push his advantage while he can."

"And what are you going to do about it?" The attorney raised his eyebrows, looking as startled as if I had reared up and bitten him. "Does he have any right to demand more? Can you put him off, at least until this year's crop is sold?"

"Easiest thing would be to give him some more money," he said finally.

I was about to tell him that there was no money, but I held the words in my mouth. I did not trust this lawyer with the button mouth and eyes that refused to meet my gaze. If I told him the truth, I guessed it would not be long before word got back to Mr. Olders.

"Easy is not always right," I said instead. "Please tell Mr. Olders that he has already accepted his due from us. There will be no more money until my husband returns."

I watched his eyes slide away from me and knew I was right. This man of the law who my husband trusted was as reliable as a snake.

"I'll tell him, Mrs. Beaumont. Daresay he won't be best pleased, though."

I shrugged as if was nothing to me and wished the attorney a polite good day. As I walked away, I was seething.

But Tom and Mr. Olders were only a part of the discomfort that was my lot each day. The worst part of my life without Simon was Mama Simone.

A few days after Simon left for Japan, she suddenly decided it was finally time to cast aside her mourning. Perhaps it was the dreary, dusty black that had made her appear so thin, so delicate, but as soon as she donned her half-mourning mauve, she looked to me as if she had shed ten years overnight.

No longer were visitors told that she was unable to attend any events or return their visits. Now, she told me that I was expected to accompany her on the morning visits to our neighbors.

"Don't worry, you won't be expected to join in the

conversation," she assured me with cruel disdain. "Just sit and smile and drink tea." She glanced at me and played her trump card. "If Simon were here, he would expect you to come with me."

I shrugged and let it go. Let her play the grande dame, if it pleased her. All that would change when Simon returned with my dearest Kazhua. I prayed for my daughter's return daily. Prayed to the gods of my childhood and Simon's god for good fortune. With every day that passed, I counted it as one day less until she—and Simon, of course—would be back with me.

I soon found that my optimism for the future was just about the only pleasure left to me. Mama Simone was right. It was as if I had been reduced to less than a shadow without Simon at my side. I was given tea and offered cakes, but other than that nobody said a word to me. When we rose to leave, Mama Simone was embraced. I was given a polite nod. I shrugged it off, pretending I had not noticed the deliberate discourtesy.

Before long, Mama Simone tried to bully me into wearing Western dress.

"You stand out like a sore thumb in a kimono," she snapped. "Do you wonder people find it difficult to make conversation with you? They probably think you don't even speak English!"

"They must have short memories then," I responded tartly. "They knew it well enough when Simon was here."

She stared at me, drawing in breath through her nostrils until I thought she might burst.

"Everything was different before Simon left here." Her voice rose to a whine. "If he hadn't brought you back with him, he would have married a nice, high-class American lady. I would have had grandchildren by now! But no, you got your claws into him good and proper, didn't you? You enchanted him with your heathenish ways. But it'll all be different when he gets back. Once he's away from you, he'll come to his senses. Why can't you understand that? Why don't you just go away before he gets back? Save us all trouble?"

"You're wrong," I spoke quietly. "We're married, Mama. Or have you forgotten that? And when he comes back, we'll be together again and we'll have a family of our own."

I didn't mention Kazhua to her. Obscurely, I felt if she knew it would somehow bring down bad luck on Simon's efforts to find our dear daughter. I was glad I had not as I saw her glaring at me, her mouth working soundlessly. Too full of bile to speak, she turned away and I felt myself cursed silently.

I was puzzled when Mama Simone insisted I attend the many functions she was invited to. I thought about refusing to go, but then saw the gloating look in her eyes and understood she enjoyed thinking I was uncomfortable in society. She was right. The balls and "soirees"—as she referred to the long, long list of events where everybody listened to below average performances on the piano by local belles and danced—would have been unbearable if it hadn't been for Callum Niaish.

Given Simon's deep dislike of him, I was surprised to find he seemed to be much liked by the rest of Virginia society. He was invited to every event we attended. And sooner or later, I always found him by my side.

"You don't dance, Terue-chan?"

"I don't know the steps," I said simply. The tuneless—to my ears, at least!—music still made my feet itch to dance. I watched the society girls swirling about in their partners' arms with envy.

"Would you like to try?"

I accepted his offer eagerly and allowed myself to be clasped gently in his arms. I concentrated carefully on following his feet and found to my delight that all I had to do was follow those feet and the sway of his body. So easy! So very enjoyable.

Nobody else invited me to dance. I thought, often, that one or other of the men was about to rise and ask me, but always they thought better of it when they were pinned by their women folks' incredulous glance. It didn't matter. Callum asked, frequently. And in between dances, he was at my side, chatting happily in Japanese.

I was deeply hurt when suddenly he was no longer there. If he had gone away on business, I would have expected him to have at least mentioned it to me. I had thought Callum was my friend, but I had obviously been wrong. I was a fool. He was best forgotten. It didn't matter. Soon, Simon would be back. With Kazhua.

That mattered.

I listened idly to Mama Sydney's and Mama Simone's gossip. My heart beat a little faster as I suddenly realized they were discussing Callum.

"Did you know Mr. Niaish was back with us?" Mama Sydney asked. My mother-in-law shrugged.

"That so? He's been gone so long, I thought we'd seen the last of him."

"You know what happened to him?" Mama Sydney's voice was so excited that Mama Simone stopped her vigorous fanning and raised her eyebrows in question. "Turns out he ain't plain *Mister* Niaish at all. He's really a titled aristocrat!"

"No!" Even Mama Simone was clearly shocked. Johanna's mother smirked, obviously delighted to be the first to pass on the news.

I was completely confused. Hadn't Callum told me himself that his uncle had inherited the title, and that if anything happened to him, yet another uncle would inherit? I pretended I wasn't listening, knowing that if I showed even a glimmer of interest, Mrs. Sydney would save her gossip for when I was out of earshot.

"You're sure?" Mama Simone looked skeptical. "I thought he was a slave trader. And I know I heard gossip that he was only doing that to kick over the traces because his papa was a missionary someplace close to where *she* comes from." She nodded meaningfully in my direction, but Mrs. Sydney was too full of gossip to contain herself.

"Yes, that's so." She dropped her voice to a hoarse whisper. "But I heard that the relative who inherited the title not long ago dropped dead suddenly, and it was only after he was buried that it was found that the next in line had actually been killed in battle just before the elder son died. There! What do you think of that! That's why Mr. Niaish— or I suppose I should call him Lord Niaish now—" She tittered in her excitement. "—had to leave us for a good while. His papa refused to come back from being a missionary to sort things out, so it was down to Lord Niaish to do the right thing and go sort things out in England or wherever."

Callum had been my special friend. I had tried to forget my disappointment when he had disappeared without warning. And now it appeared that everybody except me knew what had happened. I was deeply hurt all over again. But of course, now that Callum was a member of the aristocracy, could I really expect him to be interested in a foreign nobody? My hurt deepened until it was a bitter taste in my mouth.

I could see the dawning interest on Mama Simone's face.

"You don't say? Well, I always did think Simon was a mite hasty in telling him off that time. If the man's a true gentleman, I think I can say on behalf of Simon that he's welcome in our house. *She* won't mind." Mama Simone spoke as if I didn't understand a word she said. "Mr. Niaish —I mean, Lord Niaish—must be very clever, as I know he speaks her language."

"Really?" Mrs. Sydney looked at me with interest. "You think maybe his parents are missionaries where she comes from?"

"His parents are missionaries in China." I spoke quietly, but from the way Mrs. Sydney goggled at me, I might as well have burst into song. "But I believe his nursemaid was Japanese, which is how he comes to speak my language. And he isn't English. He's Scottish."

She stared at me with avid interest. For a moment, I felt just as I had in Japan when Auntie had paraded me before the patrons.

The thought made me shiver.

THIRTY-THREE

Cold tea and cold rice
Are bearable, but cold words
And cold looks are not

"Are you still hoping to make an offer for some of my slaves, Lord Niaish?" I sighed as I realized I had said "my" slaves. Had I spent so long with Mama Simone I was beginning to think like her? He smiled at me, but said nothing. "It's been so long since I've welcomed you to this house, I imagine that's the only reason you're here today."

In spite of my stinging words, his smile widened. "I'm sorry I had to leave so suddenly, Terue-chan. I promise you, I had no option. I would much prefer it if you would call me Callum, but if you are intent on being formal, my title is actually Lord Kyle."

I was angry with him. My anger deepened as I listened to his amused voice. I understood he had had to go back home to sort out his family business. But was it right that I should have heard about it secondhand, and from Mrs. Sydney of all people? He should have told me himself! My angry thoughts trembled in the still air of the uncomfortable best parlor. With canine intuition, Oscar cleared his throat and raised his head from my visitor's foot, looking at me appealingly. I refused to bend.

"I was surprised that you didn't tell me you were going back to Scotland, Lord Kyle," I said coldly.

"I did try. I came to tell you, but you were out visiting with Mrs. Beaumont. It was too complicated to leave a message. I guessed word would soon circulate on the grapevine. Besides, I was gone for far longer than I expected. You missed me, then?"

"No," I snapped. "I was just angry you had gone without saying anything to me. I thought you were my friend."

"I am your friend, Terue-chan. And I want to be—in fact, I promise you, I'm going to be—the only man who matters in your life."

I stared at him. I should have told him to go at that second. I knew that, but for some reason, entirely different words came from my lips.

"Really? You're overlooking the inconvenient fact that I have a husband?"

"Not for one second. You asked me if I had come to make you an offer. Indeed I have. An offer of sorts, anyway. There's only one slave on High Grove Plantation that I want to set free. And I think you know who that is."

I shook my head. "My husband told me after your last visit that you were never to be admitted to this house again, *Lord Kyle*." I put as much emphasis as I could on his title. "I should have heeded his words." My voice trembled and I was angry with myself.

"Yes, I know he did. But it's far too late for that now. We both know that. And by the way, if you call me Lord Kyle once more, I shall put you across my knee and spank you until you remember that my name is Callum."

"Please go." I ignored his words and spoke coldly. I sat straight and looked past him. I was shaking slightly, although whether it was with excitement or anger, I didn't know myself. Did he really think he could leave me for months, disappear without so much as a farewell, only to walk back and talk to me as if there was some sort of bond between us?

"Do you really want me to go, Terue-chan?"

"My name is Mrs. Beaumont," I reminded him.

"So it is. For the moment, anyway. But you must know, *Mrs. Beaumont*, that I intend to steal you away from your husband. That's why he forbade me to come back here. I told him I was going to take you. And he knew I meant it. He didn't tell you?"

I glanced at his face and saw he was smiling. For no reason I could think of, I began to smile myself.

"Of course Simon didn't tell me. He must have thought you were mad. For myself, I think perhaps your profession has gone to your head." He frowned and I raised my eyebrows in question. "Is it that the slave trader thinks he can buy anything he fancies? In this case, I'm afraid not. I'm not for sale, Lord Kyle. Not to you or anybody else."

"Is that because you already have an owner?" My head rocked back as if he had slapped me. "I found myself wondering from the first time I saw you with Simon Beaumont if you truly loved him. Oh, I could see he was besotted with you. Everybody could see that. But as to whether you loved him, or you were just grateful to him, I wasn't at all sure. But I think I know the answer now. If you truly loved him, you would have made him take you back to Japan with him. You wouldn't have been able to bear being away from him all this time. I'm right, aren't I?"

I shook my head. He had no right to know my past. I was not about to tell him.

"You're talking nonsense. Please leave, Lord Kyle." I stood to make my point. Callum stood with me, but he did not go. He moved, but not toward the door. A heartbeat later he had picked me up and carried me—hooked under his arms as if I were a parcel—back to the sofa. He sat down, pulled me over his knee and, true to his word, gave me three firm smacks on my bottom.

It was too much. The blows hurt not at all, but the indignity flooded me with fury. I kicked and wriggled until I was free of him and on my feet.

How dare you?" I thrust my face toward him. I could barely get the words out, I was so angry. "You may be a lord now, but you're nothing in this house. Get out. Now," I said thickly. "Get out of my house and don't ever come back."

"You really want me to go? I don't believe you. I suppose I should apologize for the spanking, but I did warn you I was going to do it, and you should know I'm a man of my word. Now tell me the truth. You missed me as much as I missed you, I know you did."

"I missed the man I thought was my friend. I told you that. Now go away, Mr. Niaish. Or Lord Kyle. Whatever your name is, I don't want you here. Simon will come back to me, and when he does, he will bring my—our—daughter with him." The sound of Kazhua's name in my thoughts made me long to talk about her. I spoke without thinking about it. "She was newly born as we had to flee from Japan. She would never have survived the journey. If we had stayed, it was likely that all three of us would have been executed for our crime of being lovers. You understand?"

"Yes," he said reluctantly. "It would have been much the same in China. My parents are barely tolerated. I speak much better Chinese than they do, and I understood how they are mocked and laughed at behind their backs. Worse than that, it was made obvious to me that if they put a foot wrong, the authorities would have taken great pleasure in having them executed as an example to all the other stupid foreigners. Is that why you stay with Simon? Because of your daughter? You don't love him. I know you don't. How could you, given the way he treats you? You're just as much a slave to him as the rest of them on the plantation."

"How dare you say that to me?" I flared. "Simon is my husband. He loves me and I love him. And I suppose you know all about slavery, seeing as that's how you make your money? How do you live with yourself when you trade in human flesh?"

There. It was out, finally. How could he buy and sell people as if they were nothing? Did he ever think about the misery he was causing when he wrenched mother from child and husband from wife? How could he do it, day after day, without remorse? And why did he do it, for that matter? He was an aristocrat. Surely he had no need of the money.

His position in life made no difference to how I felt about him, though. Even as I spoke, I admitted the truth to myself. In other circumstances, had he been anything but a slave trader, I could have loved him. Probably *would* have loved him.

The knowledge made me furious with myself. I raised my head and stared at him.

"Well? You say Simon treats me like a slave? Do you want to buy me, to own me as well as all the other slaves you've bought?"

I had hurt him. His eyes were full of pain. But I was right, and I would not apologize.

"I can't explain now, but you're wrong about me, please believe that. I don't want to own you, I promise you. I'll go now, if that's what you want. But I won't be far away. If—when—you decide you want me, I'll be here." He bent to pat Oscar on the head, his expression hidden from me. "Don't bother disturbing Suzanna. I'll see myself out."

I almost called out to him, asked him to come back and explain his curious words to me, but I did not. I folded my arms across my chest and wished it were his arms that were wound around me. I stared into space and tried to be angry with him. Tried and failed.

I closed my eyes and kept them closed for a long time as I realized that I wasn't in the least surprised by his visit. Nor by anything he had said. I began to smile reluctantly when I admitted to myself that the mild spanking had been not only surprising, but arousing. I pushed the knowledge away firmly.

THIRTY-FOUR

My tears are salty
As the sea. Are the oceans
Then composed of tears?

*M*ama Simone was sobbing. She was only upstairs, but it seemed to come from a great distance. I nodded politely at the well-dressed gentleman who had brought us the news.

"Thank you for coming all this way to tell us." He grimaced and I smiled at him, trying to set him at his ease. Odd that. Wasn't it me who needed reassurance, not him? "Could I get you some tea or coffee? Something to eat, perhaps?"

"Thank you, Mrs. Beaumont. That's very kind. But I must be on my way. I have a train to catch."

He shuffled his way out, leaving a trail of condolences behind him. I wondered if I should go up to Mama Simone, but even as the thought crossed my mind I heard her shout hoarsely for Suzanna to bring her cordial and I knew she would take far greater comfort in her laudanum.

I stared at the letter. The handwriting was, I thought, truly awful. I had problems reading it. Then I realized it was not the fault of the words, but rather that I was shaking so much the paper trembled in my hands.

Why hadn't I known? Why hadn't I sensed that my husband had been taken from me? Surely, at the moment of his death, I should have felt his pain. But I had not. My life had gone as usual. The daily round of discussing business with Tom, talking to Mama, even though she rarely replied to me. Slipping out for a chat with William, taking Oscar for a walk when I felt I had to get out of the house. Lately, spending far too much time thinking about Callum Niaish.

I wept now, but whether my tears were for Simon or Kazhua or myself, I had no idea. I concentrated fiercely on the letter in my hands.

It was brief to the point of abruptness. Had the unknown government official who had penned it struggled to find the words? Perhaps he had composed draft after draft, finally giving up and resorting to giving me the bare facts with the minimum of polite regret. What did it matter anyway? Simon was dead, killed the day before he was due to sail back to America, his body left on the harbor for the early rising sailors to discover. I tried to take comfort from the bald statement that he had been killed by a single stab wound to the heart, and that his death must have been instant. The letter informed me curtly that it had been impossible to bring his body back to America, so arrangements had been made to have Simon interred in the Catholic churchyard in the Dutch colony. It didn't matter. The body was no longer Simon, no more than the discarded skin of a snake carried any trace of its former inhabitant. Although I thought that Mama Simone would probably be comforted by the fact that he had been given a Christian burial.

Who had done it? Had he been robbed? Did he fight back and lose? Or—and I knew it was far more likely—had our enemies found him and taken their terrible revenge? Not Auntie, I knew instinctively. Had it been Auntie, Simon would simply have disappeared. Forever. She would have taken pleasure in knowing that I would have been left wondering what had happened to him until the day of my own death. Perhaps Lord Dai or one of his important friends had been responsible. That was more likely, I thought. The loss of face would have been a constant shadow for them. They would have wanted Simon's body to be found so everybody would know that revenge had finally been taken. The whole of the Floating World would have respected them for their actions.

Finally, I laid the letter and my thoughts aside and fingered the silk bindings on the fat diary that accompanied it. Simon's diary. I was shaking too much to untie the threads with my fingers and finally had to use Mama Simone's wickedly sharp embroidery scissors to cut the knots.

Simon's familiar handwriting made reading his words feel almost as if he was sitting next to me, telling me of his adventures

The diary began before he boarded the ship. I read of his excitement at being back in Washington. Smiled at his boyish delight in the adventure to come. Blinked back tears as he wrote of his determination to find Kazhua and bring her back, no matter what. And my hot tears spilled out as he spoke of his love for me. His pen had sputtered under the pressure as he had written. *My poor Terue. I brought her to a foreign land and expected her to turn into an American lady overnight. And would I have loved her if she had? Of course not. When I get back, it will be different. I'll make it up to her.*

"But you never came back, Simon," I said softly. "The Floating World took you and claimed you for its own."

I skipped pages and pages dedicated to the voyage. The only thing that caught my gaze was when Simon wrote of the seagulls that followed the ship sounding like wild geese. *Yes*, I thought. *I remember them.*

As soon as his ship neared the Japanese coast, the tone of the diary changed. Suddenly, all was anticipation. Soon after the ship docked, Simon wrote of boarding a Japanese ship with Biddle and how the captain had misinterpreted a samurai's greeting and had drawn his sword in defense. I felt his delight as he recorded how he was sure that if he had not been there to smooth things over, Biddle's head would have left his shoulders in a second.

But that was the last moment of optimism in the diary's pages. Suddenly, Simon appeared to be seized with doubts. The mission was not prospering. Biddle was talking of setting sail for home after only a couple of weeks in Edo. And it seemed to Simon that the whole of Edo was suspicious. He felt he, in particular, was being watched. He barely dared venture into the Floating World, even with an escort of sailors. I felt his rising desperation as he wrote how he could not even try and approach the Hidden House, as he was certain that Auntie knew of his presence. *I'm sure Hana knows I'm here. Of course she does. She always knew everything that was going on. Does she remember me? I guess she'll have had many lovers since I left. But apart from that, will she ever have forgiven me for stealing Terue from her? Stupid question. Of course not. Oh God, please reveal to me some way I can make contact with the geisha from the Hidden House. Please let Gin and Hiromi and Nami still be there. Let me get a message to them somehow. Make it possible for me to bring our daughter back to where she should be, safe with her mother and father.*

I flicked the pages over, but there was nothing more. That was it then. Simon had been unable to even get word of my poor Kazhua. I was drained, limp with weary sadness.

For a long time, I could do nothing but sit and stare into space blindly. My mind was as empty and quiet as the room around me. Slowly, I came to understand that the melancholy that filled me was only a shadow of what it should have been. Word had just come that I had lost my husband. That he had been murdered in the most cowardly way and his body left a world away. I could not even visit his grave to speak to his spirit. I should be sobbing. Screaming. Overflowing with grief.

Instead, I was simply sad. Almost absently, I wondered if true grief would come later, when I came to understand that Simon was gone from me forever. I sighed as I knew I was fooling myself.

I had already grieved when the man I had loved had been taken from me by the good people of Virginia. The friends and neighbors who had gasped in horror when he married me. The same people who had made him ashamed of me. Would it have been any different if he had come back? Perhaps. But I knew it would not have lasted. Weeks or months later, he would have learned to become ashamed of me all over again. Would it have been different if Simon had found Kazhua, brought her back with him? Perhaps. Perhaps not. I would never know.

The diary slipped from my absent hands and a loose sheet of folded paper fluttered to the floor. I picked it up listlessly, my hopes rising as I saw the message inside was written in Japanese characters. A moment later, I understood that the gods had, indeed, turned their faces from me.

The message was terse, and had obviously been flicked onto the paper by a feminine hand, unused to writing.

The geisha you asked after are not here. Nami was bought out by her danna. Gin is dead of the fever, last year.

"No!" I cried the word out loud in my distress.

I do not know a geisha called Hiromi. There is no maiko or geisha in either house by the name of Kazhua.

The end of all my hopes, in those few, hurried words. I had been wrong. Somehow, Simon had managed to get word to the Hidden House. Had he read the message? Or had it been delivered after his death? I prayed it was the latter and that he had died full of hope.

Finally, I threw the letter on the fire and watched it curl and blacken. Felt all the joy in my life die alongside it.

As did Mama Simone's life. Once more, she retreated into deepest black. Even in the house, when we were alone, she hid her face behind a veil. I thought she was going to strike me when I refused to go into mourning.

"It's not the Japanese way," I explained. "Or at least, not the way of my religion." Mama Simone flashed me a glance of pure hatred; I remembered far too late that I was supposedly a Christian these days. I would not be cowed. I held her angry gaze and spoke slowly and carefully. "I became a Christian to please Simon. But I never forgot my own gods. In Shinto, the religion I was born into, the period of mourning lasts for forty-nine days. Simon has been dead for far longer than that. His memory is in my heart. There is nothing to be gained by mourning him for any longer."

"You ruined his life the day he bought you here." I shook my head, but Mama Simone was not to be silenced so easily. "It's all your fault he's dead. When he told me the government had asked him to go back to Japan, I was pleased. I knew he would forget all about you, if he could only get away from you for a while. I was wrong about that. It would have been better if you had gone with him. If you'd been there, maybe you would have died instead. He would have come back to me and we would have been happy again."

She had thrown her veil back and her face was contorted with hate. I shook my head and spoke quietly.

"Simon went back to Japan because he wanted to go. He intended to find our daughter. He was going to bring her here. Our daughter. Your grand-daughter."

She spoke through clenched teeth, barely moving her lips. "You're lying. Simon would have told me."

"I—we—have a daughter," I repeated. "She has green eyes and hair as red as her father's. She is alive somewhere in Japan." No matter what the unknown geisha who had dared to write to Simon had said, I knew that Kazhua was alive. If she were not, then my heart would have died with her.

Mama Simone stood abruptly and walked over to me. "You're a lying bitch. Simon would never have inflicted such shame on me. He would never have acknowledged a half-breed as his legitimate child. If he left her in Japan, it was because he didn't want anything to do with her. He sold Shula's daughter. Why should your bastard be any different?" I met her gaze calmly and her face twisted with fury as she realized I knew about Shula, and that her words could not hurt me. "You're nothing but a beautiful, deadly spider. You sit in the middle of your web and watch the stupid males coming for you. They might think you're lovely, but I know different. You just used Simon to get away from Japan. After that, you didn't give a damn about him. Since he's been gone, I've seen the way the men around here look at you, licking their lips and wondering what you know that their own wives don't. I wish them well of you, I really do. If one of them took you away from here, I would go down on my knees and give thanks."

I said nothing, and after a moment, she walked out of the room, banging the door behind her. Her words meant nothing to me. She had always hated me, and it appeared now that she always would. I tried to think of Simon, and I was deeply saddened when I realized that I could not see his face in my mind. Nothing but the memory of green eyes and hair as red as a fox spirit remained with me. After a while, my thoughts wandered from the dead to the living, and the face that rose in my mind was that of Callum Niaish.

Out of the whole of Virginia society, he was the only one who had not at least sent a card to express his condolences. Was it simply that he was too honest to pretend to be sorry about Simon's death? I found myself hoping that was so. I was angry with myself for even thinking about him, yet my thoughts stayed with him.

THIRTY-FIVE

Rocks break under the
Stroke of a hammer. Sand moves
Aside without hurt

*S*oon after we heard the news of Simon's death, I
noticed that William seemed to be avoiding me.
Unlike Mama Simone's icy silence—which I welcomed—I
was hurt by William's neglect. I had become accustomed to
wandering down to the kitchen to chat with him. If he was
not there, he could generally be found fishing at the lake.
Or, if all else failed, I could always ask one of the house
servants to go down to the fields or to the slaves' shacks and
find him for me. I had come to think of him as my friend,
and I missed him.

But not a fraction as much as I missed Callum Niaish. I
knew well enough he was still in Virginia. I heard the gossip
about him from all the ladies who came to comfort Mama
Simone and stayed to chat. They said that he was to be seen
at every society event and was a popular and amusing guest.
Of course he was. It was obvious that they all had hopes of

snaring the aristocrat for their own daughter. It seemed that I was the only one who had seen neither hide nor hair of him.

I finally decided with great bitterness that I had been a fool to be taken in by him. I began to think that he had spoken simply to amuse himself, thinking it was safe to flirt with a married woman whose husband was far away. Now that I was free, he had obviously taken a hurried step backward. And of course, now that he was a titled lord, he would hardly be interested in me.

Lonely and alone as I was, I was cautiously pleased to welcome even Mr. Olders when he walked into the plantation house.

He looked as if he was more at home on a horse than on his two feet, and he surveyed the parlor with an interest that bordered on rudeness. I guessed he was mentally pricing each piece of furniture. Although the room was far too cluttered for my taste, I was pleased that everything was of the best.

"Good morning, Mr. Olders." I held out my hand to him and remained seated. "This is an unexpected surprise. What can I do for you?"

I wished I had said something else as soon as the words left my mouth. He turned his greedy gaze on me and the years fled. I was once again back in the Green Tea House. A shy maiko, hiding my face behind my fan as my prospective *danna* examined me openly.

"Well, now, ma'am." He took my outstretched hand and shook it enthusiastically. His palm was sweaty and hot and decidedly unpleasant. "I decided I was tired of Jim March's havering about. Decided it was time I came to pay you a visit myself. And to express my condolences at your loss, of course."

"Thank you." It took me a moment to place Jim March. Simon had always simply referred to him as "the attorney." "And now you're here, Mr. Olders. I imagine you want to talk business with me?"

I spoke carefully, trying to find words that were as inoffensive as possible. I wanted this man out of my house quickly.

"Oh, please. Do call me Abe. It's actually Abraham, but I always say it's a fancy name for a plain man and all my friends call me Abe." He grinned and sat down without being asked. My dislike of him multiplied ten-fold.

"What's your business with me, Mr. Olders?"

Anger made his face ugly and I stayed very still.

"Now is that any way to talk to someone you owe a lot of money to, honey?"

"You'll be paid," I said crisply. "I told Mr. March that. I thought you and he had come to an understanding?"

The old man's color deepened until his cheeks were the hue of well-hung raw beef. I watched him carefully.

"Maybe. But that was before I lost a parcel of my best slaves. Spirited away, just like the rest of them from round here. It's organized by somebody, and me and my friends are going to find out who. And let me tell you, when we get our hands on him, he is going to be one sorry son of a bitch. Pardon my language. But in spite of that, I ain't what you'd call a poor man." His tone was suddenly fawning. The redness faded from his cheeks and he grinned, showing surprisingly good teeth. "No, honey. In fact, I'm maybe one of the richest planters in the area. That being so, and you being all alone in a strange country, I wondered if you and me could maybe come to some private arrangement, just between the two of us?"

I remembered Mama Simone's savage comments about

how many of the local men lusted for me and my skin crawled. But caution put a hold on my tongue and I spoke as sweetly as I could.

"I assure you Mr. Olders, I will pay you back every cent High Grove owes to you as soon as I possibly can. But you must understand, my husband's death came as a great shock to me. It will be a while before I can come to terms with things."

I let my voice trail off into silence. Olders nodded his head vigorously.

"Sure, honey. I understand. But it seems to me a woman as young and pretty as you must be missing her home comforts, if you get my drift?" He winked deliberately. "Now, I know you was married to Simon Beaumont, all right and legal, but you're a widow now. And things are different."

He paused and waited for me to speak. I said nothing, and he appeared to take my silence for encouragement.

"Let me get right down to it. You owe me a great deal of money. Old man Beaumont borrowed heavily off me. But seeing how we were acquainted, I did the right thing by him and never pressed for interest on the loan. Never got so much as a single cent off your husband either, apart from the few dollars he fobbed me off with a while ago. By my reckoning, you owe me more than double the amount I advanced in the first place."

"I'll pay you back," I said again.

Olders shook his head and patted his nose with his finger. "Honey, I wouldn't expect you to have a grasp on such things. It ain't lady-like. But I got to tell you, if you gave me the price of your entire harvest for the next five years, you would still owe me money. And if you did that, how would you feed your slaves and pay your bills?" He smiled at me, quite kindly.

"If I have to sell the plantation, it will kill Mama Simone." I spoke my thoughts out loud without realizing.

Olders' grin widened. "No need for that. No need at all. Like I said, you and me can come to an accommodation." He frowned suddenly and thrust his head forward like a tortoise peering from beneath its shell. "Unless somebody got in before me? You ain't spoken for already?"

I was so surprised, I laughed out loud. Olders seemed pleased. He chuckled with me.

"Thought not. Man got to be fast to get between Abe Olders and something he's set his heart on. So, what do you say?"

I stared at him, genuinely not understanding his question. "Are you proposing to me, Mr. Olders?" I blinked in surprise when he laughed out loud.

"Well, I suppose I am, after a fashion. But I already got a wife, honey. Well, I'll put my cards on the table. Generally speaking, I don't have a yen for colored gals. But you're way different. I heard tell you oriental gals got ways of pleasing your men our women would never believe. I'm offering you High Grove Plantation. You stay here, just as you are, and I visit whenever I've got a fancy for you. It wouldn't work to move you into my place. My Julia would never give me a second's peace. You agree to that little arrangement, and I'll just forget about the money you owe to me. What do you say?"

I said nothing at all. I couldn't. Olders stared at me, his eyebrows raised and his grin fixed. I was rarely pleased to hear Mama Simone's voice, but today was the exception.

"Mr. Olders, how nice to see you." She swept forward on silent, black-slippered feet. "I had no idea you were here. If Terue had sent word, I would have been down at once."

If she only knew how much I wished I had sent Suzanna

up for her! No matter. Olders was getting to his feet, tapping his hat on his thigh.

"Wouldn't have dreamed of disturbing you, ma' am," he said politely. "Mrs. Beaumont here has looked after me real well. But it's time I was on my way. I'm sure I'll be back soon, in any event."

He bowed himself out. Mama Simone barely waited until the door had closed on him before she turned to me. I watched her face, wondering at the animation in her expression.

"Well?" she demanded eagerly. "He came about the money, I suppose? Have you reached some sort of deal with him? He's not going to try and take the plantation, is he?"

I wet my lips with my tongue and shrugged. "He's made a proposal, of sorts." The echo of Olders words made me grimace sourly.

"You agreed?" Mama almost fell into the chair opposite me. She reached out her hand to me and I thought I could almost see the pattern of the carpet through her flesh, her hand was so pale and thin. I had never noticed before, but her fingers were cruelly bent with arthritis. I thought absently that she would never be able to force her rings past her swollen knuckles.

"No. He wants me to be his mistress in return for forgetting the debt." I spoke brutally, expecting her to recoil in horror.

"So? What did you expect? You could do a lot worse than Abe Olders. He's a wealthy man, and flashy enough with his money. He wouldn't bother you too much, his wife would see to that."

Her tone was so eager, I stared at her in disbelief.

"You want me to agree to be that man's mistress? After Simon? Have you forgotten your son already?"

"My son? My son is dead." She raised those old, old hands and pulled her veil back. Only her eyes were alive in a face that was seamed with pain. "All I have left is the plantation. Would you take that away from me as well? If you do, I will die."

I believed her. I closed my eyes and shook my head.

"I can't do it, Mama Simone," I said wearily. "I can't sell myself to that man, no matter what. I'm sorry. I can't expect you to understand what it would be like for me."

"Can't you?" Her voice struck like the flick of a whip. I opened my eyes and stared at her in surprise. "I understand, believe me. Do you think I was always old and dry and useless?"

I raised my hand to calm her, but Mama Simone was having none of it. She leaned forward, her face thrust toward me.

"Listen to me. Martin Beaumont started courting me when I was fourteen. He told me then that he was going to marry me and that I had better get used to the idea. He told all the other young men the same thing, and they listened to him and kept away from me. He had a reputation for being handy with his fists in those days, so it wasn't surprising. My mama and papa encouraged him, in spite of the fact that he was much older than me. After all, he had High Grove. He was a catch, Mama told me. The best I was ever going to get."

Shades of Auntie! I looked at Mama Simone with new respect.

"He used to have me visit here. That was no hardship, I loved the place. But I didn't love what Martin did to me. He would take me for walks outside and back me up to a tree. Feel my breasts and slide his hand up my skirt, grope at my private parts. As if that wasn't bad enough, after a while he

would take his member out and make me play with it. Told
me if I told my mama about it he would beat me. As if I was
going to say a word to anybody! I was so embarrassed, I
would have died first. I tried to think up excuses why I didn't
want to visit, but Mama insisted."

She paused, her filmy eyes staring into the past. For the
first time, I felt something for my mother-in-law. Not love. It
was too late for that. But respect. And sympathy.

"But you still married him?" I asked.

"What choice did I have? Martin told me I was going to
be his wife. My parents looked on it as a given fact and were
happy about it. What voice did I have in the matter? I was a
child!" Her voice rose in shrill anger. "Anyway, I thought it
would be better when we were married."

"Was it?"

"Was it hell as like." The profanity surprised me. I had
never heard the mildest of curses come from Mama's lips.
"He married me the day after my sixteenth birthday.
Brought me here as mistress of the house. He drank so
much at the wedding dinner, I thought—truth to tell, I
prayed—he might be incapable. But it wasn't so. As soon as
the last guest had gone, he took me by the arm and
marched me upstairs. I was shaking so hard I missed one of
the steps. If his grip hadn't been so fierce, I would have
fallen. I may be wrong, but I've always been sure in my own
mind that William was conceived on my wedding night."

My shock must have shown plainly on my face. Mama
Simone smiled without humor at my surprise.

"Surprised you, have I? Wait until I get there. Martin
dragged me down to his bedroom. Mae—William's mother
—was already there, sitting on the truckle bed. Naked as a
jaybird she was. She smiled when we came in and stood up
and stretched as though she belonged there. Martin called

something to her and she sat down again. Bewildered and terrified as I was, I could see her watching us. I think that gave me a little courage.

"'What's she doing here, Martin?' I demanded.

"He looked at me as if I were mad.

"'Where the hell else would she be?' he asked. 'Do you think I'm going to throw her out just because you're here?'

"I was frozen with shock, but I was determined not to let Martin's whore see me afeared, no matter what. Martin looked at me for a moment, absolutely gloating, and then picked me up and threw me onto the bed. Mama had taken great care to explain to me what was going to happen to me on my bridal night. She had told me I should undress behind the screen and put my nightdress on. If I was slow and careful about it, she said Martin would be between the sheets before I had finished. He would, she said, probably be as nervous as I was. I wasn't to worry too much. That the first time would probably be over and done with very quickly. It wouldn't be very nice, but things would get better when I got used to being a married lady.

"She was wrong. I hadn't finished bouncing into the feather mattress before Martin was on me. He would have torn my dress off my body if it hadn't been so carefully sewn. As it was, he got tired of trying after a few seconds and just bundled it up around my waist. He shoved his hand in my private parts and then fumbled with his buttons and the next thing I knew he was laying on top of me and his member was pushing at me and shoving until he found his way in. I screeched with pain and he threw his head back and laughed. The more I screamed, the more he obviously loved it. Mama was right about one thing, at least. It didn't last long. Martin gave a final great shove that I thought had torn me in two and then rolled off me.

"But if I thought that was the end of the humiliation, I was not just naïve, I was stupid. I was determined not to cry. I blinked back the tears, shuffling as far away from him as I could get. My eyes were bleary, but I still saw my new husband lean on his elbow and pat the bed at the side of him. Mae was up off the truckle bed and at his side like a shot. She threw me a glance of utter triumph and then wrapped her arms around Martin, kissing him and licking his face like a puppy dog. Martin ignored me, but it wouldn't have made any difference if he had ordered me to watch. I couldn't take my eyes off them. She did things to him I would never have believed a woman could. Her hands and tongue were everywhere. And now and then, she spared me a glance and I saw her grin with pure malice."

Mama Simone stopped, panting to get her breath. Her face had turned ashy grey and her lips were white. I thought her heart might truly be giving way at last.

"Mama, do you want your cordial? Shall I shout for Suzanna to bring it for you?"

"No. Let me finish. All these years I've told nobody about this. Not even Simon. How could I tell him what his father was like? How I hated him?" She was talking to herself, I thought. But I was wrong. Her eyes moved to my face and I was pinned by her gaze as surely as a butterfly caught by a lizard. "I couldn't tell anybody how he humiliated me. Every night, Mae was there. Sometimes he forced himself on me while she watched. And I could see she was criticizing my performance. That she knew I couldn't give my husband a fraction of the pleasure that she did. Sometimes he didn't bother with me at all and just took her on the truckle bed. Quite often he slept there at her side. I know he thought he was tormenting me when he did that, and I made sure he never knew how happy it made me to be alone in that great bed."

I swallowed my nausea. That great bed where Simon had made love to me, time after time. *He didn't know*, I protested to myself. It didn't matter. If I had known when I had loved my husband, it would have mattered. Now I thought of him with only a quiet sadness for things that might have been and I felt sick for Mama rather than myself.

"Why are you telling me?"

"Because you'll understand. I feel that in my bones. You've suffered, haven't you? You know what men—even the best of them—are capable of." She took a deep breath and I put my hands out in front of me. *No. Stop now. I don't want to hear what you're going to say. I'm free, at last. Don't try and chain me again!* But she went on, relentlessly. "The only thing that stopped me from killing myself years ago was love of High Grove. Love of the house, the gardens. Love of the smell of the tobacco, drying in the sun. Love of the rhythms of it all. I cajoled Martin into planting the peach arch. Got him to decorate the house in the best style. To buy only the very best furniture from the best shops. When people commented on how charming High Grove was, he loved it. When Mae birthed William barely nine months after my wedding night, and it was obvious he was a fine, healthy child, even Martin must have felt a tad guilty. I persuaded him to keep the boy about the house, and over the years I used him to grind that guilt into Martin. I lost two babies, you know," she added sadly. "I miscarried the first quite early. It was years before I conceived again, and Martin was sure this one was going to be a boy. He was over the moon, but it was all his fault I lost it. He'd refused to have anything to do with me, in case I miscarried again. He confined his lust to Mae. She was happy enough about it, and so was I. But she died about two months or so before my baby was due. She caught a fever and was gone in days. I knew what was going to happen straight away. I begged Martin to take another slave to his bed, but he wouldn't. He'd got it into his head that it would be unlucky if he did, so he kept himself to me. It didn't matter, I was relieved beyond belief to find he only expected me to pleasure him with my hands. But it didn't last. He came home one night after a card game with his cronies, roaring drunk. Shouted he had waited long enough and he was going to have me, by God! God had nothing at all to do with it. He used me appallingly, and my baby started the next morning. He was too young to survive. He lived long enough for us to have him christened, but that was it. We named him Martin, after his father.

"There was no one to replace Mae after that. My husband said he was going to have an heir, and he did his best to make sure he did. Night after night at me. Every night the same. But still no baby. It was my fault, he said. I didn't spend when he came to me, and everybody knew it was impossible for a woman to get with child if she didn't enjoy it. In the end, I started to play act. Panted and moaned just like Mae had, pretended I loved what he was forcing me to do. It had nothing to do with it, of course, but I did catch on again. And this time, Martin took his lusts elsewhere. From my first missed monthly, he moved into another bedroom. Summoned whichever slave girl he fancied to his bed and left me alone. And eventually, my lovely Simon was gifted to me. Martin kept to the other room after that, with his colored gals, so there were no more babies for me. But it didn't matter. I had Simon and I had High Grove. I gave thanks on my knees every day for my good fortune." She nodded slowly. "And now, I've lost my son. And High Grove is going to be taken from me as well."

I waited, expecting her to tell me yet again that it was my fault. I wished she had. Naked hatred would have given me the strength to argue, to tell her I wasn't going to give myself to Abe Olders, or anybody else for that matter.

"Please. I'm begging you, as my daughter. The only thing I have left in this world is High Grove. Please, don't allow that man to take my home away from me. I'm an old woman, I know I don't have long left for this world. Please, tolerate him for my sake. When I'm dead, you can walk away. But not yet. Please."

I thought of my own mother giving me away to an unknown future when I was nothing but a child myself. Of my own dear daughter, who in my turn I had abandoned. The hot tears flowed down my cheeks and dripped off my chin. Mama Simone fell to her knees and shuffled across the carpet to me. Her hand gripped mine and she leaned forward, resting her forehead on mine. Our bitter tears mingled and became one.

I put my arms around her shoulders and felt the brittle bones beneath my hands.

"Thank you," she whispered, her voice as tremulous as paper blown by the wind. "It won't be for long. I know I haven't got that much time left on this earth. God will smile on you, I promise."

I thought of Olders's red face and his powerful hands and I wept again. For myself this time.

But what option did I have? Live with Olders or live with my conscience.

At that moment, I hated Simon for bringing me here.

THIRTY-SIX

Only if I peep through my
Fingers, may I stare straight at
The brightest sunlight.

"*I*s it raining?"

A silly question, but I was barely awake, and at first I thought I was still dreaming.

I rubbed my eyes, trying to focus. I had never expected to sleep. Certainly not quickly and deeply. But exhausted as I was from the horrors of that day, I was unconscious as soon as I had pulled the sheet around my shoulders.

And now William was leaning over me, shaking me gently. He was dripping wet, so wet that the sleeve of my sleeping robe was soaked beneath his hand.

I shook my head, trying to dislodge sleep from my mind.

"William? What is it? Has something happened? Is it Mama Simone?"

I spoke louder than I had intended, and William put his finger quickly in front of his mouth to silence me.

"Shush, ma'am," he whispered. "It's not Mistress Simone, no. Will you come with me? I need your help."

The stark fear in William's face urged me out of the bed. I tugged the belt on my sleeping robe tight and followed him out of my room. I was bewildered. Strangely, the thing that still worried me most was the fact that he was soaking wet. I glanced out of the window and saw the night was clear. Suddenly, a great horror came upon me. I was sure the plantation—even perhaps the house—was on fire, and William was wet from trying to douse the flames. But there was no smell of burning, no flickering of flames.

"Ma'am, please!" I had stopped to sniff and look, and William's agonized voice urged me forward.

I was frightened. But I trusted William and I knew he would never have disturbed me except for something very serious, so I went with him. Oscar gamboled at my side, delighted by this new game. I patted him to keep him quiet.

William led me down the main staircase and out the kitchen door. I hung back, wanting to ask what was happening, but he shook his head urgently and tugged me forward. But not far.

Just around the corner, in the backyard, he stopped so suddenly I nearly walked into him. Oscar whimpered and William cuffed him gently around his ears. I heard myself make a very similar noise and wondered hysterically if William was going to hit me as well.

Callum was half-lying, half-propped against the wall. He put his hand up to greet me, but the effort was clearly too much as it fell back with a thump. In the clear moonlight I saw that, like William, he was wet. In that bright, unforgiving light I also saw a spreading puddle of black around him.

I fell to my knees, catching him as he began to slide down the wall.

"Callum? What's happened? William? What's he doing here? What's happened to him?"

He was a dead weight and I could barely hold him upright. William hunkered down beside me and together we managed to haul him back up.

"I'm sorry." William glanced across at me. "There was nowhere else I could take him where he'd be sure of being safe. He didn't want me to bring him here. It's my fault, not his."

Somewhere in the deep of my mind, I registered the startling change in William's manner. Then Callum moaned and I pushed the thought aside.

"I don't understand. But never mind for the minute. We have to get him inside so I can take a look at him. Can we carry him between us?"

"I guess so." William bent and flung Callum's arm around his shoulders. "Ready? Pull together."

We dragged him to his feet. William was very strong, taking most of the weight. I leaned into Callum, and between us we managed to drag him inside.

"Can we get him upstairs?" William asked urgently. "Nobody going to see him there. We need to get his clothes off him. I'll throw them into the hogs to leave no trace. And I got to wash away that blood from the wall. Can I leave him with you?"

I nodded. In the midst of my confusion, all I could think of was that Callum was badly hurt. Everything else could wait. Between us—with Oscar hampering every step of the way—we got him up to my bedroom and laid him on the truckle bed. It was easier than trying to haul him onto the bed proper, but I hated the thought of him lying there, where Mae and William's father had once enjoyed each other's bodies while Mama Simone was forced to watch.

William disappeared at once. Bewildered, I moved like a sleepwalker to the washbasin and wrung out a towel in water. Only then did I realize I had no idea where Callum was hurt. He seemed to be covered in watery blood. I started at his face and worked my way down. When I got to his legs, I found the wound and moaned out loud.

His left thigh looked as though the flesh had been ripped away by giant teeth. Within seconds, the towel was bloody and soaked through. I ran and rinsed it and wiped again, and again and again. When the flow of blood finally eased, I tugged Callum's clothes off, bundling them into one of my old silk shawls. Naked in the moonlight, it seemed to me that his body was so white, he could have no blood left in him.

I was shivering with shock and fear by the time William came back to us.

"You done real well," he said approvingly. "He needs to stay here for a while. Can you handle that?"

I stared at William incredulously. I had a naked, bleeding man in my bedroom in the middle of the night. I had no idea what had happened to him, not even how badly he was actually hurt. It was all so bizarre, I wondered for a moment if I was still asleep and dreaming. Then Oscar licked my hand with his warm, wet tongue and I knew I was awake. I took a deep breath.

"What's happened, William? Tell me now," I demanded.

"He got caught in a man trap." Callum, caught in a man trap? How? Why? My mouth opened but no words came out. "He was real lucky. I saw the glint of it and dived at him. I was just a bit too late, but at least it just got the flesh and not his bone. We'd have had no chance if he'd broken his leg."

"If it hadn't been for William, I would have been dead." Callum's voice made me jump. "I'm so sorry to do this to you, Terue-chan. It wasn't in the plan, I promise you."

I stared at Callum dazedly. I felt dizzy and sick. I put my hand out to stop myself from falling over and William grabbed my shoulders and shook me.

"Breathe deep," he instructed in a whisper. "Don't you go getting foolish on me. I can't cope with two invalids at once!"

"I'm all right," I said, although I wasn't. "What's happened? What's going on? Why were you both out together in the middle of the night? Tell me!"

I stared from William to Callum, watching as they glanced at each other. William shrugged finally and sat back on his heels. It was Callum who spoke.

"I'm sorry. I told William not to bring me here, but he wouldn't listen." He shivered and I wondered again how much blood he had lost.

"What happened to you? Tell me. Everything!" I demanded.

"It's a long story, but I'll cut it short." Callum paused for a moment and I waited anxiously as he dealt with his pain. "You called me a slave trader once. I am, but not like you thought. I don't buy slaves. I set them free."

His voice died in his throat and his eyes closed. I stared at William in horror. He pulled down Callum's eyelid with a gentle finger and shook his head.

"He's passed out. Let him be still for a while. I think he'll be all right."

I wanted to throw my arms around Callum, give him the

strength and warmth of my body. But even more did I need to make sense of his words.

"What does he mean, William? What's he talking about? What's happened?"

"He done told you already. Everybody 'round here thinks he's a slave trader." William sounded pleased. "Best story in the world to hide the fact that he's part of the Underground Railroad. If he got caught, wouldn't make no difference if he was king of England, he'd still be strung up."

My head was pounding with pain. I rubbed my forehead, trying to make sense of William's words. I remembered, vaguely, Simon talking to a neighbor about something called the Underground Railroad. Both men had been contemptuous, our neighbor going so far as to say that all the "colored lovers" who were involved in it ought to be rounded up and hung.

"Callum? He's been helping slaves escape?"

"Dozens of 'em." William grinned. "Oh, he bought a few as well, and then had them shipped out. But most of them he set their feet on the road to freedom without their masters even knowing they had gone before it was way too late."

I caught my breath. Suddenly, I knew. I asked anyway.

"Shula? He helped her get away?"

"Certain did. We both did. And the other slaves that got away from High Grove and hereabouts."

I was bitterly ashamed. All these months, I had thought Callum was simply amusing himself by dealing in human flesh, and now it turned out he had been risking his own life to save others. I should have known! How could I have believed him capable of such wickedness?

"What happened tonight?" I demanded.

"We nearly got caught. We knew the planters were closing in. They all speak freely in front of old William. Been here forever. He might be half-white, but he's just another slave who knows nothing. Safe to talk in front of William!" His voice had taken on a subservient whine and I felt a stab of hurt. "Not you, ma'am. Never you. I knew we could trust you, and so did he." He nodded down at Callum. "He knew it right enough, but he wasn't prepared to put you in danger, no matter what."

"Thank you." I had no idea what I was thanking William for. He grinned at me and nodded before he went on.

"Well, tonight's was going to be the last batch we got out for a while. We knew things were getting just too dangerous to go on. Still, this time looked as if it was going to be good. We took half a dozen out of Mr. Sydney's compound, sweet as a nut. Got them to the river and away on a raft." Ah, so that was how the slaves were getting away without a trace! William paused as if I had spoken and I nodded quickly, urging him to go on. "We thought we'd got clean away with it. We had horses waiting and were ready to go ourselves when we heard the dogs. The horses spooked and were off before we could mount. Don't blame 'em. Them dogs sounded like all the hounds of hell on our trail. Wasn't nothing for it, but we had to take to the river ourselves. I can swim well enough, and Master Callum better still. We took ourselves far enough downstream to be sure we were well away. Would have worked out fine it if hadn't been for that trap getting him by the leg. Master Tom must have set it without me knowing."

My own overseer had set a trap on my property and I hadn't known?

"I didn't know either. I'm sorry," I added absurdly.

"'Course you weren't to know. He'll have been told to do

it by the other planters. Daresay Tom didn't want to worry you 'bout it. Anyway, it snapped shut on his leg. I managed to get him out and back here. And that's it. You know the rest."

"No. No, I don't. William, why didn't either of you trust me enough to tell me what was going on? Did you think I'd ever betray you?"

"We both trusted you." William frowned at me. "I told you that. Weren't a question of trust. Callum insisted he didn't want you involved. He said that if we got caught it was way better that you didn't know anything at all. Besides, that's how it works in the Underground Railroad. Nobody knows more than the next link in the chain, so if you do get taken, there ain't much to tell. In any event, I told you this was the last time. After this lot, he was going away, back to his home. Back to looking after his own people. Before he went, he was going to come see you and make you listen to him. The man told me he was going to make everything right for you, but he couldn't do it until it was real safe."

"I see." And not only did I see, but I was intensely grateful. It wasn't only Papa Sydney's slaves that had been freed that night! "What will happen to him if he's found?"

"Right thing to do would be to put him on trial. Let the law deal with him. But that ain't going to happen. My guess is that he would just disappear. Plenty of hungry hogs round about to deal with the leavings."

I swallowed nausea. "We have to get him away, William."

He looked at me approvingly. "The man told me I wasn't to bring him to High Grove no matter what. Said he would rather die than put you in danger. All the time we were staggering here, he said it. Time and time again. But if you're telling me different, nothing I can do about it, is there?"

"Can we get him into the landau and away?" I was half on my feet, but William shook his head.

"Landau's a fine idea. Better than you know. But not until it's well light. They'll have found our horses by now, and Mr. Sydney's going to know he's lost more slaves. Probably found the trap sprung and bloody. Every road around here going to have men watching it. We go now and we going to get stopped for sure. Less suspicious if we wait until mid-morning. Even then, there's a good chance they going to stop us and ask our business. We need to get to the other side of town, to the Reverend Smallbone. If we can get to him, the reverend will get him safely away to the next station on the Railroad."

I had heard of the Reverend Smallbone. Even though he was not a Catholic priest, Mama Simone thoroughly approved of his hell-fire sermons. I wondered wryly how she would feel if she knew of his other activities! I glanced at Callum. He seemed to have passed into something nearer sleep than unconsciousness. I decided William was right. The rest would do him good, and in the meantime, we could make our plans. My mind was suddenly focused.

"If they stop us, the hounds will pick up on his scent." I thought of the bloody trap and shivered. "If they smell him, we're lost. I've already washed him thoroughly. That will help. But it's not enough. We need to change the way he smells. William, go to the wardrobe. All Simon's clothes are in there. Fetch me a pair of trousers, and a shirt and coat. And shoes and Simon's leather gloves."

William stared at me for a moment and then his face broke into a grin.

Callum slept like a baby, only half waking when I took the towel from his leg and helped William pull on Simon's trousers. I sniffed him carefully when we finally wrapped him in the coat, but I could smell nothing but clean clothes. But that didn't mean the hounds would be deceived. A well-meaning neighbor had given me a large bottle of violet perfume as a wedding present. I had never used it, but I was grateful for it now. I unstoppered it and sprinkled it liberally over Callum, even rubbing it into his hair. A thought struck me and I quickly patted some on my own neck and wrists. William looked at me approvingly.

"I smell like a tart's bedroom," Callum muttered sleepily. "What are you trying to do to me, Terue-chan? Suffocate me?"

"Shut up," I said firmly. "I'm trying to save your life."

"What for? It's no good to me if you're not with me."

William turned his back discreetly. I thought of Mama Simone's tears and Olders' beefy face and huge hands and swallowed hard. What was the phrase I had heard so often and never—until this moment—really understood? Ah, yes. "You've made your bed, so now you must lie in it."

"You're getting away from here. To safety. That's all that matters. Don't worry about anything else at all."

"Silly woman." Callum winced. "What do you think you're doing? If they catch us, you'll hang alongside me and I'm not having that. Where are you going?"

I nodded at William to keep Callum still and slipped out of my bedroom along to the end of the corridor. I waited, listening for a moment, and then turned the knob on Mama Simone's door as slowly as I could. The door swung open silently, and I crept across the room, one foot in front of the other like a cat stalking a bird. She coughed quietly before I reached her bureau and I froze.

"Simon? Is that you?"

I waited, sure she must hear my blood pulsing. I thought she was going to sit up, but at last she slipped back into full sleep and I lowered the top of the bureau, inch by slow inch. I grabbed her bottle of tonic and left as silently as I had entered. I held Callum's nose until he was forced to swallow a healthy mouthful of laudanum. He tried to speak, but in his weakened state the drug took him and held him in its arms like an ardent lover.

Between William and me, we folded Callum into my quilt. We half dragged, half carried him out of the house and to the stable. I was doubled up, panting for breath by the time William opened the landau door. I stared at the plush interior and confidence drained away. We could get Callum in, easily. But the floor was bare. Anybody who so much as glanced in would see him. Even bent in two, we couldn't hope to push him out of sight beneath the twin seats.

William was rubbing his hands together cheerfully. He leaned into the carriage's interior and pushed down with the heel of his hand on the floor. I stared in astonishment as the entire center of the floor pivoted and swung smoothly up.

"The old master didn't think much to paying what he called 'undue taxes.'" William grinned. "There's many a parcel of fine brandy and tea come to the plantation this way with no duty paid. I daresay the old man would turn in his grave if he knew what kind of package was making the return trip tonight. Think you can help me get him in? I'll leave the floor open a slant so he gets plenty of air. Come morning, I'll harness up the horses myself."

I hated the idea of leaving Callum alone, but when I hesitated, William tugged me briskly by the hand and took me back into the house. I sat in a chair in my bedroom, waiting for morning. I thought about how the planters would react if they did find Callum. How would they behave if they discovered he had made fools of them all? That the man they would have welcomed with delight as a son-in-law was also the hated phantom who had spirited away so many of their slaves? Their vengeance would be cruel, and the thought made me cringe.

Oscar was curled on my feet, keeping me company. I stroked his head gently.

"It's not going to happen," I promised him. "Not if I have anything to do with it."

THIRTY-SEVEN

Even a broken reed
Is precious to the grasp
Of a drowning man.

I felt every jolt of the carriage. Moving Callum's
dead weight had taken a toll. My ribs felt as if
they were broken, and my back was so rigid that every
breath was agony. I sat stiffly, propped like a child's doll.

We were well outside the plantation boundary, almost
into town. After the trauma of the night, it had all been so
very easy. Mama Simone had not woken for breakfast, and I
had simply left a message with Suzanna to tell her I had
gone to see Mr. March. Was I being unduly suspicious, I
wondered, or did I see a glint of interest in Suzanne's
normally impassive face? No matter.

We were gone!

I heard the dogs before I saw them. Heard William
mutter a prayer and guessed he thought that we were done
for. When Mr. Sydney stepped into the middle of the road
with his hand raised for us to stop, I was sure of it as well.

Even more so when his bloodhounds went mad on their leashes, baying and struggling to get to us.

"Mrs. Beaumont." His eyebrows rose so far toward his bald head, it looked ridiculously like his hair had miraculously grown again. "Sorry to have to stop you. I guess you won't have heard, but last night we nearly had the bastard —pardon my French—who's been making away with all our slaves. He just slipped through our fingers, but we guess he's still round about, so we're checking all the traffic. Don't suppose you seen anybody at all about your place, have you? Shut up, you stupid mutts."

He yanked viciously on the leashes in his hand. The hounds still milled around, but aimlessly now. One began to howl and then sat back on its haunches and scratched vigorously behind its ear.

"Haven't seen a soul. Except William here." I managed a laugh.

"Thought not. Mind if I just take a look in your carriage anyway, ma'am? Ain't gonna be nothing there, of course, but I did say I would look in every vehicle. You're up and about early this morning."

"I have to visit with Mr. March, my attorney." My voice was trembling like a leaf shivering in the wind. He would notice, I was sure. He would make me get out. Let the dogs in the carriage. The game would be up for all of us. I smiled and fluttered my hand nervously. "Please, do look. I understand you have to do your duty. Those dogs are properly under control, aren't they? They look terribly fierce to me. I was bitten by a dog once and I've always been a little afraid of big dogs since." I improvised wildly.

Sydney grinned widely, tugging on the hound's leashes in a show of bravado.

"I'll make sure they ain't gonna hurt you, Mrs. Beaumont. Well, I can see the carriage is stone empty except for you, so I'll let you go on your way. Give my regards to Jim March."

And that was it. William tipped his hat courteously and we drove off at a sedate pace. Somehow, I stopped myself from screaming at him to hurry.

The Reverend Smallbone belied his name. He was a big man, every bit as red-faced and beefy as Abe Olders. I shrank from him instinctively, but his touch was as gentle as a child's as he helped me down from the landau.

"I thank you, Mrs. Beaumont." William worked his magic with the floor and the preacher leaned inside. "Together, William. One, two, three and hup! There he goes. Can you take him into the house on your own? Good man. I'll put the carriage together again and then you can take the lady here into town." I watched silently as William draped Callum's arm over his shoulder and shuffled him through a side door into the minister's home. "God will bless you for today's work, my dear."

Even speaking quietly, Reverend Smallbone's voice was a subdued boom. I stared at him uncomprehendingly.

"What's going to happen to Callum now? His leg is badly torn. He needs to be seen by a doctor."

"I'll arrange that. I have a good friend in the medical profession who shares my distaste of making men into beasts of burden. He'll be patched up well and truly. And then later on today, I'll find it necessary to make a trip northward. I have a carriage with a similar arrangement to your own. I'll leave Lord Kyle in safe hands, and from there he can move further northward when he's recovered. I don't actually know what route he'll take, but I imagine he'll end up in Canada. I think myself the further north from here the better. There are a lot of landowners around here who would be delighted to get their hands on the phantom who has been spiriting away their slaves. And if they realized they had been made utter fools of by somebody each of their wives had hoped to snare for their daughters, it would be very bad for him. Once he's across the border, he'll be safe. He can go back to his own country as and when he wants. Scotland, I believe. If you know where that is?" he added dubiously.

"It's next to England," I said automatically. "Thank you for looking after him. If he comes around before you leave him, please...Please tell him I'm sorry."

Not what I meant at all. But I prayed Callum would understand.

William came back then, and the Reverend helped me into my carriage. As we set off, I turned my head and looked behind me, certain that I would somehow catch a last glimpse of Callum. But there was nothing but Reverend Smallbone, waving until we turned the bend heading back into town and he was hidden from my view.

"Ma'am." William spoke quietly. "I know you want to get back home, but I really think you should go visit Mr. March. If the planters get to discussing things later and it comes out somehow you never went to see him, questions gonna be asked."

I agreed. He was right, of course. We jolted along in silence until I spoke again.

"Why have you stayed, William? You could have gone with Callum, couldn't you? Got away?"

"Sure could." William stared at the road. "Mr. Callum, he offered to take me with him. Set me free. But I told him I couldn't go. I love High Grove just as much as Mistress Simone does. I was born and bred there and I done lived there all my life. The old master was my daddy, whether I liked it or no. I'd be a fish out of water anywhere else. Besides which, what's Oscar going to do without me?"

He chuckled and I managed a tired smile.

Mr. March seemed startled to see me. And pleased. He fussed around, offering me coffee, which I refused. I had decided on the journey that I would tell him that Mr. Olders and I had come to an accommodation and that I would like something in writing to support it. Nothing less than the truth, that.

But I never got the chance.

The attorney leaned back in his chair, his fingers steepled on his chest.

"Now, there's a coincidence. I was going to ride over to High Grove to see you later today and here you are!"

He already knew, then. I managed a weak smile.

"I suppose Lord Kyle has already been to see you, to give you the good news himself?"

I wasn't listening to him. I was exhausted and anxious and wanted nothing more than to get back to the plantation and sleep for the rest of the day. I started to nod and then realized what he had said. Lord Kyle. Not Mr. Olders. I felt the muscles in my neck creak as I turned my head to look at him.

"Lord Kyle? No, I haven't seen him," I lied.

"Oh? That's odd. He assured me he was going to see you first thing this morning. I daresay he's been detained by business. Well, no matter. I have here a money draft called down on Lord Kyle's account in Washington." He spoke Callum's name with such reverence I almost managed to smile. "As good as gold any day and made out to Mr. Olders by name. I calculated the initial sum and outstanding interest on Mr. Olders's loan very carefully, I can assure you. And just to be sure there's no problems, Lord Kyle was very insistent I added a little more on top. So, there you are. I'm going to take this over to Mr. Olders' bank this morning, and as soon as it's in his account you don't owe him a single cent. High Grove Plantation is yours again. Although I guess it doesn't take much figuring out to assume you're not going to be there that much longer?" he added archly.

The attorney was still speaking, but I heard nothing else at all. High Grove was mine. Neither Abe Olders nor Mama Simone had any hold on me. I was free, and Callum Niaish had given me that freedom, as surely as he had given freedom to every other slave he had released. And unlike every other man in my life, he alone had asked for nothing in return.

I heard the sound of the wings of wild geese beating the air, their joyful cries trailing behind them. I thought only I could hear it, but I was wrong.

"My word, but the geese are migrating early this year," March commented. "Nice to hear them, isn't it? Guess they must be bound for Canada."

March shuffled his papers about, smiling broadly at me. "Now, was there anything else you needed from me this fine morning, Mrs. Beaumont?"

I barely needed to think. I nodded and told him exactly what I wanted. He seemed surprised, but did as I asked.

William was waiting for me patiently.

"You knew, didn't you? Why didn't either of you tell me what he'd done, William?"

"Weren't my place to tell you." William smiled gently. "He told me to say nothing at all. He was intending to tell you himself. He'd heard what Olders was up to—seems he was bragging to all his friends that you either took him up on his offer or he was going to toss you and Mistress Simone out of High Grove without so much as a cent—and

I thought Callum was going to go crazy. Even then, he kept insisting he couldn't put you in danger. That he couldn't tell you anything at all until the time was right. Made me promise to keep my mouth shut as well. Of course, he wasn't expecting to get caught and shipped out himself. Now that we know for certain he done made his plans all right and proper, I guess you want to go back to Reverend Smallbone's now?"

"Yes. Hurry, William. We might be too late already."

"If he's awake, he ain't going to go anywhere at all without you. In fact, I do believe he would wait until hell froze over before he left you. But as it is, I guess you might be right and we should maybe hurry ourselves a little."

He urged the horses on with a click of his teeth and I waved at Mr. March's astonished face as we turned against the traffic and set off away from the road that led to High Grove. As I rattled in the landau, I hoped and prayed that it was a road I would never have to travel again. Then I heard the sound of the wild geese overhead and it seemed to me that as William took the fork that led away from High Grove, so did the geese turn with us.

And at that moment I knew my life was about to change yet again.

EPILOGUE

*W*illiam had pushed the rocker as far back in the shade of the porch as he could manage to get it. After a few minutes, the back and forth motion of the chair stopped as he sank into a doze. The moment he was still, the old dog came cautiously forward and laid his head on his foot. The labrador twitched and yelped softly in his dreams, revisiting the days when no bitch for miles around was safe from his attentions.

Neither paid any attention to the growing noise. William heard it dimly, but thinking it was the hum of the bees getting drunk on the peaches ignored it. He had to make the slaves pick the peaches, telling them that until they were all eaten they would get no food but the greens they grew for themselves and the bit of rice that the plantation struggled to produce. Even then, the slaves complained that the over-ripe fruit tasted bad and gave them the runs. Truth to tell, the festering fruit stank something awful. He could see they had a point.

The noise was growing louder. The old dog raised his head and growled. William pushed him lazily with his foot.

"What you doing, Oscar? What's all the fuss about?"

Oscar got to his feet and stretched. His tail beat lazily on the floor, disturbing the dust. The growl faded to something between a whimper and a sigh and William frowned, sitting upright and gripping the arms of the rocking chair for support.

"What? We got visitors? Some salesman trying to palm his wares off on us?" He laughed, turning his head away to hawk phlegm into the dust. He had not spoken aloud for days, and the congestion had gathered at the back of his throat. "Man must be hopeful, if so."

He shielded his eyes with his cupped hand, staring into the painfully bright afternoon sunlight. Not a salesman, no. A closed carriage pulled by two good horses. Concerned at last, William got to his feet, his bones protesting at the movement. The carriage had stopped close to the porch steps. As soon as the horses were fully reigned in, the driver jumped down and went to open the carriage door.

William put his hands to his face and dry wiped it, his fingers finally coming to rest over his mouth as he watched the two passengers climb down.

"Well, I'll be damned," he whispered.

The strange couple stood quite still, staring at the house as if they were hypnotized by it. William watched their expressions flicker from surprise to dismay. He saw the house through their eyes, the peeling paint and wild garden, and was ashamed. *Not my fault*, he wanted to explain. *Nothing I could do.*

The man put his hand on the woman's arm. She turned to look at him and shrugged and shook her head as if an unspoken message had passed between them. Oscar could take no more. He jumped down the porch steps and flung himself at the woman's feet, rolling in the dust, almost trapping his lolling tongue beneath his own ribs.

She bent to pat the ecstatic dog, apparently unfettered by the tightness of her silken kimono. William glanced from the tall man to the woman with the green eyes and the widow's peak at the front of her auburn hair and felt the years roll back as all was well again in his world.

"Welcome home, Miss Kazhua," he said softly. "I'm William. William Beaumont Freeman. I'm your uncle. Your mama always knew you'd come here one day. She told me I was to wait for you. Me and Oscar both are sure glad to have you here at last."

She raised her face in surprise, and William caught his breath as he looked into Master Simon's green eyes.

"She's not here?" The young woman's voice was heavy with disappointment. "Or my father? Neither of them?"

"No. Your papa died years ago. I'm sorry. Your mama left here not too long after."

"Where is she?"

"I don't know for sure, but I guess she would have ended up a long way from here." He saw distress cloud her face and came down the steps to offer his arm. "Don't matter none, Miss Kazhua. She always kept you in her heart, no matter what. She always said you would find each other one day, so I guess this is just a step along the way. You both come along in, and I'll tell you the story. I promised her I would soon as you turned up. You going to be real proud of your mama, I promise you. And your papa. I'm sorry the place ain't as handsome as it once was, but things have been let go a little since the old mistress passed away. Come away in. Let William tell you all about it."

The old dog thumped his tail happily on the floor and followed his people into the cool shade of the house.

THANK YOU!

We hope you enjoyed *The Song of the Wild Geese*. Volume Two of Terue's journey will be released soon! Make sure you never miss a new release by subscribing to our mailing list.

http://redempresspublishing.com/subscribe/

ABOUT THE AUTHOR

 India Millar started her career in heavy industry at British Gas and ended it in the rarefied atmosphere of the British Library. She now lives on Spain's glorious Costa Blanca North in an entirely male dominated household comprised of her husband, a dog, and a cat. In addition to historical romances, India also writes popular guides to living in Spain under a different name.

Website: www.indiamillar.co.uk

ABOUT THE PUBLISHER

VISIT OUR WEBSITE
TO SEE ALL OF OUR HIGH QUALITY BOOKS:

http://www.redempresspublishing.com

Quality trade paperbacks, downloads, audio books, and books
in foreign languages in genres such as historical, romance,
mystery, and fantasy.

Printed in Poland
by Amazon Fulfillment
Poland Sp. z o.o., Wrocław